A Touch
of Grace

Books by Lauraine Snelling

A SECRET REFUGE

Daughter of Twin Oaks
Sisters of the Confederacy
The Long Way Home

DAKOTAH TREASURES

Ruby   Opal
Pearl   Amethyst

DAUGHTERS OF BLESSING

A Promise for Ellie
Sophie's Dilemma
A Touch of Grace

RED RIVER OF THE NORTH

An Untamed Land   The Reapers' Song
A New Day Rising   Tender Mercies
A Land to Call Home   Blessing in Disguise

RETURN TO RED RIVER

A Dream to Follow
Believing the Dream
More Than a Dream

LAURAINE SNELLING

A Touch
of Grace

BETHANYHOUSE
PUBLISHERS
MINNEAPOLIS, MINNESOTA

A Touch of Grace
Copyright © 2008
Lauraine Snelling

Cover design by Koechel Peterson & Associates, Inc., Minneapolis, Minnesota

Scripture quotations are from the King James Version of the Bible.

Published by Bethany House Publishers
11400 Hampshire Avenue South
Bloomington, Minnesota 55438

Bethany House Publishers is a division of
Baker Publishing Group, Grand Rapids, Michigan.

Printed in the United States of America

ISBN: 978-0-7642-2811-7 (Trade Paper)
ISBN: 978-0-7642-0474-6 (Large Print)

Library of Congress Cataloging-in-Publication Data

Snelling, Lauraine.
   A touch of Grace / Lauraine Snelling.
      p. cm. — (Daughters of Blessing ; 3)
   ISBN 978-0-7642-2811-7 (pbk.)
   1. Young women—Fiction. 2. Norwegian Americans—Fiction. 3. Farm life—Fiction. 4. Deaf—Fiction. 5. Teachers of the deaf—Fiction. 6. North Dakota—Fiction. 7. New York (N.Y.)—Fiction. I. Title.
   PS3569.N39T68   2008
   813'.54—dc22   2007043451

DEDICATION

To Marcy, Kathleen, and Cecile,
who help and encourage me far more than they realize.
Thanks is never enough.

LAURAINE SNELLING is the award-winning author of over fifty books, fiction and nonfiction, for adults and young adults. Besides writing books and articles, she teaches at writers' conferences across the country. She and her husband, Wayne, have two grown sons, a basset named Chewy, and a cockatiel watch bird named Bidley. They make their home in California.

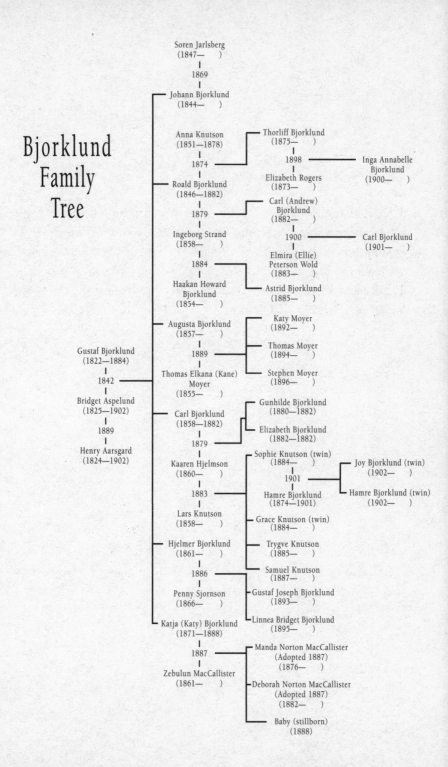

Bjorklund Family Tree

Soren Jarlsberg
(1847—   )

1869

Johann Bjorklund
(1844—   )

Anna Knutson
(1851—1878)

1874

Thorliff Bjorklund
(1875—   )

1898

Inga Annabelle
Bjorklund
(1900—   )

Elizabeth Rogers
(1873—   )

Roald Bjorklund
(1846—1882)

1879

Carl (Andrew)
Bjorklund
(1882—   )

1900

Carl Bjorklund
(1901—   )

Ingeborg Strand
(1858—   )

Elmira (Ellie)
Peterson Wold
(1883—   )

1884

Astrid Bjorklund
(1885—   )

Haakan Howard
Bjorklund
(1854—   )

Augusta Bjorklund
(1857—   )

Katy Moyer
(1892—   )

1889

Thomas Moyer
(1894—   )

Gustaf Bjorklund
(1822—1884)

1842

Bridget Aspelund
(1825—1902)

1889

Henry Aarsgard
(1824—1902)

Thomas Elkana (Kane)
Moyer
(1855—   )

Stephen Moyer
(1896—   )

Carl Bjorklund
(1858—1882)

Gunhilde Bjorklund
(1880—1882)

1879

Elizabeth Bjorklund
(1882—1882)

Kaaren Hjelmson
(1860—   )

Sophie Knutson (twin)
(1884—   )

1901

Joy Bjorklund (twin)
(1902—   )

1883

Hamre Bjorklund
(1874—1901)

Hamre Bjorklund (twin)
(1902—   )

Lars Knutson
(1858—   )

Grace Knutson (twin)
(1884—   )

Hjelmer Bjorklund
(1861—   )

Trygve Knutson
(1885—   )

1886

Samuel Knutson
(1887—   )

Penny Sjornson
(1866—   )

Gustaf Joseph Bjorklund
(1893—   )

Katja (Katy) Bjorklund
(1871—1888)

Linnea Bridget Bjorklund
(1895—   )

1887

Manda Norton MacCallister
(Adopted 1887)
(1876—   )

Zebulun MacCallister
(1861—   )

Deborah Norton MacCallister
(Adopted 1887)
(1882—   )

Baby (stillborn)
(1888)

June 1902
Blessing, North Dakota

WHERE IN THE WORLD AM I?

Jonathan Gould stared at the open window with a sheer white curtain puffing in a slight breeze. While the world outside had light, the sun had yet to blue the sky. The voice came again.

"Jonathan, time for milking."

Milking. He lifted his head enough to focus around the room. That's right; he was back in North Dakota at the home of the Bjorklunds. And this time wouldn't be like the first. That had been a brief visit for the graduation before heading to San Francisco, where his father had a business meeting. This time he was here for the summer to find out what manual work was like. The thought sent him burrowing back into the pillow.

He heard steps creaking up the steep stairs and then a knock on his door.

"Jonathan, the others are leaving for the barn." Mrs. Bjorklund's voice caught him by the nape of the neck and threw him from the bed. Not that she screamed or scolded, but she'd had to make the trek up those stairs just to wake him. After his father had admonished him to not make life any harder for these good people. People who'd been his father's friends for many years and who were doing him a favor to employ his son for the summer. All he needed was for them to report to his father that he wouldn't get out of bed in the morning. Then his father would believe the rumors he was becoming a wastrel.

"I'll be right down."

"Good. The coffee is hot if you'd like a cup before you go."

He could hear her descending the stairs as he pushed his feet into denim pants that should have been washed at least fifty times to soften them before he tried wearing them. Stiff was a weak word for the rigidity of the heavy cloth. At least his long-sleeved shirt had been worn plenty of times. They'd said to bring old clothes to work in, but he hardly had any. He slammed his feet into his boots, threaded his belt through the loops, glanced in the mirror long enough to run a comb through his dark curly hair, and headed downstairs.

Was it Astrid, the Bjorklund daughter, who called him the first time when he thought it a dream? Last night when she'd told him that he'd be learning to milk the cows in the morning, he'd smiled and wished he'd headed back to New York on the train. While they didn't look like dangerous beasts, he'd not had even a petting acquaintance with similar animals. His idea of cattle was the long-horned steers he'd seen in paintings, animals that roamed the Wild West along with the buffalo.

"Good morning. I hope you slept well." Mrs. Bjorklund, garbed in a white apron from neck to ankle, turned from the huge cast-iron stove with a smile.

"I must have. Did someone call me earlier?"

"Ja, Astrid did, but she said you didn't answer."

"I thought I was dreaming." *Actually I thought it a nightmare, but . . .*

"You'll get used to the early mornings. I think it's the most beautiful part of the day, when the earth is waking and the sun peeps over the horizon." She handed him a steaming cup. "Did you want cream and sugar?"

Her Norwegian accent reminded him of their cook at home. "Thank you, no," he said as he shook his head. Not that he was a big coffee drinker, but right now he needed all the help he could get. He took a swallow and stifled a cough. Hot and strong enough to stand his hair on end. From now on he would ask for cream and sugar, although he suspected none of the rest of the family did. *"Fit in,"* his mother had advised him. Some fitting-in things would take a real effort, like straight coffee.

"Can I get you anything else?" Ingeborg was now breaking eggs into a large bowl from a basket of eggs she had sitting on the counter. The heat from the cookstove had already removed any coolness from the air.

"No, thank you." He drained his cup and set it in the sink. More advice from his mother: *"Put things away. There will be no help to follow after you like you've had here. You don't want to cause them extra work. They have enough to do."* He'd not been sure if his mother was in favor of his coming west or not, since she had been so set on his spending the summer at the shore and then abruptly changed her mind. Maybe she felt responsible for the rumors flying around, since at her request he'd begun the party scene at prep school. "Is there anything I need to take to the barn?" he asked Mrs. Bjorklund.

"No, all the buckets and milk cans are already there. Breakfast will be ready when you are finished." Her gentle smile made him feel welcome all over again.

He headed out, leaping down the three steps of the back porch. He jogged toward the big red barn, where the sound of cows and slamming wood, people laughing and a rooster crowing reminded him to hurry. He was late for his first day on the job—a mortal sin, according to his father. This was not going to help prove he could be responsible.

Other than the laughter, the smell hit him when he entered the dimness of the barn. His nose pinched, and he swallowed. He'd never been tolerant of smells. When Mr. Bjorklund had given him a tour of the place the afternoon before, the barn hadn't reeked like this. He'd identified hay and grain when they opened the feed bin and an overlay of this odor that now drove other senses right from his head.

"I was beginning to think you were going to sleep all day." Astrid grinned up at him, her blue eyes twinkling. Her sun-streaked wheat-colored hair hung in a thick braid down her back; a faded apron covered her from just below her neck to halfway down her skirt. "Pa said

I am to teach you how to milk. We saved the gentlest cow for you."

He hoped she wasn't teasing on that point as he took a bucket and three-legged stool from her hands and followed her down the aisle. Andrew—one of her brothers—and Samuel, Trygve, and Grace—the Knutson cousins who lived next door—were already milking away, filling their buckets with foaming white milk. Others were milking on the opposite side of the long barn.

Jonathan still wasn't sure how this whole family worked together. He knew Mrs. Knutson ran the school for the deaf and Mrs. Bjorklund the Blessing Cheese Company, but the arrangement of the farming between the two families still confused him. Obviously all the milk cows were here.

"This is Bess. Most of us learned to milk on her. She is more patient than any of the others. She's never kicked anyone." Astrid set the stool down, gave the brown and white cow a couple of pats, and sat down herself, so close her head was right next to the cow's flank. "You need to be close enough to be comfortable or your back will begin to hurt after a cow or two. Then you put the bucket between your knees like this." As she spoke, she did each action. "Using a squeeze and pull motion, starting with the rear teats, although it doesn't matter which two you do first, you grasp firmly but gently and squeeze and pull." Milk pinged down into the metal bucket.

He stared from her face to her hands, watching the rhythm and smelling the warm fragrance of fresh milk, a more comforting odor than the rest of the barn. A black and white cat padded down the aisle and sat by his feet, pink tongue and white needle teeth showing with a yawn. She chirped a sound like a question mark. He stared in awe as Astrid turned her hand and a teat and squirted milk right into the cat's wide open mouth.

"The cats like their share."

"Ah, I see."

"Your turn." She smoothly twisted and, in one motion, handed him the bucket and stood.

Is this what prisoners feel like when led out to the firing squad? "Are you sure you shouldn't show me again?" *Preferably for the rest of the summer.*

"I'll coach you. This is the worst time; it'll get easy after a few cows."

He sat down, his tongue gluing itself to the roof of his mouth. He took the bucket and set it between his knees. It slipped out, and he barely caught it before it tipped the milk covering the bottom.

"You have to clamp your legs on it."

He swore he could hear laughter in her voice. The thought made him squeeze his legs and lean forward to take the two teats she'd started with. Warm and soft, but when he did what he thought she'd done, nothing happened. He squeezed again. Nothing.

"You have to remember to pull gently but firmly at the same time as you squeeze."

He nodded and tried again. He got a few drops from one hand, none from the other.

"First one hand, then the other. Think of a calf sucking."

He glared at her. He'd never seen a calf sucking. He'd never petted a cow nor thought he wanted to.

"Sorry. Think squeeze and pull."

Squeeze and pull, he muttered to himself. How come it looked so easy when she did it, and he couldn't get more than two drops? "She doesn't like me."

"This has nothing to do with the cow's opinion. Squeeze and pull."

He gritted his teeth and pushed his head harder against the soft hide of the cow. Actually, she didn't smell so bad. He squeezed and pulled his right hand, then his left. Repeating the motion did nothing. He clamped his jaw and repeated her instructions. Squeeze and pull. Nothing.

He turned his head to see her forehead wrinkling. "What am I doing wrong?"

She motioned with her hands as she repeated, "Squeeze and pull in one firm but gentle motion, first one hand, then the other. You'll get it."

Not a good way to start the summer, he grumbled to himself, concentrating on what his hands weren't accomplishing.

"Do you want me to show you again?"

"I guess so." He handed her the bucket and rose from the stool. As she settled herself back next to the cow, he leaned closer to watch her hands until he realized how close his cheek was to hers and jerked back. "I, ah, surely I can do it now." The flaming in his face would probably light up the barn. He took bucket and stool back and inhaled a deep breath that included a fresh odor from the splats as a cow up the aisle released a green stream. He swallowed hard. *You will not puke*, he ordered himself. *Squeeze and pull.*

"It works better if you try to relax." Astrid's voice wore no hint of teasing, all concern.

Right. Relax. Squeeze and pull. Two more drops oozed from one teat. *Squeeze and pull.* A thin drizzle of milk made it into the bucket. "I did it."

"Now you're getting the hang of it."

He glanced at her to see if she was punning at his expense, but her smile was nothing but encouragement. This time he did four patterns in a row, and sure enough the milk flowed strong enough to even make a sound as it foamed into the liquid.

"Just keep it going until nothing more comes out and then move to the other two teats."

He did exactly as she told him, and when nothing more would come out, he started again, aware that the muscles in his forearms were already complaining. Playing lawn tennis had not done a whole lot to prepare him for this. The bucket was half full when he could pull no more out.

"Now squeeze using your thumb and fingers to strip her out, and you'll be done. If any milk is left in the udder, she might get mastitis, an infection in her glands. We don't want any in our herd."

When he tried and wasn't doing it right, she leaned in and showed him how. "You did a good job. See, I hardly got any."

He did the same with the other three teats and tried to push his stool back. *Nope, that didn't work.*

"Here." She reached for the bucket. "You want to get the bucket out of the way so she can't kick it over or put her foot into it. You get pretty good at telling when that might happen after you've done this for a while."

He stood and picked up the stool. Far as he could tell, all the others were on their third cow. "How many cows do we have to milk?"

"Oh, thirty to thirty-five." She carried the bucket to a metal can that had handles on either side of a narrower neck with a rack on top. She poured the milk slowly through the strainer into the can and watched it drain through. "See, there's no hay or dirt to speak of. That's because we wash our cows' udders before we milk. Grass and dirt catches on the hair on their skin and would contaminate the milk."

"Who washes?"

"One of the boys takes a bucket of warm water with soap in it and goes down the line washing them all. You'll get your turn at that too, I'm sure."

His stomach grumbled as he followed her back down the aisle to a new cow. He'd picked up his stool on the way back from the milk can, so now he set it in place and, trying to remember everything she'd taught him, set the bucket between his knees. While it took a couple of pulls, the milk came more easily, and the ping soon muted into a deeper frothing sound, rich with promise.

"You're doing fine. I'm going to get a bucket and start the one right behind you. Ask for help if you need it."

He felt like he'd conquered a mountain. There was little talking except when someone changed cows, not that milking took a lot of mental concentration, but maybe that was the way of it. Jonathan stripped out his cow, dumped the milk into the can, and found Astrid to ask which cow he should do next. His arm muscles burned and his hands wanted to cramp, but he would not back down. If the others could keep going, so could he.

"Skip this one—she's still young—and take the next one." Astrid motioned to the one behind her. She raised her voice. "How many more to go?"

"Your two over there and three more on this side. We'll finish about the same time."

Jonathan wasn't sure who of the others answered, but gratitude that this would be his last made him heave a sigh of relief as he sat down to begin again. He flexed his hands and rubbed the lower arm muscles. He'd just settled into a rhythm when the cow raised her tail and a green river rained down into the gutter. He grabbed the bucket to keep the precious milk safe, but his boot and one pant leg got splattered. He choked and reverted to breathing through his mouth. How was he supposed to sit here and continue milking when even his clothes were now imbedded with that smell? Eee-uuu.

Summoning all his willpower, he kept from plugging his nose with one hand. When the cow finished, he set the pail back in place and continued milking. He hoped this was the worst that would happen. He heard the others begin to talk as they finished their cows. Would he never be done? He blew out a breath when he stripped the last drop into the bucket and finally stood. Ignoring the splats on his pant leg and boot, he carried his bucket up to the milk can and poured the three-quarter-filled bucket slowly into the strainer.

"You did well," Haakan said, lifting the final milk can onto a low wagon with foot-high racks on the sides.

"Thank you." *If you only knew.* Jonathan turned around and watched as the other men flipped back boards that held the stanchions closed, and as if choreographed, each cow backed out, turned toward the back wall, and followed the other cows out the door to the water trough and pasture. He turned back to find Haakan watching him. "How do they all know what to do?"

"The older ones train the younger ones. Old Boss is our bell cow, meaning she leads the herd. In Norway the cows wore bells so they could be found in the high pastures. Here, we don't need bells. Barney, our cattle dog, goes and gets the stragglers, but you'll find most of them lined up at the door about milking time."

"How do they know the time?"

"I don't know, but they do. Animals are wiser than we give them credit for. Here, grab the handle and let's haul this load to the well house to cool. Later we'll load up and let the horse pull a wagon over to the cheese house."

Jonathan took hold of the wagon handle and leaned into the weight. Stretching his shoulders felt good until he lifted off one of the milk cans to carry it into the low-set stone house, where a trough of cold water waited for the cans. It was heavier than he'd thought it would be, or his arms were weaker. By the time they'd set all the cans in the water, his admiration for the man working with him had doubled. He might look old, but he was still strong and never wasted a motion.

"Ready for breakfast?" Haakan clapped him on the shoulder.

"Yes, sir." *Probably more ready for a meal than I've been in my entire life.*

Grace and Astrid were already in the kitchen helping to get the food on the table when Jonathan, who had just learned to wash up at the outside wash bench, including rinsing off pant leg and boot, followed the others inside and took the chair that Andrew pointed him to. *All this work they do and no running water in the house.* Another one of those things he'd taken for granted in New York. The outdoor privies had been another lesson from the day before.

As soon as everyone was seated, they bowed their heads and joined in a grace that he'd heard his father say at times, but he'd never learned the Norwegian words. His father had learned it from a young Norwegian nanny when he was a boy.

Astrid set a bowl of oatmeal in front of him, and Trygve passed the cream and brown sugar.

"Thank you."

As soon as the oatmeal bowls were empty, Astrid removed them, and Grace helped Ingeborg set platters of fried eggs, ham, and pancakes on the table. He watched as they moved like a dance, smooth and light. These girls were just as attractive as the New York society crowd but had a complete lack of airs, which he found refreshing. They managed to combine openness and modesty. His little sister Mary Anne would be impressed.

At first arrival he had not remembered that Grace was deaf until she spoke. Though he had to listen carefully to understand her, her tonal speech had a softness to it. A big bowl of applesauce passed from one to the other along with a pitcher of hot syrup. Ingeborg and the girls finally sat down, and when he started to stand as his mother had taught him was polite, the others looked at him with questions. He sat back down and looked up to see Ingeborg smiling at him. Another lesson for the morning. Some manners were different out here.

When Jonathan could stow in no more, he listened while Haakan gave out the assignments for the day. Jonathan was to learn to harness the horses with Andrew and Trygve. Samuel was to work with his father, Lars, on the tractor plowing, one team pulling a seeder and another discs.

"When you're done with harnessing, you can help with spading the garden and raking." Haakan nodded at Jonathan. "This afternoon we'll give you lessons in driving a team, unless you've learned that already."

"I have a feeling that driving on city streets and roads out on the island is far different than driving a team pulling machinery."

"You are so right. What have you driven?"

"One horse with the buggy and the team at my grandfather's. We don't keep a team at the house in the city any longer."

"I see. Never four up or six?"

"No, sir."

"We need to finish fencing that pasture at my house also," Andrew said.

"I know, just as soon as the oats are all planted." Haakan looked at Jonathan. "Our wheat is already up, but the barley, oats, and corn that we use for cattle feed get seeded last."

"You don't make flour with anything but wheat?"

"No. We grind the other grains into feed. Sometimes people make flour out of rye and I guess other grains, but wheat has gluten that helps bread to rise. The others either don't or it is much less. Other grains can be used for food like cereals when they are rolled or cut or ground."

Jonathan shook his head. "I had no idea."

Astrid paused right behind him in her table clearing and whispered loud enough for the cows in the pasture to hear. "That's why your pa sent you to us."

Jonathan managed to keep from rolling his eyes, on the outside at least. Did she think she was superior because she knew more of farming than he did? "Wait until you come to New York." He couldn't see her response but figured the giggle was aimed at him. He glanced up to see Grace smile at him. What a difference there was between the two cousins—Astrid so outgoing and Grace so quiet but in a restful way. He knew Grace had been born deaf. His father had told him as much about the families as he knew from all the correspondence through the years between him and Ingeborg. At the graduation and the celebration afterward, Jonathan had seen many people using their hands to sign, and he knew that Mrs. Knutson had started a school for the deaf years earlier.

"All right, let's get going." Haakan pushed his chair back and stood. "Takk for maten."

Astrid caught Jonathan's questioning look. "Takk is thanks. He said thank you for the meal or food."

"Thank you, Mrs. Bjorklund. I've never eaten that much at one sitting in my entire life."

"You are most welcome. You'll find you need every bite for energy to work like our men do."

Did she think she did nothing? At home they had Cook and her assistant to feed only five people, while here, Mrs. Bjorklund's helpers were out in the barn milking, so she did most of the preparation alone. Jonathan followed the men out the door. Milking cows, harnessing horses, speaking Norwegian—what else was he going to learn here in Blessing?

2

"I SAW YOU WERE VERY PATIENT with him in the barn," Grace said in her careful way as the men left the kitchen. While they'd all learned to sign when they were children, Grace had fought and struggled to learn to speak like those who could hear, along with learning to read lips.

"Thank you. I was so sure he was going to be . . ." Astrid made a face, searching for the right word. "You know, snobbish, thinking he is better than we are because he comes from New York." She drawled *New York* and rolled her eyes, making both her mother and Grace chuckle. "His hands and forearms were really hurting by the end of the third cow, but he tried not to let it show."

"Wait until he spends a couple of hours on the end of the spade and rake. I wonder if he brought leather gloves." Ingeborg squinted, thinking. "Not sure if I included that in my letter. Do we have any new gloves?"

"Why new? He can use some old ones out of the box like we do." Astrid stood at the stove to wash dishes and poured hot water from the reservoir into the rinse pan. Grace took a towel off the rack behind the stove, and the two girls did the dishes while Ingeborg scalded milk for making bread. While she had sourdough starter growing all the time, now they often used prepared yeast purchased at the grocery store. Like a fine perfume the yeast, when stirred into warm water, filled the room with fragrance.

"If we work on our garden today, we'll do yours tomorrow," Astrid said, setting another plate into the rinse pan.

Grace watched Astrid's lips, since signing was difficult with their hands in the dishwater. "Or the next day. Mor and Ilse are cleaning the bunk rooms today. George is building new shelves for those rooms, and we are making new curtains too. Mor wants to refurbish a lot of the school building."

By the time they had the kitchen cleaned up, Ingeborg had browned the three rabbits Samuel had snared and cleaned, and had them baking in the oven.

Grace saw Jonathan knock at the back door. Tante Ingeborg's face was turned from Grace, but from the look on his, she was already telling him he was family.

"Sorry." He cleaned his boots off at the brush boot scraper on the porch and removed his hat as he came through the door.

"Did you by any chance bring leather gloves?" Astrid asked.

"Yes. They're upstairs in my trunk."

"Good. Go get them, and we'll get on out to the garden." She started for the door and stopped. "There are rakes and spades and hoes down at the machine shed on the south wall, if you'll fetch a couple of each, please."

"Of course."

Grace smiled at him as he made his way to the staircase. She leaned close to Astrid. "That young man has fine manners, and he is really trying hard."

"He's the same age as you are. How come you call him a young man?"

Grace shrugged. "I don't know. Strange, isn't it?"

"Strange or not, let's get the seeds and get out there before it gets any hotter."

"Put your sunbonnets on," Ingeborg reminded them, as she had many times before.

"Mor, you know I hate sunbonnets."

"Then take that wide-brimmed straw hat or you'll burn your nose again."

Grace and Astrid wrinkled their noses at each other. Grace snagged a blue calico sunbonnet by the strings, and Astrid clapped one of her brothers' old straw hats on her head. They both grabbed the bags with seeds and headed out the door.

"I wish I could put on men's britches like my ma used to wear," Astrid said as she and Grace strolled to the garden at the back of the house.

"You wouldn't dare. Can you imagine what Mrs. Valders would have to say about that!"

"Lots, but why do I care?"

"Because all the women would go atwitter and complain to our mothers and raise all kinds of ruckus." Grace looked down at the apron covering her faded brown calico skirt. "Besides, men's pants would be heavy." She thought a moment, spreading her skirt with her hands. "What if we cut up the front and back of a skirt to about here and sewed a seam from hem to hem?" She looked up to see delight dancing in Astrid's eyes. "Then it would still be full like a skirt but with the ease of pants."

"I have an old skirt we could use."

Grace nodded, scrunching her mouth as she thought. "We need to both do it at the same time." She tucked an escaping strand of honey, aged to amber, hair back behind her ear.

"You think we could sew them tonight?" Astrid asked.

"Ask Tante Ingeborg if you can sleep over."

Astrid twirled her seed pouch around her head like a sling. "Look out, Blessing, we have a new style coming."

"Wouldn't Sophie love to be in on this?" Even with Sophie back now from her flight to marriage and Seattle with her new husband, Grace missed her. Just being in Blessing was not the same as her being at home. Actually, even being with her now wasn't the same. Everything they talked about felt stilted. *Or I guess I feel stilted because Sophie still says whatever is on her mind.*

"She's so busy taking care of the boardinghouse and the twins, she hasn't time to sneeze. She has to be a proper lady now." Astrid looped her seed pouch over a fence post and, picking up the two sticks with string wound on them, pushed the end of one stick into the soil they had raked the day before and started unwinding the string as she walked backward to mark the row.

Grace started laughing. When Astrid looked up, she signed, "Sophie . . . proper?"

"Why can't we use the frozen bean plants as the row markers?" They'd planted much of the garden several weeks earlier. A late frost had turned the bean shoots brown and dead. They'd managed to cover the potatoes, and the peas could take a frost and survive.

"Good idea. Mor said that besides replanting these, we needed two more rows. We'll do the carrots after that." Astrid nodded toward Jonathan, bringing in more tools.

Grace turned and smiled at him. "Thank you."

"Where do I start digging?"

"Well, it's not exactly digging. Spading turns the soil so we can break up the clods with a rake and hoe." *Why is he staring at me like that?* Grace took a step backward. *Surely he knows I can read lips. Or is he even aware I cannot hear?* "You start over there." She pointed to the corner where the plow and disc pulled by one of the teams had, as always, missed turning the soil.

"All right."

She reached up and touched the brim of her sunbonnet. "Do I have mud on my face or something?" *I can't believe I said that.*

"No. Sorry. I've not seen a hat like that before. You look lovely in it."

Grace could feel heat streaking up from her neck, and it wasn't due to the sun. "I . . . ah . . . thank you." Her fingers fluttered into motion as her tongue stumbled over the words. Whew, she needed a fan. Where had the breeze gone? Then remembering that he couldn't sign, she clenched her hands together.

He started working close to the fence, pushing the shovel in with his arms.

Grace and Astrid stared at each other. With a mischievous smile Astrid motioned with her head for Grace to go help him. Grace gave a quick shake of her head and mouthed, "You." Astrid pushed the second stake in at the end of the row, picked up her hoe, and started trenching back to the other end of the garden, effectively ignoring Grace by keeping her back to her.

Grace *humphed* and stomped over to where Jonathan had turned over three shallow shovelfuls. *Remember, this is just like teaching Trygve or Samuel.* But when he looked up from what he was doing, his smile made her swallow. "I-I could show you an easier way, if you'd like." She hardly had enough spit to talk with.

"There is an easier way?"

"Ja, here." She reached for the spade and moved back to the edge that was already plowed. "If you start here, that helps. And then you push the spade into the ground with your foot, like this." She demonstrated the motion, paused, and continued. "Then you turn the soil over and put it right back where it was." She looked up to see him studying both her and the ground intently.

"But why put it right back?"

"The purpose is to turn this grass under so it dies. Then we can break up the dirt to make it smooth enough to plant in. Like Astrid is doing."

"All those rows are already planted and growing?" he asked.

She nodded and pointed. "Peas go in first, then potatoes and onions. After that we do small seeds like carrots and lettuce. We had another late frost that killed the beans, so we are replanting them. As it warms up, we plant corn, and a couple of weeks later we will plant more corn. Cabbages that Mor started in the house are ready to transplant, and the tomatoes will go in last."

"This is a big garden. What will go in the corners?"

"Squash, cucumbers, and tomatoes over there along that fence. We have more potatoes and corn planted on the edge of the field. We have another plot this big at our house."

"I see."

But she could tell from the look on his face that he had no idea how much food they would grow. "Don't you have a garden at your house?"

He shook his head. "Only a little spot where Cook grows herbs and specialty things. And there is the cutting garden with flowers for the house."

"Where do you get your food?"

"At the market. Farmers bring their produce in, and Cook goes and buys it."

"Cook?" Grace tried to stop her surprise. She'd read about families that hired cooks and maids, but other than stories Elizabeth had told, she'd never known anyone who had servants. She handed him the spade and motioned for him to follow her example. *Why did he come to Blessing, then? He could pay to have anything done.*

He stuck the spade in next to her spot, rammed it in with his foot, and turned it, just like she'd shown him. "Good enough?" He had one eyebrow raised, giving him a devilish air.

"Ja, good." Grace forced herself not to spin around and flee like she wanted. Why was she feeling so flushed again? Instead, she walked back to where Astrid was bent over dropping in beans and thumped her on the shoulder as she passed. Then she jerked up one end stake, measured three steps, and stuck it in the ground, as Astrid had already done.

By the time she had dug her furrow, she was feeling calm again. *How silly,* she told herself. *You know that you care for Toby and always have, so behave yourself.* Dropping beans into a furrow, she remembered one of their girl parties when the others had been talking about the newly arrived Geddick young men and other single fellows in the area. All she ever thought about was Toby Valders. And yet she couldn't tell the others that. Even though he was a man now, Toby did not have the best reputation, carried over from all those years in school when he'd tease some of the smaller children until cousin Andrew got fed up and punched him. As a way to teach them to control their tempers, Pastor Solberg, who also taught in the one-room school, made them both chop wood. Sometimes there was a huge woodpile for both the school and the church. Then when Toby and Andrew got in that big fight after the barn burned and Toby almost died, she'd cried herself to sleep more than once and spent hours praying for him.

One time he'd held her hand and stared deep into her eyes. She thought he might kiss her, but he turned away. She knew he'd kissed Sophie, but then Sophie was a flirt back in those days. If Mor and Far had gotten wind of it, Sophie would have been in terrible trouble. The thought of Sophie's antics tightened her jaw, especially when they involved Toby. She'd never said anything, though, and then Sophie ran off with Hamre, a distant cousin who'd left Blessing to go fishing out in Seattle.

Would she be willing to run away with Toby if he asked her? He wouldn't have to. Blessing was his home just like it was hers. Although, since graduation she had not seen him at all, which seemed odd.

She turned at a hand tapping her shoulder. One thing about not hearing, she could go off in her own little world and not pay attention to anyone else. Or maybe it was just part of her. Sometimes she had seen Tante Ingeborg look as if she was returning from somewhere else.

"You want to help me move the string?" Astrid asked.

Grace nodded and rubbed her hands together to get rid of some of the dirt. Together they marked and furrowed three rows, and she went back to covering the beans in her row, this time using her feet to tamp the ground down on the seeds. Done with her row she glanced over to see how Jonathan was progressing. Sweat darkened the front of his shirt and the sleeves where he had wiped his forehead. He grimaced as he forced the blade into the dirt with his booted foot.

His legs or feet must hurt, but he'd steadily turned over the clumps that now lay with black faces to the sun. Grace knew other girls in Blessing were all giggly about how handsome Jonathan was with his dark curly hair and laughing deep brown eyes. While he wasn't anywhere near as tall as the Bjorklund and Knutson men and boys, he had a grace about him that caught the eye. Astrid said he probably learned that in dance class, but their friend Rebecca Baard had shushed her.

Sometime later Astrid tapped her shoulder again. "Mor's calling us to come help get dinner on the table."

Grace got to her feet and brushed the dirt off her apron. The only way to sow small seeds was on hands and knees, using one's fingertips. She caught a smile from Jonathan and sent him one in return. *He must feel very odd here. Maybe he just needs a friend. Sometimes it's hard to be marked as different.*

Astrid paused at the garden gate and turned back toward Jonathan. "Mor will be ringing the triangle in a few minutes for the men to come in. I think Pa would be pleased if you were at the barn to help unharness the teams, so keep watch, and when they are nearing the barn, be there to meet them. Then everyone washes at the bench, like this morning, before coming in."

"Thank you for telling me."

Grace followed Astrid and glanced out at the land, where the teams, heads nodding, continued their rounds of the fields. The tractor belched black smoke, and a flock of blackbirds ebbed and flowed over the newly turned soil, searching out the exposed worms and bugs.

They reached the porch just as Ingeborg beat the iron bar around the triangle, sending the clanging signal across the land. One of the men lifted his hat in response to let her know they'd heard it.

"He didn't know how to use a spade," Astrid said when they entered the kitchen.

"But he learned quickly." Grace spoke carefully as she washed her hands. Everyone was so used to turning to include Grace in the conversations when they weren't signing that Astrid had turned to face her automatically.

"And he is willing to take instructions, even from a girl."

Ingeborg smiled at her daughter's emphasis on the word *girl*. "Your brothers would not be so gracious."

Grace and Astrid turned to each other and grinned, then rolled their eyes. Many an argument had occurred through the years when they tried to teach their brothers something.

Grace set the table while Astrid sliced the fresh bread that was still warm. The fragrance of it melded with the rabbits baking in the oven.

Grace looked up to see Ingeborg pull out the roasting pan and set it on the cooler end of the stove.

"I'll make the gravy, and you cut up the meat, Astrid." Ingeborg reached for the flour canister on the warming shelf of the stove.

"Do we need anything from the well house?" Grace asked.

"Ja. Cream, buttermilk, and take a knife along to slice a wedge off that cheese out there."

Grace did as she was told, as always pausing on the top step to lift her face to the sun. Like her tante Ingeborg, she needed the warm sun to drive away the memories of winter. She often thought of raising her arms to the sun just as the plants did their leaves, seeking the warmth to grow by. She glanced over to the garden to see Jonathan leaning his spade against the fence along with the other tools. He lifted his straw hat and wiped the sweat from his forehead with the back of his arm. His skin was olive toned and didn't burn as easily as hers, instead, quickly tanning with the sun. He really stood out in the midst of so many fair-haired, light-skinned Norwegians. Not that all of them were blond, but there was a difference. Thinking on these things, she followed the dirt path, now edged with ankle-deep rich green grass, to the well house.

When she opened the door, the cool air rushed out, caressing her face in the passing. Hams still hung from the rafters, along with smoked haunches of venison, mutton, and a couple of geese. The milk cans from the morning milking were still in the trough, and baskets of eggs sat on the shelves, along with crocks of butter, jugs of cream, and leftovers waiting to be made into stew or soup. She sliced a wedge off the half wheel of golden orange cheese and set it in a basket, added a full butter mold, and tightened the lid on a jar of cream so that it wouldn't spill in the basket. Then carrying a crock of buttermilk in her other arm, she headed back for the house.

When she saw Jonathan coming toward her, she smiled.

"Can I carry that for you?" He held out his hands.

She shook her head. "I am fine, thank you."

A frown blew across his brow as he stepped off the pathway to let her pass.

I should have let him, she thought. *Maybe that would have been more polite. But carrying these is what I always do. That's what baskets are for.* She could feel his gaze drilling into her back but refused to let herself turn around to check. If he kept volunteering to help them, when would he have time to do his own work? This promised to be an unusual summer. Now, if Toby had been there and volunteered, would she have let him take the basket? And walk beside her?

KNEADING BREAD ALWAYS GAVE her time to dream. Ingeborg flipped the dough over and continued the rhythm of pushing with the heel of her hand, turning the elastic dough with the other, rolling in a portion, and heeling again. Sometimes she used both hands to force air out of the dough. Always she found herself humming. She sprinkled more flour on the board and continued. She used much of her kneading time for praying. The Bible spoke so often of bread, the staff of life, and Jesus, the Bread of Life. In kneading bread she felt she had a part of that life; in taking baked bread from the oven, she knew it.

"You sound happy."

She turned to smile at the young man silhouetted in the doorway. "Baking bread always makes me happy. Even if I start angry at something or someone, when I am done, that is all gone." *Uff da. What made you answer like that?* "Do you need something?"

Young Gould had been with them for a week now, and she had yet to regret their choice to host him for the summer. He never hesitated to try a new task or complained of the aches he must be feeling. He fit into their family like a newfound cousin.

"Andrew said you would bandage me up." He held up his hand wrapped in a handkerchief.

Ingeborg stopped her kneading and pointed him toward the sink. "How bad is it?"

"It was bleeding a lot."

She washed her hands and took his hand in hers, unwrapping the bloody cloth. "Uff da. How did you do this?"

"The knife slipped."

She studied it, trying to decide if she should put a couple of stitches in to close it up. "Let's get it cleaned and see how bad it really is." She pressed against the veins in his wrist to help stop the bleeding. "See what I'm doing?" At his nod, she continued, "Use your other hand to press here so I can get some things together."

By the time she had poured hot water from the reservoir into a basin, added soap, fetched her medical bag, and set supplies to boiling to sterilize, he had pulled a chair over to the counter and sat with his hand over the dry sink.

"You feel dizzy?" she asked when she saw his white face.

He nodded.

"Then put your head down between your knees." The last thing she wanted was him flat on the floor in a faint.

"But the blood . . ."

"Don't worry about that." She placed a hand firmly on the back of his neck and helped him get his head down. "Better?"

"I guess so." His muffled voice reminded her of Andrew years before when he'd had a similar accident.

Shame Astrid was helping Elizabeth today, when she could have used her here. Of course she could load the boy in the buggy and take him to the surgery, but knowing that Elizabeth was feeling puny with her pregnancy made her decide to take care of it at home. "Feeling better?"

"Yes."

As soon as she touched his hand, blood welled up again. "Keep your fingers hard on the wrist while I wash this." She pulled her boiling pan of silk thread and needle from the hot part of the stove to cool and rubbed a small scrub brush over a bar of lye soap. The water turned red immediately, so she cleaned around the wound as quickly as she was able. "How did this happen?"

"I was repairing a harness like Andrew showed me, and the knife slipped. It would have been a lot worse had I not been wearing my leather gloves. Can you stitch up gloves too?" Jonathan flinched but held his hand steady.

"I can patch a glove all right. Now this will sting." She took the threaded needle from the water and slid it through both sides of the cut and deftly tied a knot. "One down, one to go." She looked at his pale face. "You need to put your head down again?"

"No. I'm fine."

She took another stitch in the heel of his hand, tied the knot, and watched for a moment to see if blood would leak. "There, that's all. I'll put some ointment on it and wrap it. You have to keep it clean, so wear gloves while you're out working. Looks like a clean cut, and you're a healthy young man. It should heal well."

"Thank you." He looked from the wound to her face. "You are amazing."

"One learns to do all kinds of things on a farm. I've stitched up dogs, cows, and horses, and sometimes I even sew clothes, although we use our sewing machine for much of that. This ointment I'm using contains honey and will help too."

"Honey?"

"Surprising, I know, but honey helps speed the healing." While they talked, she wrapped his hand in strips of white cotton and tied the ends neatly on the back of his hand.

"Did you take medical training?"

"No, and that's why I am so grateful we have Dr. Elizabeth here now. I'm not called on for much doctoring anymore." She gathered her supplies and put each back in its proper place in her leather satchel. "This bag has seen many miles."

Jonathan stood and glanced over at the table. "Your bread—it's about to fall on the floor."

Ingeborg turned and her laughter trailed over her shoulder as she crossed the room to retrieve her rising bread before it slipped off the table. "Obviously the yeast is working well." She quickly washed her hands then flipped the dough back into the crockery bowl. "Could I prevail upon you to bring in several armloads of wood? The woodbox is nearing empty. But don't pick them up with the bandaged hand."

"Of course."

"You'll find gloves in a box on the shelf to the right of the door on the porch. Leave your cut one here, and I'll find some leather to patch it with."

She went back to kneading her bread while Jonathan filled the woodbox and left the house whistling. She should write and tell his parents how well he was doing and what a fine young man they had raised. Her thoughts returned to the cheese house and the bumper crop of waxed cheese wheels she had growing out there. The shelves were rapidly filling with aging cheese, and with the new cows both she and some of the other farmers had bought; she might have to add on again. She'd been right in insisting they add to the milk herd, even though she hated for her and Haakan not to be in accord.

After wiping a trickle of perspiration from her forehead with the back of her hand, she turned the dough in the bowl, laid a clean towel over it, and set it to rise on the shelf in the sun. The extra kneading would make it a finer grained bread. She checked the roasting haunch of venison from a young buck Andrew had shot as it grazed in the wheat field, and then closed the oven door before pouring herself a cup of coffee and going out to sit in the sun on the back porch.

She should be hoeing potatoes, weeding carrots, or doing any number of chores that waited patiently, but instead, she lifted her face to the sun's caress. Always after the long winter, she craved the sun as a starving child craved bread. She noticed Grace did too, even from when she was a small child. Almost like an instinctive reaction to warmth. She sipped her coffee and glanced toward the barn, where Jonathan and Andrew were repairing harnesses, one of those ongoing necessities that usually got done in the long months of winter. Where had the time gone, or was it just that there weren't as many growing children at home to help with the daily chores? Or was Haakan slow-ing down?

That thought had been nagging at her. She hesitated to call it a fear because she believed what the Bible said when it commanded *Fear not*. Fear not, so simple and easy to say, but actually doing it was the hard part. While Haakan never complained, hadn't she seen him flinch sometimes when twisting? Or was her imagination trying to run off with her? It had happened before. She held her cup in both hands and closed her eyes.

"Please, Lord, take care of Haakan. If there is something wrong, bring healing, give him the strength to do what he feels needs to be done. I know you love him better than I can. I thank you for giving me such a fine man to love and grow old with."

Uff da! What's with all this thinking on getting older? Just get busy and quit sitting in the sunshine. It's making you feel as lazy as those cats sleeping in the sun by the barn wall. She tossed the coffee dregs on the rosebush, which already had buds. Once spring came, plants in North Dakota rushed to grow and bloom just like the people did. *Now if I had a table set up here, I could bring out all the bookwork.* The front porch faced west, so it was still in the shade. The cottonwood she'd planted as a sapling so many years ago now shaded the south side of the house, as did the clump of birches Haakan had brought her from Minnesota one year and planted by the back porch. They'd planted a line of elm trees and one of pines to the north as a windbreak, filling it in with Juneberry bushes, chokecherries, and wild roses, making it a haven for grouse and pheasants. Samuel ran one of his snare lines for rabbits there.

The chore of bookwork was never appealing. Her ledgers lined a shelf over the desk Onkel Olaf had made before he took his family and furniture crafting business off to Grafton. Thinking of that reminded her that she owed Goodie a letter. What she wouldn't give for a visit from her friend of so many years. She returned to the house, checked the rising bread, put more wood in the stove, and defying all the work awaiting her, retrieved a tablet and pencil from the desk.

After pouring another cup of coffee, she headed back outside to the wash bench, where she sat down and leaned against the sun-warmed wall.

Dear Goodie,

How I wish you were here to enjoy the sunshine with me. There is just enough breeze to be comfortable. Mrs. Robin is sitting on her nest in the cottonwood. I can see the nest easily because I put out bits of red and yellow yarn, and she and her mate snatched them right up to weave in with the twigs and grasses.

I just bandaged Jonathan Gould's hand. I did tell you he was spending the summer here in my last letter, at least I think I did. This is Mr. Gould's second son—actually his first son with his second wife. He had one son and one daughter by his first wife, and then his first wife died in childbirth, along with the baby. Mr. Gould had twin boys and another girl with his second wife, so Jonathan has younger brothers and a young sister. Mr. Gould believes this son needs to learn about manual labor.

As we know, there is plenty of man-ual and woman-ual labor to be done around here.

She smiled at the play on words, knowing it would make Goodie smile too.

I am so grateful that Ellie shares her letters from home. You raised a fine young woman there, my friend, and I am grateful she is married to Andrew. I am just sorry you don't get to watch little Carl growing up, as we do. He is a ray of sunshine in our lives. Such a happy baby.

We have quilting tomorrow, and Grace and Astrid have agreed to cook for the men so that Kaaren and I can both go. Did you hear yet of Sophie's two little ones? Hamre, after his father, and Joy. They are a handful. They bring back memories of Sophie and Grace as newborns who were so much smaller.

Ingeborg paused for a moment, remembering their grief when they realized tiny Grace could not hear. *And yet what a wonderful joy she is to this family. And how true to her name.* May the new little Joy also grow into her name.

I know Ellie feels torn whether to stay with the girls or take her part as one of the married women who will continue the work of our church. She is thinking of helping with the Sunday school class for the littlest ones when fall comes, but I'm sure she has told you that.

In your last letter you asked if things are better with Hildegunn Valders. One would think she'd be happy as a cat with a mouse since she hears all the gossip first thing at the post office. But no matter how hard I try, she cannot seem to forgive me and mine. She made a snide remark at the last quilting, and Mrs. Magron, bless her little heart, stood up and, hands on her hips, told Hildegunn to let bygones be gone and be grateful she has two fine men for sons and she'd better learn a lesson or two in gratitude. We were all so shocked that all we could do was stare. Hildegunn, of course, humphed and glared, but what could she say? I take that back, the day Mrs. Valders is tongue-tied is the day I know we should be checking to see if Jesus arrived unannounced. I should cross that out, I know, but we can laugh together at least.

Well, I better get back and set the rice to boiling. I cannot wait for the new potatoes. I was going to make noodles but ended up stitching a certain young man's hand instead. Oh, I read the cleverest thing in a magazine. Make your noodle dough like usual but without quite as much flour. Then, using a wooden spoon, force the dough through the colander and into boiling water. Boil for five or so minutes until the noodles rise to the top, drain and put into cold water, then drain again and brown in butter with some chopped onions and whatever seasonings you desire. Serve with a meat or under roast chicken. Everyone raved about my new noodles.

Graduation went beautifully; all our little girls now think they are grown up.

I always look forward to letters from you but would be overjoyed with a long visit. Cook up lots for Onkel Olaf, and then you, Arne, and Rachel get on the train and come kiss your grandson.

With love and joy,
Your friend, Ingeborg

She read it through, added a word here and there, and folded it so she could put it in an envelope as soon as she went back into the house. After making a face at the cold coffee in her cup, she tossed the liquid under the rosebush and stopped for a minute on the top step to shade her eyes and search the fields for the teams. Haakan was cultivating corn with the new cultivator he and Lars had designed during the winter. Four up could pull the machine, which covered three rows at a time, with Haakan riding instead of walking behind. Hoeing corn would be a thing of the past, or at least that's what they hoped.

A hammer on metal rang from the machine shed, telling her that Lars was either tearing apart or repairing another piece of machinery.

She patted her fairly new washing machine as she walked past it. The men weren't the only ones to have new machinery. Penny, who loved having the latest household tools, had shown her a new kerosene-heated model of the flatirons she'd heated for so long on her kitchen stove. Because the new iron stayed hot, ironing would go faster without repeated trips to the woodstove.

When she rang the triangle for dinner, five loaves of cooling bread waited on the counter. She'd made gravy to go over the rice, sliced the venison, and cooked the dandelion greens Astrid had picked for her before she left for the surgery. Fresh greens were such a treat before the garden produce was ready, especially when cooked with bacon left over from breakfast. With the table set, she sliced the bread, holding a heel to her nose to inhale the wonderful fragrance. Nothing smelled as good as fresh bread.

Barney's barking would have let her know the men were at the barn if the jangling of harness hadn't already informed her. She set the platter of bread on the table, sliced the cheese she'd brought in from the well house, and pressed the butter out of the mold and onto a plate.

By the time she could hear the men at the wash bench, all was ready, and she stood back to see if she'd forgotten anything.

"We found us a pilgrim," Haakan called from outside, "so you better put another plate on the table."

Without checking the window to see who it might be, she took a plate from the cupboard and set out the silverware. Company was always welcome. She quickly changed her dirty apron for a clean one and went to the screen door.

"Why, Hjelmer, I didn't know you were home again." She pushed the door open and welcomed the traveler in. As usual, Hjelmer's grin made her smile more widely. As the youngest of the Bjorklund brothers and the legislative representative from their district, Hjelmer was away more often than he was home, much to the dismay of his wife, Penny.

"Just got back yesterday." He hung his hat on the rack by the door and inhaled. "Ah, Ingeborg, you've been baking bread. I came at just the right time." He leaned forward and dropped his voice. "Did you save the heel for me?"

"How could I, when I didn't know you were coming?" Something was up. She could tell by the look in his eyes. Always one with forward-thinking ideas, Hjelmer often came to ask Lars and Haakan for advice or blessing on his latest venture, whatever that might be. "Besides, I didn't hear your automobile drive up."

"I came on horseback."

"You mean that smoking monster wouldn't start . . . again?"

"Now, don't go make disparaging remarks about my Oldsmobile."

"Why not? Everyone else does." Haakan hung up his hat too. He looked to Ingeborg. "I hear you've been doctoring today."

Ingeborg nodded and smiled at Jonathan, who trailed in after Andrew. As the men took their places at the table, she slid a heel of bread onto Hjelmer's plate, earning a wink from him and a headshake from her husband.

After Haakan said grace, she set the platters on the table and stood back a moment to watch them help themselves and pass the food around the table.

"So what brought you out this way?" Haakan asked.

Hjelmer looked up from his full plate and caught Ingeborg's gaze. "Come sit down, Ingeborg. You need to hear this too."

At the look in his eyes, she caught her breath. Something was afoot, and she had a feeling she would not be happy with the news.

Hjelmer laid his fork and knife on his plate. "I've been offered a position in government that requires me to move to Bismarck. I told Penny about it last night, and now I'm talking to the rest of you."

"And Penny said?" Ingeborg's voice broke on the words.

Hjelmer sighed. "Penny is having a very hard time with this."

"Have you accepted the job?"

"No. I knew I had to come home and see if we could make arrangements. We have a lot of questions. Do we sell the store and the machinery business, find someone to manage them for us, or . . . ?"

"Or stay here."

"Right. But if I take the position, I would have to resign my seat in the legislature or at least not run again in the fall." He sighed again. "It is a good opportunity."

"But you would have to move." Ingeborg used the corner of her apron to dry her eyes.

"Either that or never see my family. You know how Penny already feels about my being gone so much."

"She loves her store."

"I know."

"Would you have to sell it? I mean, can you afford a house in Bismarck without selling the businesses here?"

Hjelmer buttered the heel of bread, staring at it longer than necessary before raising his head to look directly at Haakan. "I don't know. Most of our money is tied up in the businesses."

You can't move away. Lord, don't let them move. But what if this is the plan you have for them? Ingeborg tried to unscramble her thoughts, but they tumbled over each other in spite of her good intentions. Penny couldn't leave. They were all used to Hjelmer being gone, but Penny and her store were part of the warp that held the tapestry of the town together. Newcomers were threads in the picture, but without strong warp, the piece would not continue to grow. Ingeborg glanced around her kitchen. The zinc dry sink came from the Blessing General Store, as did the jars that held her canning, the crocks of all sizes, the cast-iron frying pans and pots, her sewing machine, the new washing machine, the gingham she had turned into curtains for the windows. Penny loved stocking new inventions for the women of Blessing. Hjelmer brought in the latest in machinery, and his blacksmith shop not only reset wheels but repaired some of the farm machinery. His windmills dotted the countryside, providing fresh water for humans and animals.

"You can't leave Blessing." Ingeborg tried to put a touch of teasing in her voice, but the cracking was a dead giveaway. "Please don't leave."

4

As June danced with blooming lilacs and the issue of whether Sophie would sell the boardinghouse was settled, the new chief discussion of *Will they or won't they?* held the folks of Blessing in thrall. While the men seemed to think Hjelmer had to go where he could do the best, the women were tearfully praying that Penny would not be forced to leave.

When Grace entered the store, she studied the stony look on Penny's face. Did she really have a choice? Didn't the Bible say women were to go where their husbands led? At least that's what her mor said, but no one wanted to even think of that.

Penny saw her and half smiled. "Good morning, Grace. What can I get for you today?"

"I have a whole list." She laid the paper on the counter. "I thought maybe I would go see Sophie while you filled this."

"That will be fine. She is some tired."

"I know."

"How's young Mr. Gould doing?"

"He is working hard. He said he even likes milking the cows. He is over helping Tante Ingeborg in the cheese house again today."

"Did you bring a wagon in or walk?"

"The buggy. Why?"

"Some parts came in that Lars ordered. I thought perhaps you could take them back to him."

"Of course, if there is room." While she wanted to ask Penny about her decision, she couldn't bring herself to ask the questions. Sometimes things were better left unknown. "I'll be back later, then." Once out the door, she took a deep breath, as if she'd not taken one since she'd entered the store, and exhaled. The sorrow failed to follow her outgoing breath. She realized it was selfish to want everything to stay the way it was. Sophie had come home, and no one else should leave. People moving in was fine. It was the leaving that tore her apart. *I don't ever want to leave Blessing,* she told herself for more than the second time.

Does that mean never to travel or only never moving away? Grace knew Sophie still dreamed of traveling again and that she wanted Grace to go with her. So yes, traveling was different than moving. And school too. Astrid would be leaving in the fall for nursing school, but she would be coming back like Elizabeth did. She cut off her thoughts as she approached the boardinghouse. Though how they would travel with twins was beyond her. And deep down Grace had a sense Sophie was not telling her something about Garth Wiste. Most likely Sophie was just dreaming about the traveling. *Maybe I should come in and stay with her.* Grace let her thoughts roam again. She might have a better chance of seeing Toby if she was in town. But sitting out on the front porch of the boardinghouse might be a bit obvious. He'd not come to the graduation festivities after the ceremony. She jerked the screen door open with a bit more force than necessary. What was she supposed to do? Trip him on his way home from work?

She checked Sophie's room. It was empty, so she headed into the dining room, also empty, went through the kitchen, empty, and out to the back porch, where she found everyone. Even Mrs. Sam was sitting down, for a change.

"Miss Grace, I'll get you a glass." Mrs. Sam started to heave herself out of the rocker, but her daughter, Lily Mae, beat her to it. The older woman sank back into her chair with a sigh and a thank-you while Grace and Sophie greeted each other. Newborns Hamre and Joy were sleeping in a large basket next to Sophie. Hamre kept making sucking motions with his lips.

"Here. I bring strawberry swizzle, prettier than lemonade." Lily Mae set a tray on the low table. "Last of the canned strawberries."

"Good thing the berries are coming on pretty soon." Grace loved strawberries . . . well, berries of any kind but strawberries the most. She loved the smell, the color, and the taste, and that they were the first crop of the summer. While those growing in the gardens were bigger, the flavor of the small wild ones haunted her.

"Are any ready yet at Mor's?" Sophie asked.

Grace shook her head. "Not in the hollow either."

"Have you talked with Penny?"

"Only a bit. I stopped at the store and left our order."

"I thought you might have done that." Sophie looked around. "I feel so left out of everything." She gave herself a bit of a shake. "No, enough about me. Tell me how Penny looked."

Grace stared at her sister. Was this a new Sophie?

"She is sad, not like herself."

"The whole town is sad." Sophie waved off a loose fly from above the babies. "I know it's sad to say good-bye, but it can be interesting too to start a new life in a new place. Maybe Penny will be happier in Bismarck."

Away from all her family and friends? Seems to me you're talking about yourself again.

Grace took a good swallow of her drink and helped herself to a lemon cookie. *Where are these thoughts coming from? Why is Sophie's attitude bothering me?* "Any other news?"

"Mr. Wiste's house is nearly finished, and Rebecca's ice cream parlor should open on the Fourth of July, just like she hoped."

"Who is going to make her ice cream?"

"I forget. She's going to carry some of the new kinds of candy too. Hershey bars, just think."

"How do you know?" Grace asked.

"She came by and showed me pictures from a catalog where she ordered tables and chairs and a refrigerated chest, something like they use on the trains." Sophie stroked Joy's back as she began to wiggle a little. "We are getting telephones here in Blessing soon."

"Telephones?"

"Like they have in Grand Forks and Grafton. They are looking for someone to be the operator. Penny was going to let them put the board up in her store, but now if she is going to sell the store . . ." The words hung on the air, broken only by the sparrows chittering up in the cottonwood tree.

"Are you going to have one here at the boardinghouse?"

"Of course. People will be able to call for reservations like in a hotel."

"Maybe I should apply for the position of operator." Grace paused, waiting for her sister's reaction.

"Grace, you can't—" Sophie gave a hoot. "You are so funny." She stopped and stared at Grace. "Oh, how I wish you could. Do you ever dream of hearing real sounds?"

"I used to but not anymore." She set her glass on the tray. "I'm sure Penny has the order ready. If you'd like, I could come and help you awhile tomorrow."

Ask her if she's seen Toby. I can't. Sure you can. Be casual. The two sides of her thoughts engaged in fisticuffs while she talked. *I want to see Toby, and when I do, I shall just ask him flat-out what is going on.* With that firm resolution she stood and smiled at Mrs. Sam and Lily Mae. "Thank you."

Mrs. Sam fanned herself with her apron. "Cooler weather sure would be a big help."

"I know." Grace stopped at her sister's side. "You behave now."

"What choice do I have?" Sophie looked up at her sister. "I want to give them everything I can."

"Oh, Sophie, you are." Grace leaned down and hugged her sister. "I'll tell them one day about your summer of the double Bs."

Sophie gave her a confused look.

"You know, bench and bed." Grateful at the bark of laughter from Sophie, Grace headed back to the store, made sure all of her supplies were loaded, and climbed up in the buggy to back the horses. While tempted to drive by the flour mill construction, instead she took the road past the schoolhouse and on toward home.

Samuel and Mr. Gould—she still couldn't call him Jonathan, it was not proper—met her at the barn to remove the parts from the rear of the buggy and rode with her to the house to unload the kitchen supplies. "Mange takk," she answered when they offered to take the buggy back and unhitch it. She could feel eyes studying her back as she made her way up the steps to the house, the packet with sewing notions and flannel for more diapers to hem under one arm.

You weren't very friendly, one voice reminded her. *You were polite but barely*. She rubbed her forehead. Having two voices arguing was tantamount to a headache at times. This was a fairly new thing, these voices arguing in her mind. Of course she thought with her mind and dreamed there too, but argue? No. She tried to think when it had started. After Sophie ran off and married Hamre was as near as she could figure. But that was also when the deep down loneliness started. How grateful she was when Sophie came home, yet the arguing voices didn't go away and neither did the empty feeling, even when she was with Sophie. Had they both changed so much? Only when she was with Astrid now did she really feel like herself. But fall would be here soon too. *Then who will I be?* Grace, assistant teacher for her mor or Grace, preparing to marry Toby Valders?

The house seemed still without all the schoolchildren running up and down the stairs or slamming doors when they went outside, sending the vibrations up her legs. Even though they couldn't speak without their fingers, they could create a restless busyness. Grace followed her nose to the kitchen, where her mother was taking a chocolate cake out of the oven.

Kaaren set the cake pan on the wooden cooling rack on the table and turned to smile at her daughter. "Did you get everything?"

Grace nodded. "And some parts for Pa that were in." She paused. "Sophie looks very tired."

"Did she say anything about Mr. Wiste?"

"No. But I didn't stay a long time." *Because I was hoping to see Toby, and that didn't happen. I fear I am becoming as self-centered as Sophie used to be. Why is everyone asking about Mr. Wiste? Rumors must be spreading if even Mor is asking.* "She said Elizabeth is not feeling well."

"I know. Astrid was in helping in the surgery today?"

Grace nodded. "Penny wasn't herself either."

"These changes will be so hard on everyone."

❧

A couple days later Lemuel galloped up on a borrowed horse. "Dey needs you, Miz Knutson. I tole Miz Bjorklund. She say she be here in de buggy. Them babies is crying up a storm."

"I want to go too." Grace clenched her hands.

"We need you and Astrid here to cook for the men. Today they are eating at Ingeborg's, so you run on over there."

"But Sophie needs me."

"Sophie is so busy she just needs to get through one minute at a time." Kaaren grabbed her basket, and after dropping a kiss on her daughter's cheek, she said, "Pray hard" and flew out the door. Grace banked the fire, emptied the crock of cookies she'd baked into a basket, and after tucking a cloth over it, walked across the small pasture to find Astrid rolling out noodles. Fresh bread was cooling on the counter, and the fragrance of beef stew wafted from the cast-iron roaster simmering on the back of the stove.

"Separate these for me, please, and hang them over that rack." Astrid gestured to the rack on the warming shelf of the stove. She looked more closely at Grace's face. "What's the matter?"

Grace shrugged and shook her head. "Nothing."

Together the two girls set the table, dumped some of the noodles into the simmering stew, left the rest to dry for another meal, and sliced the bread. Finally Astrid rang the triangle.

"Let me guess," Haakan said as he came through the door. "The mothers are off on baby duty."

"The galloping horse?" Lars followed right behind Haakan.

Grace and Astrid both nodded.

"God dag," Jonathan said with a nod to both the girls.

Grace felt her mouth drop open. "You are learning Norwegian?" Her fingers flew faster than her tongue, which she had to force to make the right sounds.

"He asked, so we are teaching him." Trygve took his place at the table. "Along with hoeing and mounding the potatoes."

"What else can you say?" Astrid asked as she set the big crockery bowl of steaming stew in the middle of the table. "There, now, that's all."

"Let us pray." Haakan bowed his head and waited for all the others. "I Jesu navn . . ." They all joined him in the traditional Norwegian grace, ending with amen.

"Sorry, I couldn't say all that." Jonathan reached for the bread platter and took the heel, which made Andrew send him a teasing glare, and then passed the platter on. "But I am learning. Mange takk." He took the bowl of bacon-freckled greens from Samuel and looked to Grace. "If you could find the time, I would like to learn to sign also."

"In Norwegian?" Astrid's comment made the others smile.

"No, English." Jonathan dished noodles and beef onto his plate. "If you can find the time, that is."

Grace nodded as she passed the bowls and plates past her, putting some on her own, but she really wasn't hungry. Would it be proper to teach him sign language? Or would that just start up rumors about her too. She really didn't want Mrs. Valders upset with her.

Conversation flowed around her as the men discussed the afternoon's work and which crops needed cultivating and who should go help with the fencing. Jonathan and Trygve were delegated to help Andrew fence and Samuel to help hoe and pull weeds in the gardens with the girls.

Grace laid her napkin on the table and, rising, excused herself. It was a strain to follow the conversations today. To keep her hands busy, she dipped a bucket of water from the rain barrel and watered the tomato plants that were using the fence for a trellis. Several buckets later she felt a sudden release and sat down on the back steps to inhale. The day's heat washed down inside her, spreading warmth. When she returned to the house, the men were gone again and Astrid was at the stove washing dishes.

"Sorry."

"Are you all right now?"

"Ja. I just needed space."

"You and my mor. Is there something wrong?"

Grace hesitated. Would Astrid understand? Maybe, but she also had no use for romantic notions right now, and Toby was not a favorite after what happened with Andrew. "No, just the heat, I think."

Astrid quirked a brow at her. "Okay. I'll start the pie dough. You go to the cellar for the canned apples. We'll get these pies made and then go help Samuel."

"What are we making for supper?"

"There's enough stew left over. We'll put biscuits on top and bake it. The pies will make it seem better. I wish someone would go fishing. Maybe a fish fry for Sunday supper."

Maybe Toby would come. Should I invite him? If only I had someone to talk to about whether I should go find him and talk to him or keep waiting for him to come to me. She'd had that wish more than once. Sophie would be the obvious choice, but she had enough on her mind at the present. *Why do I care about him?* Two misfits was the way she'd seen them through the years. Besides, he'd needed someone to care when he and Andrew got into it. Toby had teased the other children, but he'd never teased her. Instead, she'd found him backing her up more than once, never saying anything but being right there when someone hurt her feelings. He cared for her; she cared for him. Had he outgrown that and left her behind? How would she know if this was really love or just the silly dreams of a young girl, especially if she couldn't even talk to him?

5

JONATHAN FINISHED ADDRESSING the envelope and yawned. He could hardly keep his eyes open, but he knew his parents would be anxious to hear from him, so he shook his head and smoothed the blank piece of paper.

Dear Mother and Father,

I had meant to write to you before now, but there has simply been no time. Work starts before sunrise, and by the time we've eaten supper, I only want to collapse on my bed. Tonight I am putting that off long enough to write. They say telephones are coming here soon, but I am sure I will be back in New York before that happens. I have learned to milk cows, feed calves and pigs, repair harnesses, spade a garden, hoe potatoes—did you know that you have to mound the dirt up around the plants to make sure the spuds, as they call them, are not sunburned? I will never take vegetables for granted again. Buying them at the market is easy; growing them is not.

I can harness and unharness a team as quickly as anyone, and tomorrow I am to learn to drive four up. We are preparing for haying. It is a good thing my hands are callused now, so I shouldn't get blisters again when we fork hay up onto the wagon. Trygve says haying will be easier and faster this year due to a new piece of machinery called a loader.

Sophie's baby twins, a boy and a girl, are doing well but seem to have a touch of colic and are keeping the family busy. The big news is that Penny and Hjelmer Bjorklund are moving to Bismarck, and people are wondering if the Blessing General Store will go up for sale. This is making everyone sad. Such intimate knowledge of one's neighbors' lives is so foreign to me. People in Blessing really care about one another—even those like Mrs. Valders, who manages to offend everyone on a regular basis. She wants to run their lives, as both busybody and bossy.

There are new houses going up, and the men are hurrying to get the flour mill back in business before harvest starts. That brings up something else. I had no idea there was such animosity between the farmers and the railroad. It looks to me like our railroads are gouging the very people they were designed to serve.

Well, my eyes are shutting, so I will close now. Oh, Grace is going to teach me to sign, and everyone is teaching me Norwegian.

I have learned of muscles I didn't know I had.

Your affectionate son,
Jonathan Gould

He slid the folded paper into the envelope and dropped a bit of wax on it to seal. Perhaps someone going to town would mail it for him. He groaned as he rolled into bed. He'd promised to write every week, and it was now past one week. So much for living up to his word, one of the lessons he knew his father had hoped he would learn.

Locking his hands behind his head, he stared up at the ceiling. While he attempted to think on his family in New York, Grace took over his thoughts, as she so often did lately, which kept surprising him. What pluck she had not only to learn sign language but to learn to speak like she did. Granted, sometimes he had to listen very carefully to understand what she said. But still, what would he have done had he been born with such a difficulty? How aptly they had named her. Her hands so nimbly fashioning the signs were a song in motion. When she walked, she glided; no finishing school could have taught her with more expertise. And her smile was enough to melt the hardest of hearts. He found himself thinking up things to say just to see it. What fresh air she was compared to the silliness of so many of the girls he met at social parties back home in New York.

Sometime in the night he awoke with shoulders aching from his hands locked behind his head.

No longer did he wait for a second call. His feet hit the floor before Astrid could finish saying his name. They were used to his pouring cream and sugar in the coffee that he gulped down before heading out the door. Still the last one out, he paused and inhaled the morning: the cool air, the lilac- and rose-scented dew, and the birdsong that made him want to whistle too. The wren building her nest on the front porch eave, the meadowlark from the fields to be hayed, and the rooster announcing dawn all sang to him in songs he'd not heard "before ND," as he called those days.

Following the others, he took his pail and three-legged stool and sat down at his assigned cow. He buried his forehead in her flank and fell into the rhythm he could hear all around him as the milk splashed into the buckets. All his senses were tuned to the young woman milking the cow behind him. Grace. He'd gone to bed thinking about her and arose with her name on his mind.

With a strike faster than a rattler, the cow's tail caught him around the head and mouth while in the same flash, her foot filled the milk bucket. Milk showered him, and the words that flew through his mind almost made it out his mouth. His pants, his shirt, his face, and his hands were drenched. The urge to pummel the mean and nasty bovine fled as he lumbered to his feet. He glared at her, and she stared back, placidly chewing her grain, her tail still twitching.

Never mind the guffaws of the other milkers, chagrin dripped from him along with the milk.

"Just give her a nudge to get her foot out of the bucket and save whatever you can to feed to the pigs." Haakan covered his laugh well. "It's happened to all of us. And we all know exactly how you feel."

"But what did I do wrong?"

"Nothing, most likely. She just had an idea to move her foot. The tighter you keep your forehead in her flank, the easier it is to read her intentions."

"Yes, sir." He grabbed the handle of the bucket, gave the cow's hindquarter a shove, and snatched the pail before she could kick it clear over. The once white milk looked more green now. And they wanted him to feed this to the pigs? Of course, the pigs ate sometimes with their front feet in the trough, he reminded himself as he headed for the pigpen.

"Just pour it in with the mash," Haakan called. The pigs heard him coming and crowded around the gate, squealing for him to hurry.

"Sorry, not yet." After he dumped the milk out, he dipped the bucket in the water tank to rinse it out, but Haakan called for him to get a clean one from the wagon. He made sure he was thinking about the cow and the milk from then on, no matter how enticing it was to think on Grace.

"You're now an official member of the milkers' association," Andrew teased as they scrubbed later at the wash bench. "Actually, you've done well for this to be your first time getting tricked by a milk cow."

"My first accident," Trygve told him, "the cow kicked me and the bucket into the gutter. I was so mad I coulda slit her throat right then." Trygve dried his hands on the towel hanging from a hook on the wall.

"Tell him how old you were," Lars said with a nudge.

"Oh, five or six. Young enough to bounce but old enough to get really mad. Didn't help that they all laughed at me."

Jonathan glanced at the young man next to him. Trygve's shoulders were already broadening to match the older men, and the golden hairs on his arms glinted in the sun—even his hands already wore some scars and the look of wear. Trygve had been working like a man ten years already, and he was a year younger than Jonathan.

As always, the girls had gone before to help get breakfast on the table, and now to regale Mrs. Bjorklund with his mishap. She gave him a commiserating look when he filed into the kitchen, but he could tell she caught the humor in it too.

"You all right?"

"Only thing hurt was my pride, besides the waste of good milk."

"Wasn't the first time, and I'm sure it won't be the last." She handed him a cinnamon roll along with a tender pat on his arm.

Jonathan stared at the roll. She might as well have given him a medal of honor. He stopped his grin by filling his mouth with a bite of pure heaven.

"Leave it to Mor to spoil the hired help," Andrew muttered with a sideways grin at his mother.

As the end of the meal neared, Ingeborg stood. "I have an announcement." As all eyes turned her way, she smiled at each of them. "Kaaren and I have decided we will have a fish fry for supper Sunday. That means all you fishermen better dig a bunch of worms because we are going to need a lot of fish—cleaned fish."

"And ice cream?" someone asked.

"Of course." She glanced at Haakan. "If we have enough ice left in the icehouse."

"We have plenty. Might make it clear to August."

"According to Thorliff, we will have refrigeration in homes before long, like the railroad cars." Andrew reached for the last cinnamon roll. "Gas now and electricity eventually."

"I'll take running water in the house before that."

"Just think, if we had running water in the house, we could have one of those flush toilets. No more privy."

"I can guess what Lars and I'll be doing this winter," Haakan muttered, pushing his chair back. "All these fandangle new ideas . . ."

"Enjoy your cultivator," Ingeborg said sweetly and patted his shoulder.

Lars and Haakan led the laughter as they each snagged their hats off the rack and trooped out the door.

"You go on over to Andrew's soon as you're done with the driving lesson," Haakan ordered Jonathan and Andrew. "I've got a few more rows with the cultivator, and I'll be along. See if we can get that last section fenced today."

Barney's barking spun them all around.

"The pigs are out!" Andrew headed for the barn but yelled over his shoulder, "Go shut the garden gate. Ma will kill us if the hogs get in there."

Jonathan headed for the garden, slamming the gate to the yard as he ran by.

"What's the matter?" Astrid called from the back door.

"Pigs are out." Jonathan dropped the wire loop over the post of the wire gate and trotted back toward the barn, where pigs of all sizes were darting out in every direction.

"What happened?"

"They took out one whole section of fence," Trygve grumbled. "That old sow must have been working on that post forever. Someone ever tell you pigs are dumb animals, they don't know what they're talking about."

"Leastwise it didn't happen when none of us were here." Andrew whistled for Barney to round up a couple of deserters, as the herd was now digging in the soft dirt in front of the barn, grunting in satisfaction, tails coiled or flicking in delight.

"We need to get those weaners cut soon."

"Weaners?"

"That last batch we took off the sow. Need to castrate the males so the meat doesn't taste rank."

"So who does that?" *This is one chore I do not want to learn—ever.*

"Usually Andrew. He's best at it. Give him a sharp knife and we'll have mountain oysters for supper." Trygve grinned at the look of confusion on Jonathan's face. "Ask Andrew. He'll give you a better description."

"Okay, Pa's got the fence ready," Andrew said. "Let's herd 'em back nice and easy."

Arms wide spread, moving slowly, they eased the pigs back around the corner of the barn. With Barney darting ahead of the sow, the hogs poured back into their pen and headed for the water trough. Lars, Andrew, and Haakan nailed the two-by-sixes back in place, adding another one right at ground level.

"That's to keep that old girl from getting her snout under the board. Give her an hour, and I swear she could take the barn down."

"But why? They have all the food they can eat, plenty of water, and a wallow to sun in."

"Grass is always greener on the other side of the fence. Besides, animals, like people, get bored. If they were out in the wild, they'd have to spend all their waking time foraging for food. Here they get fed good twice a day. If that old girl weren't such a good mamma, she'd have been made into ham a long time ago. She just has this perverse attraction for fences—and their destruction."

By the end of the driving session, Jonathan had mastered handling four lines instead of two, weaving the lines between his fingers so as to have control over four bits in four horses' mouths. He backed the hay wagon, turned going forward and backward, and set the wagon bed right under the hay lift outside the barn wall. Andrew's praise rang in his ears, the kind of accolades he'd wished to have heard from his father.

But there was no team driving at home, nor any other of the manual things he was showing such an aptitude for. He thought on this as he drifted off to sleep that night. If the choice were studying or working here with this family, he feared he would choose this sort of work quite joyfully. Whatever would his father and grandfather think of this? Would they be pleased he chose a path for himself or see it as a desertion from the family business?

❧

Sunday gave him even more time to think. He attended church with the Bjorklunds as he had before. While he knew some of his church's background, his family did not attend services often, only on specific community occasions, and they'd not told him he couldn't attend church in Blessing. The hymns and the liturgy all were unfamiliar, but he had no trouble following along in the hymnbooks. The psalms he'd been taught by his grandmother on his mother's side. Any spiritual heritage had come from the little he learned from her. He wondered if the Bjorklunds knew of his background, but he had no desire to share it unless someone asked him.

The words of the Scripture for the day were read in Norwegian. His mind leaped forward two rows to where Grace sat next to her father with Trygve on her other side. Would that he were sitting in her brother's place. *Do I have a crush on her?* The thought jerked him upright in his seat.

Pastor Solberg caught his attention when he read the verses again in English. "Jesus was talking with the disciples when one of the leaders of the synagogue stood and asked him this question. 'Master, which is the great commandment in the law?' Jesus said unto him, 'Thou shalt love the Lord thy God with all thy heart, and with all thy soul, and with all thy mind. This is the first and great commandment. And the second is like unto it, Thou shalt love thy neighbour as thyself.' Simple, isn't it?" Solberg continued. "We're asked to do only two things—to love our God and to love those around us." He smiled out over his congregation. "So simple and so easy to say, but what about when someone disappoints you? When someone gets angry at you or you get angry at them? And the last line, 'love thy neighbour as thyself,' does that mean you have to love yourself? And how do you do that without seeming prideful, a nasty sin according to other Scriptures?"

Jonathan waited for him to answer his own questions. He knew he had disappointed his father on many occasions, often no matter how hard he tried. He knew that sometimes he was jealous of his older brother Thomas, who it seemed could do no wrong. He shifted in his seat. His mind took off across the continent to remember one of the times he'd stood before his father's desk, knowing he deserved the scolding but wishing for one word of approbation. He remembered the sorrow in his father's eyes. Was God like that?

Last Sunday the pastor had talked about how much God loves His children. Did he believe in a God who loved His children or in a God who set up rules too numerous to be fully obeyed? And most important, wasn't this the same God of the Old Testament and, according to Pastor Solberg, the New Testament also? *So go talk to him*, he heard himself thinking. *I will. Or maybe I should ask Ingeborg.* While he always called her Mrs. Bjorklund to her face, in his mind she'd always been the Ingeborg of his father's memories.

As everyone rose for the final hymn, he watched Dr. Elizabeth, who was playing the piano. She looked to be a bit green around the mouth and eyes. *Go tell her you could take her place and play for Sunday services if you could have some practice time on the piano.* He flexed his fingers. He'd not played for more than a month, but that was one thing he did well—even his father said so.

As the congregation was dismissed, instead of playing until everyone was out of the church, Dr. Elizabeth got up and hurried out the back door.

Within a few minutes, while the men gathered in small groups talking, the women had brought the food from their wagons and were setting dishes and pans out on the long tables set up on sawhorses in the shade of the cottonwood trees planted years earlier. The children ran between the church and the schoolyard, laughing and playing.

Jonathan kept watch, and when Dr. Elizabeth rejoined her family, taking Inga from her father's arms, he approached her. "Dr. Bjorklund?"

"Yes, Mr. Gould, how can I help you?" She looked better than she had in the church.

"Well, I'm thinking that perhaps I could help you, and please, I am not Mr. Gould. That is my father."

"Jonathan, then. How is it you could help me?" Her smile welcomed him closer. Her little daughter leaned her head against her mother's shoulder, eyes drifting closed.

"I saw that you weren't feeling too good, and I thought . . . well, I have played the piano since I was six, and with a bit of practice I could learn the service and play the hymns."

"Have you ever played for church before?"

"No, but I read music well, and I'm sure Pastor Solberg would translate or tell me what to do. If you want some help, that is." He held his hat in his hands and reminded his fingers not to crush it. Perhaps this wasn't a good idea after all.

"Jonathan, I would be most grateful if you could do this. Let's go find Pastor Solberg and ask him about it."

"I'd best ask Haakan too. I mean, I really would need practice time, and there isn't a lot of that lying around."

"You go get Pastor Solberg, and I'll meet you at our buggy. I'm going to lay this sleepy one down before she breaks my arm."

Pastor Solberg led the singing of the grace and then joined them at the buggy as he said he would. "So you could be a replacement for Dr. Elizabeth for a while. Is that right?"

"I think so. I mean, if you would like we could go inside and I'll play for you."

"The only problem would be the liturgy. You don't know Norwegian, but I could write it out in English so you could follow along." He rubbed his chin as he spoke and nodded, obviously giving it some serious thought. "Have you mentioned this to Haakan yet?"

"No, but here he comes."

Within minutes they'd all agreed on the new plan and joined the others for Sunday dinner. Jonathan would be staying after church to practice for a couple of hours, giving up his first chance to go fishing with all the young men that afternoon. His gaze sought Grace's across the gathering. She nodded and smiled wistfully. How had she already learned what was decided? And why was she looking so sad?

6

"WE NEED PARTIES MORE OFTEN."

"I agree." Kaaren swiped the hair from her face with the back of her hand. "Good thing our fishermen did well." She took a cake pan from Ingeborg's warming oven and added the four fish she'd just finished frying to the growing stack.

"So Sophie and the babies and the boardinghouse are doing well?" Ingeborg put glasses on a tray, along with silverware, to be taken outdoors.

"Ja, Mrs. Sam is making her toe the line. Not that nursing twins gives Sophie much time for anything else. That little Joy latches on and sucks her mother dry. Hamre has to be encouraged more."

"I've noticed that with boy babies. I think girls are stronger."

"Only because they have to learn early to fight to live." Kaaren laid another cornmeal-coated fish in the frying pan and pulled it back to keep from spattering grease so wildly. "Ingeborg, I know I loved my children, but there is something so special about holding grand-babies."

"I know. It's hard to keep from spoiling Inga something terrible. When she screws up that little mouth and narrows her eyes when she doesn't get what she wants, I have to swing her up in my arm and kiss the daylights out of her. Then we both giggle, and she is back to being her sunny self. I watch little Carl and wonder what he will be like. Right now he is more content to sit on my lap and cuddle and watch his cousin running on her tippy toes."

"I am so glad and grateful that Sophie came home, and I get to be there with her. I might have had to take that train to Seattle more than once a year." She turned the fish in the pan and went back to dusting more.

"Here's the last of them," Thorliff said as he set another half-full bucket on the table. "Do we have enough?" He scratched at a mosquito bite on the back of his neck. "Pesky things near to ate me alive."

"How's the ice cream doing?"

"You'll have to ask Pa. I was in charge of fish. But they have three cranks going. The cranking contest is between Trygve and Jonathan." He looked around. "Where's Elizabeth?"

"Lying down with Carl. Inga is out with the big girls, so she's happy as a little pig in the mud."

"You want me to start taking things out?"

"Please." Ingeborg watched him pick up the tray laden with glasses and utensils and leave by the back door, whistling as he went. Was it wrong to be so proud of her elder son she was sure her apron strings would pop? Often she wondered if Roald was watching down from heaven and rejoicing in this son. Thorliff and Andrew were so different but both such fine young men.

Haakan came in a bit later, announcing, "Ice cream is all packed in ice. When do we eat?"

"Any time. These are the last pans of fish. Are Penny and Hjelmer here yet?"

"Nope." He snatched a fish off the top of the stack, dodged his wife's playful attack with the pancake turner, and grabbed the handles of the two biggest baskets of food waiting on the table. "Anything in the well house?"

"Potato salad and rice salad. And please bring in a jug of milk too."

As he went out, Astrid came in. "Need anything else done?"

"The pan of rolls in the oven is done. Butter the tops and turn them out. That basket is for the rolls." Ingeborg motioned to a cloth-lined basket on the counter. "Where's Grace?"

"Swinging with Inga. Good thing Pa put the swing back up. Inga loves it." Astrid set the oven-sized pan on the table and, dipping her fingers in the butter, spread the golden butter over the hot rolls and then flipped the pan over onto the waiting dish towel, sticking one finger into her mouth.

"That's why we have pot holders."

"I know."

"Please make sure the tables are set right. And ring the triangle. We're ready to serve."

"You will miss Astrid come fall," Kaaren said as they took care of the last tasks. "And I know this will be hard on Grace again too. If not for Astrid, Grace would not have managed Sophie's elopement."

"They are good for each other. But Grace knows Astrid will return, and now Sophie is here."

"But she's retreating again even with them both here, and that's not like her."

Hearing footsteps, Ingeborg switched to signing. "Give her time. She has great depth to her. She just needs space to make this adjustment to being grown."

Barney's barking told them the other Bjorklunds had arrived. Ingeborg glanced at Kaaren. "Perfect timing."

"Should I wake Elizabeth?"

"No. Let her sleep. She's looking mighty peaked. Between her and Thorliff they do enough work for three people."

"Look who's talking."

"I've been slowing down some. What about you?"

Kaaren half shrugged. "That's what we have children for, to help pick up the slack when we get older." Using two pot holders, she lifted one of the pans of fish and headed for the door. "Let's eat before this gets cold."

After the pause for grace, everyone served themselves at the food table and found a place to sit, the young people using the stairs to the front porch and the railing too while the folks took the chairs at the other tables.

Ingeborg made sure everyone was taken care of before she filled her own plate and took the chair between Haakan and Penny. "My, that breeze feels good."

"Keeps the mosquitoes away too." Haakan sighed on his first bite of fish. "I don't know why we don't have fried fish more often."

"There's no one with the time to go fishing since you put Samuel in charge of feeding all the young stock. He hardly has time to run his snares either. Sophie was asking when she could have rabbit on the menu again."

"Maybe that's another thing young Gould should learn."

"I'd love to get that buck that took out part of a row of corn." Ingeborg glanced over at the porch to see Grace feeding Inga, who was sitting on her pa's lap. A burst of laughter said someone had told a funny story. Interesting how Jonathan fit in so well when they'd been expecting him to be a problem. She watched his face and realized he was watching Grace. Come to think of it, he watched Grace a lot. Was Kaaren aware of that? And did it matter? After all, he'd be heading back to New York at the end of August and Grace would start teaching with her mother at the Blessing School for the Deaf.

"I thought I'd come tell you first."

Ingeborg jerked her attention back to the conversation going on around her. She stared at Penny, sure she knew what was coming.

"I have agreed to sell my store to move to Bismarck. I really debated on finding a manager, but I think a clean cut might be better—" Her voice broke. She blinked and raised her chin. "Better in the long run. Otherwise, I will be tempted to give up and come back."

Recognizing how hard it was for Penny to keep from breaking down, Ingeborg willed her own eyes not to leak. While she wanted to take Penny's hand, she clenched her own in her lap. She and Penny were much alike, not wanting to weep in public. And these would be not only tears of sorrow, but tears that tore one's heart out and dashed it against a stone wall.

Even Hjelmer stammered when he said he was grateful that Haakan and Lars were buying the machinery business, since that made it so much easier for him to part with it.

Ingeborg stared from Hjelmer to Haakan. When had that transpired? And without talking it over with her? She glanced at Kaaren to see a look of astonishment on her face too. Here, she'd been wanting to talk to Haakan about the possibility of their buying the store with the agreement that Penny could buy it back at the same price if she so desired down the road. Meaning if things didn't work out in Bismarck for Hjelmer.

Shock and disappointment moved on to disgust, finally flaring from a bed of burning coals. Hadn't they always discussed everything? Hadn't she depended on that for trust and wisdom? "I think I'll go check on Carl." She felt like she had a steel bar up her spine and she was chewing on glass. *Lord, please help me get through the rest of this day without letting the others know of my anger—no, resentment—no, I am so mad at him I could scream. I haven't been this mad for years. I thought I was over such displays of temper. Temper, my right foot.* Both small child and Elizabeth were still sleeping soundly. She heard footfalls on the back steps and steeled herself, took a deep breath and let it out slowly. One more and she could turn and be civil.

"You didn't know that, did you?" Penny's voice sounded soft in the twilight.

"No, and neither did Kaaren. When did it come about?"

"Just this afternoon, I think. Hjelmer has said he hoped they would do that. He went to them with a good offer."

Ingeborg turned, shaking her head. "I was hoping to buy your store, but now I don't see how we can swing both. At least not for cash, and I know you need the money to buy a house."

"Everything I have is tied up in my store." The tone of her voice said far more than money was involved. Penny had loved her store ever since she first dreamed of it, long before it actually came about.

More steps and Kaaren pushed open the screen door. "You might as well fill me in too."

"It happened just a little while ago."

"Was there such a hurry they couldn't wait to talk with us? It's not like we were gone or something. Or that Hjelmer was leaving tomorrow."

"Not tomorrow, but the day after. They'll sign the papers at the bank tomorrow, and then he'll take what he has and go looking for a house for us. He needs to start work next week."

"Hjelmer Bjorklund is not going to like working in an office on someone else's time schedule. He likes his freedom too much."

"You know that and I know that, but he has to learn that for himself." Penny mopped her eyes with a tatted-edged handkerchief. She reached for Ingeborg and collapsed against her shoulder, tears soaking the soft calico and her own shoulders shaking.

Ingeborg's tears dripped off her chin as she stroked Penny's back and murmured comforting mother sounds.

Kaaren gave the grate a good shaking and added small sticks to the glowing coals. She opened the draft, added bigger chunks, and slammed the lids back into place. "They don't deserve fresh coffee." Her mutter pierced the heavy gloom and made all three of them sniff.

"You could make it with dishwater." Ingeborg clapped a hand over her mouth. *Uff da!* What was she saying?

"Adding pepper was more along my way of thinking." Kaaren dumped the grounds from the bottom of the pot into the bucket for compost. They didn't feed the coffee grounds to the chickens for fear it might taint the eggs. After rinsing the pot, she filled it with water from the reservoir so the coffee would be ready sooner.

"Mor, is the lemonade—?" Astrid stopped and stared at the three women. "What happened?"

"Nothing. We'll talk about it later." Ingeborg's hands fluttered in a shooing motion, as if she were herding chickens. "The lemonade is in the well house. There should be ice out there too to put in it." She reached out and patted her daughter's shoulder. "Don't worry, all right?"

The look Astrid gave her said she wouldn't let it drop forever, but she headed back out the door.

That evening after all the others had left and the house was closed up for the night, Ingeborg sat on the edge of the bed and grimaced when her brush caught in a tangle. She gave it a jerk rather than gently disentangling the recalcitrant hairs and clamped her teeth together. *I will not bring it up. He has to know how angry this makes me.* She caught his steady gaze in the mirror.

"I know you are angry with me."

"That I am." She turned to look at him. "What was the hurry that we couldn't discuss it?"

"I knew you wouldn't want to."

"How did you know that?" She tried to speak sweetly, but it sounded more like vinegar.

"You don't want them to go."

"And you do?"

"Not at all, but Hjelmer needs to do what he thinks best. Don't you agree?"

"Yes. If this is God's will for them, then they must be about it." *If you don't sound sanctimonious.* Her strokes softened, then picked up speed again. "But I am not convinced this is what God wants them to do. They are rushing into it." She watched his eyebrows go up.

"You think God will run things by you?"

"Haakan Bjorklund, what a thing to say." Her eyebrows rammed against each other in the center of her forehead. Her jaw ached from the clamping teeth until her thoughts careened back to their discussions on buying more cows and how bullheaded she'd been. She still thought she was right. "I was hoping that we could buy the store and machinery all at once, so if they wanted, or needed to, they could come home again."

"What is stopping us? Just because you are angry that I went ahead . . . if that is what you were thinking, why are you . . . ?" He shook his head slowly, his jaw askew. "Ingeborg, sometimes you just have to trust me."

"You think this is about my trusting you?" It was her turn to shake her head. The newly purchased cows stood in a row between them. "It seems more like you not trusting me."

She braided her hair much too tight but tied a ribbon at the end and threw the braid over her shoulder. A gentle tug told her Haakan wanted to turn out the light and let this be done with. She clenched her teeth again and heard a voice in her head so clearly she dare not argue. *Do not let the sun go down on your anger.* The sun had gone down long ago, but the voice reminded her that she and Haakan had agreed early in their marriage to follow God's Word, and this was one point they'd agreed to honor. She sucked in a deep breath. *I cannot say I'm sorry. This isn't my fault. It is Haakan's.*

"Come, my Inga, let us put this on the shelf for now. I am sorry I didn't talk with you first."

She followed the tug on her braid and scooted back into his welcoming arms. "I forgive you."

"Good. And I you."

"But I—" He cut off her argument with a gentle kiss. "'Night." Though it was awhile before they went to sleep, she felt the comfort of his arm over her waist and listened for his first gentle snore that told her he was really asleep. *God, I wish there were easy answers at times. One thing settles out and something else comes up. I don't like changes like this. I will miss Penny and Hjelmer dreadfully. Besides, how could I run a store with all the other things I have to do? But what do you want us to do?*

7

COULD THERE BE ANYTHING more precious in the whole world?

Grace stared down into the basket, where the twins slept cuddled together. Hamre's hair was so fine as to look bald, while darker wisps feathered little Joy's head. She traced the tiny perfect fingers on a baby hand with a tender touch. Her heart swelled with a love she'd not known before.

"They are so perfect." She signed the words so the sound wouldn't wake the babies.

"I know," Sophie signed back. "But they are not so perfect when they both demand to be fed at the same time."

Grace smiled and settled back in the rocking chair. Sophie had moved into Bridget and Henry's quarters after having the woodwork repainted, new curtains hung, and the furniture rearranged. Perhaps when the twins were older, they would have a room of their own, but for now the basket sat on a trunk at the foot of the bed.

She couldn't get over the difference in her sister. Already she'd slimmed back to half the size she'd been before the delivery. Black circles under her eyes testified to lack of sleep, but their mother said that was normal for a new mother, even more so with twins.

"Do you have enough milk for both of them?"

"So far, although they want to nurse every two hours. Hamre eats and falls asleep before getting full enough, I think. Then he wakes up first. Dr. Elizabeth said to keep him awake to make him eat more. Ha! I can't keep me awake, let alone him. Thank God for Mrs. Sam."

"You could go take a nap now while they're asleep."

"But you are here to visit, and I so long for something besides babies."

"Sophie!"

"I know. I love them so much, and I'm grateful they are all right, but I'm even more grateful they are all right and now outside of me."

"You were huge." Grace pantomimed how big Sophie had been.

"I know. Believe me, I know." Sophie leaned forward and signed, "Can you keep a secret?"

Grace pulled back. "You're not running away again, are you?"

"Don't be silly. How could I run away with all this, and besides, all I want now is right here in Blessing."

Grace stared at her sister—the dreamy look in her eyes, the gentle smile. "So the rumors are true."

Sophie's eyes popped open. "What rumors?"

"That Mr. Wiste and you . . . that you're . . ."

"What? That he loves me?"

Grace nodded. *And why* she wondered yet again, *didn't you tell me?*

"I wanted to tell you, dear Grace, but Garth asked me to wait until he could talk with Far." Sophie clenched her hands harder. "Please don't be cross with me. I love him. We are going to be married as soon as his house is finished, and Mrs. Valders is going to have not just one fit but many, for it won't have been a full year since either his wife or my husband died, and I don't really care." Sophie reached for Grace's hands and folded them in her own. "I know it is soon, but his children need a mother and mine need a father. His sister will bring Grant and Linnie out as soon as the house is finished, and she and her family will live with us until their new house is ready. Did I tell you Garth's sister Helga and her husband are moving to Blessing?"

"I think you might have mentioned it. Have you talked with Far and Mor—about getting married?"

"Garth is going to talk with Far tomorrow night after the board meeting for the flour mill."

"And Mor?" Did Sophie not realize that if Grace had heard the rumors so had their parents? Had she become so distant from all of them that their feelings didn't matter? Grace tried to push down the seed of resentment.

"I was hoping she would come in today with you."

"She and Ilse are canning strawberries and making jam. I should be helping them, but I wanted to come and be with you."

"Thank you. Well, are you happy for me?"

Grace tamed her thoughts before nodding and giving Sophie a gentle smile. "Yes, I am. Mr. Wiste is a fine man." She paused again and then grinned. "And he's not likely to take you away from Blessing."

"So what about you?"

"What?"

"Astrid says Jonathan Gould can't keep his eyes off you."

"Astrid is being a gossip." But she could feel the heat rising up her neck.

"You are blushing." Sophie fanned her neck with her fingers along with a teasing grin. "He is very handsome."

"He wants me to teach him to sign, so I gave him one of our alphabet charts."

"I'd think he'd rather you formed his fingers into the proper shapes like you do the little children."

"Sophie Knu—Bjorklund! What a thing to say." Grace's fingers warmed clear to the tips to match her face. She stumbled over the words in her confusion and resorted to fingers only. "How can you even think such things?"

"Do you like him?"

"Of course. He's a very nice young man."

"Does your heart pick up speed when he walks into a room?"

Grace shook her head. *Ah, Sophie, if only you knew. My heart is already tied up with a knot and a bow. I just wish I could get a chance to talk with Toby and find out what is going on.*

"Do you look up and find him watching you?"

"Sophie, that is quite enough. Besides, he will be leaving to go back to New York at the end of August. And that will be the end of that."

"You can always write letters." Sophie gave her a droll look and sighed. "So then, have a good time but be aware that what you think and what he thinks might be two entirely different things. Doesn't the name Mrs. Jonathan Gould have a nice ring to it?"

"Very nice but not for me. I will help Mor in teaching the new students. We will open the school to five more pupils this year. That will be about twenty, if that many inquire."

"Doesn't Mor have a waiting list?" Sophie turned toward her babies. "There he goes again. Hamre, you just ate."

Grace leaned over the basket. "I'll take him up so he doesn't wake Joy." She lifted the squirming baby. "Oh, you're soaked."

"Ja, his system works very well. Cover him up when you change him, or you'll get squirted."

Choking back a retort, Grace laid the now whimpering baby on the padded top of the chest of drawers. She unpinned his diaper, remembering how the same thing had happened when Samuel was a baby. She and Sophie had thought their baby brother the most fascinating creature. And it was she, not Sophie, who had tried to help Mor change his diapers then. They were too little when Trygve was born to pay much attention. After dusting Hamre with powder, she pinned a new diaper in place and added dry soakers and finally a clean dry gown, tying the ribbons at neck and chest. By this time Hamre was throwing in a howl or two. She carried him to his mother, who had a hemmed flannel blanket to throw over him and her shoulder while he nursed.

Sophie settled her son into the crook of her arm and smiled down at him as he latched on to the breast. "Now, don't go to sleep on me."

She glanced up at Grace. "Calves and lambs are cuter than human babies, don't you think?"

"Don't let Mor hear you say that."

"Well, they are. And a lot more independent too. A calf wouldn't lie around whimpering. It would go bop the cow on the udder and help itself." She settled back in the rocking chair. "Have you walked through Mr. Wiste's house?"

Why is she asking me that? "No. But it looks to be a big one."

"I wondered why he wanted me to look at the different plans and help him choose. But he had already decided he wanted to marry me, and he wanted me to like the house. Isn't that just the most thoughtful thing?"

Grace nodded, not sure she'd caught everything Sophie said, but signing right now was a bit difficult. She got the idea that it was all about Mr. Wiste, however. *Sophie, Sophie, this sounds like last September all over again. Hamre this and Hamre that.*

"I know you think I'm going on like I did over Hamre, but my dear sister, I have learned a few things. One of them is that life can change faster than you can blink your eyes. I'd rather grab hold and go along for the ride than stand on the sidelines and watch life pass me by. Both Garth and I have lost someone dear, and that makes us not want to waste a minute." Her serious look turned to a grin. "Besides, just think of all the conniption fits Mrs. Valders is going to have over this. Why, she might as well write to President Roosevelt and complain." Her eyebrows wiggled, setting Grace to grinning back.

"You really believe this is what God has planned for you?"

"I do, and we have prayed about this a lot. We will have the wedding in the church, and I want you to stand up with me. Garth is having his brother with him. We haven't talked with Pastor Solberg yet, but we are hoping for mid-July. Maybe I'll be able to wear one of my newer dresses by then."

"Well, if we need to sew one, we better get on it."

"You could wear the dress you sewed for graduation."

"All right."

Sophie glanced down at her baby. "Sure enough, sound asleep. Here, you tap on the bottoms of his feet while I pat his cheeks. Hamre, wake up." They got him to nurse a bit more, but his little mouth would just slip away from the nipple. Sophie held him to her shoulder and rubbed his back until he burped and then laid him back in the basket next to his sister. "At least Joy didn't wake up."

"Why don't I go and get us some lemonade."

But when Grace came back, Sophie was on the bed, sleeping as peacefully as her children. Grace went back to the kitchen and set the lemonade in the icebox. "I'm going over to see Elizabeth," she told Mrs. Sam. "I'll be back in a little while."

"They's sleepin'?"

"For the moment."

Before leaving, Grace took another look at Sophie sleeping, once such a familiar sight and now so different. *You ran away but now have two beautiful babies and are about to marry again. If you are like the prodigal son, I guess I am the stay-at-home brother. I definitely have his attitude today. Why am I feeling jealous of my own sister?*

Grace set her straw hat with the tulle ribbon back on her head, using a hatpin to hold it in place, and pausing on the front step, made a lightning decision. She'd walk the long way, around the flour mill and then back to Thorliff and Elizabeth's house. Just perhaps she would see Toby, and just perhaps he would take a moment and come to talk with her. While the men waved from high up where they were putting the roof on the concrete building, Toby didn't bother coming down. But then, what silly idea made her think he would? The men would have teased him forever. *Don't be such a ninny, Grace. You'll embarrass yourself and him too.*

Instead of going in the front door and passing Elizabeth's surgery, she let herself in the back screen door.

"Is anyone home?"

Thelma, her hair covered with a white dish towel, came up the stairs from the cellar brushing a cobweb off her arm. She nodded at Grace. "Don't know how those pests move in so fast. We need a cat.

Mouse droppings all over the place."

"Our barn cats take care of the house too. We could bring in one of the half-grown kittens, but they are pretty wild." Grace glanced about the immaculate kitchen. "Is Elizabeth out on a call?"

"No, she's lying down. You want I should get her?"

"No. I know she's not feeling well. I'll go on back to the board-inghouse. I'm spending the afternoon with Sophie, but she fell asleep too."

Thelma looked up. "That's the doctor's bell. I'll go see what she needs and be right back."

Grace waited, glancing around the room, admiring the gas stove and the hand pump at the sink so they needn't carry water. Mor and Far wanted to put that in at their house too, but so far it had not happened.

Thelma charged back into the kitchen. "Doctor says to go for Ingeborg. Can you harness up the buggy and go?"

"I can run faster than harness the horse and buggy, but I could ride the horse."

"Please, go."

Without asking more, Grace tore out the door. What could be wrong that Elizabeth needed Ingeborg? Her baby? What else?

8

INGEBORG HEARD THE HORSE galloping up the lane and went to the door. What was Grace doing on Thorliff's horse?

"Tante Ingeborg, she needs you!" Grace slid off the horse as soon as it stopped. "Dr. Elizabeth."

"Oh, dear God. I'll get my bag. You run down to the barn and ask the boys to harness the buggy." Ingeborg whipped her apron over her head as she ran for the bedroom and her bag, although why she'd need it at Elizabeth's, she wasn't certain. Badly bruised bag in hand, she stopped long enough to grab a sunbonnet from the coatrack.

"What is it?" Astrid came down the stairs from where she'd been rocking Inga to sleep.

"Dr. Elizabeth needs me. Good thing we have Inga here. You'll have to finish up supper. Perhaps Grace can stay and help you."

"We'll be fine. Go on and don't worry."

"I'm not worrying. God has everything under control—just thinking out loud."

Grace charged up the steps and burst in the door. "They'll be ready by the time you get to the barn." Her fingers did her talking so she could catch her breath.

"Takk." She paused before the door. "We'll plan on keeping Inga

75

overnight if this is what I think it is."

"She's losing the baby?" Astrid asked, following her mother out the door.

"Possibly. This pregnancy hasn't been right." Ingeborg looked to the barn, where Jonathan and Trygve had the horse backed into the buggy traces. "Take care."

"Go with God."

"I do. Thank you, my dear." She kissed her daughter's cheek, gave Grace a hug, and let Jonathan hand her into the buggy. "Thank you too." She picked up the reins, clucked the horse forward, and driving a tight circle, turned down the lane in a quick trot. *Please, Father, protect Elizabeth. Restore her health. Comfort her.* Her thoughts roamed back to 1880, when she and Roald immigrated to this new land. She'd had to fight to learn to forgive herself for losing their baby. She'd taken a fall when out hunting, something Roald hadn't wanted her doing anyway. And then with Haakan, when she never conceived again after Astrid, she often thought perhaps God was punishing her. Thankfully those terrible days were done and gone, and she now knew with all certainty that God had forgiven her.

But Elizabeth would most likely suffer the same doubts, especially since this was her second one to lose, although she had carried this baby longer. Doubt and guilt seemed to be the way of women when they lost a baby. Now she figured some babies died early because something was wrong with them and this was nature's way of taking care of things. It didn't help the hurt of the hour, however.

She prayed her way into town and upstairs to Elizabeth's side.

The bloody sheets and towels told their own sad story. Thelma nodded to her and bundled the evidence up to wash.

"Oh, my dear." She sat on the edge of the bed and held Elizabeth in her arms to let her cry out her sorrow.

"I lost my baby boy," Elizabeth sobbed. "I-I can't find Thorliff, and I . . ." Her mutterings dissolved in shuddering tears.

Ingeborg's tears of comfort slid down her face as she murmured mother things and stroked Elizabeth's hair back from her sweaty forehead. When the storm lightened, she asked, "Are you still bleeding?"

"I guess. I had Thelma help me."

"Not overly heavy?"

"No. Just a few contractions and it was over. I want to bury him."

"You shall. And we'll plant a tree for him, in memory."

"You think I did too much? Maybe I should have gone to bed or—"

"You know that's not true. You've been feeling ill for most of the pregnancy. Something just wasn't right." Ingeborg dipped a cloth in a basin of cool water and sponged Elizabeth's face. "How about I give you a basin bath and you put on a clean nightdress? Then I'll mix my brew. You drink that and you'll sleep for a while."

"Inga?"

"Astrid will keep her at our house, and I'll stay here as long as you need me."

"Dearest Ingeborg, what would I do without you?"

Ingeborg kissed her daughter-in-law's forehead. "God gives us each other for such times as this and for every day."

Sometime later, with Elizabeth resting, the room straightened again, and the evening breeze puffing the sheer curtains, Ingeborg sipped the iced tea that Thelma had brought up and thought about the little boy who would never know his bestemor and bestefar, who would never run in the grass with his big sister, and who already knew the joys of heaven. "Father, I know you love him more than I could, but give him some extra love, please. He didn't get to discover what a wonderful earth you have given us, but I realize you know what is best. I know that he is healed now of whatever was wrong, and while we are all sad, he is in your mighty hands, safe and home." She wiped away her tears and swallowed some more tea. The footsteps she heard coming down the hall were heavy, a man's steps. Thorliff.

Her son came through the door, saw his wife in the bed and his mother at the window. "I'm sorry; I came as soon as I heard." His whisper sounded like a shout in the stillness. "Is it over, then?"

"Ja. Elizabeth just needs to sleep. I gave her something to help her relax. Now we need to pray for healing for her. Losing a baby that never lived has its own sorrow."

"But we will have more babies?"

"I don't see why not. But she will grieve this one too."

"What can I do?"

"Fix a little box, and we will bury him in your backyard. He can have a cross there, and then we'll plant a tree for him. I thought maybe an apple tree."

"He. A son."

"Ja."

Thorliff stared out the window.

Ingeborg knew he wasn't seeing the yard any more than she had.

"But Elizabeth will be all right?"

"I believe so. She is strong."

"I-I can't lose her. If we never have any more children, I can't lose her." He raised his tear-streaked face to stare into his mother's eyes.

"I know how you feel, but only God knows the future."

"Thorliff?" Elizabeth sounded sleepy.

"Ja, I am here." Thorliff sat on the edge of the bed and gathered his wife into his arms. Ingeborg left the two of them to cry together. Roald had not cried with her. Roald had never cried that she remembered. Perhaps he did after his brother Carl died, but not in her presence. Good thing that God never shared the future with His children. They wouldn't want to go on.

She made her way downstairs and to the kitchen, where Thelma was mixing biscuits.

"Supper will be ready as soon as these are done." Thelma patted the dough out on a floured board and, using a glass rim, cut the dough. "I put cheese and dill in—thought some extra might perk up the doctor's appetite. She ain't been eating good the last couple days. Now we know why."

"Thank you for your care of her."

"Just wish I could do more, but . . ."

"So do we all, but we can be content knowing we do our best."

"That little Inga, she's the best thing that ever happened to me. You think there'll be more little ones?"

"Yes, I do, and I'm sure you'll be able to enjoy Sophie's twins as they get a bit older."

"I had a baby once. Cholera took him and my man."

Ingeborg swallowed her surprise. Thelma had never said anything about her past life before. "I'm sorry to hear that."

"Long time ago."

Ingeborg stared at the woman sliding the pan of biscuits into the oven. She had no idea even how old Thelma was. Or what her last name was. And considering all the hours Thelma had spent here in the surgery and just visiting, it was amazing that nothing had ever been said. "Where did you come from?"

"Fargo."

Ingeborg waited until she realized no more words were forthcoming. Thelma never took part in any of the family events, even when they were here. She always remained in the background. The only time she'd seen her away from the house was in church. Strange how they just accepted her as part of the woodwork.

"I'm setting the table in the dining room for you and Mr. Bjorklund. I'll take a tray up to the doctor when she wants it. I thought biscuits and soup might be good for her."

"I'll go see if she's awake. Perhaps we'll all just eat on trays with her if she feels up to it." Ingeborg mounted the dark walnut stairs. Maybe she should suggest that Elizabeth invite her parents to come visit. While Thorliff and Elizabeth had gone occasionally to visit them in Northfield, Mr. and Mrs. Rogers had not come west. And if her father didn't feel he could leave his newspaper, perhaps her mother would come. She met Thorliff coming out of the bedroom.

"She's sound asleep," he said softly.

"Good. That's the best medicine right now." She tucked her arm in Thorliff's. "Thelma has supper nearly ready. I think I will go home after that."

"You want me to come for Inga?"

"Not on your life. We get to keep her. She's all excited about sleeping with Tante Asti." She smiled as she said Inga's name for Astrid. "Just think how quickly she is growing up."

"I know. She told me the other day that printer's ink is stinky and I should wash my hands better."

Thelma served them in the dining room, refusing an invitation to join them, and returned to the kitchen and the little room off the kitchen, where she slept. If she slept.

"I'll come back in the morning to check on Elizabeth and perhaps bring Inga then."

Thorliff laid his fork down and rested his elbows on the table, leaning forward to gaze at his mother. "I never dreamed that one little girl could become so important to me. I mean, I knew you and Far loved me and that someday I would love my own children, but not like this." He waved his hand in a gesture that included the entire house. "Right now, this huge house seems empty without her laughter and the slap of her little feet. I am looking forward to more children, and I know losing another one is crushing Elizabeth, but Inga . . ."

"She's your first, and your firstborn always has a special place in your heart. But thanks be to God, the more children there are to love, the larger grows the heart of love, so there is always enough for everyone. We're like our heavenly Father in that way." Ingeborg smiled at her son, who was not of her loins but always of her heart. "I think that is one of those things that people without children never comprehend. They never realize what they are missing out on."

"There are still things beyond our understanding too. How did Tante Kaaren cope when they realized Grace was deaf?"

"With love and prayer. And it shows in Grace's character now that she is grown."

"But what about when your children do something that really disappoints you?"

"How often do you think we disappoint our Father?"

"Point well taken, but He is better at forgiving than I am." Thorliff buttered his bread and took a bite of potatoes and gravy to go with the bite of bread. Silence smiled in benediction. "I guess you have to be a parent to begin to understand what your parents went through."

"I guess that is very true." She cut a piece off the roast pork and chewed. "Thelma is such a good cook. You are fortunate to have her."

"Elizabeth was moaning one day that she wasn't being a very good wife because she rarely cooks and seldom cleans."

"And what did you tell her?"

"That I hired men to do the jobs that I haven't time for and saw nothing wrong with that, so why shouldn't she do the same? After all, my work rarely takes me out in the buggy to spend the night delivering a baby or fighting to keep someone alive."

"Thorliff, you are a man among men, and I am so proud of you at times that I nearly burst with it. I know your far would have been so very proud of you too."

"Can I get you anything else?" Thelma asked from the doorway.

"Mor?"

Ingeborg shook her head. "Thank you, no." She wiped her mouth with her napkin and laid the napkin back on the table. "I'm going to check on Elizabeth, and then I will head home. The supper was delicious."

"Can you take a few more minutes?" Thorliff asked his mother.

She settled back in her chair. "Of course, if you need something."

"I would like to buy Penny's store."

"So would I. Haakan and Lars are buying the machinery and blacksmith business, and I don't see how we can do both."

"What if we all went together on it?"

"Who would run it? None of us has time to be in a store all day."

"We could advertise for a manager, like we did for the flour mill."

"I keep hoping they won't leave."

"Have you heard Mrs. Valders wants to buy it? People are saying she's trying to argue Penny down on her asking price."

"No, really?" Leave it to that woman. "But Penny has the price at rock bottom already."

"I know. That's why it sticks in my craw too. I think if we buy it, we should ask Gerald to run it."

"Perhaps that is what Hildegunn plans."

"Perhaps. I think we all need to get together and talk about this."

"Tomorrow night at our house?"

"I'll ask around. No, let's give Elizabeth a couple of days. She'll want to be there."

On the way home Ingeborg thought about the conversation. Why was she feeling like they needed to hurry?

9

"SHE DID WHAT?" Grace couldn't believe her eyes.

Sophie signed along with speaking more slowly. "Penny sold her store to a man from back east."

"But I thought . . ." Grace stammered to a stop. "Do Haakan and Far know?"

"I don't think so. Mr. Harlan Jeffers stayed overnight here, and I heard him talking with one of the other men. He was really pleased with the purchase but said that Ms. Bjorklund was a hard negotiator. She wouldn't come down on the price one bit."

"Good for Penny." Grace leaned back in her chair. The slight breeze on the back porch of the boardinghouse rustled the cottonwood leaves and cooled the girls' faces. With her foot Sophie set the cradle by her chair rocking gently. The twins had been asleep since their latest feeding, Hamre with one arm over his sister. Grace smiled at them, remembering her mother's stories that she and Sophie had been most content that way too. Would she and Toby have twins too? The thought made her jerk her attention back to Sophie's conversation.

"Penny said she got fed up with Mrs. Valders' haggling, and none of the family had enough ready money to buy her out. Hjelmer was being impatient, so she sold it to the highest bidder."

"Does Hjelmer have a house for them yet?"

"I guess so. She's leaving most of their furniture here. Mr. Jeffers said he could move right in, another thing that pleased Hjelmer mightily."

"Have you seen Toby lately?" The words leaped off her fingers.

"No. Why?" Sophie stared at her. "You've asked me that before. Is there something you're not telling me?"

Grace hid behind her glass of lemonade. *Why did I ask her that? I know better.*

"Grace Knutson, what is going on? Astrid says Mr. Gould is taken with you, and I think that could be a wonderful thing. And you're asking about Toby."

"I just haven't seen him for a while, and you know he's been my friend for years. That's all." *And now I'm telling a lie too. I have to tell someone. Can I trust Sophie? If I can't trust my sister, whom can I trust?* But Sophie didn't trust me about Garth either. Grace glanced up to see a frown marring Sophie's forehead.

Sophie's eyes narrowed. "You think you're in love with Toby?" She both signed and spoke, her fingers showing her agitation.

"I don't think so. I know so." There. She had said it. She laid her shaking hands in her lap.

"How do you know?"

"How did you know?"

Sophie heaved a sigh and then shook her head. "I couldn't think about anything else. I couldn't eat. I had a hard time sleeping. I was terrified Hamre was going to leave without me, and I couldn't abide that. I didn't think I could live without him." A silence fell with both young women studying the babies in the cradle.

"Do you regret going?" Grace stammered on the words.

Sophie looked up from the babies, shaking her head all the while. "Not one bit. I regret hurting all of you; that is my only regret."

"But now you are in love with Mr. Wiste?"

"Yes, and now I know again what love is. Sometimes it is like I dreamed Hamre and our so very brief life together. I had a letter from Mrs. Soderstrum, and it brought it all back. I sat and cried for Hamre and for what he is missing in not seeing his babies and not getting his boat. But then I thought of what Mor and Tante Ingeborg would say." She smiled at her sister. "They'd say that Hamre is in heaven and there are no regrets in heaven. He has more than a boat of his own, and he is watching to make sure we are all right."

Grace nodded. "That's what they'd say."

"But you, my dear sister, just very cleverly got the attention off you and back onto me. I have a feeling you've been doing that for a lot of our lives. So here's my question: what makes you think you care for Toby as more than a friend? And second, do you think he feels the same way?"

Grace answered, "I have always loved him."

"But what makes you think it is love."

"I can't picture being with anyone else. I am comfortable with him. I love watching him, talking with him. He has always been kind to me. . . ." Both her voice and fingers trailed off. "And I see love in his eyes when he looks at me."

Sophie shook her head. "Sounds more like good friends to me." She shook her head. "Has Toby ever said or done anything like take your hand or lean close when he talks with you or . . ." She closed her eyes.

"N-no."

"Does your heart pick up the beat when he is near?"

"Well, sort of. I mean, I guess. I haven't paid much attention to that."

"Do you have this deep desire to touch his arm, take his hand, stand closer to him?"

"I've thought of those things a few times, once or twice." Grace retreated into her chair. She did feel like she was burning when Jonathan looked at her, but that couldn't be what Sophie was talking about. Where was Mrs. Sam when she needed her? How come they'd had all this time alone together without someone needing something?

"And besides all that—" Sophie leaned closer and stared right into Grace's eyes—"do you really want Mrs. Valders to be your mother-in-law?"

Grace clapped her hands over her mouth, feeling her eyes grow round at the laugh bubbling up. "Sophie."

Sophie shrugged, then laughed too. "Just thought I'd ask."

"Do you feel all you said with Mr. Wiste?"

"Oh my, yes." She closed her eyes again. "I know this is so right, and we both agree that life might be too short. Look what happened to both our mates. We don't want to waste any of the time we might have together. In spite of what etiquette says." She shuddered. "Who made those rules anyway?"

Grace grinned at her sister. "They're not in the Bible."

"See? That's what I mean."

They both looked up as the screen door opened. Mrs. Sam nodded over her shoulder. "Gentleman here to see you."

"Can he come out here?"

"I think you better come in."

Sophie dusted crumbs off her gown and followed Mrs. Sam into the kitchen.

Grace moved to Sophie's chair so she could continue to rock the cradle. She watched as Joy stretched and then settled back into sleep. Good thing, since her mother was busy at the moment.

The screen door slammed, the babies flinched at the bang, and Grace caught the movement from the side of her eye. Sophie, furious, didn't need signs or words to let her sister know something was wrong.

"What is it?" Grace asked.

"That insolent creep Mr. Cumberland—the man who wanted to buy the boardinghouse and spread rumors that I agreed to sell—is back. This time with another offer he is so sure I will take that he even offered, mind you, to go talk with Haakan and Thorliff for me so that no one can say he took advantage of a poor widow, young as I am." She stomped up the porch, then down.

Grace could feel the force of her sister's fury right through the soles of her feet.

"And then he had the nerve to request a room here for the night." She glanced in the cradle to see the babies twitching and making faces.

"And if I don't calm down, I'll have babies to feed, and maybe my milk will be curdled." She threw Grace a half smile. "Do women get mastitis?"

Grace shrugged. "So what are you going to do?"

"I don't know. Any suggestions?"

"You could write a letter to his company, telling them to leave you alone, that due to his mismanagement, you would never consider selling to them."

"He is one of the owners."

"Oh."

"Now look what I've done."

Grace watched Sophie swoop down and pluck Hamre from the cradle.

What if I have a baby, and since I can't hear it when it cries, something terrible happens? Where had a thought like that come from?

"Shush, shush. Let your sister sleep." Sophie looked to Grace. "Joy has been awake for a couple of hours each night lately."

"Fussy?"

"Screaming. I'm afraid she'll wake the men who are sleeping. Mrs. Sam has helped me walk her."

"Still the colic?"

"I don't know. Ask Mor for me, will you?"

"You ask her. She's planning on coming in tomorrow. If you want me to, I could spend the night." She inhaled the wonderful fragrance of strawberry preserves wafting from the kitchen.

"I need to go change him. Keep your eye on Joy, will you please? I'll be right back."

Grace leaned her head against the back of the chair, the rocking motion soothing her as much as the baby. How she would have loved to pick little Joy up and rock with her, but Sophie wanted to feed Hamre before this one insisted. After spending the entire day here, Grace realized Sophie was right. Feeding babies was what she did most of the time. How had Mor managed with the two of them?

She closed her eyes, and as usual Toby came striding across her mind, greeting her with a smile. He tucked her arm in his, and they walked up a path lined with green grass and bright yellow buttercups on both sides. Bluebells danced on their slender stalks; a meadowlark heralded them from the meadow. They paused under the shade of a big old oak tree. Toby turned toward her, looking deep into her eyes.

Grace, I—

She knew he was going to kiss her. She leaned forward and—

Her eyes flew open as she felt Sophie return.

"All right, we are back. I see Joy is still sleeping. Thank you, Lord."

Grace could feel a flush start up her neck. Good thing Sophie couldn't read her mind or decipher her dreams. What would Toby's lips feel like on hers? How would she breathe if he ever kissed her a long time? Was her heart beating extra hard like Sophie had asked?

She watched Sophie settle Hamre in to nursing. "Is he staying awake longer so he doesn't want to eat as often?"

"Somewhat." Sophie peeked under the blanket at her son. "Garth can never seem to hold these babies enough. Every evening he sits and rocks them, one in each arm. He says it helps make up for when he was away from Linnie. That little girl of his would have nothing to do with him when he went to Minneapolis to visit at Christmas, but she warmed up to him a bit sooner when he went back to sell his house."

Since Joy was still sleeping, Grace stood. "Think I'll go on home. Wish you could come with me." *Should I offer again to spend the night, or did Sophie not answer before on purpose?*

"Me too. But even more I wish I could show you Mr. Wiste's house."

Why don't you want me to stay the night, and why do you keep talking to me about his house? Her head ached a little at the many twists and emotions their conversation took.

"It's going to be your house."

"Soon, but for now it's not."

Grace waved and walked down the steps to the grass Lemuel kept mowed. The garden was huge, and she waved to the young black man out hoeing. She should have been doing the same today. The large round leaves of hollyhocks filled a bed on the eastern side of the house, while lilies of the valley sent a sweet fragrance to welcome her as she reached the street front. It immediately relaxed her. She noticed a man walking toward her from the direction of the flour mill and waved when she realized it was Toby. *Maybe he'll offer to walk me home.* She waited for him to meet her. He looked tired, even with his fedora shading his eyes, eyes that did not brighten with his smile.

"Hello." *Please be happy to see me.*

"You visiting with Sophie?"

She nodded. "You were working at the mill today?"

"Yeah, it's almost finished."

"You didn't come to the fish fry." Her hands clenched the paper-wrapped rhubarb bread Mrs. Sam had insisted she take home to Mor.

"No time."

Toby, talk to me. What is wrong? "Why don't you come to our house for supper?" She couldn't believe she'd suggested such a thing.

He shook his head. "Sorry. I've agreed to help my mother tonight."

"How about tomorrow night?" She reached out and touched his arm. Her frustration made her tongue thick, the words harder to say. *Grace, if your mother heard this, she would be appalled. Why am I doing this? It must be because of what Sophie said.*

When he stepped back away from her as if he'd been burned, she swallowed hard. *He can't even bear my touch.* Pain seared her soul.

"Sorry, Grace, I just don't have time right now." He touched one finger to his hat brim and nearly broke into a run getting away from her.

He didn't have to be rude. She stared at his sweat-stained back. *Here I think I'm in love with you and you can't even spend five minutes in my company. Even friends don't treat each other like that.* Grace thought over the list of questions Sophie had asked. She honestly wasn't sure how to answer them with Toby, although she was clear about her thoughts concerning Jonathan—she knew she wasn't in love with him. Did her uncertainty mean she really wasn't in love with Toby? But he was—she thought he was—her best friend, at least her best male friend, and she had often heard Mor and Tante Ingeborg say how important friendship was in a marriage. Grace rubbed her forehead as the headache returned.

10

JONATHAN LATCHED THE GATE to the pigpen and then checked it again. Embarrassment and guilt still rode him like spurs. He'd never realized how important a garden could be to a family until the rampaging pigs did so much damage. He'd never realized a lot of things until he came west. Tonight he needed to write to his family again and share his list of learned things. One of which was that money could buy a lot of comforts, and did in his family's case. Something else he had learned—but not something he felt he could tell them— was that money did not buy love in a family.

He picked up a stick and leaned over the wooden fence to scratch the big sow's back. She'd stand there grunting in contentment for as long as he'd take time to scrape the stick up and down her arched back. He'd also not known how smart pigs were or any of the farm animals, actually. But then, his knowledge had been restricted to dogs and horses.

On Saturday there would be a house raising for Garth Wiste's sister and her family, who were moving to Blessing from Minneapolis. The idea that half the community would turn out to do such a thing intrigued him. Astrid said there would be a party that evening after the house raising. Perhaps he would be able to dance with Grace.

Always lately, it seemed, his thoughts turned to Grace.

Jonathan picked up the buckets and took them back to the barn. The whey from the cheese house filled two barrels a day, which they fed twice daily to the pigs and chickens. He'd hauled four barrels down from the cheese house the day before—two for here and two to Andrew's barn. Today he was to take the wagon and pick up full milk cans at three other farms, then deliver them to the cheese house and dump them into the tank, where the first stage of cheese making began.

Life was never dull around here, that was for sure. If his mother could see him now, she would be appalled. The idea made him smile.

Up at the house he found all the women in the shade shelling peas—the peas that weren't in the abundance needed due to his carelessness with the gate, so the hogs got out and into the garden. "I'm on my way with the milk cans." He watched as Grace popped open a pod with her thumb and tossed the peas into her mouth. "Those aren't cooked."

"Didn't you ever eat peas straight from the garden?" Astrid looked at him like he was missing a body part, a look she had perfected and he saw frequently. Grace's eyes twinkled as she munched and then handed him a full pea pod.

He started to slit it open. Grace shook her head, as did Astrid.

"No, this is the easy way." Astrid held up a pod, ran her thumbnail down the seam, and laid it open, then scraped the peas into her bowl. "See?"

He followed her example and tossed the peas into his mouth. The crisp crunch and sweet flavor made him want more. "So why don't we eat them this way instead of cooking them?"

Ingeborg laughed. "We are canning these for winter. The creamed peas we had last night were cooked. Are you saying those weren't as good?" Like mother, like daughter. They did love to tease him.

"No comment." He grinned back at her. At this time of day, his mother would be in the morning room, enjoying a cup of tea and perhaps writing letters or planning the next week's menus or the guest list for a party. If the peas they ate came in pods, only Cook or her helper would know. "Do you need anything from town?"

"Thank you for reminding me. There's a stack of mail on the kitchen table to be mailed."

"I'll take care of that."

"And take a couple of cookies that are cooling there." Her comment followed him into the house.

The sun was edging close to vertical by the time he'd picked up full milk cans from three farms and dropped the mail off at the post office, dodging Mrs. Valders' questions, as he'd learned the extent of her inquisitiveness on previous trips. His dealings with Mrs. Valders gave him a vague sympathy for the son he'd heard about who tended to lose his temper easily. He heard the ringing of the triangle when he turned the team into the lane. The cans rattled and clanged as he urged the horses into a slow trot. He needed to get the cans into the cool of the cheese house before he went in for dinner. More and more this way of life felt so natural and New York a foreign place where he had been raised but never really belonged.

Saturday morning breakfast wore an air of hilarity. While raising a house sounded like a lot of work to Jonathan, the other men talked like this was a huge party. Haakan had spent the evening before sharpening saws, and he'd explained that while there were usually teams that raced to build the walls of a barn, this house had come ready to put together like a jigsaw puzzle.

"You'll see what we mean when we get there. You ever used a hammer and saw before?"

"Only on the fencing." Pounding in staples took a different skill than nails, as he'd learned at Andrew's.

"Make sure you bring your leather gloves." Haakan held up his cup for a refill. "We'll go on ahead, and the women will bring dinner in by noon. Astrid, are you and Grace the water girls today?"

"Most likely." Astrid turned from the dishpan on the stove. "We'll come in an hour or two."

"Don't forget that tomorrow is the farewell for Penny and Hjelmer at church." Ingeborg set the coffeepot back on the stove. "This surely is a busy time."

"I don't want Penny to leave." Astrid dumped a plate in the rinse water with enough force to cause a splash that spread across the stove, steaming and sizzling as it hit the hot part.

"No one does." Ingeborg's voice thickened.

Jonathan glanced up to see Haakan's jaw tighten. None of the Bjorklunds had been happy with the precipitous sale of the store to an outside buyer. There had been some rather heated discussions around this kitchen table, but Penny said the deal was done and that was that.

When Andrew drove up in the wagon with the Knutsons, Haakan and Jonathan tossed their tools in and joined the others. Other wagons arrived at the same time they did, and the older men moved from stack to stack of lumber, checking supplies against the manifest, the instructions, and the plans. Within a few minutes, the assignments had been made and Jonathan joined a crew of Haakan, Pastor Solberg, Gus Baard, and Samuel to begin laying the floor joists across the basement.

As soon as Astrid and Grace arrived, they called for a coffee break, serving both hot coffee and lemonade. The men and boys gathered around, joking about which was the slowest team.

The sun beat down as the walls went up. Jonathan handed the proper lumber to those on his team and pounded a few nails into place. At least he could usually drive a nail in straight with four slams now, not like Haakan with three and sometimes two. Milking cows and moving milk cans had vastly strengthened his arm and back muscles, so this work wasn't as miserable as his first.

They had the first floor framed in by noon, including some of the lower siding.

Jonathan observed Grace watching someone during dinner. When he realized she was surreptitiously observing Toby Valders, he felt a stab in his heart. Was this the reason she didn't seem interested in him? *Oh, Grace, please . . .* He wasn't sure what he was asking Grace for, since he was in no position to ask her for anything, but his reaction caught him by surprise. He was concerned too, based on what he'd heard of the other man. He thought Grace deserved someone more caring. Toby Valders was so busy talking with the men around him that he was paying her no attention whatever. Toby accepted a piece of the cake that Rebecca was scooping out onto offered plates, laughing up at her and making her cheeks blush rosy.

Grace slumped for a moment then straightened her spine and turned to say something to the woman beside her.

Jonathan mentally applauded her spunk. If she wasn't sitting between two women, he'd have gone over there and sat down beside her. When Haakan called for the work force to get back to the house, he stood and pulled his leather gloves back on. Settling his hat securely in place, he joined his team members.

Astrid carried on a continuing banter with the workers that afternoon while she passed dippers of water up to the second floor of the house. Jonathan nailed siding on the wall his team was finishing, accepting the drinks that came by but always looking for Grace.

"She went over to see Sophie for a bit," Astrid said while she waited for him to finish with the dipper.

Jonathan knew it wasn't sunburn heating the back of his neck. *Am I that obvious?* He handed back the dipper. Should he ask Astrid? Why not? "Does Toby . . . I mean is he . . . or she"—He rolled his eyes. "I mean . . ."

"She and Toby have been friends since school days."

"But . . ."

"Hey, Gould, would you bring me that saw?"

He turned back. Now wasn't the time to even be thinking like that. Giving Astrid a thank-you nod, he did as he was asked.

After a cold drink break midafternoon, which Grace helped serve, two teams moved to the roof, using pulleys to hoist the rafters up to the workers.

Jonathan paused to watch one long two-by-six rise in the air. Grace walked underneath it, her bucket and dipper in hand. The rope snapped, someone shouted, and Jonathan dove at Grace, knocking her to the ground, shielding her with his body. The end of the wood slapped across his back and glanced off his head before clattering to the ground. Dizzy from the blow to his head, he rolled to the side.

"Are you all right?" Haakan knelt beside him.

"H-how's Grace?"

"She's all right—a bit mussed but not injured, thanks to your quick action. Thank God some other wood broke part of the force or you could be—"

"Seriously hurt." Pastor Solberg finished the sentence from the other side of Jonathan.

Haakan probed the back of Jonathan's head with gentle fingers. "You're going to have a big knot, but I think your hat protected you. There's no blood."

"Maybe we better have Dr. Elizabeth look at him."

"No, no. I'm fine." Jonathan accepted a hand that reached down to pull him up, but when he moved, pain shot through his shoulder. "I better do it myself."

Haakan stood and eased an arm about the young man's waist. "Let's do this real easylike." When they both stood upright, a cheer went up from those around them. "Let's get you on a bench. Astrid, bring the water bucket."

Jonathan looked to find Grace. She stared at him, her face as white as the apron had been before he sent her crashing into the dirt. "Are you all right?"

She nodded, her fingers flashing signs that he couldn't begin to interpret. She stopped, sucked in a deep breath, and said, "Thank you." Her focus flew to the pulley overhead and back to the piece of wood, then to him. She turned to her father standing right beside and burst into tears.

"If that hit her in the head, it mighta killed her," one of the other men commented.

Jonathan wanted to take her in his arms himself, but when he took a step toward her, he staggered.

"Come on, let's get you sitting back down. You dizzy or nauseous?"

"Some." He twisted his shoulders and winced at the pain in the right one. He clenched his fingers and moved his arm; all seemed in working order. Haakan on one side and Pastor Solberg on the other, they walked him to the closest bench and sat him down.

Astrid held out the dipper of water. "You sure were fast."

Seeing there was nothing more they could do, the rest of the crew went back to work on the house.

"Astrid, is there any ice here?" Haakan asked.

"There would be some at the boardinghouse. The ice we put in the lemonade is all melted."

Haakan glanced around and beckoned to one of the younger boys. "Go over to the boardinghouse and bring back some ice in a wet dish towel. Run, now."

He scurried off.

Jonathan rested his head in his hands, wishing the drummer inside would cease and desist. His back ached but not the stabbing pain of before. His knee must have slammed into a piece of wood, or else the ground was rock hard, for it pulsed too. He felt like throwing up, but another drink of water helped settle his stomach.

"I'm all right. I'll just sit here a bit, and then I'll be back." *Grace might have been killed there.* The thought beat worse than the pain. She hadn't heard the shout. *She shouldn't be in a dangerous place like this.* He opened his eyes when he felt someone lay something against the back of his head.

"Just sit still and I'll hold this in place."

Pastor Solberg stood behind him, his voice as gentle as the one in Jonathan's head was strident.

"Hurt?"

"Yes, sir."

"Cold penetrating does that. Feels worse before it feels better. Doesn't feel like your skull is cracked, however."

"My father always says I have a hard head."

"Good thing. Thank God this wasn't any worse."

Jonathan forced himself to think of something besides the burning at the back of his head. Grace, was she hurt and they weren't telling him? After all, he'd slammed her into the same hard ground that had bruised his knee. He gave a sigh of relief when the ice pack was lifted from his head and flinched when it was returned.

Staring at the ground, he heard someone walk up and saw the hem of a skirt enter his line of vision. Trying to roll his eyes to see higher wrinkled his forehead, which wrinkled the skin on his head, which made the wound hurt more.

"Have you ever had a big knot on your head before?" Dr. Elizabeth owned the skirt.

He started to shake his head and then answered instead. "No."

"I'm going to look at it. It includes some probing, and it will hurt."

What could he say? No, I'm chicken? Instead he said nothing, just held his head more firmly. She was right; it did hurt but not unbearably. When she finished he let out the breath he didn't realize he'd been holding.

"All right, now let me look at your eyes. If you have a concussion or skull damage, it can show up there."

He raised his head to see her smile and stare first into one eye and then the other.

"Looks good. I would say both you and Grace were protected by your guardian angels today."

"I guess."

"Anything else hurting?"

"My back, especially the right shoulder." He didn't bother to mention his knee.

She moved behind him. "No bleeding. Do you mind taking your shirt off this shoulder?"

He did as she said and flinched again as she palpitated his shoulder.

"You have an abrasion here, but I don't think anything is broken. Can you move your shoulder? Good. Now make a fist. Excellent."

She stepped around in front of him. "Pastor, why don't you move what's left of that ice pack to his shoulder. Good. Now, Mr. Gould, you are welcome to come over to the surgery and lie down for a while if you like. It might help the headache."

"Can't I go back to work on the house?"

"You won't be able to wear your hat. And if you get dizzy, you could get hurt worse."

How embarrassing.

"They're going to be stopping soon, at least those that have to go milk cows, and then we'll all be back here for supper and the party."

A wave of weariness deluged him. All of a sudden the only thing he could think of was lying down. He looked up to see her studying him.

"Come with me." She reached out a hand. "We'll walk slowly."

Once in her surgery he collapsed on the bed and was asleep before he had time to thank her.

When he opened his eyes again, dusk softened the room. He slowly lifted his head from the pillow, where he'd been lying face down, since the back of his head sported the most obvious of his wounds, and winced at the pain in his shoulder. But other than a dull ache, the timpani player inside his head had gone home and taken his instrument with him. Even more slowly he rolled over so he could sit up on the edge of the bed. His boots sat by the wall, so someone had been in to help him. The last he could remember was the walk that took forever from the new house to the doctor's house, him leaning more on her shoulder than he'd wanted.

Since the drum was no longer playing, he could hear music floating in on the same breeze that lifted the sheer curtains. The party had begun. Which meant he'd missed chores—a definite mark against him. He glanced around the room to see a note propped against the water pitcher on the washstand and slowly stood to reach it. When he saw the water, he immediately realized he suffered from a raging thirst. After guzzling a glass of water, he unfolded the paper and read, *We are all at the party. If you would like supper, Thelma will fix a plate for you. If you would rather just sleep on through the night, that is probably the best. I expect you still have a fierce headache.*

He gingerly felt around the swelling on the back of his head, wincing as he did so. Using his left arm eased the pain in the back of his right shoulder. That timber must have whacked him on both head and shoulder. Gratitude that it didn't hit him in the neck knocked him back down to sit on the edge of the bed. *I could have been killed. Grace . . . Grace is all right too.* He thought back to the accident. He'd just acted instinctively, not pausing for a moment's thought. All because she couldn't hear that shout when the rope started to go. The miracle? She'd not been hurt before. She must always be in places that could be dangerous, living on a farm.

She needs me to take care of her. Where had that thought come from? But wasn't that what love did, take care of the beloved? *My beloved.* He wrapped his tongue around the idea and spoke the words softly into the deepening dusk. "Grace, my beloved. I am in love with Grace Knutson." Something started in his toes and worked its way upward, swelling as it surged. It paused at his heart, gathered more warmth, and swirled around his head before slipping out on another whisper. "Grace, such a perfect name for the most gallant young woman I've ever met. I came to Blessing for this purpose, to love Grace and spend my lifetime showing her how much." Lifetime. That meant marriage. Would Grace be willing to leave Blessing and move to New York? Or could he come back to Blessing?

As he pulled on his boots, another thought hit him, this one not nearly as pleasurable. He couldn't say a thing to Grace without first getting her father's permission to court her. And he couldn't do that without talking with his own father first. A four-year-long courtship while he attended college was not unheard of. But what would his mother say? Bending over to tie his boots made him so dizzy he nearly fell headfirst onto the floor. His stomach roiled, hot and violent. Closing his eyes, he tried putting his head between his knees, but that was only worse. Slowly, carefully, he eased his foot out of the boot and lowered himself to lie on his side, bringing his feet up to join the rest of him on the bed.

Maybe Dr. Elizabeth had been right. Staying put seemed the better part of valor. Fainting if he tried to dance would not be very impressive—if he made it back there at all. As he drifted off to sleep, he once again saw Grace looking at Toby Valders. Nausea returned as the question stood in front of him like a large fence—just what was their relationship?

11

Rain ruined the Fourth of July celebration.

Pouring rain at that. It started early in the morning, crested about noon, and drizzled most of the afternoon. After dinner was served at the church, they called off the ballgame, and when the clouds looked to have taken up residence right over Blessing, everyone gathered back inside. All the men could talk about anyway was the hay crop and would it remain standing or at least not be laid so flat that mowing would be impossible.

As the women cleaned up the leftovers, they talked about how they missed Penny and hoped all was well with her, about the new man at the general store, who brought out a wide variety of opinions, and about Sophie's coming wedding.

Ingeborg tucked a dish towel around the bread and cheese left in her basket. As the other women found their own dishes and pans, she did the same, all the while fighting against the sadness watered by the rain. Penny's leaving had torn a hole in her heart, as if she'd lost her own daughter. In a way she had. Penny had been part of her life ever since that day so many years ago when the Baards stopped their wagon near the newly finished sod barn and introduced themselves to the Bjorklunds. So much had filled the years since then—Roald dying, her remarrying, their children growing up together. Agnes, the sister of her heart. Good friends like that didn't come along every day, and then she was gone long before her old age. Death had visited them all, and while she knew Penny was alive and well, her heart still ached for the miles separating them.

She hadn't felt like celebrating today, and now no one did. Thunder grumbled off to the west and lightning forked the black clouds.

"As soon as the storm front passes, I think we'll head on home." Haakan looked to her for confirmation.

She knew by the way he was watching her that he was concerned about her. She forced a smile to go along with the nod. Being at home would be better than here. It wasn't as if she didn't have plenty to do, although this rain would be hard on the berries. Good thing she'd picked the ripe ones last night. The sooner she got them canned, the fewer she'd lose.

The storm passed to the south, and as the rain let up, they headed for their wagons, ignoring the mist blowing under umbrellas and into buggy seats.

"Good thing we got the roof on that house," Lars said as he helped Kaaren onto the wagon seat.

With their buggy and team tied right next to the Knutsons', Haakan answered, "And the windows in."

"What are you going to do with all your free time until chores?" Lars asked, his lips stretched in a slight smile to say he was teasing.

"I might just take a nap."

Ingeborg glanced at her husband in surprise. Her first thought, *Is he feeling all right?* Haakan rarely took a nap, except on a Sunday afternoon if they didn't have company.

"Don't worry," he said, climbing in beside her. "I'm fine. A nap on a rainy holiday just sounded like a fine idea."

Ingeborg waved in response to the farewells and slid a bit closer to her husband. While she had brought a shawl, still the chill penetrated, along with the moisture, which dripped off her straw hat and trickled down her back. Much as they needed the rain, it sure did ruin a rare holiday.

"Where did the young people suddenly disappear to?"

"They're over at the school. I think they asked Jonathan to play the piano, and they'll probably push back the desks for some dancing."

"But they didn't invite the old folks." He clucked the horses to pick up their feet a little faster. Water splashed from the spinning wheels.

"I'm sure we'd be welcome if we wanted to join them." She tucked her arm through the crook of his. "Do you want to?"

"Not at all." He clamped her hand against his side and turned to smile at her. "I'm sure we can find something to do."

The shiver that ran up her back had nothing to do with the chill of the air. She rested her head against his shoulder. The strawberries would last another day in the cool of the well house.

The rain let up in time to bring the cows up for milking. As Haakan stepped out on the back porch, he called for Ingeborg.

"What is it?" She wiped her hands on her apron as she joined him.

Haakan pointed toward the gray-clouded east, where a brilliant rainbow arched across the sky, the colors so vibrant they made her catch her breath.

"Ah, a whole arch. Look at that." Ingeborg smiled up at her husband. "Thank you for calling me." *Thank you, Lord, for painting us such a gift.* The prayer rose without her volition.

The sound of clopping hooves and laughter made her glance down the lane. The young people were returning just in time for chores, and it sounded like they were still having a good time.

Andrew was striding across the field alongside Lars and George, with Barney running in front of them. The evening clan was gathering, and she needed to get going on the supper.

"You won't believe what happened." Astrid rushed into the kitchen.

Ingeborg looked up from measuring flour into the biscuit dough. "What?"

"Toby walked out when Grace asked him to dance."

"Oh, poor Grace." Ingeborg thought a moment. "What a rude thing to do. That doesn't sound like Toby at all." She paused again. "Grace asked him to dance? That doesn't sound like Grace either."

"You know she has a crush on him?" Astrid dipped water from the cool bucket and drank her fill, watching her mother over the rim of the long-handled dipper.

"I was afraid of that. Her mother will not be pleased." She knew Grace loved Toby but kept hoping she'd outgrow it. He'd been a friend for so long, and Grace was always loyal. A childish crush, as Astrid said. But the old saying "Still water runs deep" could have been written about Grace.

Astrid started to say something else, but Jonathan walked in just then, and the conversation ended as Astrid headed up the stairs to change into chores clothes. Ingeborg smiled at Jonathan and turned the bowl of biscuit dough out on the floured board to knead it.

"Do you need anything from the well house?" he asked.

"The ham that is hanging on the beam, please, and the crock of cream. I need to churn in the morning."

"Be right back."

She watched him go out the screen door, keeping it from slamming. *Interesting how I was so concerned about his coming, and now I know how much I'm going to miss him when he leaves. I need to write to his mother and tell her what a fine young man she has raised.* She patted out the dough and dipped a glass in flour before cutting each shape. Setting them on the cookie sheet, she molded the small leftover bits into a circle to cut again, then patted the last together. The final biscuit never did look as perfect as the others, so after she baked them all, she kept that one off the serving plate and ate it herself.

Did Kaaren know about Grace's quandary? Even more concerning, did Lars know? He'd had such a hard time when Sophie left, and now his dependable daughter was going to break his heart if she really did want Toby. While Toby had always been a good worker, his reputation as a troublemaker still clung to him like a starving leech. For a town that heard forgiveness preached so wondrously, many still struggled with it personally. Or even more frightening, perhaps not thinking on it at all. *Lord, help us all.* Ingeborg wondered how often she prayed that prayer.

"Don't worry about it, Mor," Astrid whispered in her mother's ear as she kissed her cheek in passing through the kitchen on her way to the barn.

"I'm not worrying. I never worry." Ingeborg hoped that was true. While she thought she turned everything over to her heavenly Father, sometimes things had a way of cropping up all over again, in spite of her good intentions.

Jonathan held the door for Astrid, getting a saucy grin and an over-the-shoulder mange takk for his gallantry as she passed him. His velbekomme made her laughter flutter with the breeze.

"Good for you." Ingeborg smiled at his efforts and added tusen takk when he set the ham and crock on the table.

His forehead wrinkled and he made a face. "Is there something different I should say to that?"

"No. Velbekomme works for both. How are your language lessons doing?"

"Bare hyggelig—my pleasure. Hallo allesammen—hello everybody."

He tossed those behind him as he headed upstairs to change into work clothes.

He was diligent in his sign lessons too, she thought, but probably more for Grace's smiles. Ah, what a combination. He thinks of Grace as she thinks of Toby, but he will be leaving. Still, perhaps he can widen Grace's world a little.

Ingeborg took out the big carving knife and sharpened it before slicing thick slabs of ham to fry for supper. Creamed peas would taste good on the biscuits. She paused and headed out the door for the garden. Kneeling beside the potato plants, she dug into the soft soil with her fingers, searching for small new potatoes to add to the cream sauce with the peas.

Feeling like a victorious hunter with tender-skinned red potatoes in her apron and the potato plants still intact to keep producing, she glanced up to see remnants of the rainbow to the east as the sun disappeared behind a bank of clouds in the west, outlining the tumultuous clouds in gilt. "Uff da," she muttered as she looked down to see the mud crusted on the front of her long apron. The black Red River valley soil could stick like the hardiest of glue. She'd have to change her apron and set it to soaking before the milkers came in for supper.

"Grace is in trouble," Astrid whispered when she'd scrubbed her hands after milking. The men were still finishing up with the chores. "Samuel told his pa about the dancing, and now Trygve is mad at him for blabbing and everyone is mad at Toby for hurting Grace's feelings. Onkel Lars gave Grace one of his father looks. I'm glad I'm here and not at their house tonight."

Ingeborg closed her eyes. Leave it to Samuel. He'd take on the world to protect those he loved and often got in trouble himself because of it. He reminded her of Andrew and his championing of the underdog. Look where it got him that summer still labeled The Big Fight. Shame the younger ones couldn't seem to learn some lessons from the older.

"Well, aren't you going to say anything?"

Before turning to her daughter, Ingeborg checked on the biscuits she'd put in the oven. "What can I say other than I'm so sorry this is happening?"

"Me too. I don't like it when people are unhappy." Astrid took the silverware from the drawer and set the table. "Do you mind if I go help Dr. Elizabeth tomorrow?"

"After washing clothes and picking the last of the peas?"

"I guess." Her sigh said what she really thought of the situation.

"If it is too wet to cut in the morning, I'm going to put Jonathan to work up in the cheese house again. He is such a big help."

"He is really interested in making cheese. I told him to ask you all his questions, not me." Astrid turned at the sound of the men talking at the wash bench. "I imagine he would learn Norwegian a lot faster if we spoke only Norwegian around him."

"Between Norwegian and signing, he'll be multilingual before he goes home."

"He already speaks French, and he's had both Latin and Greek." Astrid finished putting the biscuits in the basket and set it on the table. She looked over her shoulder. "And between you and me, he likes Grace—a lot."

"I was afraid that was what I was sensing."

"Why afraid?"

"Because someone is going to have hurt feelings, since she has always championed Toby."

"Not anymore."

Ingeborg kept the rest of her thoughts to herself. Grace was not one to let go easily. If she really thought she was in love with Toby, one brush-off would hardly deter her. And after all, Toby had become a polite young man and a hard worker, and Ingeborg had caught the glances of other young women who thought him handsome, with his dark curly hair and flashing eyes. If only he could be freed from his past reputation. And his overbearing adoptive mother. Ingeborg glanced up to see Astrid watching her. It was a good thing her daughter could not read her thoughts.

The opening door cut off Astrid's questions before she could ask them. Ingeborg sent a simple prayer for help heavenward as she donned a smile for the entering men.

That night after the house was quiet, Ingeborg sat in her rocker, bathed in the light of the kerosene lamp, and flipped through pages of her Bible, looking for something to comfort her anxious heart. *Why art thou cast down, O my soul? and why art thou disquieted in me? hope thou in God.* She paused there at a verse so easy to read and yet sometimes so difficult to do. *For I shall yet praise him.*

She laid her hands on the Bible and leaned her head against the back of the chair. *Lord, am I anxious? Or is* uneasy *a better word? There is trouble brewing, I'm afraid, and people will be hurt. Yet I know that you are in control. I trust that you have a plan for Grace, as you have said you have a plan for each of us, a plan for good and not for evil. I put my worries and fears for Grace, for Kaaren and Lars, for Toby, and for Jonathan too in your mighty hands. Now please give me the grace to leave them there and not try to fix things myself.*

She sat quietly, listening to the night noises as the house settled into the cooler evening. A breeze fluttered the sheer white curtains at the open window, an owl hooted on its nightly patrol, both it and the bats leaving their haunts in the top rafters of the barn and swooping out to hunt. A dog barked somewhere in the distance. June bugs clattered against the window screen, seeking the light, and a mosquito whined around her head.

She reached up to cup her hand around the chimney lamp and blew out the flame, releasing an odor of smoke and kerosene. Leaving her Bible on the table by the chair, she rose and made her way into the bedroom. At least if she was sleeping, she would quit thinking about all the ramifications. Leaving today's troubles with this day was excellent advice. After all, she had enough to do tomorrow already. Happy Fourth of July. At least it had started out happy.

She had to smile at the memory of little Inga. Now, that one could light up a whole room with her smile. Quicksilver for sure. On that happy note she hung her clothes on the peg on the wall and slipped her cambric nightdress over her head, shimmying out of her underthings as the dress fell about her ankles. The chill on the moist breeze tingled up her back, and sliding under the sheet and light blanket felt like a luxury. She turned on her side and laid her arm over Haakan's upper arm, his gentle snoring pausing a moment as he shifted from his side to flat on his back.

"You all right?" His voice came soft in the dark.

"Ja, I am now."

"Good." He brought her hand to his lips for a kiss and was snoring again before she could respond.

Thank you for Haakan too. She added more to her thank-you list and fell asleep some time along the way.

❧

"Where's Grace?" Ingeborg asked Astrid in the morning when she returned from milking.

"I don't know. I hated to ask." She set a small crock of butter she'd brought from the well house on the table. "This was the last one."

"I know. We'll churn today too. Why did you not ask Lars?"

"He wasn't smiling."

Ingeborg nodded. While Lars was not one to say a lot, he always greeted you with a smile. Except when Sophie left. "Are the boys here?"

"Ja, but Trygve didn't have much to say either. He grumbled at Samuel." Astrid dried her hands after washing them in the dishwater.

"I think I'll go see Kaaren while you hull the strawberries." She nodded to the flat baskets she'd already brought in from the well house. "I did enough to go on the pancakes. That will make your father happy." Haakan loved strawberries. She planned on strawberry shortcake for dinner, his favorite.

It didn't sound like God had taken care of the whole matter overnight. Ingeborg stepped up her praying. With the shadow of Sophie's runaway wedding still lingering, she hoped Lars would not overreact with Grace.

I DON'T HAVE TO TALK *if I don't want to.*

Grace dropped the too soft strawberry in the pail for the chickens and picked up another to hull. The fragrance of bubbling strawberry jam filled the room and her senses. Ignoring her mother's questioning looks was easy if she didn't look at her. Kaaren had tapped Grace's shoulder once and, laying a gentle finger under her chin, forced her to look up. But when Grace shook her head, her mother nodded, her brow furrowed, her eyes filled with concern.

"When you want to talk, you know I want to listen."

Grace nodded and went back to her strawberries. Instead of going to the barn for milking, she had gone out to the garden to pick what was left of the ripe strawberries. She should have been home picking the berries yesterday, in spite of the rain, rather than going to join the dancing. Whatever had possessed her to ask Toby to dance? It served her right when he turned away. What man would want to dance with a girl so forward as she had been. Mor must be appalled and her father furious. Girls just did not do such a thing, especially *his* girls. First Sophie runs off, and now Grace is chasing a man. If it wasn't so pathetic, she might think it funny.

If only her heart didn't hurt so much.

And here she had scolded Sophie for being so foolish as to think her heart would break if Hamre went back to Ballard without her. Broken hearts hurt terribly. The pain was like slicing her finger with a knife, only deeper. She sniffed back a tear. Or a river of tears. Surely she had cried enough last night.

She dumped the hulled berries into another saucepan, added the sugar, and mashed the berries with a potato masher. She set the kettle on the back of the stove to heat slowly. Stirring the other kettle, where the thickening jam bubbled gently, she eyed the jars lined up and waiting. Keeping the jam from burning on the bottom kept her hopping. Her mother and Ilse had gone out to pick the peas.

If she cut rhubarb to add to the second kettle, that would extend the berries. Pushing the fuller kettle to the back of the stove, she headed outside, knife in one hand to cut off the rhubarb tops and a basket in the other. She paused on the steps and raised her face to the sun. The warmth on her face made her close her eyes. At least the sun liked her.

But I don't want Toby to just like me. I know he's my friend, although what kind of friend would be so rude. I want him to love me. Like I love him. Like I have always loved him.

A rooster crowing broke her concentration. If she didn't quit looking at the sun, she'd get freckles, and no man wanted a woman with freckles. She stomped down the steps and strode out to the south side of the garden, where the rhubarb grew lush with big leaves. Pulling out the stalks and whacking off the leaves gave her a perverse sense of pleasure. She stuffed the leaves back under the plants to help keep the weeds down and stomped back to the house. Men!

The fragrance of cooking strawberries met her at the door, reminding her to stir the kettle contents. Then she added wood to the stove, pulled both kettles out to a hotter section, and stirred them again. After washing the stalks, she chopped them into small pieces and dumped them into the smaller kettle, adding more sugar. Rhubarb took a lot of sugar, but it still cut the sweetness of the strawberries.

She sensed someone coming into the kitchen by the reverbera-
tions of the floor, thought about greeting whoever it was, and decided
she wasn't ready to talk yet. Perhaps she'd never be ready to talk. She
lifted a ladle of jam to see if it was thick enough. No longer did the
jam pour back into the pot in a stream but now clumped with the
bright red deepened to carmine. After pulling the pot to the cool end
of the stove, where she skimmed the froth off the top and into a
saucer, she flipped the waiting jars upright and began filling them
with the rich preserves. As she filled them, she tapped each jar on the
wood surface to make sure there were no air bubbles. Grace glanced
out of the corner of her eye. Whoever had come in had left again.

With the jars sealed with melted paraffin and lined up, she
stepped back to appreciate the sun glinting on the shoulders of the
jars. The deep red made her wish for a dress of the same hue. A dress
that would catch Toby's attention and . . . *Do not do that*, she ordered
herself and dabbed at her nose and eyes with the corner of her apron.

At a tap on her shoulder, she turned to face her mother.

"Tell me what is wrong." Kaaren kept her hands on her daughter's
shoulders so she couldn't leave.

Grace shook her head. "I will be all right," she signed, then
ducked out of the grip to go stir the other kettle. In a passing glance
she caught Ilse shaking her head. Knowing the way gossip flew about
Blessing, the probability of everyone knowing of her rebuff made her
clamp her teeth. Perhaps she should get on the train and head west.
Surely Penny could use some help, and in a big town like Bismarck,
no one would know that Toby left the schoolhouse rather than dance
with her. They'd just look at her strangely, like new children did when
they moved to Blessing, because she talked funny. She gave the jam
such a ferocious stir that the kettle rocked.

After the second kettle of jam was bottled, she took out a loaf of
bread, sliced off three pieces, smothered them in the skimmings, and
set them on a plate to take outside on the porch, where Ilse and her
mother were shelling peas. Remorse for the way she'd acted rode with
a heavy hand on the bit.

"Here. Would you like buttermilk also?"

Kaaren shook her head and patted the wooden step beside her. "But thank you for asking."

Grace fought with herself over her mother's gentle action. Then she sank down and, setting the plate on the low table, picked up the remaining slice of bread and jam. The flavors exploded on her tongue, making her close her eyes to savor them more fully. At least she could make good—no, make that excellent—strawberry jam. She felt her mother's shoulder leaning into hers. If she kept her eyes closed, she'd not have to respond. And since her hands were busy with the bread, she couldn't sign.

But years of being the dutiful daughter caught up with her, and she leaned her head on her mother's shoulder. "Please don't say anything, because then I'll cry some more, and I don't want to do that." She felt her mother's nod.

When she finished her bread, she automatically picked up a pea pod and dropped the empty pod into her skirt lap after tossing the peas into her mother's pan. She ate the peas out of the second one. Focusing on shelling peas worked about as well as stirring jam at keeping others out.

Her mother finally tapped her wrist. When Grace looked at her, she signed, "Where did you go this morning?"

"To the river. I couldn't face Astrid."

"They were all worried about you."

"I know." The words flew from her fingers. "Did Samuel tell you too?"

Kaaren nodded.

"I guess everyone in all of North Dakota knows by now."

"I doubt that even all of Blessing knows. Your friends are very protective of you, as are your brothers."

"I am so mortified."

"I can guess so."

"You'd never do anything so stupid."

"Perhaps that's why we have rules of etiquette."

114

Grace blinked and then nodded when her mother signed the last word again. "And I broke them." She reached down and wrapped her arms around her legs just above her ankles. Sitting on steps allowed one all manner of positions. She laid her cheek on her apron and skirt-clothed knees. One minute she was so angry she could spit horseshoe nails, the next she wanted to fling herself into her mother's arms and cry her eyes out.

"What can I do?" she finally muttered.

"You could go help Sophie with the children. I'm sure that—" She stopped. "Why don't we both do that." She called to Ilse, "Would you mind canning the peas by yourself? The men are all eating dinner at Ingeborg's, so Grace and I will take the afternoon and go help Sophie. With the wedding coming up in a week, I'm sure she'd be glad of some extra help."

Grace spent the night before the wedding at the boardinghouse with Sophie. They shared a bed like they had for so many years, returning to their secret hand signals to talk before they fell asleep. When the babies cried for their very early morning feeding and Sophie motioned a sign, Grace rose and brought them to her to be nursed. When they finished, Grace changed them and put them back in their cradle on their sides, spoon fashion like she and Sophie had slept. She rocked the cradle with one foot, sitting on the bed where Sophie lay propped against the pillows.

"Will you miss the boardinghouse?" Grace signed.

"I'll still be here a lot of the time. And Lily Mae will come for me if there's a problem in the evenings."

"I know, but . . ." Grace motioned around the bedroom with her hand. "You won't sleep here, and you'll be making a home for Garth and his children."

"I know. They are such good little ones. When the Larsons

arrived with the children, Grant asked if he could call me Mama."

"And you said?"

"Yes, of course." Sophie picked at the hem of the sheet. "Sometimes all this scares me."

Grace made a face. "Nothing scares Sophie."

"You have no idea. Being alone in Ballard and sick to death pregnant. No Hamre. You can be very sure that I was terrified."

"But you knew you could come home."

"Did I? What if none of you would ever speak to me again?"

"But we sent letters. Of course we'd speak to you." Grace shook her head. "And look how well everything turned out." She peeked at the sleeping babies and crawled back under the sheet. Leave it to Sophie to make her feel . . . feel what? Irritated? Frustrated? "Good night again." She rolled on her side, away from her sister, and tucked her left hand under the pillow. Morning would be here before they knew it.

&

"What is Garth's sister's name?" Grace signed.

"Helga, and her husband is Dan. Garth is so relieved they arrived in time."

Mor had arrived early enough to join them for a cup of coffee and some of the coffeecake Mrs. Sam had made special for the wedding day. With Garth living at his new house now, they had not had to figure out how to keep Garth from seeing the bride before the ceremony, which was scheduled for ten o'clock at the church.

"I put the bouquets of snowball blooms on the altar, and Ingeborg is taking care of setting up for the dinner, so all we need to do is get you and your groom and Grace and Dan dressed and to the church on time."

"That's hardly a problem, since the church is only two blocks away." Sophie cocked her head. Sure enough, one of babies was crying. "I'll be right back."

I'll never be able to hear my baby cry, Grace thought. *How will I know if my children need me? But then, I most likely won't be getting married, so there is nothing to worry about. After all these years of praying for Toby to love me, he doesn't. I guess you just can't make someone love you.* Tears burned, and she both sniffed and rolled her eyes to keep them inside. *God, couldn't even you make him love me?* But God was silent, not that she'd ever heard Him speak to her like her mother said He did. Did one need to be able to hear for God to speak? He'd healed both deaf and blind people in the Bible, but she guessed He didn't do such miracles any longer. At least not in her case.

Later that morning Grace stood beside Sophie at the front of the church, filled with people, and watched Pastor Solberg carefully so she would know how the service was progressing. When he said Garth could now kiss his bride, she turned to watch. Love shone from his eyes as he leaned forward to kiss Sophie.

A little barb of jealousy made Grace clamp her teeth together. Sophie had now been married for the second time. Two men loved her. And she couldn't even have one. As her mother often said, life is not fair, but right now that wasn't much of a comfort. Grace turned to follow Sophie back down the aisle, nodding at the man who held out his arm for her to take. Garth's brother-in-law smiled at her, making the exit easier. If Toby had only cooperated, perhaps she and Sophie could have had a double wedding, something they had talked about what seemed like years ago.

Would she ever stop thinking of Toby?

As the town gathered to celebrate the wedding, she put on an apron and helped set the food out. Sunny skies and a gentle breeze helped make the day perfect. She could see people laughing and talking but decided not to watch. If she stayed in her own little world, she could almost pretend the party was for her—and Toby. She knew she didn't even need to keep an eye out for him because her heart always told her when he came near. When everyone had been served and sat down, she took the filled pitcher of lemonade and made the rounds to fill glasses. Astrid carried the coffeepot.

When she came to Jonathan Gould, his friendly smile made her sniff.

"Mange takk," he said carefully.

"Velbekomme." She nodded her approval as he signed an English thank-you at the same time. She'd never signed in Norwegian, but here he was using both of the skills she and Astrid were teaching him.

"Come on. It's our turn to eat." Astrid set the coffeepot down.

"No, I'll—"

"No you won't. I know you're mooning over Toby, but—"

"I am not mooning!"

"Sorry. Feeling sad, then. If he comes, I swear I'm going to sic the boys on him."

Grace almost smiled. She knew *the boys* meant Trygve and Samuel. She shook her head. "That's right. Have a fight going on right here at Sophie's wedding."

Astrid grinned back at her. "Would sure give some excitement."

Grace put a slice of chicken and some other things on her plate just to keep Astrid quiet. She glanced up to see her mother swaying gently with a baby on each arm. Ingeborg reached to take one of them, and the two grandmas swayed in unison, talking about the wedding. Sometimes there was an advantage in lipreading. You didn't need to be close enough to hear.

After the food was cleared away and the cake served, Grace was left without anything to do again. Sophie and the two grandmas took the babies over to the house to be nursed. Lars was tuning up his fiddle while the piano from the school was rolled out onto the porch. Grace looked around just in case Toby had arrived and she'd missed him. At least if he wasn't there, he wouldn't have to worry about dancing with her.

Dr. Elizabeth sat down at the piano, and Haakan announced that the dancing would commence.

Trygve appeared on one side of her and Jonathan on the other.

She glanced from one to the other. Trygve bowed, motioned to Jonathan, and with a wink, left her.

"I hope that means you will dance with me?"

She caught the last part of his sentence and nodded. He took her hand and led her out for the first waltz. *I will not think of Toby. I will not think of Toby.* Keeping a smile in place took effort until she lost herself in the smooth motions, counting the beat she could not hear so that she would not step on Jonathan's feet. As they turned and swirled, she smiled up at him. "You are a good dancer."

"Mange takk. I had lots of lessons. So are you. How did you learn?"

"Thorliff taught Astrid, Sophie, and I together."

His smile made her neck warm. Astrid's insistence that Jonathan was interested in her made her feel slightly uncomfortable, but she decided to ignore that and just enjoy herself. She could feel others watching them, and the thought made her break stride and stumble. Jonathan held her firmly, paused to let her get the correct foot going again, and gave her a smile that caught in her throat. Didn't it seem a lot like the one that Garth gave Sophie? Could Astrid be right?

13

If HE COULD HOLD GRACE in his arms forever, it would not be long enough.

"My turn." The male voice interrupted Jonathan's reverie, as did the tap on his shoulder.

Jonathan paused in the dance, smiled at Grace, bowed, and handed her off to one of the Geddick sons. He didn't smile at the interloper. At least Toby hadn't shown his face. If that man hurt Grace's feelings again, Jonathan wasn't sure what he would do, but remaining silent wasn't one of the options. He moved out of the way of the dancers and turned to search the circling couples for Grace. Cutting back in immediately, which he'd like to do, was not proper, nor polite.

"So how are you enjoying the festivities?"

He turned to smile at Thorliff standing beside him.

I'd be enjoying it more if I were still dancing with Grace. But he kept his thought to himself. "People here know how to celebrate. Looks like the entire town turned out."

"Most likely. How is your summer going?"

"Very well. Far better than I thought it would in the beginning."

"I wondered if you were as enthusiastic about coming here as your father was for you to come."

Jonathan smiled again and raised one eyebrow, which made Thorliff clap him on the shoulder.

"I hear you are a great help in the cheese house especially, but everyone has been complimentary."

"I'm glad to hear that. I never had any idea of all the intricacies of farming or how hard farmers worked. Reading about it in a book doesn't begin to detail a day that starts before sunrise and doesn't end until you collapse in a bed so tired you are sure you won't be able to get up in the morning and go again."

"What have you liked about it?"

"Everything."

Thorliff turned to stare into Jonathan's eyes. "Really?"

"Really. The thought of returning to the life I used to lead in New York no longer appeals to me at all."

"Does your father know this yet?"

Jonathan shook his head. "I've been very honest with my parents about the things I've learned and the experiences I've had, but I know that I am committed to go to college whether I want to at this point or not." He turned as the dancers clapped at the end of the song, automatically searching out Grace.

"Are you thinking of staying?" Thorliff lowered his voice, surprise having raised it.

"I wish I could. I wish I'd thought fast enough to buy Penny's store. But I just wasn't thinking quick enough. Not that I'd planned on being a storekeeper, but—"

"Let me get this straight. You want to stay in Blessing?"

"Or come back here."

"Why?"

Jonathan raised his hands. "See these callouses? The hardest thing my hands ever had to do was grip a tennis racket, turn book pages, or write an essay. That first day, when Astrid taught me to milk a cow and I learned to dig in the garden, I thought my hands and arms were killing me. At home I would have told a gardener to do the digging had I wanted a hole in the ground, not that I ever wanted such a thing. But here you live on the food produced in that garden and the animals I've learned about taking care of . . ." He paused a moment. "Somehow this seems far more important in the grand design of life."

"But you haven't gone through haying or harvest yet. That might change your mind."

"I don't know, but I doubt it. Life has purpose here, and I like that."

"Is it the farming or—" Thorliff paused and nodded toward Grace and Astrid, who were teasing Trygve—"the people?"

Jonathan followed Thorliff's glance. At least Grace was smiling now. "Pardon me, I'm going to ask her to dance again and turn the other way if someone tries to cut in." He left Thorliff chuckling and stopped beside the girls.

"Go dance with him and leave me alone." Trygve nudged his sister with his elbow.

"You can hand it out, but you can't take it." Astrid laughed at Trygve. "Just because she's a new girl in town."

"Well, Maggie's not really new. She and her family came last fall," Trygve said after a moment's thought.

"See? What did I tell you?" Astrid grinned at Grace. "He's been keeping track. Go over and ask Maggie to dance. Don't be so bashful."

Jonathan smiled at Grace. "If you would come dance with me, you wouldn't have to endure your brother's miseries."

Grace nodded and then said to her brother, "Go ask her." She let Jonathan take her hand and lead her back to where the dancers were fanning themselves and waiting for the next dance. "Thank you."

"For saving you?"

"No, for saving Trygve. He is such fun to tease. Even his ears get red."

The music started and they swung into a schottische, following the same pattern as the other dancers. Cottonwood trees lent their dappled shade, encouraging the party with whispers stoked by the breeze. Jonathan wished he could just spend the time watching Grace, but making sure no one jostled her and that they didn't bump into another revolving couple took too much concentration. At the final flourish they followed the rest to the table where ice chunks still floated in a tub of lemonade.

Mrs. Valders handed Jonathan a cup, which he handed to Grace. At her raised eyebrow look, he smiled and said, "Mange takk." Her nod failed to hide pursed lips. Obviously he'd done something to gain her disapproval, perhaps the last time he picked up the mail.

He led Grace over to a vacant bench under the trees. When they'd sat down, he looked upward and then tried to sign, "Were these here when they built the school and church?"

She shook her head. "Mor and Tante Ingeborg insisted that we plant trees. You'll find one by every house. Mor says when they came here the grass was taller than a man on horseback in some places. When Andrew was just a little guy, he got lost in the grass and Wolf saved him."

"Wolf?"

"Metiz became Ingeborg's friend. She lived near here—an old woman who was Sioux and French Canadian. They called people with that background Metiz, but she kept the name they mistakenly gave her. She had saved the life of a young wolf from a trap, and he stayed nearby. Thorliff says we all became part of Wolf's pack."

"A pet wolf?"

"He was never a pet, but at least one time, he drove a wild wolf pack away from the sheep. We knew his footprints, because one front foot was deformed."

"I think life in New York back in those days must have been boring compared to life on the prairie."

"It probably depends on how much money you have."

"True. My great grandfather started out with nothing, like many of the immigrants, but he eventually amassed a considerable fortune. My grandfather and my father keep working to grow it larger."

"What will be your position in the business when you graduate from college?"

He shrugged. "I have no idea. As firstborn, my older half brother

Thomas is, of course, the most important. He was graduated from Harvard and works in the family business already. He has the kind of brain that thinks in numbers, and he has always planned to follow in Father's footsteps."

"And you?"

Before he could answer, Samuel came up to them. "Jonathan, we're starting a baseball game. Come on."

"You better go play."

I'd rather stay with you. We never get time to talk like this.

"Come on," Samuel insisted.

Jonathan unbuttoned the cuffs of his shirt and rolled back the sleeves. He untied his tie and draped it over Grace's extended hand. "I think I should have worn other clothes."

"You look very nice."

"Thank you. So do you." He blew out his cheeks. "I like talking with you." *Dancing with you, watching you, dreaming about you.* "Coming." He pushed a lock of hair off his forehead—the pomade didn't hold up well when dancing in hot weather—and trotted toward the field, where a diamond was laid out.

"You're on my team," Andrew called with a wave. "We're up first."

Jonathan nodded and joined the line of men, glancing back to see Grace joining her sister and mother with the other women. Some of the younger girls were making their way to cheer their favorite team. He wished he'd invited Grace, or rather dragged Grace along with him to cheer.

That night after chores were finished, Jonathan took out pen and paper to write an overdue letter to his family. His conversation with Thorliff had stayed on his mind all through the milking. What was it he really wanted to do? He knew what he didn't want to do—return to New York City and go to college. But did he want to own a farm like Andrew and the other Bjorklunds did? Or did he want to have another kind of business out here? If so, what would it be? Would his father be open to new ideas? That was the most important question of all.

Dear Father and Mother,

That part was easy, but what to say next?

Today was the big day for Sophie and Garth. The wedding went very well. The celebration afterwards involved everyone in town and the surrounding countryside, and a good time was had by all. The red team beat the black team in baseball. I was the pitcher, or at least I tried to pitch. My arm will be sore tomorrow, I am sure.

We will begin haying tomorrow. We should have had it cut by now, Haakan says, but a rainstorm flattened a lot of the fields and we had to wait for the grass to dry out. The morning after the rain much of the field was standing tall again. I was exceedingly amazed.

Would you please see if you can find some information about the deaf school somewhere in that vacinity? I've been thinking that Grace might like to know more about that school, as she helps her mother teach, and they are hoping to increase the number of students.

I've been working a lot in the cheese house. I had no idea how much cheese such a small herd could produce. I usually drive the wagon around to pick up the full cream cans and leave empty ones at various farms that provide milk for making the cheese. Mrs. Bjorklund mentioned the other day that she is looking for someone to help manage the business. I see where the business could be expanded with additional capital if they had access to more milk and cream. That, of course, means more dairy herds, and I now understand the amount of work involved in dairying. Most of the farmers around here have ten head or less.

I hope you are all having a good summer. I'm sure the family is at the shore by now. My time here is going by fast. I'm grateful I will be able to see at least part of the wheat harvest.

Your affectionate son,
Jonathan

He stared at the sheet of paper. Had he said too much or too little? His father was astute at reading between the lines. While the ink dried, he addressed the envelope. He would take it to the post office on his milk route. If Haakan and Lars began cutting as soon as the dew was off the ground, they said they'd be raking and turning hay in two or three days. He and Andrew would be driving teams for that. One more skill he'd not only never done before but had never heard of before coming west.

❧

I see Grace in a few minutes. The thought was always a good one to wake up to. But neither Grace nor Astrid showed up at the barn.

Haakan handed him his stool. "The girls are up at the house. Ingeborg had an emergency call last night, so Astrid and Grace are fixing breakfast."

"I hope everything is all right."

"Not sure. It may be a problem from Dr. Elizabeth losing her baby."

Jonathan could feel his ears redden. While the forthrightness of these farmers was something he admired, the mention of such private matters still caught him by surprise. "I-I'm sorry to hear that."

"Why don't you take the Holstein that Astrid usually milks and the Jersey Grace milks that is nearly dry. This way we all take on extra."

"I will." A month ago the thought of two extra cows would have set his muscles to screaming, but now that he milked five every morning and night, two more didn't seem such a challenge. He set his bucket and stool down at his first cow and, planting his forehead in her flank, set to milking. Poor Dr. Elizabeth. She took such good care of everyone else; it seemed unfair that she should have problems like these. He knew his mother had lost a baby between him and his younger sister. His older brother and sister Lillian's mother had died giving birth, and the baby along with her. Life was hard for women. That was for sure.

The ping of the milk in the pail deepened to the thrum of a bucket filling. Someone was whistling, most likely Samuel. Once in a while someone said something to the cow he was milking, but as usual, peace filled the milk barn. The cows chewed their grain; splats of manure filled the air with an odor that was no longer so offensive to him. The cow shifted her back feet. "Easy, boss." His voice assumed the same cadence of the others. How would he ever explain the joy he found in milking cows, in driving a team, in pitching hay, in digging in the garden? Eating vegetables fresh from the garden, eggs right from the henhouse, fish right out of the river? He'd heard tales of what butchering was like, and while he knew he would be gone, he was sorry he would miss the experience.

How would he explain all this? Did he really want to farm, or was he still in some kind of euphoria because it was a different life? He'd never worked so hard, learned so much, or eaten so much, for that matter. His mother had warned him that he would miss the ease of their wealthy home and life, but he hadn't. Was there any school he could attend that taught about farming? What would his father say to that? And he thought of Thorliff's comment too. Was it the life here, or was it Grace that drew him? Would he still want to be here if there were no Grace?

14

Dear Mrs. Bjorklund,

Thank you for your letter regarding Jonathan. I so appreciate your letting me know how he is, as he seldom writes and the letters are brief. I am surprised that he has fit in so well, as he has always looked forward to summer and our months at the shore. North Dakota is a long way from the sea.

We are all well here. Thank you for asking. Mr. Gould insists on staying in that hot city and coming out here only on the weekends. I try to convince him that he has others who can do some of the work for him, but both he and Thomas, his eldest son, are committed to taking the company into the new century with force and success.

The girls, the twins, and I love the beach and the life here. There are parties almost every night, and we always have a houseful of young people and other guests.

Since Lillian will be leaving for Europe soon for an entire year with her aunt, we are also preparing for that. Mr. Gould said he heard that Blessing would be getting telephone service soon. I find that strange instrument such a time saver. That, along with electricity, will change our country and our lives dramatically.

Again, thank you for writing and for hosting Jonathan for the summer.

> Sincerely yours,
> Mrs. David J. Gould

Ingeborg read parts of the letter again. Months at the shore, parties nightly. If Jonathan missed his life back there, she had seen no sign of it. Or else he was an exceptionally good actor. The few times he talked about leaving, she was sure he was not looking forward to going at all, that he would rather stay in Blessing.

"Mor, I'm going in to help Elizabeth now." Astrid stuck her head around the doorway. "Is there anything you need from the store?"

"Yes, I have a partial list."

"Garrisons' Groceries or the general store?"

"Both."

Astrid came into the parlor, where Ingeborg had been working on the books for the cheese house. "I sure wish Penny was still here. That Mr. Jeffers—"

Ingeborg looked up from adding to her list. "Mr. Jeffers what?"

"I don't know. Do you like him?"

Ingeborg thought a moment. "I don't like or dislike him. I hardly know him. Why don't you invite him out for supper—see if he's busy tonight. Here, let me write him an invitation. We need to be hospitable. I'm sure he's been slighted by about everyone, since he just isn't the same as Penny. Poor man."

"Shame he doesn't have a wife and family. Then he would fit in better."

"True." Ingeborg looked up. "Can you think of anything else we need?" She read off the list she had.

"We're almost out of salt."

"Thank you." She tapped her pencil on the paper. "Why don't you invite Thorliff and Elizabeth too? The more the merrier."

"Tante Elizabeth isn't very merry right now."

"I know. The visit might do her good." She handed the paper to

Astrid. "Get some peppermint sticks too. Inga loves chocolate pudding with mashed candy on top."

"If I can, I'll bring Inga back with me in the buggy. Jonathan isn't back with the wagon yet."

The thought of her granddaughter coming with Astrid made Ingeborg smile both inside and out. "I better make some cookies. Would you please bring in some butter and the buttermilk? I feel a baking spree coming on."

"Good thing the men are eating at Tante Kaaren's."

"I know."

Astrid headed out the door to harness the horse and popped back in. "Mor, there's a man coming up the lane with two cows. I'm sure he hopes you'll buy them."

"I'll be out in a minute." Ingeborg closed her account books and slid them into the vertical slots in the desk. She cleared the papers into one drawer and the pencils into another. If Inga was coming, things needed to be put away from her inquisitive fingers. She glanced out the window to see that the man was in the yard and the two cows were already grazing on the short grass near the well house. Heading out the door, she grabbed her sunbonnet as she went.

The man looked about as tired as the cattle he drove. "Howdy, missus. I heard tell you might be in the market for another milk cow. The heifer is carryin' too, by a real beefy bull. Cow's been a good milker."

"Looks like you've been on the road some time." While they talked, she looked the cow over for any injuries. "How long since she calved?"

"Three, four months. She's bred back too."

"Why are you selling?"

"This land just takes too much. My wife and daughter are gone. I can't stay here any longer. I'd give 'em to you if'n I didn't need some cash so bad. Folks around here say you're always on the lookout for more cows."

"What do you want for the pair?"

The man named a price higher than she wanted to pay, but her heart got in the way.

"I'll give you sixty dollars and a good meal."

The man tipped his fedora back, scratched his several-day-old whiskered chin, and hitched his overall strap higher on his shoulder. "Guess I'll take it."

"You can put them in that corral by the barn. Give them a good drink at the water tank first."

"Thank you, missus. Lord bless you."

Ingeborg returned to the house to fix a plate of food and fetch the cash from her strongbox. After slipping the bills into her pocket, she sliced bread and cheese, poured a glass of buttermilk from the crock Astrid had brought in, added the last of the gingerbread from the night before, and headed back outside. The cows were still drinking, and the man had soused his head in the tank too. Water drops darkened his shirt, but he looked a mite refreshed.

"Why don't you sit down in the shade of the well house and let them graze while you eat. Then you can put them in the corral."

"Be glad to do that." He took the plate and the money and sank down cross-legged in the shade. After a couple of bites he looked up. "You know what time the train comes by going east?"

"About another hour or two."

"Good. I'll be on it." He held up a piece of bread with cheese. "Mighty fine, ma'am. Mighty fine."

Ingeborg returned to the house, and the next time she looked out the window, the cow and heifer were in the corral, and the man was down the road on his way to town. She found the glass sitting on the plate on her back porch. Glancing out over the fields, she saw the two teams mowing hay, one slightly ahead of the other, the way they'd always done it. Lars and Haakan would move from field to field, the sickle bars laying the grass out flat behind them. The breeze carried the fragrance of newly mown grass and clover across the fields, a summer scent that promised a bountiful year. She probably should have gone out and asked Haakan what he thought, but one milking and one due to freshen soon didn't make a whole lot of difference in the milking time. Surely he wouldn't mind. Besides, the cheese house could always use more milk.

When Haakan came in from the fields that evening, she told him about the man and her purchase. "He looked so down and out, I couldn't refuse."

Haakan shook his head. "Leave it to my Inge." He lifted his hat and wiped his forehead with his forearm. "You got something cold to drink?"

"Buttermilk?"

"Sounds good."

"I'll bring it out. They look to be a good addition to the herd. They're both bred. I was going to ask him if the heifer was out of the cow, but I forgot."

"They look similar enough. I'll get the harnesses off. The boys are milking already."

"They started early."

Ingeborg brought a glass of buttermilk out to her husband, thinking he looked mighty tired himself. But she knew better than to suggest he let the young men finish off the chores and he take it easy. At the sound of a trotting horse, she looked around to see Astrid turning into the lane, Inga waving beside her. When Astrid stopped the buggy, Ingeborg held out her arms and swooped Inga into her embrace.

"Gamma, I come see you."

"I know. I am so happy, I could squeeze you forever."

"Mr. Jeffers said thank you and he'll be out as soon as the store can be closed. Thorliff and Elizabeth will be along soon. What did we bring for Grandma?"

"Candy. Good candy."

"I see you already had some."

Inga held up one finger. "One, that all."

"Andrew and Ellie are here too," Ingeborg told Astrid. "Ellie brought a rhubarb pie. And yes, the chocolate pudding is ready for the topping."

"I see you bought the cows."

"Ja, I couldn't help it."

"Down, Gamma. See Gampa."

"You stay with me until he gets the horses unharnessed."

Astrid backed the buggy into the shed and jumped out to release the horse. She stripped the harness off, handing it to her father, and led the horse to the corral, where he couldn't get a drink yet. "You want me to put the cow in the barn?"

"Ja, thanks." Haakan lifted the harness onto pegs on the barn wall. "You go on and help your mother if we're having all this company. We'll finish the milking."

Ingeborg stretched the table out to its longest length in order to seat all the guests. Ellie did her best to help with Carl on her hip. He gave a huge yawn and laid his head on Ellie's shoulder.

"Why don't you go lay Carl on one of the beds, Ellie," Ingeborg suggested. "His eyelids are looking heavy."

"I'll give it a try. He didn't sleep long enough this afternoon."

Inga helped Astrid set the table while Ellie took care of Carl.

"Each plate gets a spoon," Astrid said as she handed Inga spoons and set the rest on the table, where she could reach them.

"For pudding?"

"How do you know there is pudding?"

"Gamma said." Inga placed the spoon very carefully on a plate and looked up to Astrid, who shook her head.

"Beside the plate."

Inga moved the spoon. "Here?"

"Good."

"She talks more every day," Ellie commented as she sliced the bread. "Carl has someone to keep him on his toes. When he starts walking, that is."

"Don't rush him. At least you can catch him when he's crawling." Ingeborg pulled a pot of beans from the oven and checked on the roast. "We're going to have to butcher one of those steers pretty soon. I'm running out of meat."

"One of the sheep is limping. Pa said he'd butcher it and hang the hindquarters to dry in the haymow."

"Some venison would taste good."

"They won't take time to butcher now that haying is begun." Astrid watched as Inga, the tip of her tongue showing between her lips, placed each spoon precisely.

"Now I do knives?"

Ellie glanced at Ingeborg. "How does she know all this so soon?"

"She's helped Astrid set the table before. You only have to tell her something once and she'll remember."

"Are all children this smart?"

"Not that I know of." Ingeborg dropped a kiss on the little towhead at her side.

"Takk, Gamma."

The three women burst into laughter, making Inga giggle too, her little hands clapped over her mouth.

"Oh my, what a good girl you are." Ingeborg wiped her hands on her apron and swung her granddaughter up onto her hip.

Inga looked toward the door. "Gampa coming." She pushed away to be set down, and when her feet hit the floor, she ran to the screen door. "Gampa!"

"Coming." Haakan's voice floated through the screened kitchen window above the wash bench, where the milkers were cleaning up.

Inga pushed against the screen door and, when it opened, started out.

"No, you stay inside. Watch your fingers." While Ingeborg cautioned, Astrid swooped the little one up and danced around the room with her.

"See Gampa!" Inga glared up at her aunt, making Astrid laugh again.

"He'll be here in a minute." Astrid spun them in a circle, bringing a smile back to the stern little face.

When Haakan came through the door, Inga ran to him, her face beaming and her arms raised. "Gampa, up."

Haakan lifted her and kissed her cheek, holding her against his chest. "Your pa and ma are here," he said when he heard a buggy. She nodded but kept her arm around his neck, even when Thorliff and Elizabeth came through the door.

"Smells good in here." Thorliff sniffed deeply a second time.

"Pudding," Inga informed him.

"You don't say. Did Grandma make you chocolate pudding?"

"Uh-huh." She stuck a forefinger in her mouth and leaned her forehead against Haakan's chin. "Gampa milk cows."

"Did Pa help milk cows?" Astrid asked.

Inga shook her head. "Pa no milk cows." Her serious look at her father made them all chuckle.

"She has that right." Thorliff held up his hands, still ink stained from printing the newspaper. "But I never had hands like this milking cows."

"No matter what he scrubs with, we all know when it is printing day." Elizabeth reached for her daughter. "You come sit with Ma."

They were all taking their chairs when they heard a buggy nearing the house. Ingeborg looked out the window. "Mr. Jeffers is here, just in time."

"Welcome, Mr. Jeffers," she said, meeting him at the door. "Please come in."

He looked short next to all the Bjorklund men as he shook hands around the table and said howdy to them all. Extra girth usually hidden by his shop apron added to the impression. With his mouse brown hair pomaded to stay back and his slightly darker mustache newly trimmed, he'd obviously cleaned up to be company. A wandering left eye made one wonder where he was looking.

"Thank you for the invitation," he said, turning to Ingeborg. He handed her a brown wrapped parcel from his other hand.

"Why, thank you." Ingeborg almost said, "You didn't need to do that," but restrained herself and slipped off the string instead. She laid it on the counter to add later to the ball of string she was saving and unfolded the paper to reveal two packets of needles—one for hand sewing, one for the machine—and several yards of inch-wide eyelet. "How nice of you."

"Thought perhaps you could use those."

"I surely can. Please, won't you sit down?" She indicated a chair next to Haakan.

As soon as the guest sat, Haakan folded his hands. "We'll say the blessing. I Jesu navn, går vi til bords. . . ." With all of them joining in, they finished with "amen." Inga said it after they all did, setting a chuckle around the table.

"So how's the store going?" Haakan asked after everyone had helped themselves from the bowls and platters that circled the table.

"Fair to middling." Mr. Jeffers laid down his fork. "Guess it takes some time for folks to adjust to a new owner, Miz Bjorklund being part of the family and all."

"Our Penny ran a good store all right and catered to everyone around. If she didn't have something in stock, she'd order it right quick," Ellie said.

"She loved finding new gadgets, especially for housekeeping." Ingeborg buttered half a slice of bread and handed it to Inga, receiving a wide grin in return.

"I'm hoping to move out some things been sitting there awhile."

"Well, we hope you join into the life of our town," Thorliff said. "We'll be putting up some new houses if you decide to bring your family out."

"No family to speak of," Mr. Jeffers told them. "I was hoping there might be some marriage-minded ladies out here. Although my sister from Wisconsin said she'd come out to help me if I needed her."

"Is that where you're from?" Dr. Elizabeth asked over Inga's head.

"Oh no, back east. Had no idea about life in the west."

"How did you hear about the Blessing General Store being for sale?" Thorliff asked.

Wonder why he didn't say where exactly he was from. Ingeborg started the meat platter around again. "Here, help yourselves. I don't want anyone to go away hungry."

"As if that would happen." Thorliff gave his mother a teasing grin.

"Oh, a friend been through here on the railroad told me about the store."

He's very tight-lipped, yet he doesn't appear to be shy. *You don't look like the kind of man who would have amassed a nest egg. Where did the money come from to buy Penny's store?* Ingeborg kept her thoughts to herself, knowing she and Haakan would discuss this conversation later.

"You been a storekeeper before?"

"Worked in one since I was old enough to push a broom. Our family's been keeping stores since they come from the old country." He passed the bowl of baked beans after spooning more onto his plate. "This is the best meal I've had since I left the boardinghouse. Never been much of a one to cook for myself."

"You come to church on Sunday and we'll make sure you're introduced to the rest of the folks." Ingeborg nodded to Astrid to get the coffeepot. *Didn't say which country his family was from either. He is a man of few words.*

"Don't see how I can do that and keep the store open too."

"You're going to be open on Sundays?" Andrew asked.

"Nothing is open on Sundays except the boardinghouse." Thorliff paused in slicing his meat.

Mr. Jeffers laid his knife across the top of his plate. "There a law against a man keeping his business open on Sunday?" His tone had tightened.

"No, not really. It's just the way things been done here. The Bible says Sunday is a day of rest, and—"

"I see some of the farmers working on Sundays."

Wait until the women get wind of this, Ingeborg thought, rolling her lips together. *I can hear Mrs. Valders now.*

"Well, I'll say you just might get some opposition from the folk around here, but what you do with your store is your business."

Haakan spoke slowly and easily, dousing a possible fire rather than adding to it.

Talk turned to other matters, and not long after they finished the meal, the guests headed homeward, since it was nearly dark already. Haakan and Ingeborg waved from their back porch, and Ingeborg blew sleepy Inga one last kiss.

Astrid and Ellie were finishing up the dishes while Andrew held his still sleeping son.

"Don't imagine he'll get much business on Sunday," Andrew said. "He'll be boycotted for sure."

"Got to let a man learn his lessons whatever way he chooses." Haakan settled back in his chair, pipe and tobacco in hand. "You milked the new cow tonight. How'd she do?"

"Stood there without a twitch. Needs some feeding up, but she gave better than half a bucket. Good-looking heifer." He looked to his mother. "I think you got a real bargain with the two of them."

"Glad to hear that. Felt sorry for the man." Ingeborg smiled across the lamplight to her son. Andrew had little Carl on his shoulder, the baby now sucking on his fist. *He must be ready to eat again by now.*

"You can put her in the pasture with the dry cows and heifers tomorrow. How close is that sow to farrowing?"

"Any day. She started pushing her nest together, so I put her in the farrowing stall."

Ingeborg helped put away the dishes, letting the easy conversation roll over her. Something bothered her about Mr. Jeffers, but for the life of her, she couldn't put a finger on it. Perhaps Haakan would have the answer. More changes, and this one didn't feel good. If only Penny hadn't left. It was obvious she hadn't wanted to go. Maybe Hjelmer would find life in the city less than he thought and want to come back. But that didn't mean Mr. Jeffers would give up the store. She sighed. Wishing things undone never helped. *Only you do, Lord.*

15

"THAT NEW COW IS LIMPING A BIT," Haakan told Ingeborg when he came in for breakfast a couple of days later. "I'm going to check her hooves tonight. Maybe she has thrush or something."

"If you leave her in the stanchion, I can have Jonathan help me check her."

"We already let them all out. Tonight will be soon enough."

When they finished eating, he announced, "We start raking today. Jonathan, you ride with Andrew for a while, see how he does it, then you can take over that team and Andrew can ride with you. Then finish cleaning out the haymow. Samuel will help you. Trygve will take out the other rake."

"That's good because I need to check on the sow a couple of times," Andrew said. "She's restless."

Jonathan looked over to Andrew. "What does that mean?"

"Well, when a sow is about to farrow, which means have her babies, she starts pushing the straw or grass into a mound for a nest. Then she starts to pacing, quits eating, lies down, gets up—does this over and over until finally she lies down and we start getting piglets. I keep a close eye on them, because it's really easy for a sow to roll over on her babies. Or step on them. We have a board across one corner of the stall, and after the babies nurse, I herd them under it and into the corner for protection. Cuts down on piglet mortality. When it is cold out, we keep a hot water bottle in the corner and they snuggle up against that."

"They can see and walk when they are born?"

"Ja. When she starts, I'll come and get you, and you can watch. Seeing anything being born is a real privilege."

"Andrew has always been our animal doctor," Astrid filled in. "He often spends the night in the stall when a cow is calving or a sow is farrowing."

"Ja, Mor takes care of humans and some animals. Andrew would make a good veterinarian did he not love farming so much."

"I never wanted to go away to school like some do around here."

"Thorliff did and I want to, so it's a good thing someone wants to stay home and farm." Astrid patted her brother's shoulder as she refilled the coffee cups. "You'd be lost without your animals, wouldn't you?"

"Well, he does have a baby boy now, so maybe that will change." Ingeborg looked to her son to see him shaking his head.

A few minutes later Haakan drained his cup and slapped his hands on the table. "Let's be at it."

As the men filed out, Ingeborg silently blessed each one of them, something she'd started doing years before, praying for their safety.

"Since it is our turn to make dinner, I'll knead the bread down, and you start making pie crust." Ingeborg began clearing the table. "I figured two rhubarb and two custard."

"What else are we having?" Astrid carried a stack of dishes to the sink and, after shaving soap into the dishpan and adding hot water, began the age-old task.

"Samuel left three rabbits hanging in the well house. I'll cut them up, brown the pieces, and set it to cooking. We can let it simmer on the back of the stove while the bread is baking. I think we have some sour cream out there. I'll put that in when the men are on their way up. Should make noodles too." Ingeborg nodded. "That's what we'll do. Along with leaf lettuce with sugar and vinegar. Sure am looking forward to fresh beans." She picked up a dish towel and began drying those ready.

"They'll be another week, at least."

When the dishes were done and put in their places, Astrid set the lard crock and a large crockery bowl on the table, then went for the flour. Measuring enough for six crusts, she cut the lard into the flour and salt until it was the size of peas, then added water. With the dough in a ball, she cut it in six wedges and, forming one into a flat round in her hands, dusted the board with flour and began rolling the crust. She flipped it over, patched a small tear with extra dough and a bit of water, and started rolling again. When the crust reached the correct size, she lifted it into a pie pan. She'd just finished the first two that were for the single crust custard pies when her mother returned from the garden with the rhubarb.

Together they chopped, beat the custard mixture of eggs, sugar, and cream, and poured most of it into the two pie shells and the rest over the rhubarb. With the top crusts rolled and spread over the rhubarb filling, Astrid crimped the edges, cut slits in the top, and slid the pies into the oven.

The fragrance of rabbit browning in bacon grease permeated the kitchen. Astrid rolled out the remaining bits of pie dough, sprinkled them with cinnamon and sugar, and set the tin on the upper rack of the oven. She and her mother would have piecrust cookies in time to take a back-porch break. After she took water and food to the men.

"Where's Grace?" Ingeborg asked as she shaped the bread dough into loaves.

"She was going to help Sophie today."

"What are they doing now?" Ingeborg realized she hadn't had a talk with Kaaren lately to catch up on all the news since the wedding.

"I guess some furniture arrived on the train from Onkel Olaf and Sophie wanted her to see it. And—" Astrid paused for effect—"they are wallpapering the babies' room so the furniture can go in there. I hope he made a cradle big enough for both of them."

"I still remember how Sophie and Grace would only sleep well when they were in the same bed. One was always touching the other."

"Do twins always have more twins?"

"Not necessarily, but some do."

"Grace is the closest I have to a sister."

"You have Ellie."

"But she's different since she and Andrew got married. We never have time to talk about things anymore. Especially since Carl came." Astrid paused in her sandwich making to look at her mother. "You and Tante Kaaren make sure you have time to talk."

"I was just thinking how we've not done so lately. Usually one of us crosses the field almost every day in the summer but not this year."

Silence but for the birdsong from outside floated in the kitchen.

"Mor, do you mind if I go away to school this fall?"

"Of course I mind, but that can't keep you from going if that is what you really want to do."

"I don't want to go clear to Chicago like Dr. Elizabeth wants me to do. I could never come home then."

"You don't have to do that. You can go to the nursing school in Grand Forks, or you can get what training you need right here in Blessing. Elizabeth said she can train you, and she already has been. She thinks you could possibly go for only one year, you are so far ahead of other students."

"I wish I knew what was going to happen."

"Ja." Ingeborg nodded. "We all wish that, but God in His mercy opens the door only far enough so we can see the next step. That way we don't get frightened and run and hide."

"If I go away for school, home will never be the same again, will it?" Astrid tucked the sandwiches into a basket, added a napkin of cookies, and hoisted the can she'd already filled with water.

"No, home won't be the same, but it will still be home until you marry and begin your own home."

"There's no one here I want to marry. I'd be back soon. I think I will miss everyone more than Sophie did. And how hard will it be for

Grace by herself?" Astrid asked, heading out the door.

Ingeborg went to the window and watched her daughter stride out to the fields. So capable and strong and yet still young inside. *Lord, thank you that I don't know what the years will bring. But please put a hedge of protection around her, both body and heart. I know you love her even more than I do, but I can't figure that much. So thank you.*

She removed the pan of pie-crust cookies from the oven and set it on the counter. One of the rhubarb pies was running over, sizzling on the oven floor. The crusts weren't brown enough yet, so she closed the oven door and put more wood in the firebox. She wiped away the sweat on forehead and neck with her apron and turned the pieces of rabbit over. The dough for noodles lay rolled flat on the board, so she gave it another couple of passes with the rolling pin, then dusted the surface with flour, and starting at one edge, rolled the dough into a long tube. She washed the scissors and cut the tube into half-inch sections and flipped each roll loose. After hanging as many of the noodles as possible on the rack behind the stove, she fluffed up those left on the table so they could dry too and headed for the garden to pick the lettuce.

With an apron of lettuce she returned to the house, dumped it in the sink to wash, and checked on the pies. The rhubarbs were done. She moved them to the counter and took a table knife to cut into the custard pies to see if they were done. The knife came out clean, so she took them out, removed one of the racks, and slid the four loaf pans of bread inside.

Back in the garden she pulled some of the crowded stalks of corn from each hill, and once she had a handful, she wandered out to the pasture. The new cow lay off by herself under one of the oak trees. Ingeborg opened the gate and, after closing it behind her, strolled toward the cow, taking her time so the animal wouldn't bolt before she got close enough to look at her.

The dusty brown cow with a few white markings watched her with ears forward, head up. Ingeborg held out the stalks of corn and slowed to a creep. Whenever the cow threatened to move, she stopped and rustled the corn. Several of the other cows stood, and one took a few steps toward her.

"Easy girl, how about some fresh corn? Beats anything in the pasture." Not that they'd grazed all the pasture down either. She stopped a few feet away from the cow, who had yet to stand, and looked her over. She seemed healthy. Extending the corn, she edged closer.

The cow heaved her rear end in the air and rose slowly to her feet. She stretched her head forward, took the corn, and chewed while watching Ingeborg. The other cows gathered round, and Ingeborg gave out the rest of her bounty before returning to the gate and thence to her kitchen by way of the well house, where she picked up a full butter mold from the shelf to serve at dinner. She should have made the cow walk to see the limp.

Astrid breezed back into the kitchen a bit later and snatched up three of the pie crust pieces. Talking around the one in her mouth, she invited her mother to join her on the back porch. Which she did.

"So how is Jonathan doing?" Ingeborg asked.

"His windrows are looking straighter as he goes along. He said Andrew is a good teacher."

"We all know that. How's the mowing going?"

"Lars has his mower up in the machine shed. I don't know what happened. Pa said thanks, drank, took his sandwich, and kept on going."

Ingeborg ate her cookie and dusted her fingers on her apron. "Some things never change."

Later that afternoon she went back out to look at the cow, only to find her in about the same place, lying down again. "Well, girl, we'll give you a good looking over tonight when you are in the stanchion. Maybe you have an infection in your hoof or something." She tossed another corn treat in front of the cow and headed back for the house. She would cut up the leftover rabbit into the noodles with a cream sauce and throw in a jar of canned beans.

That night after milking, Haakan and Ingeborg brought out a lantern to look closely at the cow's feet. Haakan prodded the bottom of the hoof, and the cow tried to pull it away.

"It's tender, but I can't see anything. There's no cut." He sniffed the foot. "No infection." He felt her ears and nose, but all seemed normal.

"How about we soak that foot in a bucket of warm soapy water? If there is an infection, that might draw it out."

"I'll try that. At least it's a front hoof. We'd most likely have to throw her to soak a back one."

"I'll send Jonathan out with a bucket of water." Ingeborg headed back to the house. Supper should have already been on the table, and here she was out with a limping cow. But then, which was more important? Healthy livestock or hungry men? She was glad she didn't have to leave out either.

The next morning the cow didn't eat her grain, and Andrew reported the heifer was limping too. Haakan held the cow's head while Andrew pried open her mouth. Ingeborg stood behind Andrew, trying to see over his shoulder.

"What are you looking for?" Jonathan asked.

"Spots on her tongue. Looks kind of like big cold sores."

"Put her in the corral and bring the heifer back here too," Haakan directed.

"What do you think it is?" Ingeborg asked.

Haakan shook his head. "I hope to heaven it isn't what I'm thinking. Hoof and mouth disease."

"But that's contagious, terribly so," Andrew said. "Cattle die from it."

"I know."

"So what do we do to treat it?"

"I don't know if there is any treatment."

Ingeborg heard the despair in his voice. What had she done by buying the cows?

When Grace left the boardinghouse and turned toward home she saw Toby, standing almost as if he'd been waiting for her. In books she'd read about feminine wiles to be used on men. While she was sure Sophie knew what they were, right now she'd give about anything for one.

"Hi, Grace," he signed. "Can I walk with you a bit?"

She nodded. A little ripple seemed to run through her stomach. Finally he had come to find her.

They walked a while without talking, and then he stopped and turned to look at her.

"Grace, there's something I've been meaning to tell you."

Oh good.

"First, I'm sorry I didn't dance with you. That was no way to treat a friend. But I was so surprised, I wasn't sure how to act."

Grace was confused. Did she understand his words correctly? Why would he not know how to act?

"I thought, since we've been good friends for a long time, you'd like to be the first to know."

Already she could tell this wasn't what she wanted to hear.

"I met a woman from Grafton, and I think I'm in love."

She focused on his chin, unable to get her gaze any higher for fear he'd see the tears fighting to burst forth. "Oh." She forced herself to at least look at his mouth, so she could see what he was saying, but his fingers continued the signing and she didn't have to let him see what he was doing to her.

"I wanted to tell you, thanks for being such a good friend all these years. You stood by me, and I value that."

"I wish you all the blessings you deserve." She forced herself to smile. "Guess I better get on home, Mor will be wondering where I am, after all she needs help, and I . . ." She knew she was running on like water from the pump when the wind was blowing the windmill. Unable to get more words past the lump that bounced up from somewhere, she signed good-bye and headed down the road to home. The urge to turn and look at him one more time fought with the tears that coursed down her cheeks. Toby loved someone else. No wonder he was never around. All she wanted to do was curl up in a ball and cry herself so dry she'd blow away like dandelion down on a puff of breeze.

Suddenly she realized she was almost home, and Astrid was in front of her. There was no way she could hide her tears.

"Oh, Grace, you've already heard. It is so frightening. I don't remember ever seeing my parents look so worried. What will our families do if it's true?"

Grace tried to absorb that the breeze she wished for had suddenly become a storm.

16

H**AYING DIDN'T LET UP** for the tragedy going on around them.

Haakan sent a telegram to the agriculture department at the college in Grand Forks. Ingeborg prayed that the diagnosis was not what they feared, but this time God either didn't respond or failed to hear. She wasn't sure which. The reply: It was the dreaded hoof and mouth disease that had wiped out the cattle of entire nations in other parts of the world. While the letter that followed was long and full of statistics, the remedy remained the same. Since the disease was so contagious it could be carried on the wind, the only way to keep it from spreading eastward was to destroy all cloven-hoofed animals.

Reports were trickling in from the west of other outbreaks, but the news did nothing to cheer Ingeborg. She had bought the diseased cattle. Haakan had not wanted more cows, but she had gone ahead anyway. Guilt was a bitter bed partner.

"It would most likely have come here anyway," Haakan told her more than once, but she couldn't seem to hear him.

The men were bringing the first load of hay into the barn when the sheriff from Grafton rode into their yard.

"Mornin', Mr. Bjorklund," he called from horseback.

Haakan sank the tongs of the hay sling into the hay and signaled for the lift. "Morning." He slid to the ground and approached the officer. "What can I do for you today?"

The man shook his head. "I hate to do this to you, but I been so ordered. All cloven-hoofed animals are to be destroyed. I see you've not started that yet, and every day you resist, the disease can spread further. You got to shoot 'em all and burn or bury the carcasses, and you got to do it now."

"Has it spread more?"

"We're hoping to stop it at the river, but you're not the only one that's got it. It came from the west. We think from some steers brought up from Texas on a train." He tipped his hat back. "I got to say, this is about the hardest job I've ever had to do."

"Sheep and pigs too?"

"And goats. What could carry it over is deer. We can stop the transport of cattle, but the wild animals—that's a different story. I have hunters out shooting all they can find. I know you got to get your hay up, but this has to be taken care of right away."

"Not much sense in haying if we have nothing to feed it to." Haakan turned to Andrew. "Go get the guns and ammunition."

Ingeborg stood back from the others, listening to the sheriff's edict. Did he not understand he was destroying her cheese house? A good part of their livelihood? And that of their neighbors? Tears rained down her face and choked her throat.

She turned back to the house, one step ahead of Andrew, and marched up the steps. Going to the gun cabinet, she opened the door and handed the rifles back to Andrew. Drawing out the box of bullets, she filled the remaining gun she'd held back.

"You don't have to do this, Mor." Andrew's jaw wore the look of steel.

"Ja, I do."

"It would have come even if you'd not bought those two. It isn't your fault. The sheriff said so."

She nodded and held on to the rifle. "Let's go."

Haakan took one look at her face and kept his thoughts to himself. "We'll herd them to that depression out in the pasture. Bring some grain, Jonathan. We'll scatter it so they settle down."

"What about the sheep?"

"Same thing. We'll have to shoot the pigs in the pens and haul them out there. I hope Mr. Jeffers has plenty of kerosene. Astrid, take the wagon and go to the store. Get what you can."

Astrid nodded, rivulets of tears streaking her face. "Where was the sheriff going from here?"

"Calling on all the farmers. He didn't single us out. Just one of those things that has to be done. Let's get at it."

"Can't we milk first?" Astrid asked.

"It's too soon. They wouldn't have enough to make it worth our while. Let's just get it over with."

Ingeborg walked beside him, feeling stiff, as though none of her joints wanted to bend. The rifle hung heavy in her hand.

Jonathan brought two buckets of oats from the grain bin and joined the group. His face looked frozen cold. They stopped at the fence to see the milk cows grazing, the scene peaceful like any other day. Gunshots resounded in the distance. Some of the cows smelled the grain and ambled over to the free meal, a few of them limping. Several looked but didn't bother to get up. Barney barked and nipped them until they staggered to their feet and over to the rest.

Within five minutes, the entire herd lay dead. Barney and Andrew brought out the sheep, and in spite of their milling and bleating, they dropped at the volley.

Ingeborg threw down her rifle and headed for the house. *Lord, this is too much. You've taken away it all. I thought you were a merciful God and protected your people. We have tried to do what you say, but this is too much.* She sat down on the edge of the bed and stared through her tears at the floor. Now the shots were coming from the barns, Andrew's barn and Lars', where they kept the weaned calves.

The stench of burning flesh hung over the region in a pall of smoke.

Pastor Solberg called a special service to try to comfort his people.

"I can't go," Ingeborg told him when he came by to announce it.

"Yes you can. And you will." He took her hand. "God has promised to walk through the valley with us. While this is not our own death, this is surely a valley of death, and He is here, right in the midst."

Ingeborg shook her head. "I can't find Him."

"No, but He is finding you. Just like He is finding all of us. He has seen us through floods and blizzards, through sickness and despair. God has said, 'I will never leave thee, nor forsake thee.' He never changes. He lives up to His Word." Pastor Solberg looked her in the eye. "I'll see you tomorrow night at seven."

"Huh, you might as well make it earlier. We don't have any chores to do." She turned away and set each leaden foot on the next step up.

The next day she filled and set the last cheese presses. Granted that while she had a lot of cheese for this time of the year, the house would not be full come fall. And after she filled the orders, there would be no more.

When the paper came out that day, Thorliff had written an article about the catastrophe and the far-reaching effects. The government had decreed that all cloven-footed animals be destroyed west of the Mississippi River and east of the Rocky Mountains and that there be no cattle imported or transported. The Red River hadn't stopped it.

The people of Blessing gathered at the church only due to Pastor Solberg's insistence. With eyes red-rimmed from the smoke, the men removed their hats and nodded to one another as they sat down. Women held the little children on their laps, and the older ones sat silently beside them. Mrs. Valders glared at Ingeborg.

When it looked like everyone was gathered, Pastor Solberg stood up and moved to the center in front of the carved altar, Bible in his hands. "Dearly beloved, let us hear what the Word of God says to us." He flipped pages and began reading. "Isaiah 43:2: 'When thou passest through the waters, I will be with thee; and through the rivers, they shall not overflow thee: when thou walkest through the fire, thou shalt not be burned; neither shall the flame kindle upon thee.'"

When he stopped, he closed his Bible. "Let us pray, and tonight I ask that those of you who are able, to please pray aloud, so that we can all be blessed. I'll begin and then you join in." He paused and the rustlings settled. "Lord God, heavenly Father, we have heard your word of promise and mercy. You have promised to restore the years of the locust. We've lived through those, and you have restored us. This horror is like unto another locust, taking what we have built and burning it away. But our hearts are on you and your kingdom, where moth cannot make holes, nor can disease, where rust does not destroy any earthly thing. We are your children, the people of your kingdom. Heal and restore us, O Lord, we pray."

Ingeborg heard someone sniffing and mopped her own eyes. *Lord, these were your cattle, hogs, sheep, and goats. Your hills around here are now empty. I know you can restore, but right now I'm not sure you will choose to.*

Haakan cleared his throat. "Lord God, I can't say I understand this, for I don't. I just know that evil does not come from you. And this has been a great evil. But I do know that your love never changes and that you have promised to bring good out of bad. Only you can know how to do this. I give you my heart, knowing that it is safe with you and you will live up to your promises." He paused. "I know that." His voice carried a conviction that caused murmurs of agreement to float around the room.

Ingeborg slid her hand into his and rested her cheek against his shoulder. "You are right," she whispered and squeezed his hand. He covered their two hands with his other one.

Several others prayed, and the room seemed to lighten. A breeze blew through the windows, a clean breath of air.

Pastor Solberg said, "And all the people said . . ." They all joined him on the amen. He lifted his hands. "Say this with me. The Lord bless us and keep us." The congregation joined one by one. "The Lord make His face to shine upon us and be gracious unto us. The Lord give us His peace. In the name of the Father and of the Son and of the Holy Ghost, amen."

Only a sniff broke the silence. Ingeborg sucked in a deep breath that caught on the lump in her throat. It was Grace crying next to Astrid.

"'Blest be the tie . . .'" Surely it was Kaaren's voice but still choked up and hard to identify. One other joined in, then another.

Ingeborg fought the tears and tried to join, but no sound came from her throat. Haakan's rich baritone voice picked up the harmony. She mouthed the words, singing with her spirit, even though her vocal chords would not function properly.

"'Our hearts in Christian love.'" By now all those around her were singing. "'The fellowship of kindred minds . . .'"

Her voice finally returned. "'Is like to that above.'"

All together they surged into the second verse and after Haakan stood, the others followed. "'And perfect love and joy shall reign through all eternity.'" As the last verse sung in full harmony reverberated off the walls, a small voice from behind her said, "Pitty, Ma."

Pretty indeed. If heaven sounded half as good, it would be worth the trip, let alone to see the Savior. Ingeborg wiped her eyes again and turned to beam through her tears at her little granddaughter. "Leave it to Inga."

Thorliff's eyes shone bright, and Elizabeth hugged her daughter close.

Astrid held out her arms, and Inga reached for her, so Elizabeth let her little one loose. "You liked the singing?"

Inga nodded. "More?" She placed her hands on Astrid's cheeks and stared into her eyes then laid her cheek on Astrid's shoulder and sighed.

"Someone is tired." Thorliff smiled at his mother. "I have a feeling she is not the only one."

"No, that's for sure. Sadness makes you more tired than twelve hours of pitching hay." Haakan turned to greet Pastor Solberg.

"Thank you. Although I didn't want to come, I'm sure glad I did."

"God indeed met us here tonight. Times like this I am not only renewed but more deeply amazed than ever at the power of His Word and how gathering together to hear it brings healing to souls and spirits. 'Where two or three are gathered together in my name, there am I in the midst of them.'" He patted Haakan on the back of his shoulder. "Thank you for coming."

Back at the house Ingeborg added wood to the stove and drew the coffeepot onto the soon to be hotter part. "There's cake left. I could whip some cream and put raspberries on it."

"How about putting raspberries on it and pouring the cream on top?" Haakan sank into his chair and clasped his hands on the red-and-white checked tablecloth.

"Fine."

"I'll get the raspberries and the cream." Astrid headed out the door.

"I'm sorry you had to go through such an ordeal," Ingeborg told Jonathan as he took a seat at the table.

"Me? I didn't lose my livestock. I don't know how you are all going on like this." His voice grew more intense with each word.

Haakan leaned forward. "One thing you learn about farming, son. Any number of things can nearly wipe you out—floods, fire, drought, disease, an accident—but if you love the land and can't see yourself doing anything else, you put your trust in the Lord above and keep on going. Somehow, we will buy more cows, plant more wheat, cut more hay. Loss and death are part of life, but not the most important part." He smiled at Ingeborg. "When you have family and loved ones around you, you can get through most anything together."

Jonathan stared deep into the older man's eyes and nodded.

Ingeborg wondered what he saw there. She knew what she would see: love, patience, and fortitude, but mostly love. Such love for this wise man sitting in the lamplight at the table welled up in her that she went to stand behind him and placed both hands on his shoulders. She laid her cheek on the top of his head and inhaled his scent, a fragrance like no other. Soap and sweat and Haakan.

The sound of sputtering on the stove cut off the moment. The coffee was boiling and spattering out the spout. "Uff da." She grabbed a potholder and dragged the coffeepot off the hottest part. Astrid came through the door and set her basket and the cream pitcher on the counter. She brought out plates from the shelf, and she and her mother fixed and served the dessert.

The last of the cream, Ingeborg thought. Where would they get milk to drink or cook with? While they had butter to last awhile and buttermilk, what would they do?

"I'll find us a cow if I have to go to Chicago for one." Haakan had read her mind again. "As soon as it is safe to bring one home."

"How will we know?"

"I'm sure the agriculture department at the college will have good advice."

"The school there, is it a regular college?" Jonathan asked.

"Ja, they have more than just the agriculture program."

"That's where I'm going for nursing school—someday." Astrid licked the cream from her fork. "Why?"

Jonathan shrugged. "Just curious."

Ingeborg watched him draw lines along the checks in the table-cloth with the tines of his fork. What would Mr. Gould have to say if his son wanted to go to school out here? She looked up at Astrid as her "someday" caught up in her mind. This fall was not someday.

WOULD THE SMELL NEVER GO AWAY? Grace wondered.

The stench had been hanging over Blessing like a heavy cloud for several days. And though rain would've helped if it came, they needed to get the hay in first. Her mother had said that perhaps the fat melting down into the earth was what still smelled, but all the bones had not burned up either. The men were digging a hole by the burning place to bury the remains. Perhaps then the air would be clean again.

Grace squatted down to reach three green beans hanging together. She had long before realized that her sense of smell was far superior to those around her, but now that was a burden. She was in a constant state of nausea, and any attempts to eat only made her gag. Although she had been able to munch on the more tender beans as she picked them, which interrupted the smell for a few moments. She'd come to realize the close connection between smell and taste. Being outside, which usually gave her a sense of peace, was now something she avoided. Perhaps if she tied a scented handkerchief over her nose it would help.

With her basket full, she settled onto the bench on the back porch. Shame Astrid wasn't here to help. Someone to chat with always made a job go easier, although it might be harder to keep up a cheerful attitude. All she felt was tired these days. If she didn't know

Mor needed her, she wasn't sure she could get out of bed in the morning. And she wasn't the only one. Astrid said Elizabeth told her that grief was more exhausting than any physical labor.

As she snapped the ends off the beans and broke them into bite-size pieces, she let her mind roam. As always it went back to Toby and how he wouldn't dance with her. Then learning why didn't help at all. She closed her eyes against the stab in her heart. But others liked to dance with her, like Jonathan. She clamped her jaw, recognizing the anger that danced and popped like drops of water on a hot stove. As Astrid said, Toby had been terribly rude even though he had a reason. Not that the reason made any of this easier to bear.

She'd loved waltzing with Jonathan, his strong hand at her back, her right hand lost in his. And when he spun her around, her feet hardly touched the floor. What would it be like to kiss him? His lips were firm and carved like the lips she'd seen on a picture of a statue. *Where did that thought come from?* Of course, she could ask Sophie how it felt to kiss Toby. The one person she cared about she'd never kissed, but her sister had. That thought brought her back to reality with a thump. She bit into a slim green bean as if she were chomping nuts. What if Jonathan cared for her like she cared for Toby? She mustn't treat him like Toby treated her, but how could she keep his friendship without leading him on?

She felt the thud of footsteps on the stairs and looked up to see Jonathan smiling at her. He looked a little pale. "You want a bean?" She held out one of the slender, more tender, ones. She felt the blush moving up her neck, glad he couldn't read her thoughts.

"But it's not cooked."

"Haven't you eaten raw string beans before?"

"No." The twist of his mouth made her smile as she bit off part of the bean.

"You are missing out." She held out another, and this one he took, obediently biting down and chewing.

He cocked his head slightly. "Not bad."

"No, very good."

"Well, I wouldn't go that far. Perhaps raw beans are an acquired taste." He reached for another. "But it does help a little."

Grace tilted her head in a question.

"The smell." Jonathan looked embarrassed.

"Me too."

"But it is such a small discomfort compared to what your families are facing."

Grace nodded. Her parents, Tante Ingeborg, and Onkel Haakan, even Andrew, all walked as if they were carrying heavy wood. And Astrid said Onkel Haakan sometimes took a short nap in the afternoon "I thought you were fishing with the boys?"

"I was, but I didn't catch anything except mosquito bites." He scratched one on his arm. "Where's Astrid?"

"At Dr. Elizabeth's." Her fingers continued snapping beans while they talked. "Did you hear we are going to have a party?"

"When?"

"Sunday."

"Isn't this an odd time to have a party?"

"Well, it will bring the community together to remind us of joy as well as sorrow, Mor says."

"Can you get ready for a party in two days?"

She drew back, looking at him with one eyebrow raised. "We can get ready for a party in two hours. Or make one up on the spot." She handed him another bean.

"What are you doing to them?"

"See, you snap off the ends, without wasting any of the bean, and break them up. Did you really never help with the garden?"

"No, never." He tried to sign but mixed up his fingers.

Grace moved them in the right way and had to hold her breath at the tingle that shot up her arm.

"At home a party takes at least two weeks to organize. You have to make up a guest list, send out invitations, get the responses back, decide what you want to serve, and give Cook plenty of time to purchase the supplies. Then the housekeeping staff must clean extra good, not that the house isn't always immaculate, or heads will roll under Mrs. Smithston." At Grace's questioning look, he added. "She's the head housekeeper and in charge of hiring and firing the maids. If one isn't doing her job, she is let go immediately."

Grace shook her head slowly. Every time Jonathan revealed bits and pieces of what life was like in New York City, she was always grateful she didn't live there. "Can't you ever just have people over?"

"We do more of that when we are at the shore during the summer." He sat down on the wide porch railing and wrapped his arms around one raised knee. "There, all of us, including houseguests, kind of float from one house to the other, depending on what we want to do."

For the most part he was speaking, but from time to time he tried to fill in a few words with sign language.

"We go to the Bloomquists' if we want to go riding, the clay tennis court is best at our house, croquet at the Mitchells'. If we decide to do a . . . bake, we need at least one day for the food to be purchased."

"What kind of bake?"

"A clambake. You've never had clams?"

She shook her head and signaled for him to come over to her chair so she could help him sign the word *clambake*. After he had it down, she handed him some beans. "Women can snap beans and visit at the same time." This way she could avoid touching him again.

"Then how can I practice?" he teased but rolled his eyes and followed her suggestion. "Well, I'd never had raw beans or peas before coming here, so I guess we're even." He got settled on the railing again and started snapping beans. "Clams are bivalves, meaning they have two shells with a strong muscle to hold them together. Like fish, they come from the ocean, and when they are cooked in a kettle— steamed—they open up, and you dig the meat out with a fork and dip it in melted butter. We do potatoes and corn on the cob and sometimes lobsters or big shrimp." He watched her eyes. "You have seen pictures of such things, haven't you?"

"Maybe, but I might not have known what I was looking at."

"When you come to New York, I'll make sure you get to try all kinds of new things. . . ." He paused.

She could feel him staring at her. But she couldn't nod and smile like she could tell he wanted her to. Instead she shook her head. "Whatever makes you think that I will come to New York City?" She shook her head again, smaller movements but nonetheless emphatic. "I have no desire to leave Blessing at all, let alone travel all across the country to a huge city that I can't even begin to imagine the size of. Sophie is the one who wants to travel, not me. Not me at all."

Jonathan stiffened slightly. "My father and I are hoping your entire family, you and the Bjorklunds, will come visit us to allow us to repay the hospitality all of you have shown me. There is an incredible school for the deaf that I think you would be interested in." He got off the railing and dumped his broken pieces into her basket. "It is one of the leading schools in the world for deaf people and it trains people who work with the deaf. I thought perhaps you would like to learn new things to use in the school here."

Grace tried to soften her reaction. He was just being considerate, and she was being rude. "I think Mor has corresponded with someone there. You'll have to ask her." She tumbled the ends of the beans into a bucket to feed to the chickens. "How do you happen to know about such a school?"

"I wrote and asked my father what he could find out."

"How kind of you." She knew she was being more formal than she'd been with him before, but the thought of a trip like that and visiting a house like he'd described made her shudder. Nothing about it appealed to her—or did it? What if she could indeed learn something to help the students here? Would it help or hurt her family financially with the school? "I'd like to learn new things to help Mor, but I don't think I'd like to go there." She stood. "But I think you are very kind to offer."

Grace took her basket of snapped beans into the house and rinsed them with water from the bucket kept clean by a dish towel that covered it. The water ran into another bucket set under the drain in the dry sink. Perhaps this year the men would have time to run a pipe from the well like they had at the well house, and they could have running water in the kitchen. Especially since they'd have no stock probably for a long time to come. Running water had been one of her mother's dreams for years. Just like making the school even better was one of her dreams. If that school could help here, why was she being so pigheaded about looking into it? Grace stared out the kitchen window to see Jonathan walking down to the machine shed, where her pa was going over the steam engine to get it ready for harvest. While the wheat was nearing harvest time, there were still greenish patches among the gold. She'd read somewhere that the wind blowing the wheat looked like a golden sea. What would it be like to see the Atlantic Ocean? What would it smell like? she wondered.

They officially announced the late-afternoon party after church, but most people already knew about it and were planning on coming. Grace looked around the people gathered outside, but Toby was nowhere to be seen. Did he not even come to church anymore? Maybe that's when he went to Grafton.

Talk of the slaughter was avoided by discussing the wheat harvest in the men's circles, and gardens and canning dominated the women's conversations. Grace joined the gaggle of girls, staying toward the outside. Ellie joined the women, and Sophie returned immediately to the boardinghouse. Grace looked for Astrid, but she was missing too.

Rebecca Baard wore a long face, and Grace watched her talk. "I was almost ready to open my ice cream parlor, but you can't make ice cream without milk or cream. I don't know when it can happen now."

"It looks really pretty inside," one of the other girls commiserated.

"The book I read said the ice cream parlor is an ideal place for young people to meet."

We meet all the time. Why do we need something like that? Grace took the thought out and looked at it again. That really wasn't a very nice comment, so she was grateful she'd not said it. Blurting out something before thinking was more Sophie's trait than hers, but even Sophie had changed a lot. Between the children and the boardinghouse, she was so busy, she rarely had time to talk. Besides, Grace had tired of hearing how wonderful Garth was.

A tap on her shoulder caught her attention. Jonathan smiled at her.

"May I walk you home?"

"We can take the wagon with everyone else."

"I know, but I thought a walk might be nice."

Grace thought a moment. "But we need to get ready for the party." *We don't have cooks and maids to do the work for us.* She was glad she hadn't said that too. What was the matter with her today? Much as she looked forward to the party, she was really in a crabby mood.

"I see. Maybe next Sunday, then." He bowed slightly, reverting to his more formal demeanor, and turned away.

She watched him go. The sun caught the dark curls that tumbled over his forehead, and his face held a darker tan than the rest of the men's. Had his shoulders broadened this summer too? It looked as if his shirt was tighter. He walked with an easy grace and joined the group of young men who'd gathered under one of the other trees. Where earlier he'd stood back, now he was a welcomed member. Trygve clapped him on the shoulder and said something that made them all laugh. She didn't mean to hurt his feelings, but she couldn't let him get the wrong idea about her either. But he was leaving soon. Surely she could be a friend. It seemed like every thought she had lately had to have an argument to go with it.

Grace gratefully climbed into the bed of the wagon when her pa motioned it was time to go. Maybe planning a party for this afternoon wasn't such a good idea after all. Curling up on the porch swing with a book to read sounded much more appealing. Now that she thought of it, walking home with Jonathan might have been a pleasure. He at least made her laugh. Sometimes. Except when he looked at her like Garth looked at Sophie.

Even without ice cream, all those who came to the party at the Knutsons' had a good time. The raspberry swizzle tasted just right. It was like there was a silent rule that no mention be made of the disaster they were still reeling from, and everyone played ball, teasing the other team as well as the spectators. When they started the bonfire, the mosquitoes left and food arrived. Haakan brought the last of the smoked sausages from the well house, and they stuck them on the end of sticks to brown in the flames. The noodle salad disappeared as quickly as the hot dogs, and the pans of chocolate cake followed suit.

Grace sat on a log next to Astrid, and Jonathan placed himself on her other side.

"So how is this party compared to yours on the beach?" Grace asked, trying to make up for her rudeness earlier.

"What do you mean?" Astrid leaned forward. "I'm missing something here."

Jonathan began telling about house parties on Long Island, and soon everyone was grouped around, listening.

"Don't you ever have chores to do?" someone asked.

Jonathan paused and shook his head.

"Who does them?"

"The help."

Astrid patted his arm. "You poor thing. No wonder you didn't know how to work a shovel when you came."

Everyone burst out laughing, including Jonathan.

Trygve clapped him on the shoulder, nearly knocking him off the log. "You have learned a lot, Cityboy. I wonder if your family will even recognize you."

"Well, I haven't changed that much. On the outside at least."

"Shame you still can't catch fish, though," Samuel said, making everyone laugh again.

"Looks like this is tease Jonathan night," Haakan said from across the fire. "But I have to say that I am right proud of the way you pitched in and never complained."

"On the outside, that is." Jonathan held up his hands. "Those first days my hands were shredded and my arms screamed all night long, not that I could stay awake to hear them."

"You aren't who we thought you would be." Astrid poked her stick into the coals. "Funny how things work out."

"Speaking of work . . ." Haakan groaned as he got to his feet. "We'll be helping the Baards with haying, so morning will come early."

"Thank you all for coming," Kaaren said from beside Lars. "We'll just take the pans and dishes into the house and wash them in the morning." Everyone picked up something to carry back to the house, and the boys took shovels and threw dirt on the fire, then tipped pails of water over it.

Grace walked beside Astrid, aware the others were talking but not making an effort to take part. Communicating in the dark was near to impossible, other than the secret codes she and Sophie had devised using arm tapping. Sophie and Garth hadn't come tonight. Come to think of it, the only time she saw Sophie was when she went into town and visited her. Somehow there seemed a vast gulf between being one of the young people and having a husband, four children, and a boardinghouse. But Andrew and Ellie came and Thorliff and Elizabeth. The little children were sound asleep in the house and would be carried home most likely without waking up.

She chewed on her bottom lip. If Toby had come, the evening would have been perfect. He would have realized he was making a mistake with the girl in Grafton and Grace was the one he really cared about. Grace paused. Maybe that was really true. He had no idea about her true feelings because she'd never told him. Maybe she should talk with him. If only she had someone she could ask for advice. She knew what her mor and far would say. Tante Ingeborg? Or would Tante tell her mother? Dr. Elizabeth? Grace wasn't sick unless you considered an aching heart an illness.

WHILE JONATHAN HAD THOUGHT haying hard work, shocking the bundles of wheat was another exercise in endurance.

He, Samuel, and Trygve walked behind the binder, grabbed two bundles of wheat, leaned them against each other, then stood another three to five against the shock and moved on up the field. Trygve made it look easy, but getting the rhythm took some doing, and having to go back to stand up a collapsed shock made him more careful. To put it mildly, wheat was a dusty and prickly business. His neck, under his shirt, itched like fire.

The girls bringing out water jugs were a most welcome break both morning and afternoon. He had the feeling that Grace was avoiding him by not making eye contact. He wished he had introduced the possibility of coming to New York in a more gentle manner. The look on her face had reminded him of their dog's yowl when Mary Anne, as a toddler trying to walk, stepped on his tail.

At the end of the day, Jonathan collapsed on the ground, almost too tired to clean up and eat supper. Even worse than being hot and dirty, the bits of wheat spears that dug into the skin, especially under his shirt collar and pants waist, itched worse than a hundred mosquito bites. When Mrs. Bjorklund passed around a salve she'd made, he smeared it on immediately.

"You should market this," he said as the fire in his neck died out.

"Metiz taught me how to make it. Have you heard of her?"

"The Indian woman with the wolf?"

"Yes. She taught us all so many things about living on the prairie. We might not have made it through that first winter without her. People rail about the Indians, but she was a true friend. I miss her still." Ingeborg stared out the window. "She knew all about the herbs around here, which things are medicinal and which are good to eat. I keep a box of simples of my own now, and Dr. Elizabeth has been writing down all my receipts for the uses and mixtures."

As the family sat down to supper, Jonathan couldn't help but relive the shock he'd had that afternoon when he'd grabbed a shock and felt something moving in it. When the rattlesnake stuck his flat head out between the stalks of wheat, Jonathan dropped the shock with a yelp and leaped about five feet in the air and straight back.

"What's the matter?" Trygve dropped his bundles and came running. Together they watched the snake slither away.

Jonathan laid his hand over his heart, hoping to keep the thundering organ in his chest.

"Yep, prairie rattler all right. Sometimes they get tossed up on the wagonloads of hay too. They like the cool of the shade." He turned to grin at Jonathan. "Good thing they can't strike without coiling. Saves us from plenty of bites that way."

"That was too close for comfort."

"As pa says, a miss is as good as a mile."

But it wasn't your arm that felt that critter moving. "Shouldn't we kill it?"

"Why? Did no harm, and they eat plenty of mice and field rats that do harm when they get in the granary and corncrib."

"I see." One more bit of information he filed away for future use. That, along with a vow to be more careful. "You could have warned me."

Trygve half shrugged and dropped his gaze. "Sorry. I forget you don't know all this stuff."

Jonathan decided to take that as a compliment and looked up to see how far ahead of them the binder had gotten. "We better get back to it before we can't catch up."

The snake surprise turned into a huge joke around the supper table when Trygve teased Jonathan about it. Everyone had a snake story to share, including Haakan, who had been bitten once.

"But I thought a rattlesnake bite was fatal." Jonathan paused in the act of buttering his bread.

"Not always. Sometimes there's even such a thing as a dry strike. A rattler can hold his venom if he so chooses. If you can get the venom sucked out before it gets into the bloodstream, the wound makes you really sick and miserable but it's not always fatal. Depends too on where you're bitten. Up around the face and neck or upper arm are the worst. We all wear boots and heavy pants to protect our ankles and legs." Haakan passed the meat platter again. The deer that Samuel had shot before the disease struck made for good venison roast. Haakan had smoked part of it, so the meat should last them through a few weeks yet.

"Just the shock of it could give a man a heart attack." Jonathan thought back to his pounding heart. He raised a hand before Astrid could say something. "I know, just one more thing to get used to."

"You don't have to make snakes your friends, however." Astrid grinned at him. "And a skirt can be good protection too. A snake struck at me one time and got a mouthful of skirt. I was screaming so hard, I think he panicked and vamoosed as fast as his belly could wiggle."

"You get used to listening for the rattle. They hiss too."

But what about Grace? The thought made him nearly choke on his bite of venison. She couldn't hear a rattle or hiss. Did he dare ask? Did no one try to protect her?

"Oh, I forgot to tell you. There's a letter for you," Ingeborg said as she refilled his coffee cup, her hand on his shoulder like she did all the others. "I left it on the table by the desk in the parlor."

"Mange takk."

She squeezed his shoulder, sending warmth down his arm. "Velbekomme." Her smile as she moved on to fill Haakan's cup made him smile back.

Funny how that simple gesture made him feel like all the hard work was worthwhile, just so they could gather for a meal like this. Jonathan glanced at the faces around the table. Lars, Samuel, and Trygve were as at home at this table as at the one at their house, as if both families were melded into one. This alternating houses to cook for the men gave the woman a day to keep on canning, since putting up the garden was the major event going on besides harvest. Actually it was another form of harvest.

He'd never paid any attention to where his food came from before. It appeared on the table, and he ate it. What would Cook think if he went into her kitchen and started asking her where she got the carrots and shouldn't they have more of a garden than just flowers and herbs? What would the gardener say if he asked for a plot to plant himself? Or asked him to plant corn and green beans and potatoes? What would his mother say if he dug up part of the landscaped yard behind or beside the house to plant a vegetable garden? Perhaps he could plant carrots between the roses and use the boxwood as pea poles.

Thinking of the letter he wanted to read and answer, he excused himself while Haakan was lighting his pipe. After offering "Mange takk for maten," he picked up his letter and trudged up the stairs. He never dreamed he'd miss milking the cows. And if it still bothered him, what about the others? Was that why Ingeborg's smile did not come as readily, and if caught unawares she stared at the wall, her face tight with sorrow?

He slit the envelope with his pocketknife, one of the many things he'd purchased here since he'd arrived, and sat down to read. But instead he stared at the knife in his hand. Like the others, he realized the Blessing General Store was not the same welcoming place it had been under Penny's ownership. Ingeborg had mentioned several times that Mr. Jeffers wasn't carrying the amount of stock Penny had, and he didn't volunteer to order right away what was missing.

He'd even heard the women discussing it after church, a safe place to talk about it, as the store was still open on Sunday. Not that any of the people he knew would go there to buy on Sunday. Would their boycott make a difference?

Unfolding the paper, he began to read his father's letter.

Dear Jonathan,

Thank you for your letter, and I am pleased with the things you write. I had hoped this summer would be a life-altering experience for you, and it seems to be so.

Jonathan paused and looked out the window over the wheat shocks that stood like Indian teepees dotting the fields. Little did his father know how much his life was changing and that his new dreams would change it even further. He mentally composed a telegram. *Dear Father, I am staying here to attend college in Grand Forks to learn more about agriculture and farming, which is what I want to do with the rest of my life. Stop. Your steadfast and most appreciative son, Jonathan.* He shook his head and returned to the letter.

Everyone is having a normal summer season at the shore. I go out for long weekends whenever possible. I believe your mother and sisters have a surprise for you when you return home.

That thought made him shift forward a little. Too many of Mother's surprises involved meeting people he had no interest in spending time with. But if his sisters were involved, it might actually be interesting. Maybe some new music.

I heard mention that they have not received many letters from you, but I have an idea of how hard you are working, thanks to Mrs. Bjorklund's very complimentary letter. I have told your sisters to be patient and that you might like to hear of their escapades. From what they tell me, the summer is flying by too fast.

I did the research on the Fenway School that you requested. The school's reputation is impeccable. If Grace would like to attend there, I will gladly pay her tuition, although as proud as my friends in Blessing are, I doubt they will permit that. I am sending the printed information from the school to you under separate cover.

Again Jonathan paused. His letter regarding the animal slaughter had probably not reached his father yet. Money could be a serious issue for these folks this fall. Surely there were cows to purchase further east. Although the price would be high, due to demand.

If you would like, I will write to Mrs. Knutson and extend our invitation for their daughter to visit here and perhaps attend the school, if that is what she would like to do. I know your mother has been making lists of the articles you will need for college. I suggested she not order clothing for you yet, as I have a feeling you have filled out some with all that heavy labor.

Jonathan rolled his eyes and glanced in the mirror. "Won't they be surprised?" His dress coat was too tight in the shoulders and upper sleeves, so he had taken to wearing a dress shirt and vest to church. The shirt was at least wearable, though not comfortable.

Thank you, my son, for living up to my expectations for you this summer. I know you went out there solely to please me, and you have.

Your loving father

Jonathan read the last paragraph again and went to stand at the window. The curtains hung still. The evening breeze had not come up, but since his room faced the north, the air was cooler here than in the rest of the house. With the windows open at both ends, the draft helped alleviate the suffocating daytime heat. He'd earned his father's approval. This was one letter worth keeping, not that he'd thrown any of them away. He tapped the folded edge on the fore-finger of his left hand. But would the cost be worth the confrontation?

A yawn caught him and nearly cracked his jaw. Writing a letter right now seemed beyond the realm of physical possibilities, but he knew if he didn't do so immediately it might be days before he could find the time. They were to start the actual threshing in the morning.

∽

He'd finished his letter the night before, but the next morning he awoke at dawn, wondering if there was a better way to say what he had written. Taking letter in hand, he stood again at the window; this time watching the rising sun set the tops of the shocks on fire and throw shadows behind them. What critters had taken up residence in the ready-made houses during the night and would later startle those pitching the bundles up on the wagon? Ignorance might be bliss, as the old saying went, but he'd learned quickly that in working with animals and machinery, it might also be dangerous.

He reread his letter, one ear listening to the clanking of stove lids and the murmur of feminine voices. Did the women ever sleep? Feel-ing uncomfortable at his less than charitable thoughts regarding his own mother and the things she called tiring, he put that thinking aside and sat back down to rewrite his letter. He even thought of tearing the last part of the letter off and signing his name small, but that might let his father know he'd been editing. Senior Gould was a master at reading between the lines and reading people.

He copied the first section of his letter, where he'd shared the general news and the events around Blessing, and then rewrote the final paragraph. He crumpled up the original, which would make Mrs. Bjorklund shudder at the waste.

I have some serious things to discuss with you when I come home, and I look forward to hearing your opinions. In the meantime I have another favor to ask. Since all the cattle were destroyed around here, would several head of milk cows and a bull be an adequate gift for my months of living with the Bjorklunds? I tried to refuse payment when Haakan was handing out wages, since I thought the agreement was that I would work for my room and board. But he was adamant, and it would have been churlish to refuse, so I will add what I have earned to the cost of the cattle.

With gratitude,

Your son Jonathan

This time he slipped the folded sheet into the envelope and addressed it. Perhaps if Astrid was going in to town, she would mail it for him. He finished dressing, picked up the crumpled paper, and headed downstairs, lifting the lid on the stove to drop the paper into the flames.

☜☞

After another long, sweaty, itchy day of harvesting, it was finally time to start threshing. Jonathan finished helping unload the first of the wagons carrying wheat bundles and then stood by the spout and watched golden kernels of wheat flow into a gunnysack. As soon as the sack was full, Andrew pulled it to the side and Haakan slid an empty sack into its place. Andrew used a needle and hemp line to whipstitch the sack closed. When finished, he knotted the thread, cut it, stuck the needle into a pouch, and swung the completed sack up into a waiting wagon.

They didn't spill a kernel.

"Care to try this?" Haakan asked, indicating his position.

"Think I'll stick with pitching, at least for now."

"This is easier on the back."

"Could be, but not on the mind. I'd hate to spill and waste any of this precious gold that we've worked so hard to get to this point. I will never look at bread the same way again."

"Have you ever been through a flour mill?"

"I walked through the mill with Garth one day, and he explained the principles. He promised me a full tour if it opens before I leave." Jonathan turned back to take out the wagon just emptying. They were running three wagons, with Knute and Gus Baard helping them.

When the triangle rang at noon, the silence after Lars shut off the roaring steam engine kissed the ears. Lars squirted oil in several orifices of the monster before climbing down and wiping his hands with a rag he kept in his back pocket. He wiped his forehead with the back of his arm.

"Shame we can't save some of that heat for the winter." He motioned toward the engine that turned the long belt that made the separator blow chaff out one pipe and pour cleaned wheat down into the waiting sacks. The straw stack was already several feet high, with Samuel spreading the straw evenly, as they had the haystacks of haying season. The stacks were leftover hay that wouldn't fit in the barns.

"You know how pa was so tough about being careful around the belt, especially with all that machinery?" Andrew kept step with Jonathan. "Well, Mr. Valders lost the lower part of his arm one year when his sleeve caught on something and he got drug into the blade. Pa said that one time a belt broke and a man lost his head—cut it right off. That's why we are all so careful."

Jonathan stared at him. "You're kidding."

"Nope, not a bit. I was there when it happened to Valders. I had to go throw up in the bushes. Mor spent days doctoring him so he wouldn't die."

That explains a lot about Mrs. Valders and Toby too. The pain and bitterness must have affected the whole family.

"Guess I'll stay on the wagon end of the process. Most I could do is stab myself in the leg with the pitchfork or fall off the wagon."

"Or get snake bit."

"Andrew, you are just a barrel of comfort today. Remind me to come and talk with you when I need a dose of encouragement."

"At your service." Andrew sketched a bow. "How long until you have to leave?"

"Not long enough."

Andrew paused in midstep and stared at Cityboy, as he had called him at first, but the name never stuck. "Are you serious?"

"Perfectly."

"Well, I'll be—"

"You'll be what?" Samuel stopped beside him. "A slowpoke."

Jonathan laughed and ran on ahead until Andrew's hand caught his shoulder.

"What do you want to do?"

"What do I *want* to do, or what do I *have* to do?" Jonathan started walking toward the house again.

"I take it they are not the same?"

"Not in a lifetime." Jonathan and Andrew waited in line to get to the washbasins. "I don't want to attend Princeton, even though I argued to go there over Harvard. My father's selection was Harvard, and I was accepted there first. But now I've decided I want to go to the college in Grand Forks and learn all I can about farming."

Andrew whistled under his breath. "And . . ." He drew the word out and studied Andrew's face, the pause stretching like the belt that connected the engine and the machine. "And what will your father say about that?"

Jonathan shook his head and stepped up to pour clean water into a now empty basin. He scrubbed his face and hands without answering. He had no answer, only a suspicion that he was sure was right. Never in a million years might be along the lines of his father's opinion.

19

W<small>HY IS HE SO NICE TO ME</small>?

Grace stared after the broad-shouldered young man who had just presented her with a yellow rose bud. She sniffed the flower in her hand absently, concentrating more on her thoughts than her senses. She knew he'd picked the rose from the bush at Tante Ingeborg's, and that meant he'd gone out of his way to bring it to her. He'd also broken off all the thorns.

Grace mounted the back steps and ambled into the kitchen, sniffing the rose all the while. Such a rich, fruity scent, with petals like the finest velvet. She'd touched some like it on the trim of one of Elizabeth's hats. Were roses edible? Not wanting to spoil the petals by taking a nip out of one, she found a small glass, filled it with water, and put the rose in it, the emerald sepals setting the yellow to gleaming.

"How lovely." Her mother bent to sniff. "Ah, that rose has always smelled so sweet. I don't know why I don't go over and pick a bouquet now and then."

"Jonathan brought it to me." *And he must have come very early.*

"How nice. He is such a considerate young man."

"But why bring it to me?"

"Because he likes you, and he realizes how much you enjoy things that smell good."

"Nobody ever brought me a flower before." Did Toby take flowers to Grafton for his girlfriend? Whoever she was?

"Your father brought me a bouquet of bluebells once. I nearly cried I was so happy."

I should bring my mother more flowers. Next year I'm going to plant more flowers in the garden. They don't take up that much room, and with all the space we have, we could surely afford a few rows of flowers. She sniffed the rose again and set the glass on a table in the parlor, resolving to take it upstairs with her the next time she went up. In the meantime she needed to be picking beans again. She'd lost count of how many jars they'd canned so far, but the shelves in the cellar were filling up. And they'd already finished two boiler loads today. Beans took a long time in the boiling water bath.

As she went down the row picking beans, she wished she still had the britches she and Astrid had made, but her mother made her take hers apart and make a skirt again. Although both she and Tante Ingeborg thought it was a good idea, Kaaren had explained, "As teachers, we cannot create dispute." The baking sun made rivulets of perspiration run down her cheeks in spite of the sunbonnet or maybe because of it. No breeze, if there was any, could get to her face around the wide brim. At least the smell had become more tolerable, and her nausea had stopped. She finished one row and started down the next. The way the beans were still blooming, she'd be picking a long time yet. She sat back on her heels to watch a yellow and black butterfly taste the bean blossoms then try the pumpkin, creeping halfway into the orange trumpet. Her knees ached from kneeling in the rocklike dirt.

They needed rain for the garden but were praying for the rain to hold off until after harvest. The community couldn't handle another crisis. The pain over the livestock was dulled but not spent. She could smell the smoke from the coal fire that kept the steam engine blazing. Usually it bothered her too, but this time it was a relief. Probably in two or three more days, they would move the whole rig over to the Baards'. In less than two weeks Jonathan would be returning to New

York. She would miss him, she realized. He always managed to make her smile, even now. She couldn't take her pain from Toby's rejection out on Jonathan. If Astrid was right and he did like her, she wouldn't treat him as harshly as Toby had her. Somehow she would just be a friend and not encourage any other possible ideas. Was that what Toby had been trying to do to her all summer? A tear slid down her cheek.

That was either one of the good things or the bad things about picking beans. There was too much time to think.

Sitting on the porch snapping beans held the same difficulty. The need of brain power was negligible. Her mother and Ilse were in the hot kitchen cooking for the threshing crew, as were Ingeborg and Astrid. Feeding the workers three full meals and two lunches a day took a cooking crew. This year Mrs. Geddick and her daughter would run the cook shack that traveled with the threshing crew, same as last year.

Again Grace's mind flitted back to Toby. On Sunday Pastor Solberg had preached on the verses about taking every thought captive to the Word of God. He'd said that worry was a sin, which didn't sit well with some of the congregation. But when he explained that worry was lack of trust in our heavenly Father, it made sense to her. So she wasn't worrying exactly, but her thoughts had a habit of becoming unruly. After all, what good did thinking about Toby do her? Other than to make her sad. *Take every thought captive.* He'd said use the name of Jesus, that the mind, like everything on earth, will bow at the name of Jesus.

Jesus, I don't want to think about Toby anymore. But if only I could talk to him one more time, perhaps I could make him understand that what I feel is more than friendship and that I thought he felt the same way. Maybe he just thinks he's in love, but if he knew how I really feel . . .

She glanced up when she felt the floorboards resonate with someone coming and smiled at her mother.

"So here you are. Want some help?"

"Of course. And it is cooler out here than in the kitchen, that is for sure. Not as steamy either."

Kaaren sank into a rocking chair and fanned herself with her apron. "Uff da. I don't know how the men keep going, hot as it is."

"Pa says this is good threshing weather."

"I know. Maybe we should take him up on his offer to hire someone to help around here." She reached for the basket and, using both hands, dumped a pile of beans into her lap.

"Who would we hire?"

"That's the problem. All the girls are helping at home. We need more people to move into Blessing. But until we can replace the livestock, many things will need to wait."

"Thorliff said he was going to write an article for a Minneapolis paper about the booming town of Blessing."

"Well, the ad for a manager for the mill brought a mighty fine man here."

"I haven't seen Sophie since before harvest started."

"I know. But things will settle down again when they move on from here."

"Mor, has Pa said anything about buying more cows?"

"No, but if we don't get some livestock, I don't know what we'll eat all winter. You can't live on rabbit or we won't have any of them either."

"Two of the hens are broody again."

"Good thing. Rabbit and chicken. I'm going to have to buy a side of beef from the east to feed the students when school starts—once it is cold enough. It is amazing to me that, thanks to refrigerated train cars, we can buy beef that way now."

"I miss the calves in the pasture, and I even miss milking. I never thought that would happen."

"We're out of butter; Ingeborg is almost out too. And we won't have lard much longer. I need to go to Garrisons' Groceries to buy those things. I have never in my life bought lard in a bucket."

They snapped beans in silence for a minute.

"Go tell Ilse to bring some lemonade out and come sit here with us for a bit." When Grace rose, Kaaren said with a smile. "Thank you, Grace. You are always so helpful."

Why did the word *always* seem to chew on something inside her? "Always Grace." Now there's a nickname. Even from her own mor.

                                                   ~

The first night they left the steam engine and threshing machine at the Baards', Jonathan rode home in the wagon with Lars. With Samuel and Trygve dangling their feet at the rear, he had some time to talk with Grace's father. *Ask him.* The little voice inside had prompted him before, but for a change he had the opportunity. *What do I say?*

"Ah, Mr. Knutson."

Lars looked at him. "You sound mighty serious."

"This is." Jonathan sucked in a deep breath. "I want to ask your permission to court your daughter." The words came out in a rush, but at least he'd said them.

Lars stared out across the backs of the two teams pulling the wagon, his arms resting on his upper legs, hands easy on the reins. "Does Grace know about this?"

"No. I knew I had to ask you first."

"You think she will agree?"

"I don't know. I know she has cared for someone else, but I'm hoping that is over."

"Toby Valders?"

"How did you know? She said she'd always kept her feelings a secret."

"I may be getting a mite creaky in the joints, but I'm not blind." He turned to look at Jonathan. "I suspect she thinks we wouldn't approve, and that's why she's tried to keep it a secret."

"I suspect so too."

"Toby's made some mistakes, but he's a good man."

What could he say to that? He wasn't here on Toby's behalf, so he kept quiet.

"But that's neither here nor there regarding your question. As far as I'm concerned, if Grace is willing, I am, and I'm sure I can speak for her mother too. You are a fine young man. Our only problem is that you would be taking Grace so far away. Your big problem would be whether Grace can accept the way you live your life. I don't want her to be hurt." He looked Jonathan in the eyes, as if peering into a deep pool to try to see the bottom. "I can't abide the thought that moving east would cause her pain."

Jonathan took in another deep breath and let it out. "What if she didn't have to move away?"

"What are you saying?"

"I want to go to agricultural school in Grand Forks and become a farmer—like you."

"My land, boy, have you talked with your father yet?"

"No, sir. But I will as soon as I get home."

"Well, I never." Lars chuckled softly. "You have my permission to court Grace, but I have me a feeling this will be a long courtship since you have a lot of school ahead of you."

"Yes, sir. Thank you, sir." He felt like jumping out of the wagon and dancing all the way back to the farm. "I want you to know that I did, on my father's suggestion, invite Grace to go to New York. There is an excellent school there for the deaf. Perhaps she might want to go there for a time and learn some new things to help with the school here."

"I see you've been doing some serious thinking on all this."

"Yes, sir, I have."

Lars extended his hand. "My best to you, son. You've cut yourself a deep furrow."

"Thank you, sir." Jonathan thought to ask him exactly what he meant by that, but he got the gist of it. His plans and dreams most likely would not come easy. He leaped off the wagon at the bottom of the lane to the Bjorklund house and waved good-bye as he trotted the track. He had permission to court Grace! Another thought sobered him. How to convince Grace?

I cannot ask his mother about him. Heaven forbid. Grace thought some more. Nor wait for him in front of the flour mill. But I need to try to talk to Toby at least one more time.

The porch at the boardinghouse seemed the most probable place to see him. She hoped he'd come by alone. Once the threshing crew moved away from Blessing, she could take some time to go visit Sophie and, hopefully, talk with Toby. With her mind made up, she carried the basket of carrots she'd been picking to the well house and dumped it all in the bucket of water. Sitting and scrubbing in the cool of the well house would be a welcome reprieve from the hot sun.

But what about the school Jonathan had told her about? She'd asked her mother, who said she had received excellent advice and assistance from the teachers there.

"Have you ever thought of going there?" Grace had asked her mother.

"Dreamed of it a few times, but I knew there was no way I could leave my family in the summer nor the school in the winter. It's just never been possible."

"Jonathan has invited me to go east with him and either attend or visit the school." She watched her mother's face.

"Really." It wasn't a question. Her eyes took on that faraway look that said she was thinking hard. "Do you want to go?"

"Not really." *Not if Toby . . . You cannot . . .* The interior argument started up again.

As if it ever quit. Grace stuck her hands in the scrub water to rinse the dirt off. At least if she was working with deaf students, she would be accomplishing something of value. "Would it help you and the school if I went?"

"That is something to think about. I can't answer that right off. I'll have to pray about it. Perhaps it would be nice to learn some new methods so we can help our students more."

Grace nodded. "I'll have to pray about it" was one of her mother's stock answers. Perhaps if God talked with her as much as He did with her mother, she might be more inclined to pray more frequently. She almost made that comment to her mother but thought the better of it. Right then she hadn't felt like listening to a sermon.

❧

The threshing crew pulled out at daybreak to be ten miles south by the time the dew was dry. Jonathan grinned at her and waved from the seat on a wagon. Since no one was needed at home to milk and work in the cheese house, he was going along for the first two days, and then he'd ride back and get ready to leave for New York City.

Grace waved back and glanced up at her mother, who, as always, had tears in her eyes and was praying for the safety and success of the entire venture. She tucked her arm through her mother's and turned her toward Ingeborg's house. With her on one side, Astrid on the other, and Ingeborg on Astrid's far side, the four of them locked arms and headed for the house. Coffee and a long chat were long overdue.

Later in the morning she and Astrid walked toward town, Grace to the boardinghouse, Astrid to assist in the surgery.

"When do you leave for school?" Grace signed.

"I'm not going."

"What?" Grace spoke and signed both, a sure indication she was startled or concerned. She stopped so Astrid had to turn to look at her. "When did you decide this?"

"The last few days." Astrid picked up a lump of dirt and heaved it out into the field. "I think Mor needs me here. I'd rather they spent every dime from the harvest on replacing the cattle, and I can learn all I need to know from Elizabeth. She's always said that, but she wanted me to go to Chicago. I don't want to go there."

"Have you told Tante Ingeborg?"

Astrid shook her head. "So keep this secret, all right?"

"Sure." *You could talk with Astrid about Toby.* She brushed the thought aside. She'd kept the secret this long. A little longer wouldn't hurt. Except that Astrid was going to be hurt by her not talking about this all along. However, after the earlier fiasco, most likely everyone knew about her feelings anyway. Why did things have to be so difficult?

The two girls split and went their separate ways. Grace understood how Astrid felt but she also knew Astrid really wanted to be trained, and school was her best opportunity.

Grace continued her musing as she neared the boardinghouse. Was she being selfish by not going to New York? Could she learn enough there to help her family? But first she needed to settle this with Toby, to tell him her real feelings. Grace wished she'd worn shoes, instead of coming in barefoot, and had put on a nicer dress, but then she would have had to answer a barrage of questions. At least she had pinned up her hair, ostensibly because it was cooler, but really because she hoped it made her look older. She'd left her apron at home too. As she walked around the boardinghouse to the back porch, she admired the black-eyed Susans and delphiniums that bloomed along the base of the porch. While Bridget had planted some of the flowers, it looked like Sophie had added others. The pink and red hollyhocks along the back were helping to shade the porch.

Mrs. Sam sat in the big rocker, fanning herself and rocking the twins' cradle with one foot. "Mornin,' Miss Grace."

"Mrs. Sam, is that really you sitting down?" Grace mounted the three steps.

"Now don't you go gettin' a smart mouth like that sister of yours. She said I was to take a rest. Huh!" The final word said what she thought of the order.

"It's nice out here with the shade from the tree." Grace peeked in the cradle, where the two babies were lying spoon fashion, in spite of the heat, and wearing nothing but diapers. Cheesecloth draped the cradle to keep the flies off them.

"You go on in but watch your step. That sister of yours is on a toot today."

"What's the problem?"

"No fresh milk, no cream, that what she ordered din't come in on the train. She got into a huff with dat new man at de store." Mrs. Sam leaned forward. "He offered to sell her hard liquor to serve here." Her eyes rounded. "Dat man not good for Blessing, you mark my words."

Grace drew back. "You are not serious?"

"I am de most serious. My Sam, workin' in de blacksmith shop, he heard rumors 'bout someone buyin' some there."

Grace almost wished she'd waited for another day but opened the squeaky screen door and headed into the kitchen, where Lily Mae was taking bread out of the oven and Sophie was chopping onions.

At the slam of the door Sophie turned and, seeing Grace, replaced a frown with a smile. "You are just in time." She mopped her onion tears on her apron.

"To do what?"

"To rinse the lettuce and slice the carrots really fine for the salad. Dinner will be served in less than an hour, and we're not quite ready." She switched to sign. "Mrs. Sam was leaning on the table, and I think she was feeling faint again, so I sent her out to take care of the twins."

"I see." Grace nodded. "Good old Grace" could always be counted on to pitch in. But ignoring the little barb, she did just that. She helped through the afternoon until just before five, when she knew the men would be getting off work. "I have an errand to run," she signed to Sophie, now nursing her babies in the chair in what used to be her bedroom but was now kept as a private sitting room.

"You'll be back?" Sophie asked.

Grace nodded. She glanced in the mirror, tucked a stray strand of hair back in her roll, and left the room, hanging her apron on the peg by the door. She closed the door behind her to give Sophie privacy and slipped out onto the front porch to sit in the rocker there. Blue morning glory climbing strings from the porch railing to hooks in the ceiling helped shade the porch, making her feel like she could peer out at the real world. Would Toby see her waiting? Would he come that way today? Perhaps she should have brought some handwork with her. Or a pitcher of lemonade. *Please, please come by yourself.*

Through the vines she watched the mill. Several men came out but not Toby. When the door opened again, her heartbeat picked up. Still no Toby. What if he hadn't gone to work today? What if he no longer worked there? The door opened and Garth walked out with Toby. Now what would she do? Could nothing work in her favor? She watched them walk down the street, still talking. Garth would turn into the boardinghouse most likely. And he would find her sitting here in front rather than in the back, where they usually gathered.

"Come on in for some lemonade."

She saw Garth's offer and saw Toby start to refuse and then change his mind. Where could she go? They'd see her run away now. She searched the porch, her eyes darting around. Nothing to hide behind. Sucking in a deep breath, she stood and stepped in front of the door as though she'd just come out.

"Why, Grace, how good to see you." Garth's smile was genuine. If only Toby would smile like that too, instead of the polite, slightly guarded look he gave her.

This was not the right or best thing to do. She wished she were anywhere but there right now. Why had she ever thought this was a good idea?

"I-I was just on my way home."

"I hope you and Sophie had a fine time. I'm just about to drag her and the babies home for the evening."

"Thanks, Garth, think I'll pass on the offer tonight." Toby touched his hat and turned to go on down the street.

" 'Night, Garth." Without further pause Grace stalked down the stairs. "May I walk with you, Toby?"

Toby nodded, but while he slowed, he didn't stop.

Grace caught up with him, wishing she had the courage to put her arm through his. With his hands in his front pockets, it would be so easy. Just slip her hand in the crook of his elbow and . . .

Instead, she broke the silence. "You must be awfully busy lately."

He nodded. "I have been."

"No time to even visit with all your friends?"

"Not much."

"Seemed strange not to have you helping with the harvest."

"I know. Felt strange."

"They left this morning."

"I saw them."

"Toby, last time we talked, I wasn't able to tell you something." Grace felt like a cat with a fur ball in her mouth.

"Grace, you didn't tell anyone about what I said, did you? That was private between us."

Grace was too nervous to speak. She signed no.

Toby instantly relaxed and smiled. "Thanks. I knew I could trust you. It's becoming really serious, and I want to make sure before I tell my mother. I might actually become a married man." He laughed. "Could you ever imagine that?"

Imagine it? That's what she had imagined all summer. All Grace's carefully thought-out words burst inside her like the fires after the plague hit. The nausea returned like shooting embers. She was too late.

She looked at his contentment and forced the words through her fingers. "I hope you will be happy. I have to go now." And then she ran.

20

"HOW DID YOU FIGURE WHERE I WAS?" Ingeborg said, lifting her tear-stained face.

"I looked everywhere—even over to Tante Kaaren's." Astrid took down a milk stool from the wall and sat down by her mother. "What's wrong?"

Ingeborg wiped her eyes with her fingertips. "I just missed the cows so much I came out here. Seemed as good a place to cry as any." She shook her head slowly from side to side, feeling as if she were pushing heavy weights. "Now with the crew gone, I guess I just have too much time on my hands. No cows, no sheep, no pigs. This farm seems empty, like all the family is gone and the barns might blow away too."

Astrid leaned her head against her mother's shoulder. "You have us."

"Good thing, isn't it?" Ingeborg put her arm around her daughter's shoulders. "But you'll be going away soon, and that leaves just your pa and me."

"You have Inga and Carl, and there'll be lots more little ones. Besides, it's not as if I'll be gone forever. In fact, maybe I won't be gone at all."

"What are you saying?"

"I'm saying I can't make up my mind. I know I don't want to go to Chicago." She ticked off one finger. "I know I want to be a nurse." Second tick. "But Dr. Elizabeth says I can train here. If I want to be a doctor, she'll teach me all she knows." Third finger. "But something in me wants to go away to school too." She laid her hands in her lap, fingers entwined. "What do you think I should do?"

"I think you should ask God what He wants for you, and then wait until you have a definite answer."

"I have and He doesn't seem to be in any hurry. And school costs a lot of money, and we—"

"Wait a minute," Ingeborg interrupted. "Are you thinking we can't afford to help you with school?"

"Well, it is going to cost a lot to replace the livestock, if we do, and I . . ."

"Don't you know that Elizabeth has offered to pay for your school, since she wants you to work with her?"

"No. But even so . . ." Astrid paused. "Did she really say that?"

"Both she and Thorliff have come to me on separate occasions and said they would pay."

Astrid cocked her head and smiled in the dimness. "We have a good family, huh, Mor?"

"That we do, and I need to get about caring for my fine family rather than crying in an empty barn." She stroked Astrid's braid, which hung halfway down her back. "I know better than to let that black pit come even close to me. But sometimes the sadness just sneaks in and I forget that God is in control and we are His sheep."

"I always wonder about those verses. Sheep aren't very smart, and they are really smelly. They get ticks in their wool, and they don't always herd the way they should. Calling us His sheep isn't really a compliment."

Ingeborg chuckled. How this daughter of hers could come up with such things, she'd never know. "But the people of Jesus' time were a lot of them farmers and sheepherders, so they understood Him when He told such stories."

"I understand that part, but—" Astrid rose and, in one smooth motion, picked up her stool and hung it back on the peg—"I don't really miss the sheep. The cows and pigs yes, but not the sheep." She reached out a hand and pulled her mother up. "Now, the chickens . . . nobody better touch my chickens."

Arm in arm they strolled out of the barn. Astrid turned and shut the door behind them, dropping the board latch into place. "Mor, do you think there is something wrong with Far?"

"Why do you ask?"

"He seems to get tired easily, and sometimes I catch him leaning against something as if he needs help."

"I know. I see the same things, and yet we are all getting older." *Dear God, I hope that is all it is.*

"But sometimes his color isn't good either."

Ingeborg smiled inside. This was her daughter talking, speaking the medical things that had always fascinated her, learning the new ways from Elizabeth, yet she had grown up on the old ways of using natural herbs to fight sickness and disease. "I will try to talk to him again, but he keeps saying he is fine, just a little tired. Maybe we should try to get Elizabeth to talk to him."

"I'll ask her today."

"I wonder sometimes what great things you will see. Changes in the medical field are happening so fast."

"And Elizabeth wants to keep up with it all, but between caring for all who come to her and her family, she just hasn't the time. Have you thought of helping her on a regular basis?" Astrid asked.

"I've thought of it, but I don't want to intrude. We don't do things the same way." Ingeborg stopped by the well house. "I'm not too old to learn new things if she is willing to teach me."

"I could share with you the books she has given me. I have almost all the human bones memorized and most of the muscles. Did you know that our hands and feet have the most joints and bitty muscles?

I'm having a hard time with the nerves."

"If I have to memorize all that, I'll stay home and knit or sew."

Ingeborg glanced up to see Grace striding up the road and past their lane. She looked like she was stomping locusts, the way her feet pounded the ground.

Astrid turned to see what she was looking at. "Uh-oh."

"I don't think I've ever seen Grace like that."

"I have. It takes a lot to make her mad, but when she is, look out."

"I wonder what is wrong?"

꒰꒱

The next morning Grace told her mother she had promised to go back and help Sophie again.

"Is there something you want to tell me?" Kaaren asked.

"No." Grace's fingers slashed the air, along with an emphatic shake of her head.

"You seem upset."

"I'll get over it." At least she hoped so. Lying awake most of the night had done nothing to make the pain lessen. Crying or fuming—there seemed no middle ground.

"Perhaps you should stay and help me and Ilse work on the lesson plans for school."

"I will tomorrow. I didn't see Grant yesterday, and I like to play with him and Linnie. Sophie spends so much time at the boarding-house that he doesn't get a lot of attention."

"Oh, his tante Helga takes good care of him."

"We need to bring them out here more." Grace grabbed a straw hat off the peg. "You could come too."

Kaaren hugged her daughter. "I hope you have a good day."

Anything would be better than yesterday. She'd replayed Toby's words so many times, they were engraved on her mind.

"Stubborn does not become you."

Grace caught the glare before it reached her face. *Talk to your mother* warred with *Handle this yourself, you're a woman now.* By the time she'd walked to town, she felt a bit more resigned. Surely she'd be able to talk with Sophie. After all, she'd been in love—twice.

Sophie was still at home when Grace opened the back screen door and entered the kitchen. Both babies were crying. Linnie looked like she was about to cry, and Grant was hiding under the table. "What is going on?"

"You take those two, and I'll nurse these two. That should settle things." Sophie, hair halfway up in the roll on one side, the other tangled and flying, pointed to the little girl in the high chair.

Grace bent down to smile at Grant, still under the table. "You want to come out and tell me what happened?"

He nodded, his lower lip thrust out. "Sissy cried."

"And the babies cried?"

He nodded again, his face solemn. "I was bad."

"I see. What did you do?"

"Spilled the milk."

"But you did not mean to?"

"No." He took Grace's hand and looked at his sister. "Her is hungry."

Grace set Grant back up at the table, buttered and sugared a slice of bread for Linnie, and breaking it in pieces, set it on the tray so she could feed herself. She did the same for Grant, and while they were eating, she set about wiping off the table and putting the kitchen to rights, setting the dirty dishes in a pan on the stove and heating water in another.

Sometime later Grant tugged on her skirt and pointed down the hall. Grace took Linnie's hand and headed for the baby room, where Sophie was changing one diaper while the other baby was squalling.

Grace picked up Joy and cradled her until she could use the surface of the chest of drawers to change her.

"Nobody is happy with anything this morning. I don't know what came over them. But one starts crying and the rest join right in. I've fed them both now, so if you will watch them all, I can go finish dressing."

Grace nodded and, with a baby in each arm, followed Grant back to the kitchen. Linnie sat down to happily spread bits of bread all over the floor. She grinned, showing her sparkling new teeth, and stuffed some bread into her mouth.

"Sissy bad."

"No, babies don't do bad things. She is just playing."

The look he gave her said what he thought about that.

Grace had long before realized that Sophie would be having problems with two small babies and two little children, very little children. Usually Garth's sister came over and helped, but something must have happened to her today. Sophie finally came out wearing a blue-and-white gingham dress with short puffed sleeves and a sweetheart neckline, and she'd gotten her hair rolled up and a smile in place.

"Thank you. One of Helga's children is sick, so she couldn't come. I have to find someone to help me here. What about you? At least until school starts."

"I can come some of the time, but Mor needs me too." Grace handed Hamre to his mother. "Have you had breakfast yet?" *Why does she expect me to drop everything and help? I guess because I always have before. Why does it bother me now?*

"No, but I did get the coffee made. Garth had to leave early for some reason, so he was going to eat at the boardinghouse. And I need to get there soon. Once breakfast is over, Lily Mae and Mrs. Sam need to work on the day's meals and don't have time for the desk work."

At the boardinghouse with the children settled down—Grant playing on the back porch, the babies sleeping, and Linnie busy with a wooden spoon and a small kettle—Grace and Sophie sat at the table with cups of coffee.

"Why did you leave suddenly yesterday?"

Leave it to Sophie to leap right in. Grace studied the dark liquid in her cup before looking up again to Sophie. "I talked with Toby."

"So?"

"He said he is in love with a woman in Grafton and may marry her."

"So? Aren't you glad for him?" Sophie paused. "You don't still think you're in love with him, do you?"

"As a matter of fact, I do. I've loved him for years."

"Oh, Grace, you're in love with the idea of Toby, not the real him. Why, the two of you have nothing in common, and . . ."

The more Sophie went on, the tighter Grace's jaw grew.

"You've always been like Andrew, forever sticking up for the underdog."

"At least I wasn't flirting with every male in sight." Fingers flashed and the words slashed.

"Grace Knutson, what a thing to say."

"Well, it's true. You have always thought only of yourself. How do you know how I feel or think?" Grace thumped her fist on the table for emphasis. She glared at Sophie, who glared right back.

"But you're my twin sister."

"You should have thought of that when you took off with Hamre, leaving broken hearts in your wake."

"But Grace, you always—"

"Not anymore. I am no longer 'Grace Always.'"

"Grace, you are shouting."

"I finally have the courage to tell someone how I feel, and you—you . . ." Grace pushed her chair back. "You can take care of your own children! Clean up your own mess!"

She was out the door and on her way back on the road to home without looking back nor left nor right. As she passed the church, it hit her. *What have I done?* She slowed when she reached the lane to Ingeborg's and turned in, each step heavier than the last. She should go on home and ask her mother to go to Sophie's to smooth things out. She should go back and make amends.

But why? I said only the truth.

Ingeborg was alone, sitting in the rocker with her Bible on her lap when Grace walked in. One look at her aunt's face and Grace crumpled to the floor, burying her face in Ingeborg's lap. Her tears soaked the dress and apron. She had no idea how long she cried, but the soothing stroke of her aunt's hand on her hair finally lulled her into hiccups and then sniffs. She mopped her face in the apron and blew her nose into a handkerchief Ingeborg handed her. When she looked up, she saw only love shining in the face above her.

"Now tell me all about it."

Grace talked with both mouth and hands, spilling out the years she'd buried inside. She told of loving Toby, of the hurt when Sophie left, of all the times she'd wanted something and Sophie took it away, of taking care so that Sophie didn't get into trouble.

"And now I don't know what to do." She stared up at Ingeborg.

"What do you want to do?"

"I don't know, but I don't like me like this, angry and shouting and saying things I know I shouldn't. This is awful."

"You need some time to get over loving Toby."

"You think I really love him?"

"I think you have for a long time, and if he loved you back, you would know what to do. But since he says he's in love with someone else, you have to let go and pray that he will be happy."

"But that's so hard."

"Of course it is, but this is where God will come in to help you if you ask Him and follow His guidance."

"God doesn't talk to me like He does to you and Mor."

"Could it be that you've not talked much with Him, not spent time in His Word? Loving God is a lifetime lesson. It never happens all at once. Think how you had to work to learn to speak. I remember you struggled so hard, yet you were so determined. And you still are. I know God has something wonderful in store for you, and if you search His Word, you will learn and grow."

"I want to be wise like you and Mor."

"We have both prayed for and sought wisdom for years. You are just seeing the end result of hours of prayer. God always promises wisdom to those who seek it."

"Mange takk." Grace rose to her feet. When Ingeborg stood, Grace wrapped her arms around her aunt and the two stood together, locked in love.

That evening when Jonathan drove the wagon in from threshing and stopped by the barn, he saw all the women gathered under the trees. Ellie, Astrid, Grace, Ingeborg, Kaaren, and Ilse.

"Welcome home," Ingeborg called.

He waved back and stepped down to unharness the team.

Astrid and Grace ran to help him. While Astrid hung up one of the harnesses, Grace asked, "Is the invitation to visit in New York City still open?"

He stared at her. "Are you serious? Of course it is."

Grace nodded, her jawline set. "Then I would like to go with you." All of her insides screamed at her to take back her words, but she ignored them.

"Can you be ready in time?"

"Can you wait one more day?" Her heart felt like it was going to jump right out of her chest.

New York City, New York
September 1902

GRACE SWALLOWED HARD to keep from throwing up.

Jonathan touched her arm to get her attention, and she turned so she could read his lips.

"Are you all right?"

Her desired nod got stuck on a shake, and she kept her eyes down, certain the fear that was eating her from the inside out would be visible should she look at him. Why had she ever decided to leave the safety of Blessing and come with him on this trip to New York City? Sophie was the one who wanted to travel, not her. She wove her gloved fingers together to keep them from shaking, certain he could sense her trembling anyway. Shivers stormed up and down her rigid spine, in spite of the heat in the train car.

Sophie. This was all her fault. If she'd not been so . . . so Sophie, perhaps she'd never have blown up at her. And made such a radical decision. She had let her personal grief override common sense. But why hadn't Mor stopped her from leaving? Instead, she'd seemed almost relieved. Why? She turned from her inner world at the insistent tap on her arm to see Jonathan peering at her, consternation furrowing his brow and tightening his jaw.

"How can I help you?"

She shrugged. He was trying so hard to make this easy for her. They'd practiced his signing for hours these days of swaying train travel. While he could form all the letters and create simple words, they still depended too much on her speaking ability. Another sigh escaped before she could force her lips to smile. "I do not know."

Four little words that conveyed all her heart's confusion. She'd always known how to answer, how to do most anything. Especially how to make others around her comfortable. She'd caught the stares from other passengers when she spoke, and while she knew she didn't speak the same as everyone else, no one in Blessing had paid much attention. Had the stares held pity or repugnance? Not that it much mattered. She didn't care for either.

"We'll be going under the river soon and be at Grand Central Station before you know it." He paused and studied her face. "What didn't you understand?"

Grace fought to still her trembling again. "Speak slower, please." She kept herself from responding to the stares she could feel from the two children across the aisle.

When she saw Jonathan whip around and glare at someone, she knew there'd been a comment he didn't like. She glanced at the small boy talking to his mother, who was shushing him with a finger to her lips and a worried glance at Grace. He'd been the culprit. If only Jonathan could sign better, she would not be subjected to such scrutiny. *Lord, help me, please. I am in over my head, and I'm drowning.* She sucked in a deep breath. No, she wasn't drowning. *I am swimming in peace.* The thought washed her in a comfort she'd not felt since leaving her bedroom several mornings ago. *I am swimming in peace, Lord, your peace. Why did I not ask for help before?* Was that a heavenly chuckle she sensed? Her mother had often said God must chuckle at some of their worries and concerns. After all, He knew what was coming next and what His plans were. She felt her shoulders leave off bumping her ear lobes and settle back where they belonged. The vibration of the train changed and their world went black.

Jonathan had taken her hand in the two of his, and she was grate-

197

ful he had warned her. Of course, the tunnel. How could men build a tunnel under a river without it leaking? Oh, so much she had to learn. She forced herself to take another calming breath and tried to look straight ahead. Never in her life had she felt such a darkness. Even in the darkest night at home, one could see shapes after the eyes adjusted. Was this what being blind would be like? She sucked in another breath of air overwarm already. Here, she'd sometimes thought being deaf was the worst thing that could happen. At least she could see the myriad colors of green on a spring day and the faces of those she loved.

With a whoosh, light again flooded the car, and she blinked several times, glancing at Jonathan to see him smiling at her. In spite of herself she wanted to reach up and touch his jaw with one tentative finger. What a beautiful smile he had. She smiled back, unable to tear her gaze from the . . . the what? shining in his eyes. Had she not known better, she might think it love. What a silly thought. They were just friends after all. He was bringing her to New York as a friend of the family who would attend a special school. But what if Astrid had been right and this fine young man was falling in love with her?

Grace Knutson, you have always been in love with Toby Valders— remember? The inner voice was changing from admonishing to strident. But Toby said he was in love with someone else. The arguments in her thoughts returned. And look at the trouble they caused last time she did not take them captive like Pastor Solberg preached. No one in her right mind could argue with that. The words had had to sink down in her mind before they could rise to the top at a time when she could think better.

Was that time now?

The train was slowing, and people around them began gathering up their things. Jonathan grinned at her, his happy-go-lucky look back in place, and said, "Welcome to New York City."

She nodded and turned to look out the window. If this was New York City, it was not a pretty sight. Soot-streaked brick buildings looked close enough to touch as the train chugged between them. Laundry hung from iron stairs that appeared too fragile for people to use. She'd read of fire escapes, and now she was seeing them in reality. A woman sat on one landing, smoking a cigarette, her carrot hair in such a tumble birds could have built nests in it with ease. One strap of her camisole hung over her shoulder.

Grace bit back a gasp. The woman wore only a chemise and knickers. In broad daylight, out in public. And the folks of Blessing, her mother included, had been appalled when she and Astrid sewed their old skirts into pants earlier in the summer. Truth to tell, the pants had made kneeling in the garden far easier.

Grace brought her wandering thoughts back to the moment as the train slowed even more and pulled to a stop between raised platforms that separated the trains already lined up on both sides of them.

Jonathan tapped her arm to get her attention. "We're here."

"I know." Grace reached up to make sure her straw hat was pinned securely. *Do I look all right?* At home she'd not given looks or attire a great deal of thought, since most everyone there wore similar skirts and waists or faded calico dresses in the summer heat. So far, she'd seen many different styles. At least the traveling suit Elizabeth had loaned her, although she'd apologized for it being out of date, looked respectable.

Jonathan removed their parcels from the overhead shelf, and tucking one under his arm, he picked up the valise and motioned for her to go before him.

Shooting him a glance that she hoped appeared confident, she stepped into the aisle, her reticule dangling from one wrist while she clutched a small valise in her other gloved hand. If only she could have washed before—*No*, she commanded herself, *don't go thinking on all the if onlys. Mor always says that is a waste of time and effort.*

She paused at the steel steps and smiled at the conductor, who held out a hand to assist her, before clutching the handrail with her free hand. What if she tripped over her skirt and went tumbling right into his arms? Now wouldn't that be a fine introduction? Grace closed her eyes for the briefest of moments, took in a deep breath, and on a silent exhale smiled again, at least she hoped it was a smile, at the conductor and took her first step down.

"You hand me that satchel and I'll take your arm, miss."

His calm direction soothed her trembling like the touch of her mother's hand. "Thank you, sir." She had to force herself to speak, conscious now of her oddity. She handed out the satchel, placed her hand in his extended one, and stepped down with ease. Once on the platform, she turned to see Jonathan smile at her. Warmth like a summer sunbeam circled her heart and caused her breathing to settle a notch or two. She saw Jonathan hand the man something that caused his dark face to widen in a smile.

"Thank you, sir." The man reached back in the train car to retrieve another bag while Jonathan set his on the platform and, taking Grace's hand, tucked it through his arm.

"Come. McHenry will have the carriage waiting."

She glanced over her shoulder to see another black man loading their bags onto a cart. Looking up at her escort, she raised an eyebrow in question.

Jonathan patted her hand. "That's the way we do things in New York."

Grace half shrugged and let him lead her through the maze of people, following the crowd that moved out of the monstrous cavern and into another, this one with marble floor tiles, marble pillars, and high arched windows around the vaulted ceiling. She stumbled once when watching the splendor above rather than her feet below.

Jonathan led her to a marble pillar of cream streaked with gray and paused to let her catch her breath. "Are you all right?"

"Ja, there is so much to see." Not only see but also smell. She touched her nose with a rose-scented handkerchief. Soot, unwashed bodies, the pungent eye crinkling smoke from the cigar of the portly man standing off to her left. Her nose wrinkled at what could only be dying garbage, overlaid by the heavy perfume of the woman in black standing next to a gentleman. No farm smell—not even the smells during butchering, which she'd always thought the most offensive—could begin to equal what threatened to overwhelm her here. Although not as terrible as the carcasses burning, her body reacted the same way. She could feel the bile rising again. She held her bit of cambric closer to her nostrils. "Can we go now?"

"Of course." Jonathan beckoned to the man with the luggage cart and led the way out the main doors to the street.

A uniformed man stood holding a flashy bay team that was hitched to a carriage resplendent in shiny black leather with brilliant brass fittings. He waved to Jonathan and motioned to the man in the box before leaving his post to open the carriage door and fold down a step.

Grace knew Jonathan's family was wealthy, but the large carriage with two men caught her by surprise. She'd not thought ahead or asked what to expect, but if she weren't so weary, she'd have tried to turn and head back to the train—a train heading west, all the way to Blessing. Instead, she managed to smile at the man with the twinkling blue eyes, the red hair, and the closely trimmed sandy beard of a freckle-bedecked Irishman.

"Good day, miss." He touched his narrow-brimmed black hat with one finger and handed her into the carriage.

As she settled into the plush black leather seat, she felt every bit of energy drain right out through the toes of her new laced boots. Tired didn't begin to describe the boneless weight of her body pressing into the seat. She studied her hand on her thigh. Lifting even her little finger was beyond her, not that lifting her little finger was necessary. Why was it that at home she was strong and could work from dawn to well beyond dusk, but sitting on a train for the last five days had drained her like a turned-over bucket?

The carriage rocked as the men put their trunks aboard, and then Jonathan settled into the seat across from her. The door was closed behind him, and the carriage rocked again as the other man swung up into the carriage box.

"Welcome to New York City." Jonathan said again and leaned forward and took both of her hands in his, gazing directly into her eyes. "I know this has been terribly hard for you, but we'll be home soon. I know Mother will have your room ready, and you can rest."

She watched his lips form the words, but the act of really understanding him took more than she had to give, so she just nodded. The depth of his caring, so visible in all he did, made the backs of her eyes burn. *You will not cry*, she ordered herself. *You will not.* She swallowed once and then again and sniffed. *You will not.*

The carriage jerked as the horses moved forward, and she turned her attention to the crowds waiting or walking on the wide sidewalk that fronted the bank of doors through which more people continued to flow from the station. Grand Central Station, Jonathan had called it. Men in black top hats, derby hats, fedoras, or flat hats, some wearing suits or jackets, others in shirtsleeves. Women wearing wide straw hats with flowers or ribbons, twirling parasols or clutching shawls. People of all nationalities and social strata, all intent on their own business, all looking as if they were going somewhere. Or at least as if they knew where they were going.

She thought back to a story her mother and Ingeborg had often shared of Ingeborg lost in New York in 1880 and Jonathan's father coming to her rescue. Grace glanced at the young man sitting knee to knee with her in the swaying carriage. Like his father, he was rescuing a young woman in need—not a Bjorklund but a Knutson, not that many people realized the difference.

The urge to reach out and take his hands caught her by surprise. She stared down at her own hands, gloved in spite of the heat and no longer resting like limp dough in her lap. Propriety said she must keep her gloves on. Propriety said she must not take his hands, for she and Jonathan were no more than friends. Had she left propriety in Blessing? she wondered as she watched her hands open and reach across the slight gap between their knees. As she extended them, he reached back and their hands clasped as if of their own volition. He squeezed her fingers, and she looked up to see him ask, "What are you thinking?"

"I am thinking that Mrs. Valders might faint if she saw me being so forward."

Jonathan threw back his head, his mouth open in a wide grin, laughter glinting from his eyes.

I wish I could hear him laugh. She knew he was laughing, because Sophie had explained laughter to her. She'd seen lots of people laughing and knew the various actions of different kinds of laughter, thanks to Sophie and their mother. But she'd given up wishing she could hear long years ago. Wishing did no good. She'd prayed for hearing more times than she could ever count, but God had not acquiesced. For a time she'd been resentful, but finally she'd given up and worked harder to read lips and sign clearly.

Until today.

He raised one finger and began to sign. Y-o-u. He pointed at her, and she nodded. He made the sign for R. She nodded again. *You are* . . . He made a B and added e-a-u-t-i . . .

She rolled her lips together and swallowed, sure of what he was going to say. How could he think her beautiful in all the disarray she felt?

F-u-l. His smile stretched wide, putting commas in his cheeks.

"Thank you." She spoke and signed at the same time. The warmth returned, this time trailing up her neck and blossoming on her face. She took her fan from her reticule and flipped it open to fan the heat from her cheeks.

He beckoned her and pointed out the window to a green field dotted with trees and some big rocks on the other side of a pond. "Central Park."

"Are we in the country?"

"No, part of the city. We are almost home. The family came in from the shore early to be here for us."

She knew they had two houses, one in the city and the other on Long Island, a summer house.

"Mother kept the summer house open so we'll be going to the beach in a few days but not for long."

"Really? The ocean?"

He nodded. "Did you bring a swimming dress?"

Her brow furrowed. "A swimming dress?"

"For going in the water."

At home she'd worn an old shift when swimming in the river. Would this be one more area where she would be embarrassed? She released his hands after forgetting she was that closely connected to him and collapsed against the back of the seat. So much change. Too much change. How would she ever adapt to life here? Even for the few months she'd agreed to come? Just a few months. Surely she could last a few months. *Please, God.* Just long enough for the pain and anger to go away so she could go home and start again as a new Grace, not a "Grace Always."

22

WHEN THE CARRIAGE TURNED between two brick pillars supporting open wrought-iron gates and drove up a brick drive, she tried to look both ways to take it all in. Tall trees and blooming shrubs dotted the green lawn that even sheep could not graze so perfectly. She'd read of mansions with groomed lawns and huge houses, and now she was fast approaching one. She cast Jonathan what she knew must be a look of panic, for at the moment she was consumed by it. Why did he not warn her? He'd tried, she knew that, but no words could have prepared her for the actuality.

Her fingers ached for the clenching. She tried to breathe deeply, but she might as well have been wearing a corset tied much too tightly. Was she going to faint?

The carriage stopped. She wished she could disappear into the upholstery.

Jonathan took her hands again. "It will be all right."

Her nod did nothing more than move her head. It had no connection to her heart or mind. *Father, please. Send that peace again.* Her hands relaxed. Her spine straightened. *All will be well.* The memory of her mother writing the words in her book one day seeped in. More comfort.

The carriage door opened, and McHenry smiled up at her. "Welcome, miss."

She nodded and took the hand he offered to help her down. Once standing firmly on the brick drive, she stared at the house before her.

Wide steps led up to a polished wooden door set with two narrow rectangular windows. Looking up, she counted at least nine front-facing windows on the two stories, not including the roof, of a style she had never seen before. Dormer windows and elaborate surrounds broke up the expanse of gray tiles.

"Jonathan!" A young girl of ten or so burst through the opened door and vaulted down the three steps. She bypassed McHenry and threw herself at Jonathan as he stepped to the ground. He caught her in a hug that lasted seconds and then stood her upright.

"I want you to meet my friend Miss Knutson." He bent closer and whispered something in her ear. "Miss Knutson, this is my youngest sister, Mary Anne, with an *e*."

Grace spoke most carefully. "I am pleased to meet you." She eyed the drop-waisted cream dress with blue trim and a wide swath of grass-green stain across the ruffle on the skirt. If this was a good dress, Miss Mary Anne, with an *e*, was probably going to be in trouble. Grace liked her already.

Mary Anne grinned at her. "Me too."

Jonathan paused in step and stared down at his sister.

She rolled her eyes, huffed a sigh, and gave a slight curtsy. "I am delighted to meet you, Miss Knutson, and welcome to our house." She looked up at Jonathan from under her eyebrows. At his nod, she gave a tug on his hand. "I've been waiting and waiting for you." She leaned back to study him. "You look different."

Grace had noticed the difference a few weeks ago. His shirts were tight across the shoulders, and his coat had hung on a peg instead of being worn to church like when he first came. One could not fault him on his looks, that was for certain, as all the single girls in Blessing had noticed.

He took Grace's elbow and guided her toward the still open front door. "Where is Mother?"

"Pouring iced tea out on the back veranda." Mary Anne skipped up the steps. "She said she was sure you would be ready for something cold and wet by the time you got here."

Jonathan ushered Grace through the door. When she caught a glimpse over her shoulder, the two men were unloading their baggage.

She'd not even said thank-you. She glanced up at Jonathan, who'd not seemed to notice the oversight. Had he thanked them? Did wealthy people not thank their servants? Was she going to meet his mother without even a moment to freshen up?

Not if she had anything to say about it. "Jon—" Was the familiar name no longer allowed? He'd introduced her as Miss Knutson. What was tolerated in the West might not be so proper in the East. "Mr. Gould." Her tongue stumbled over the *G*.

"Oh." He stopped and faced her. "I'm sorry. Was I rushing you?"

She nodded, focusing on his face instead of the palatial surroundings. "I . . ." She gestured to her clothes. "I need to—"

"Of course. Mary Anne, find Mrs. Smithston so she can show Miss Knutson to her room."

"I can show her. She's in the Rose Room, next to me. Mrs. Smithston is busy with the surprise."

Jonathan paused a moment then nodded. "All right."

"We made sure her room has everything she needs. McHenry should have the trunks up there already."

"Would you mind?" he asked Grace.

It matters who takes me to my room? Oh, this is a whole different language in itself.

"There you are." A woman in a black bombazine dress with a white apron bustled into the hall. "I'm sorry. I wasn't quite finished."

Was this Jonathan's mother? Grace let out a breath she hadn't realized she'd been holding.

"Welcome home, young sir. We've missed you around here."

Not his mother.

Jonathan introduced her as Mrs. Smithston, as Grace had already surmised.

"Welcome, Miss Knutson." Her formal smile didn't reach her

eyes. "Let me show you to your room." She glanced down at Mary Anne. "And you, young lady, had better wash up before your mother sees you."

As she moved toward the stairs that curved up in front of windows that separated floor and ceiling, Grace shot Jonathan a look she was sure was filled with panic. His smile gave her the courage to follow the leader up the steps, Mary Anne beside her.

The girl tugged on her hand to get her attention and smiled up at her. "Mrs. Smithston is really very nice."

Grace hoped she had whispered that but just nodded and kept on climbing, turning on a landing and continuing to the second floor, where a long hallway stretched before them. Paintings of stern gentlemen lined the walls lit with gilt sconces that had neither gas nor candle. It had to be the electricity they had read about in Thorliff's newspaper.

Mrs. Smithston stopped and opened a door on the left. "We thought you might like a view of the gardens, since Mr. Gould wrote that you loved to garden. This is the Rose Room, and I hope you'll be very comfortable here. This door opens . . ."

Grace lost the last of the sentence but followed the woman into a room like no other. Who would teach her to use all these things she'd only seen in pictures and drawings in catalogs?

Mrs. Smithston turned around and recognized confusion when she saw it. "Oh dear, I'm sorry, but I forgot that I need to face you when I am talking. Mr. Gould was so explicit in his letter."

Grace sensed her discomfort but could find no strength within herself to attempt to put the woman at ease. She was far too uneasy herself. Grace motioned around the room and shook her head carefully, as if it might fall off her shoulders.

With a nod Mrs. Smithston moved across the room to a counter. Facing Grace she pointed to the sink and turned a spigot that released water into the bowl. "We have hot and cold running water, both here and in the bathtub." Next to the counter was a narrow door. She pointed through it to the claw-footed tub. As Grace came closer to see, she continued, "And over here is the commode. You pull this chain to flush after you are finished. You share this bath with Mary Anne, who comes in through that door." She pointed to a door Grace hadn't even noticed. She was too busy looking at all the towels on rods, the mirror above the sink, and the rugs on the marble floor.

Mrs. Smithston led the way back into the Rose Room. "I will send a maid up to put away your things, so you needn't bother with that. She will iron whatever needs to be, and you call her by pulling this." She moved to the corner, where a tassled cord hung. "One pull is for me, two pulls for your maid. Her name is Fiona." Mrs. Smithston thought a moment. "Is there anything else you will need? Oh yes. Please join the others outside when you can. If you would like, Mary Anne will wait outside your door for you."

Grace nodded. *Oh yes, please don't leave me alone up here. I might get lost and never find my way.* "Thank you." She had to clear her throat in order to say even those simple words. Mrs. Smithston did not react to the sound of her voice at all. Grace sensed she kept a tight rein on her facial expressions. *Something I desperately need to do. Too much change. This is too much.*

Jonathan watched Grace go up the stairs. He should have gone with her, whether it was proper or not. He waved at Mary Anne as she threw him a grin over her shoulder. He knew he should clean up and change clothes himself, but instead he strode through the music room and out the French doors, untying and pulling off his tie as he went. He paused to watch his mother fussing with the serving cart. Someone had not set it exactly as she liked. She fluffed the roses that filled a short, round glass vase and turned when she sensed someone was there.

"Jonathan!" She hurried across the flagstone, and he met her halfway. She hugged him, then leaned back to study his face. "You look wonderful. So tanned, like you've been at the shore all summer." She patted his upper arms and then clasped his cheeks between her hands. "Oh, I have missed you so."

"How could you, as busy as you've been?" He hugged her again and, with an arm around her waist, led her over to the iron chairs and the serving cart.

"You know all the shenanigans I've scolded you for?" She looked up to catch his smile and quirked brows. "I missed them. The house was too quiet without you."

"So you say I'm noisy?"

She tipped her head slightly to the side. "To a degree. But there was less laughter." She stepped back and studied him head to foot. "I think my boy has become a man. I'm sure your father will be suitably impressed and as delighted as I am to see you."

"Mrs. Smithston took Grace—" He stopped himself at her raised eyebrow. "Er, Miss Knutson to her room to freshen up. Mary Anne went with them."

"Good. The poor child, traveling like that on such short notice. Does she have all she will need to live here?"

"If you are referring to the latest style in dresses, no. But I knew you would remedy that and have a wonderful time doing so." He accepted the cut-crystal glass of tea, the tinkle of ice a welcome sound.

"I sweetened it just the way you like it and added mint syrup, just a trifle."

He took a swallow and closed his eyes. "Ah, what a treat."

"They did not have tea in Blessing?"

"I'm sure they did, but the Bjorklunds are coffee drinkers. Black coffee. While it took some doing, I learned to leave off the cream and sugar. Ice ran out in July. The refrigeration was a tank of water in the well house. They used kerosene lamps for light and cooked on a cast-iron range that burned coal or wood. Everyone there works harder than I could have believed before I lived there." He set his glass down and took her hands. "And, Mother, I loved every minute of it. Well, after I got used to it, if I'm going to be honest."

She rubbed her thumbs over his hands, then picked one up and turned it over, running her finger over the callouses and the scar from where he cut himself with the knife while repairing the harness.

"Your hands tell a tale of their own. Did you not use any lotion or salve?"

"None. I was grateful for the leather gloves, but even so, I got blisters that made my hands look like chopped meat." He looked at his hands, spreading the fingers wide. "I can milk cows with the best of them, drive four-up horse teams, set posts in holes and string wire for fences, run machinery, shovel out the barn, and spade the garden, and I never knew how fascinating is the process of making cheese. Oh, Mrs. Bjorklund sent you some. No wonder the Bjorklund cheese is prized everywhere."

His mother sat down and indicated the chair next to her. "Did you not miss your life here at all?"

He started to shake his head but quickly thought the better of it and answered with a rueful smile. "I hardly had any time to think of the past. I was always busy trying to learn all I could so that I would not be a burden, and by night, I fell into bed so exhausted I couldn't think." He glanced toward the house. *Grace, are you all right? How can I help you?*

"I am so glad to have you home, yet you will leave again soon."

"I know. Did Father mention anything about the school for Grace?"

"Yes, he contacted them as you requested. They have agreed to interview her to see if she is a suitable candidate for their program." Geraldine Gould sat back slightly in her chair, straight and not touching the chair back.

"I see." *A suitable candidate, if that doesn't say a ream of thought in a few words.* He reminded himself not to push too hard and be extra charming to keep his mother on his side. He'd always known he was her fair-haired boy, no matter how dark his hair. Being her eldest son had some advantages, since the mother of his older siblings had died and she was the second wife. "Where are my brothers?"

"David is spending a week with friends at the shore, and Daniel is having a tennis lesson. He will be back soon. He wanted to skip in order to be here when you returned but acquiesced when I insisted he keep to the schedule."

"Why make him learn tennis when he'd much rather be reading?" At the slight change in her smile, he knew he'd made a gaff. Playing tennis was an important part of summers at the shore, and she expected her children to be at least adequate in all areas of sports and social graces. Proficient was more suitable. He thought of Astrid and Grace making light of working in the garden. What would they think of tennis and lawn bowling, croquet and badminton for an afternoon's entertainment, and changing clothes again for dinner and dancing in the evening? Although they loved to dance, the parties in Blessing were few and far between.

Was bringing Grace back here a wise move or a horrendous mistake?

Grace hung her traveling suit in the spacious armoire. After washing her face, hands, and neck, she felt much cooler and a bit more ready to face the unknown. At least the nausea had stopped. She stood in front of the mirror and unpinned her hair, letting the golden mass fall around her shoulders. Looking longingly at the tub, she instead picked up the brush she found lying along with a comb on a glass shelf and tried to brush the travel dust away. If only she could lie down and sleep for a week, then take a bath in that tub big enough for three, wash her hair, and sleep for another week. Instead, she wound her gathered hair around her fingers and pinned it again at the back of her head up off her neck. She felt a slight breeze coming through the open window from the park-like place behind the house. She expected Jonathan was regaling his mother with stories of his summer in Blessing. What would she think of them? Life in Blessing was so far removed from this world. How had Jonathan ever managed? How would she manage here?

She stared into the face in the mirror. "Well, best to beard the lion." The face staring back needed to smile and make sure to include the eyes. She turned away and, after shaking out her black serge skirt, took a deep breath and strode toward the door, where she hoped Mary Anne with an *e* was still waiting. *Lord, please continue your peace in me.*

23

"CAN YOU REALLY READ LIPS?"

Grace nodded with a smile. "Otherwise I would not know how to answer you."

"You can't hear a thing?" The girl frowned and shook her head when Grace shook hers. "That's awful."

"I learned to live with it. But I can also talk with my fingers." She made several signs.

Mary Anne stared at the gracefully moving fingers, then up at Grace's face. "What did you say?"

"Mary Anne."

"Can you teach me?"

"If you like. Your brother knows the alphabet and some other signs. He wants to learn too." Grace pointed at the grass stain.

"I couldn't get it out, not even with soap."

"If you scrub it good and lay it in the sunshine on the grass, the stain will disappear."

"If I scrub me good and lay me in the grass, will I disappear?" Her laughing eyes said she was joking.

Grace grinned back at her. "I most certainly hope not."

Mary Anne took her hand. "Come on. Mother is waiting."

Oh, I don't think she's waiting too eagerly. I think she's probably glad to have her son all to herself. Grace allowed the girl to lead her back down the hall to the staircase, down and out the French doors. Even with all the green grass and trees, the air didn't smell anything like that of the wide open skies of North Dakota. However, once they took a few steps out onto the flagstone terrace, the fragrance of the formal rose beds that bordered each side of the beautifully laid cut rock made her smile. Grace sneaked glimpses of vibrant reds, pinks, yellows, and whites as she walked with her escort to the decorative iron table with matching chairs and a huge umbrella.

Jonathan stood and turned to smile at her as soon as he heard them approach. "I was beginning to think I needed to come fetch you."

"I'm sorry, I—"

"No, not at all. Mother, I want you to meet Miss Grace Knutson." He took her hand and drew her closer.

"Welcome to New York, Miss Knutson."

Mrs. Gould extended her hand so Grace shook it gently. Grace had never seen a hand so smooth and unmarred.

"I hear I have much to thank you for?"

Grace glanced at Jonathan with a questioning look.

"I've been telling her of all the help you and Astrid were to me."

Grace turned to his mother. "I think the reality is all the help he was to us. Your son worked harder than anyone this summer."

"I had to prove I wasn't just a stuck-up city boy."

Grace rolled her lips together. He must have heard someone talking at home. "You proved that, all right."

"Please, won't you sit down?" Mrs. Gould indicated a chair. "Mary Anne, would you please walk nicely and ask Cook for more ice?"

Mary Anne nodded, but it was only three steps before she skipped two, sobered, sent a glance at her mother, and tried again to walk nicely.

Since Grace was facing that way, she saw it all. Did they expect Mary Anne to act like an adult all the time? What was wrong with a little girl running and skipping? When she turned her attention back to the conversation, she realized she'd missed part of it.

"Mother was asking how your train ride was," Jonathan filled in for her.

Long, hot, dirty, and ... "The scenery, especially through the mountains, was beautiful. I had never seen such variety of land before or realized how big this country is." Grace leaned forward. "Your roses are lovely."

"Thank you. The fragrance makes sitting out here such a pleasure. Did you find everything to your satisfaction in the Rose Room?" She glanced up to see her daughter carrying back a cut-glass bowl of ice. "Thank you, dear. Set it right here."

But before she could reach the table, Jonathan stood and took the bowl and set it on the glass-topped serving cart. "Now, who would like more ice in their tea? Grace, here is a glass for you." At the censorious look on his mother's face, he caught his error. "Mary Anne, would you please hand this to Miss Knutson? And the plate of cookies too."

"I'd like more ice." Mrs. Gould held her glass up. "Please." She looked at her daughter. "Were there no servants available to help you?"

Mary Anne held the plate for Grace. "No, Mother, and Cook was up to her elbows in flour getting ready for the—" She stopped, glanced at Jonathan, and set the plate back on the table after taking two cookies, one lemon and one spiced, and sat in her chair, swinging her legs as she took the first bite.

Jonathan watched his sister for a moment then turned toward his mother. "Father referred to a surprise in his letter, and I sense busyness among the staff today. Anything special going on?"

Mrs. Gould smiled. "Well, yes. I'd have rather waited until dinner, but since you've been so observant, we have some guests coming tonight. I know you're probably tired, but this was the only evening she was available, and I knew you wouldn't want to miss seeing her again."

His face flushed and jaw tightened. "Who would that be, Mother?"

"The Bloomquist niece from Chicago, whom you spent so much time with over the Christmas holidays. She was disappointed when she arrived at the shore and found you were in North Dakota, so we arranged a small dinner party this evening."

Jonathan looked like he'd swallowed bees. "Mother, I have absolutely no interest in the Bloomquist niece. I was simply being polite at Christmas, and she was the least obnoxious of all the young ladies."

Grace saw Mary Anne hide a giggle behind her cookie.

"Her family has excellent connections, Jonathan. I am shocked at your rudeness."

"I'm sorry, Mother, but I really did not expect to be social on my first night home."

Mrs. Gould turned back to Grace. "There is sugar and lemon for your tea if you prefer."

Grace set her glass down. "No thank you. This is very good." She tried to keep track of the conversation, but weariness was not only catching up with her but running her down. Also, she felt she was intruding on a family issue. She nibbled the cookies, drank her tea, and wished she were at home. Trying to hide a yawn behind her hand, she drank some more iced tea.

She glanced up in time to see a frown flitter across Mrs. Gould's forehead. Jonathan touched her arm. "Mother wondered if you would like to take a nap before dinner."

"Oh yes, please. Pardon me, I had no idea I was so tired."

"I'll take you." Mary Anne slid off her chair, stuffed a cookie into her pocket, and took Grace's hand. "Miss Knutson is going to teach me sign language. Would you like to learn too, Mother?"

"We shall see." She smiled at Grace. "I'm sure you will feel better after a lie-down. I return from a train trip exhausted. Why, it takes me two or three days to recuperate."

"Yes. Thank you, ma'am—Mrs. Gould." Grace followed her escort; sure she was as glad to be away from there as Mary Anne was.

Grace removed her shoes and lay down on the bed, wishing she could stay awake long enough to take a bath. But with the state she was in, she might fall asleep and drown. Falling asleep was like tumbling down the rabbit hole like Alice in Wonderland.

Darkness, but for a small lit lamp by the door, filled the room as Grace fought to remember where she was. How long had she been asleep? A light blanket had been placed over her, so someone had come in to check on her. She stretched and wiggled her toes. After making use of the facilities, she returned to her room and turned on the lamp by the bed only to discover a tray with sliced cheese, crackers, a little dish of blueberries and cream, and several of the cookies like those she'd had with the iced tea. A folded little piece of stiff paper lay beside the spoon. She unfolded it and read, *Since you missed dinner, I brought you something in case you are hungry.* The childish hand was signed *Mary Anne.*

For a moment a twinge of guilt for missing dinner pinged inside her, quickly replaced by relief. She thought Mrs. Gould was probably relieved too, since she had invited the young lady as a special treat for Jonathan. Not that she herself was any competition or would even be considered as such by Mrs. Gould.

Grace slipped out of her white lawn waist and black serge skirt. Since her trunk and valise were nowhere in sight, she checked the chest of drawers and located a nightdress. Once she'd divested herself of the remainder of her clothing, she hung the skirt and waist in the armoire and laid the other things in an empty drawer. No pegs on walls here, that was for certain. She climbed back up on the bed, reached over for the tray, and with her knees bent and her gown bunched around her feet, nibbled at each of the offerings, enjoying the blueberries with cream most of all. When she'd finished it all, she set the tray back, folded down the quilt cover, and slid between ironed sheets faintly scented with lavender.

With a sigh she thought of home. Her mother wouldn't believe the opulence of this house—she would enjoy the beauty, especially the roses. If only Astrid were here, she wouldn't feel so intimidated by Mrs. Gould. Had she felt that way with Mr. Gould when he came to Blessing? She thought not, but then he was the guest not the host. Did that make a difference?

The next morning the tray was gone and so were her clothes she'd taken off the night before.

A note on the lamp table said to come down for breakfast whenever she woke or to pull the cord in the corner one time to order her meal brought to her room. Grace made up the bed, making sure there were no wrinkles so that it looked the same as when she arrived, found more of her unmentionables in the drawer, and ambled into the bathroom. The bathtub was calling her name.

Turning on the taps and watching the tub fill was a delight in its own right. She didn't have to lug the water into the house, heat it on the stove, haul in the washtub, pour in the hot and cold water, and set up the screen so that no one would surprise her. Inspecting the bottles on the shelf at the high end of the tub, she found lavender, rose petal, and a fragrance she couldn't define. Bath salts—whatever were they for? She followed the instructions and tossed a handful of lavender into the steaming water. Too hot but ah, the fragrance. She turned the hot handle down and raised the cold. When she climbed in, she sank down into the foaming water and leaned back against the slanted end of the tub. What bliss. No wonder in the pictures she'd seen, the bather always looked pleased.

If only her mother could see her now. What would she say, other than "Don't waste the water," of course. So much to write home about already. She slid down to get her hair wet then applied the bottle of lavender shampoo—at least that's what the label said. Putting a dab in her hand, she rubbed it into her hair and then added a little more. This was better than the rose soap she had purchased at Penny's store to wash her hair. She lathered and rinsed, soaped herself and rinsed, then pulled the plug in the bottom and watched the water drain away.

"Mor, somehow we need to get running water into our house. You wouldn't believe all this." With a towel wrapped around her hair, she dried off and slipped into her underthings. Would sitting out in the sun to dry her hair be considered seemly? She guessed not. When she returned to her room, she pulled a matching dimity waist and skirt from the closet, holding them up to discover they had been freshly ironed. Who were the invisible people who were doing all these things? She turned from brushing her hair at the window to see a small hand waving from around the slightly open door.

"Come in."

"Oh good. You're up and dressed. I was beginning to think you would stay in the bathroom all day." Mary Anne came to stand beside her. "Would you like me to bring up a tray? Or Fiona will."

"Is it too late for breakfast downstairs?" *I can't believe I slept so long. Mor would be so embarrassed.*

"No." The girl shrugged. "You can eat any time you like. Cook will fix whatever you want, but I have to tell you, she makes the best muffins in the entire world. Today they are blueberry, my favorite."

I don't have to cook, clear away dishes, take care of my clothes. What will I do all day?

"You have beautiful hair."

"Thank you."

Mary Anne sank down on the floor with her elbows on her crossed knees, one of which wore a scab, and watched Grace fluff and brush her hair to dry it. At home she washed it in the rain or with water from the rain barrel and let the clean Dakota wind blow it dry. In the winter they dried their hair in the hot air from an open oven door.

"And you smell good."

"Thanks to the bottles in the bath." Grace kept one eye on her guest so she could see her speak.

"When are you going to teach me some signs?"

"When I get my hair dry enough to put it up."

"I think you should wear it down. It's too pretty to wear up."

"If only I could, but I must be proper."

Mary Anne jumped up and went to the door. She returned, followed by a young woman wearing an apron that covered her from neck to ankle. A white frilled cap sat on her riot of carrot hair. "This is Fiona. She is your maid."

My maid? What do I need a maid for? "I am happy to meet you."

Fiona gave a slight head bow. "Do you need help with your hair?" She spoke very slowly.

"You can talk regular. You just have to make sure Miss Knutson can see your face. She reads lips." Mary Anne leaned against the bed.

"I see." But her face said she clearly did not.

"I am deaf. That means I cannot hear, but I can see what you are saying." Grace motioned to her ears as she spoke.

"She also talks with her fingers, but none of us know how to do that except Jonathan. I'm going to learn, though."

"Would you like me to help with your hair?" Fiona pointed to the brush and Grace's head.

"Why?"

"Because part of my job is to help you."

"Did you take my clothes?" Grace wrapped her hair around her fingers and reached for one of her hairpins.

Fiona nodded. "I'll be bringing them back this afternoon." She handed Grace the pins as she needed them. "I am good with hair, miss."

Grace caught part of the sentence in the mirror. "Perhaps another time."

"Will there be anything else, then?"

"No, thank you."

Instead of going out the door to the hall, Fiona went into the bathroom and returned with the wet towels. "I'll take care of the bath, miss." And out the door she went.

"She'll make up your bed too. I have to make my own. Mother says that develops character."

Grace followed her guide out the door, down the stairs, and into a room taken up by a long table, chairs, and a credenza along the wall. One place remained set.

She caught Mary Anne's hand. "Can't I eat in the kitchen?"

"You better not. Mother insisted we leave a setting for you. I'll go tell Cook you're here." She pointed to the chair and then headed through another door. There were enough doors in this house to fit an entire boardinghouse.

Ordering breakfast was another ordeal, and then Mary Anne said her mother wanted to see Grace in the morning room when she was finished. So Grace hurriedly downed coffee, one of the celebrated blueberry muffins, slices of bacon, and more blueberries and cream. She started to pick up her dishes, but Mary Anne shook her head.

What would she do without her guide?

Mary Anne led her past the music room and the inviting French doors and into another room, where Mrs. Gould sat at a desk, still in a dressing gown, the remains of her breakfast on a tray. The tray sat on a low table in front of a flowered chintz sofa. Sunlight streamed in through tall windows like in the other rooms, dancing on brass fittings and throwing rainbows on the tables through crystal dangles.

Grace stared at the colors, entranced by the light. She smiled at Mrs. Gould. "How very lovely."

"Thank you, my dear. Please sit down so you and I can have a chat. Mary Anne, will you have Nettie bring us more tea? You do drink tea?"

"Yes, of course. Thank you for the beautiful room. I apologize that I slept through dinner." *And so late this morning.*

"You were exhausted. I am surprised you are up so early this morning."

Grace glanced at an ornate clock on the desk. Surely the hands didn't say eleven o'clock. She'd never slept so late unless she was sick. But then she'd taken a bath too. Uff da. What would Mor say?

Mrs. Gould rose and came to sit by Grace on the sofa. "I have some suggestions that I would like to share with you, so please do not take what I say the wrong way."

Grace had no idea what was coming or what she should say, so she said nothing.

"I asked Jonathan if this would be all right, and he said to go ahead. I know you had to leave without a lot of preparation, so I would like my seamstress to sew you some new gowns. We have a party coming up, and I know you have nothing formal to wear. I thought of using some of Lillian's dresses, but you and she are not the same size. She was hoping to meet you, but they sailed for London two days ago."

As Mrs. Gould kept turning away from her, Grace struggled to follow the conversation. Finally she got the sense of it. Grace raised a hand. "But I can sew and—"

"I'm sure you can, dear, but we want to have the party before Jonathan has to leave for school, and he wants you included. You see what a short time we have. My seamstress will be here within the hour to measure you and bring samples of dress goods."

"I appreciate your generosity, Mrs. Gould, but I thought I was only here for a short visit, and—"

Mrs. Gould cut her off. "Yes, but we don't want to appear too unprepared now, do we? Besides, this will help you make a good impression at the school for your interview."

"Tea, ma'am." Another maid, wearing the same uniform as Fiona, set a tray on the table and removed the first. "Anything else?"

"You may pour." She turned back to Grace. "Do you take milk or lemon?"

Grace shook her head. It seemed that Mrs. Gould had decided she did not meet their standards. And these were the people her family considered friends? Although Grace could not hear Mrs. Gould's tone of voice, she recognized her urgency. Now she knew what it felt like to be run over by a runaway six-up team hauling a wagonload of grain.

24

WOULD HE NEVER BE ALONE WITH GRACE?

Amazing how quickly he'd forgotten the strictures of propriety in his mother's house. Jonathan thought back to Blessing, where he had been welcomed as a member of the family. After only a few days they had all dropped the formality and called him Jonathan. Astrid told him to call them by their first names—the girls, that is. He'd always referred to the adults as mister and missus. But in his mind he called them Ingeborg and Haakan sometimes, wishing he could use the Far and Mor addresses the families used.

Mary Anne had adopted Grace as her own personal mentor and herself as guardian. While their mother thought it cute and he was grateful, he knew Grace was being made comfortable. He ached to touch her hand again, to resume long conversations like they'd had on the train. Living in his mother's house was like playing a game. While he knew the rules, he no longer wished to play by them. But he also knew he must not let his mother have any sense of his real feelings for Grace. Especially after the surprise dinner she'd held on his first evening home. What connection was she trying to make this time?

His only reprieve was the sign language lessons with Grace and, of course, Mary Anne, who was learning so much more quickly than he that it was embarrassing. He checked the clock and headed for the library, where they met. Sometimes, when she could get away, Fiona joined them. And while Daniel and David thought it interesting, they came and went.

His mother claimed to be too busy to learn sign language.

"Good morning." Grace both signed and spoke slowly, so they could be learning from the very beginning of the hour.

"Good morning." The words came easier than the signs, so Grace signed *good morning* again.

Jonathan watched her graceful fingers carefully and then concentrated on making his fingers do the same. When she nodded, he felt like the sun had just come out.

"I copied some signs onto paper for you to take with you, so you can practice on your own. Mary Anne, please sign your name for me and hand out the papers."

Mary Anne's fingers flew. "Mary Anne Adele Gould." At Grace's smile and nod, she did as directed.

Fiona stumbled on her middle name. Grace corrected her and complimented her when she did it right.

Jonathan found himself in a quandary. If he did it right, he'd be blessed by an angel smile. If he did it wrong, she would hold his hands to shape the letters correctly. He chose to do it right.

"Why does she"—he nodded to Mary Anne—"learn this so much faster than the rest of us?"

"She practices continually. Watch her when she is walking."

"Mary Anne," Fiona signed, then sighed and finished, "rarely walks."

They all laughed because it was so true, no matter how hard her mother tried to correct her behavior.

"I cannot . . ." Mary Anne's tongue peeked from between her teeth. "H-e-l—" She looked up at Grace. "What is *p*?"

Grace showed her and Mary Anne finished with "it." She beamed her pleasure. "I sure wish we could do this outside."

"Is there any reason we can't?" Jonathan's gaze had strayed to the window once or twice too.

Fiona looked at the clock. "Miss Knutson has a fitting in fifteen minutes."

Grace rolled her eyes.

Jonathan had a pretty good idea what she really thought of all the fittings, the choosing of accessories, shoes, hats. She'd far rather be in the classroom or out weeding the garden. The gardener had commented that he'd found her out weeding and transplanting a wayward marigold just after sunrise. He said she was most delightful company and wished she was staying for a longer visit.

Everyone seemed to love Grace except for the most important person—his mother, who still held herself in reserve. And Mrs. Smithston, who always copied her mistress.

But Father would be back soon, and that might ease their chill toward Grace. Jonathan wasn't sure whether his mother felt Grace was too below them socially or if her deafness offended her in some way.

Grace pinned up a paper with words on it. Please, thank you, ear, nose, eyes, face, and chin. She made the signs for each as she read them. "Soon some of these will be so natural you'll forget that you are signing, which is really an entirely new language."

Jonathan realized he had missed most of these words in his early lessons. But then he had been concentrating more on chores and farm items.

"Can you sign in French?" Mary Anne asked.

"Sign what you are able when you speak."

"But then I have to talk so slow." As if doing anything slow was the end of the world. "Can you sign—" she grew frustrated, wrinkling her face, but continued to the end—"in French?"

"Excellent. But no, I cannot. I did not learn that language. I had enough trouble with the two I was already working in—sign and English. I do speak some Norwegian, but I am harder to understand in Norwegian than English." Her smile was definitely teasing. She paused.

Jonathan could tell she was thinking. She always wore that same bemused look. "Signing Norwegian would not be difficult. There are only a few letters that are different." She swiftly formed a *j* and an *a* for ja. "That means yes."

Jonathan heard footsteps coming down the hall. Surely it was someone coming to tell Grace the seamstress had arrived. While he knew the party was in his honor, he wished his mother had not planned one. Especially not when this would be Grace's introduction to society, even though his mother said it would be informal. The word *informal* did not mean the same to his mother as to some other people. But a Saturday afternoon fete was definitely preferable to an evening cotillion. He would have much rather gone to the shore as he'd told Grace they would. He'd wanted to share with her all the things he most enjoyed. He thought she seemed disappointed too.

He had watched Grace manage to disappear when in large groups of people. She faded into the background and could be found making sure someone else was comfortable. As a guest of honor, she would not be able to do that at the party. She danced all right. If he could dance with her throughout the hours of the fete, he was sure he could keep something bad from happening, but that was impossible.

At the doorway Mrs. Smithston cleared her throat. When Jonathan realized Grace did not see her, he stood so Grace couldn't miss him and then nodded over his shoulder.

"Oh, thank you." She dismissed the class, making her way to the door. The brief smiles she had shared with them suddenly became swallowed up in a mask. It was the same look she had worn after Toby had humiliated her. What was going on when he wasn't around?

Jonathan caught a narrowed-eyed look from the housekeeper. Why was she having such a hard time understanding that Grace was deaf, not ignorant or deliberately impolite? He saw Grace bite her lower lip slightly and realized she'd seen the look too. How many more did she get that he did not see? Mrs. Smithston was either overstepping her authority or within his mother's boundaries. Both possibilities made him very uncomfortable.

Friday Jonathan and Grace were walking along the gravel paths in the rose garden, with her and Mary Anne pausing to inhale the fragrances of every other bush, when he saw his father step out onto the slate of the veranda. Jonathan waved, catching Mary Anne's attention at the same time.

"Father's home." Mary Anne grabbed Grace's hand and tugged her back up the path. "Come along, he's been looking forward to seeing you again." She'd paused and faced Grace so they could talk.

Jonathan felt a burst of pride, colored with delight in the caring his little sister showed to Grace. No matter how much he wished for time alone with Grace, he realized the advantages of having the three of them together. He caught Grace's glance down at her skirt, as if unsure if she were dressed right. She'd never used to worry about things like that, one of the many things he liked about her.

"Don't worry. You look lovely." When her smiled trembled slightly, it was all he could do to not take her hand and tuck it in his arm.

Instead, she allowed Mary Anne to lead her up the path, with him following.

"Ah, Miss Knutson, what a pleasure it is to see you again." His father's smile could have melted a frozen lake.

"Thank you."

"I hope your journey was pleasant."

Was Jonathan the only one to pick up on her slight hesitation? He glanced at Mary Anne, who nibbled on her bottom lip, a sure sign that she was concerned.

"Grace is teaching me to sign."

"Really? What a wonderful idea." His father smiled down at Mary Anne. He leaned over slightly and lowered his voice. "But shouldn't you be calling her Miss Knutson?"

Mary Anne rolled her eyes and heaved a sigh. "I s'pose so, but she is my friend."

"And I asked her to call me Grace."

Jonathan caught the glint in his father's eyes and kept a grin from his own face. What his mother didn't know wouldn't hurt her. Or them.

His father motioned to the garden chairs. "Let's make ourselves comfortable. Mary Anne, perhaps you would go ask Cook for some refreshments to be brought out here. Then go ask your mother if she would like to join us."

"Yes, sir."

Jonathan swallowed another smile as Mary Anne leaped over one stair and then after a quick glance at the house windows made herself walk instead of run. Irrepressible fit his little sister. And he loved her for it.

His father seated Grace, usurping Jonthan's chance to take her hand, so he sat next to her and leaned back in his chair. In Blessing they'd never had time to sit like this. Grace or Astrid would have gone inside for the tray with glasses and most likely made the swizzle or lemonade before returning.

Did Grace miss her life there? If so, she'd been good at hiding her feelings.

By Saturday afternoon, Jonathan wished he and Grace were anywhere but there. Foreboding hung on his shoulders like half-full grain sacks. The air added more weight. While many of their friends were still at the shore, some had returned to the city to attend the party. He paced at the bottom of the staircase, hearing his mother greet some of the guests and guide them to the veranda, where refreshments were being served.

What was keeping Grace? He started up the steps but paused when Mary Anne at the top shook her head. Grace appeared beside her, fashionably clad in a light blue gown sprigged with white daisies, the neckline lined with white lace. With the short puffed sleeves and a ruffle around the bottom, she looked like she was drifting on a cloud of flowers. Her hair was gathered up in back, and ringlets tumbled down from a bow matching the dress. He'd never seen her look more beautiful.

As she came down the stairs, he stepped up to meet her and offered his arm. "You look so lovely, I cannot begin to say what I feel."

"Thank you." Her smile hid the trembling he felt in her hand.

"You'll be fine." *Please, Lord, let it be so.* While he'd not been much of a praying man most of his life, he'd learned much from those in Blessing who had an honest regard for the Father and a willingness to speak their faith and voice their needs. And right now, he knew he needed divine help. Together they walked out the French doors and joined the milling guests. Should he tell people Grace could not hear and they needed to face her, tell them that was the reason for her strange speech? Or had his mother already begun to spread the word? What could he do to make this easier for her?

A business associate of his father's greeted him. "Jonathan, my boy, welcome back from the wilds of North Dakota." He reached out to shake his hand. "How did you manage, banished from civilization like that?"

"Quite well, thank you. I'd like you to meet a friend of ours who came back to go to school here in the city. Miss Grace Knutson, Mr. Simpson."

"I am pleased to meet you." Grace spoke slowly and as clearly as she was able, her hand tightening on his arm.

The man looked at her, glanced at Jonathan, and then smiled a bit too broadly. "Welcome to New York, Miss Knutson. You are from North Dakota?"

"Yes. Blessing, North Dakota."

"Blessing, did you say? Strange name for a town."

Her glance up at him prompted Jonathan to add for her, "The women outvoted the men when it was time to name the growing town. The settlement began in 1880 when the Bjorklunds arrived there to homestead." The pressure on his arm told of her appreciation.

"Sounds like you got to know a lot about the place." Simpson beckoned his wife over. "This is Miss Knutson from North Dakota, where Jonathan went for the summer."

Mrs. Simpson smiled up at Jonathan, almost including Grace in the gesture. She tapped his arm with her fan. "We missed you at the shore, young man. Delia and the other girls, especially."

"I'm sure they found someone else to devil."

"You might be surprised. They are all becoming most attractive young ladies. I hope you found time to keep your tennis arm strong. They've set up a tournament for next weekend,

"Oh, my arm is strong enough, but I'm not sure if I'll have time." He noticed Mary Anne motioning them from the edge of the crowd. Saved by his little sister. "Excuse us. Mother said we need to mingle. Greet the girls for me."

That the woman had made no effort to talk to Grace at all set his collar to steaming. Had she always been that rude? He tried to think back. She'd always been one to tell everyone what to do and made sure her daughters were mixing with the proper people. Mrs. Simpson and his mother were good friends. What had his mother told her?

Mary Anne handed Grace a fan. "Do you know how to use one?"

"It's difficult to sign if I am fanning my face."

"No one else can sign here anyway, so it don't matter."

"Doesn't." Grace and Jonathan corrected her at the same time, then turned to smile at each other. The blue dress made her gray eyes look blue. He thought he might be falling into them.

Mary Anne stared up through her fringe. Grace missed her comment and Jonathan pinched the girl, sending her away giggling.

"Would you like some refreshments?"

"Yes, please." She slipped the loop on the fan over her wrist and let it dangle. She glanced over to see Mr. Simpson look her way and read his lips.

"Pretty little thing, isn't she? But her voice has a . . ."

She felt the blush begin at her toes and work its way upward. If only she could leave the gathering. If only she could get on the train heading west. But . . . why was there always a but?

She accepted the cup of pink liquid Jonathan handed her, smiling her thanks over the rim. Hot as the weather was, she could drink the entire thing in one gulp. That would surely shock someone watching her. She felt eyes on her from every direction. She held the cup out for a refill.

Jonathan touched her arm, and when she looked at him he asked, "Are you hungry?"

She sipped her punch again and shook her head. *Let's just get this over with.*

Jonathan took her empty cup and set it on the tray of a passing servant. "Let's go back into the fray."

"When can I leave?"

His chuckle at her determined look drew the attention of those nearby.

The people she met became a blur of color, perfumes, gowns, and various degrees of curiosity and interest. One woman Grace fell in love with immediately. Jonathan introduced her as Mrs. Wooster. "With a *W*," he said, making the sign for the letter.

"You dear boy, you are learning to sign so you can help your friend. What a good idea." She turned to Grace. "I so admire your grit, young lady. Why, when Geraldine told me about your difficulty, it near to broke my heart. Come humor an old woman, and let's sit down. These slippers are killing my feet."

Grace breathed a sigh of relief. Finally someone who was not uncomfortable around her. She felt as if she should be waving her arms and crying *Unclean!* the way some of the guests were acting.

"So now—" Mrs. Wooster beckoned to one of the servants, who came over instantly—"we would like punch for the three of us, some of those tea sandwiches, and whatever else you think we are missing."

"Yes, madam." The man bowed slightly. "I will send someone with the punch immediately."

Grace glanced at Jonathan to see laughter dancing in his eyes. He liked this woman too. But then, who wouldn't? *Ah, I wonder if her directness has caused some of these others offense. How did Jonathan ever fit into life in Blessing so well when this is what he came from? No wonder Astrid was all set to not like him.*

"Thank you." Amazing how quickly the punch appeared. When that man said immediately, he meant it.

Mrs. Wooster took a long swallow. "I always say, ask for what you want and do it firmly. That way there is no confusion."

Jonathan nodded. "But I have never seen you to be anything but polite."

"Others might not agree with you, but thank you anyway." She turned to Grace. "What can I do to help you?"

"Help me what?"

"To start with—" she motioned to the people around them— "these ninnies, as an example."

Jonathan choked on his punch and had to thump his chest. "Pardon me." He coughed again. "Whew, you got me on that one."

"Good. There is hope for you, but I've always known that."

Grace locked her lower lip between her teeth. If only Tante Ingeborg and Mor could meet Mrs. Wooster. But even they would be amazed at her calling the other guests ninnies.

The woman turned back to Grace. "Now I know you read lips. That is how you understand what people are saying. I read about this in a journal that I subscribe to."

"Many people, not just the deaf, learn to do this," Grace answered. "It would be very useful for politicians."

Mrs. Wooster tipped her head to the side, much like a hen peering at a bug on the ground. "You, my dear, have a lot to offer, if only people will listen beyond your speaking." She looked around the gathering, shaking her head. "Sadly, too many won't. But . . ." She nodded to the young woman who set two plates of food in front of them. "Thank you."

So it *was* polite to thank servants. Grace tucked that away in her memory. She was glad she'd been doing so anyway. *I wonder just how bad I do sound. No one in Blessing ever said, but then, they wouldn't.*

"How did you learn to speak?"

"The same way I learned to sign. My mother helped me, and I kept at it until I succeeded."

"And your mother runs a school for the deaf?"

"Yes. Some of the students are in a sorry state when they come to us because of neglect or ignorance, but once they learn to sign so they can communicate with others, they are changed. Then they must learn skills to help them in life. When they have a good grasp on signing, they can attend the school in Blessing, where all the teachers can sign too."

"Your mother is a saint."

"Yes, she is." Jonathan motioned to the sandwiches. "Help yourself."

Grace bit into a slice of cucumber on soft cheese on a circle of rye bread. *It would take both those plates to fill one of my brothers, especially in the summer. What would they think of bite-sized sandwiches and tiny bits of cake? Why, they would laugh themselves silly over this.*

Mrs. Wooster looked at the food, then at Grace. "I never gave a lot of thought to being able to hear until recently. My hearing is not as good as it used to be. I find myself saying, 'Pardon me,' more often and, 'Will you please repeat that?' Sometimes it is easier to just nod and pretend I understand and hope I don't make too big a fool of myself."

"Yes, that is it." Grace laid her hand on the back of the woman's liver-spotted one. "Thank you."

"You are indeed welcome. Now, I hear you are giving classes in signing here at the Goulds'. Would it be possible for me to join you?"

Grace stared at her, fighting to comprehend. "B-but why?"

"Because I want to learn something new and—" she tapped Grace's hand with her fan—"I like you and what you are doing."

Grace looked to Jonathan, who said, "Of course she can come."

But will your mother be pleased with this?

Mrs. Wooster wiped her mouth with her napkin. "Now I must let you two young people go and mingle. I have used up too much of your time. I see your mother glowering at me." She took Grace's hand. "What time on Monday should I be here?"

"One o'clock?"

"Done." She made shooing motions with her hands. "Off with you now."

Grace stood and allowed Jonathan to guide her by touching her elbow. She glanced at Mrs. Gould and saw her talking with someone else. Jonathan introduced her to several other people, and she was content to try to keep up with the conversations. Being with one or two people was far easier than in groups of four or five or more.

She glanced about the gathering and saw several younger women, more her age, staring at her. One tipped her head and said to another, "Why would they let her be here? She can't even talk right. Isn't there a place for people like that?"

Grace felt like she'd been struck in the midsection and all her air forced out. She had to get out of there. "Excuse me," she said and, head held high, made her way toward the stairs. She forced the tears back. She would not let these people see her cry. *Mor, I want to come home. I don't belong here. I don't want to be here. But I know it's important for you that I see the school. Mrs. Wooster is right. What you do is important, and I can't let you down because I'm homesick. But this loneliness is as bad as losing Toby, only in a different way. Living here makes me feel like I am disappearing.*

I AM GOING HOME! *You can't go home. You have work to do here! Let someone else. I'm going home.* Grace paced the length of her room and back, caught in a world of no sound, yet her mind yelling at her.

Mary Anne came and stood inside the door until Grace saw her.

"What?" At the child's crestfallen look, Grace stopped and took a deep breath before answering. "I am sorry. What is it?"

"Jonathan is worried about you. He's right outside the door."

"Tell him to come in."

"I can't. That would not be proper, and Mother would be upset."

And we cannot upset Mother. No one in Blessing ever had time to worry about upsetting Mor or Ingeborg or any of the other mothers. Except maybe Mrs. Valders. And she made a living out of being upset. People there got upset about cattle dying and prairie fires and drought. About too much rain, a hailstorm or . . . She paused in her inner diatribe. What would Mrs. Gould do if she got upset? Grace leaned her head back and stared at the ceiling. *I am upset and I can't do anything about it. Other than to turn the other cheek.* The verse she'd learned long ago flittered like a butterfly through her mind. *Whosoever shall smite thee on thy right cheek, turn to him the other also.* She laid the flat of her hands against her cheeks. She closed her eyes and thought of more of that Scripture. *And if any man will sue thee at the law, and take away thy coat, let him have thy cloak also.*

She'd been ready to give them a piece of her mind, not the cloak off her shoulders. *Love your enemies . . . do good to them that hate you, and pray for them which despitefully use you, and persecute you.* She felt a small hand tug at the fan dangling from her wrist. She looked down into Mary Anne's sad eyes.

"I don't know what made you sad, but me and Jonathan, we want to help."

Grace knelt in front of her. "You help all the time. I do not know how I could bear to be here were you not my friend."

Mary Anne stepped into her embrace and patted her back, then leaned backward to look into her face. "Come. Let's go to the library. No one else ever goes in there but Father."

Together the two walked out the door hand in hand. Jonathan studied her face, nodded, and took Mary Anne's hand.

"We're going to the library."

"Good."

"Can you tell me what happened?" he asked when they'd sat down in the chairs in front of the fireplace that now housed a huge bouquet of roses, the perfume filling the air. Grace inhaled the scent that brought back home, and the loneliness rose up like a fog.

"I read someone's lips and they said something that made me realize how much I don't belong here and how much I miss home."

"Who?"

"It is not important. If I am to make my way in life, I need to learn to turn the other cheek."

"Then they'll smack you on that one." Mary Anne sat on a hassock with her skirt wrapped tight over her knees. "Better to punch 'em back first."

"Don't let Mother hear you say that."

"I won't." She looked up at Grace. "You're not going to leave, are you?"

"Well, I'm hoping they choose to let me into school, and then I will most likely live there."

"You could live here, and McHenry would drive you to school like he does me and the boys."

"I think it is too far for that, but thank you." *Another day here feels impossible already, except for you and Jonathan.*

"You can come home on weekends." Mary Anne looked to Jonathan. "You could too."

"I'll be too far away to come home often, but I'll write you letters."

"Like you did this summer?" Her raised eyebrows said what she thought of his letter writing.

"I'm sorry. This will be different." He leaned forward. "I need to go back outside and make another appearance. Do you want to come, Grace, or stay here?"

"Grace and me will come soon."

"And I," Grace signed and said automatically.

"I said you. Oh. Grace and I."

Jonathan left the room, his shoulders shaking in what Grace knew to be mirth. Mary Anne gave those around there plenty to laugh about. What a shame that her mother failed to see the humor in her delightful daughter.

A few minutes later, feeling calmer, she pulled Mary Anne, who was practicing her signs, to her feet, and together they returned to the patio, where fewer people made it more pleasant. The younger people had moved out to where a croquet game was laid out and seemed to be having a good time. Some of the others had set up card games at two tables, and the rest were visiting while one portly gentleman slept in a chair off the flagstone and in the shade of the mulberry tree.

Grace saw that Jonathan and his father were talking with another gentleman she was sure she'd been introduced to but could not remember his name. At his mother's beckoning, she crossed to where Mrs. Gould sat with two of her friends, including Mrs. Wooster.

"Are you all right now?" Mrs. Gould asked.

"Yes, thank you." Grace started to make an excuse but decided not to.

"I am glad to hear that. Perhaps you would like to join the others." She motioned toward the game.

"I will observe from here. I do not know how to play."

"I will teach you," Mary Anne said. She had squeezed Grace's hand to let her know to look down.

"Could I bring any of you something to drink?" Grace asked.

"That's what—" Mrs. Gould cut off her comment.

"Yes, that would be lovely," Mrs. Wooster replied, her eyes twinkling. Her nod to Geraldine prompted a different ending.

"And me."

"Make that three," Mrs. Wooster added.

Grace caught her sideways glance, realizing she had missed a comment. Bless that woman. What a kind heart she had. She brought back three cups of punch, feeling like a little girl afraid to drop what she was carrying.

She started to turn away after their thanks, but Mrs. Wooster tapped her arm with her fan. Grace was beginning to realize that fans could be used for all kinds of things. "Yes?"

"Geraldine tells me you have an interview at the Fenway School on Monday."

Grace nodded and smiled her thanks to Mrs. Gould.

"I would be interested in accompanying you, if you would permit me. I know Mr. Gould and Jonathan will be with you, but I have a great curiosity regarding that school, thanks to you, and this way I could learn more firsthand."

Grace hadn't known both Jonathan and his father were taking her, but she smiled and responded in the only way she could. "Of course. I would be delighted." At the same time she was wondering why Mrs. Wooster would want to do that.

Later, after the guests had left and the family was gathered in the music room, Mrs. Gould leaned forward. "Do you know who Mrs. Wooster is?"

She actually looked animated, Grace realized, as if someone had given her a gift.

"A very kind lady who is interested in a great many things?" Grace had no idea what was the proper answer.

"Yes, she is that, but she also owns a goodly portion of New York City. And is renowned for her philanthropic activities. Perhaps she will decide to add the school for the deaf to her list of charities."

"That would be most generous of her." She smiled at Mary Anne, who came to sit beside her. "We might have to change the time of our lessons on Monday, then."

"That's all right." Mary Anne signed as she spoke.

"What's that you are doing?" her mother asked.

"Learning to talk in sign language. Grace is teaching me."

"Miss Knutson. I had expected just a few signals for communication's sake, not ongoing sessions. Mary Anne has enough trouble keeping up with her other lessons. You are to stop now." She looked at her daughter. "Understood?"

Mary Anne slumped in a sigh. "Yes, Mother. Miss Knutson."

Oh, Lord, please may the interview go well, or maybe not, so I can go home. But I cannot live here any longer. It is wrong to accept the Goulds' hospitality and have these feelings for Mrs. Gould. She seems to admire what Mrs. Wooster owns instead of the person she is.

⊷⊶

"So, Jonathan, what is it you wanted to talk to us about?" Mr. Gould took his favorite chair in front of the marble fireplace in the room designated as the men's room. Mrs. Gould entered also and settled herself in the chair next to her husband, her needlepoint in hand. She chose a new color and, after threading the needle, began to stitch. Jonathan was too nervous to sit.

He swallowed around the lump in his chest. He'd put this off as long as he dared, and here it was Sunday evening. He'd rather be playing chess with Daniel anytime, even though he always lost. Or talking with Grace, even though Mary Anne always accompanied her.

"I thought . . . I mean, I believe . . ." He stopped. This was far worse than he imagined. He sighed all the frustration out and started again.

"Father, Mother, I think I found what I want to do with my life, and the problem is, I'm not sure . . ." He wanted to say, "I am absolutely sure," but decided to couch his words in the least offensive way possible. He sucked in and exhaled another breath. "I'm not sure you will be as excited about my plans as I am."

"Plans are a good thing." His father templed his fingers and tapped them against his chin. "What is it you think we will not approve of?"

"Father, please remember that my going to North Dakota was your idea."

"I am aware of that. I made the choice after a lot of deep thought as to what might help you overcome your undisciplined ways."

Mrs. Gould shot her husband a look that Jonathan recognized as censorship. Although they never argued or even sharply disagreed in front of their children, Jonathan had learned to recognize the signs, and sometimes, if he were honest, he'd used them against his mother to get what he wanted. This discussion was too important to waste on games, however.

"I like farming. I liked the hard work and seeing something grow because I planted the seeds. I loved the smell of cut grass that became hay. I learned to string fence and care for the animals. I saw the heartbreak of losing the livestock, and I felt like I belonged in that small town with such heart that I can't describe it. I know you've always had a great deal of respect for the Bjorklunds and what they do. I want to join them, buy land and cattle and machinery, and . . ."

He heard his mother take in a horrified breath but kept his attention on his father.

"You think you learned enough this summer to take on a farm of your own?"

"No, not at all. I learned enough this summer to know that I need to learn a whole lot more. I can begin this in one of two ways: go to work for a farmer, like I did, or go to agriculture school and then work for someone else. Or, there is a third way. School first, then hire a manager with a lifetime of experience to teach me and work beside me."

"And where would this agricultural college be?"

"There is a good one in Grand Forks, North Dakota."

"Have you looked into anything in the eastern states?"

"No. From what I understand, farming the prairies is different from farming here."

"We have dairies in New York State, New Jersey, all over. In fact, I found the cows for you in Pennsylvania."

"I'm sure there are. But out there, you can see forever. The sky is a huge blue bowl, and storms come across those plains in dancing curtains of rain."

"The north wind blows down in the winter with blizzards and cold beyond your wildest imagination," his father added.

"I heard stories of it." At least Father isn't saying an out-and-out no. He sneaked a peek at his mother. The way the needle flashed in and out of her frame said as much as her pursed lips and wrinkled brow.

Mr. Gould leaned back in his chair and crossed one ankle over the other knee, elbows propped on the chair arms. "And what would you use as money to buy this farm? If there were a farm for sale."

"I have a sizable inheritance."

"That you would use for such an outlandish scheme as this? Your grandfathers worked hard to amass the money you would so glibly throw away," his mother put in.

Mr. Gould looked to his wife with a slight shake of his head and a glint in his eyes. She returned to her needlework, her back ramrod straight.

"Do you have any idea what it would cost to set up a farm like the Bjorklunds have?"

"No, sir. I've not talked to anyone else, because I felt it honorable to discuss this with you first."

"I see." He returned his relaxed foot to the floor and leaned forward again. "I have known for a long time that you have no desire nor the affinity to come to work in the company, like Thomas has done. Without purpose, I feared you could become a rake, and that would be a terrible waste. I hoped you would find your place and interest in college, in getting a good education."

Jonathan nodded. "I have. I've not said I do not want to go to college, have I?"

"No, you haven't, for which I am thankful. But I am not convinced that your plan is the best for you."

Jonathan started to say something but his father held up a hand.

"No, we'll not have a debate here, for I know you can out-debate me."

Jonathan knew he was referring to the times he'd brought home a topic from the debate squad at school and coerced his father into arguing with him.

"You can be most persuasive."

"Thank you, sir."

"I wonder too how much your desire to farm in North Dakota has to do with your attraction to Miss Knutson."

His mother drew in a loud breath. At least that idea hadn't occurred to her until then.

Jonathan sat down on the hassock and studied his hands. "I would like to think that I love farming, not the farmer's daughter. But I have to admit that I asked her father if I could court Grace, and he said yes, if she was willing."

"And?"

"I wanted to talk with you first."

Out of the corner of his eye he saw his mother drop her needlepoint into her lap and collapse against the back of the chair.

"She is not suitable. Not at all suitable." The words hissed out through her clenched jaw, much against his father's judgment, if the stern gaze he shot her was any indication.

Oh, Mother, if you would only see who Grace is inside, instead of judging her speech and lack of the social niceties. All those young women you deem suitable are so unsuitable to me. To think of one of them washing dishes or digging in the garden . . . well, some might do that one day, but I can't imagine any of them planting a garden to feed the family through the winter.

"Jonathan, your mother and I will do some talking and thinking about what you have said. In the meantime, I would appreciate it if you would continue to prepare for Princeton as you agreed."

Jonathan felt his shoulders curve inward to shield his heart. Had his father not listened? Of course he had listened. He'd been very polite, just as he was when running board meetings. Jonathan had gone with his father and older brother to some of those meetings. While Thomas had been excited about it, he'd wished he could be anywhere but there, preferring to be out on the shore in a sailboat, tacking before the wind. He had thought at one time of becoming a captain of a ship, but that slid away, as did becoming a surgeon. He'd always figured he would have to go into the family business someday, just like his brother and his male cousins. He heaved a sigh. At least Father had not said no and given orders that would be hard to accept. But now Mother would oppose him. Was there any hope after all?

A VISIT WAS ONE THING, but an interview quite another.

The carriage turned in to a drive not far from the Goulds', and the horses trotted up a slight grade to a house three stories high and with enough dormers and turrets and arched windows to resemble a castle she had seen in pictures. The Wooster mansion only lacked a moat. And she thought the Gould house ostentatious. She could feel Jonathan watching her. If only she could take his hand and feel some sense of comfort, of someone else in this with her. Yet she hadn't seen him since the party, and Mrs. Gould was quite cool to her. Except for Mary Anne and Fiona, it was as if she had suddenly become quarantined. And she had no idea what gaff she had done to merit even more exclusion.

When the carriage stopped, she watched the carved wooden door open and breathed a sigh of relief. She hadn't dreamed up this sprightly little lady who brightened the day just by appearing.

"You look lovely, my dear," Mrs. Wooster said as she was handed into the carriage. "Isn't this a wonderful day?"

And suddenly it was. Here, she was on an adventure that would make Sophie shiver in delight: a drive through New York City with amenable companions, a chance to see more of the sights, and an interview that could change her life. Not that it had not been tossed topsy-turvy already, but since she'd come this far, she could certainly go the next mile. Or however many it took.

After greeting the men, Mrs. Wooster looked to Mr. Gould. "I spoke with Joseph Ettinger—he is on the board for the Fenway School for the Deaf—and he said that they are actively pursuing benefactors for the school, not that every school in New York and probably everywhere is not. But they are not looking to expand so much as to redo what they have to make it more functional. The school is on the old Fenway estate, which I'm sure you already know."

"My mother's school is not looking for benefactors." Grace couldn't believe she'd joined the conversation, if that's what she had done. Ever since the fete she'd been hesitant to volunteer anything for fear of ridicule.

"Really? So your family supports the entire thing?"

"Well, those who come pay tuition and room and board. Much of the work around the school is shared by family and those old enough to help."

"How old must the students be to attend there?"

"Seven, but Mother prefers eight or nine. It depends on the child. How civilized they are. Many were barely manageable until they could begin to communicate more easily. One child had to have a keeper at first. Some adults have come too."

"Most schools have both adult and juvenile programs. The Fenway School does."

Grace could feel Jonathan's gaze upon her.

She turned in amazement at the rows of maple trees beginning to turn yellow and red and orange. As if God were dripping paint on them, she thought.

They'd left the city behind and now the road traveled between farms with views of the Hudson River through the trees. At one point they stopped at an inn to use the facilities and ate lunch from a basket Cook had packed for them. The conversation continued, with Mrs. Wooster making sure that Grace could understand her. Before long, Mr. Gould announced they were nearly there.

"This was so much more pleasant than the train," Mrs. Wooster commented. "Thank you for choosing to use the carriage."

"You are most welcome. I thought Miss Knutson might enjoy this too." He smiled at Grace from his seat with his back to the driver.

Grace nodded. But the nearer they drew to the school, the more she fought to keep her butterflies under control.

A bronze sign on a brick wall announced Fenway School for the Deaf, and the carriage turned onto a tree-lined drive. The building ahead lay somewhere between the size of the Gould mansion and the Wooster castle, with more the look of an English country manor she had seen in a magazine. A large black dog came to stand by the carriage when it stopped, its tail wagging, tongue lolling. If this was the welcoming committee, this could indeed be a good place.

When Grace stepped down, Mrs. Wooster put her arm through Grace's. "Aren't you excited?"

"Something like that."

"Never fear. This is the start of something momentous for you. I have a feeling you are about to realize God's purpose for your life."

Now I know why I feel at peace with you. You speak with God. Is that why I feel such a disconnect with Mrs. Gould? But what is God's purpose? Other than marriage and children? What was wrong with her first dreams anyway? *Remember, Toby is not in your dreams any longer.* When awake, she knew that and sometimes had to overcome the sadness again. At night her dreams still included him and a house or farm in Blessing. Or did they? She tried to think when she had last dreamed of Toby. Right now, even his face was blurred as she walked up the brick-laid path to the front door. In fact, too many of her dreams recently had included Jonathan, and that just couldn't be. Their worlds had no possibility of ever blending.

Mr. Gould rapped with the knocker twice before a woman, who looked to have been in a hurry, opened the door.

"Welcome to Fenway. I'm afraid we just had a bit of an emergency that had to be seen to." She stepped back and motioned them in. "I am Mrs. Callahan." She extended her hand to Mr. Gould. "And I am sure you are Mr. Gould and Mrs. Wooster." She smiled at Grace and signed as she spoke. "You must be Miss Grace Knutson. I am so pleased to meet you."

"This is my son Jonathan. He learned some sign when he worked in North Dakota this summer."

"I take it you are able to hear?"

"Yes, ma'am, but I wanted to be able to talk with Grace—er Miss Knutson more easily."

"An admirable effort. I wish more family members and friends felt that way." She turned. "Come along. I thought we would have tea and chat a bit first. Then I will show you the school." She signed and talked at the same time, her smile making Grace feel even more comfortable.

When they were seated and tea and coffee served, she turned to Grace. "I understand you have helped with your mother's school for the deaf."

"Yes. Mother learned to sign, thanks to Mr. Gould, who sent her a book to learn from. She taught me as she learned, then she taught the schoolchildren in Blessing and our pastor, who is also the school-teacher. Blessing is a very small community, and many of the people there learned to sign. Some of us are related, so that makes it easier."

"The deaf children go to the public school also?"

"When they can sign well enough and have learned how to live with others."

"I know how that is." Mrs. Callahan turned to the others. "Some children come here who've been cooped up like pets or beasts. They have behavior problems and a lot of anger. We need a program to inform the public that deaf people are not stupid and do not need to be hidden away. I am sure if we could test many of those in institutions, we would find some are deaf rather than insane." She passed the plate of cookies. "These were baked by some of our older students who manage the kitchen duties."

"You don't incur injuries because your students—er clients cannot hear?" Mr. Gould asked.

"We teach them to be careful and watch out for one another.

Some never want to leave here. The world outside is a frightening place for those born with handicaps."

"Do you teach lipreading also?" Mrs. Wooster sat on the edge of the sofa so that her feet could rest on the floor.

"Yes. But many have already learned a modicum of that skill; they have had to in order to survive. But with signing they can communicate in return."

"If others can sign."

"Right. I learned because my sister was born deaf, and I wanted to be able to talk with her. We learned together. She is one of our teachers now." She handed each of them a brochure with a drawing of the school on the cover. "Here is more information. I mailed you a packet of information, Mr. Gould. Did you receive it?"

"Yes, but I haven't had time to share it with the others." He smiled an apology at Grace.

"Mrs. Wooster, I have a packet here for you too if you like."

The door to the sitting room burst open, and two young girls erupted into the room, signing frantically. "Mrs. Callahan, there's a cow in the garden."

"So chase the cow out." Mrs. Callahan signed and spoke at the same time.

"But she is eating the corn."

"I'll be right back."

Jonathan stood up. "I'll help you." Together they went out of the room.

"It is easier to chase cows when you can yell at them."

Mrs. Wooster laughed. "I'm sure it is, but a big stick is not a bad idea either."

Grace wished she had gone too. But she hadn't, and now it was too late, so she sat looking around the comfortable room that had at one time been much more formal. The wallpaper and heavy drapes testified to that fact, while the furniture looked sparse without any knickknacks and whatnot tables. A low table in front of the leather sofa held books and a vase with hydrangea blossoms in rich blue. Mrs.

Callahan's desk had seen better days, and stacks of books on the floor attested to the overflow from the shelves.

By not watching Mr. Gould and Mrs. Wooster speaking softly, she was able to stay within herself and think on this move. She already liked the headmistress, and if the rest of the building was like this room, she knew she could be comfortable here. What would it take to be accepted? She began to read through the brochure. They had various levels for students. She wondered where she would fit. *God, if this is what you want for me, I thank you for taking care of making it happen. If not, I'll just go back to Blessing when Jonathan leaves for college.* That resolved, she looked up when she sensed the door opening again.

"I'm sorry for the interruption." Mrs. Callahan and Jonathan returned, he grinning and she laughing. "Thank you, young man. I'm surprised that someone with your background knew how to herd a cow."

"After my summer working on a farm in North Dakota, I can milk with the best of them now, among many other skills I had no idea I needed to learn." He took his seat again, shooting Grace a smile that made her feel warm all over. He had the nicest smile.

"Come, let me show you around."

The tour of the buildings didn't take long, since there weren't many students living there yet. There was a boys' dormitory in one wing and one for the girls in the other. Smaller rooms slept one or two for the older students, and there were some single accommodations for the adults, including the staff. The rooms were quite small, but each had a window, so if there was sun there would be light. *I wonder how dark they would be in winter. What would it be like to room with a total stranger?* Several cottages were for married staff. Classrooms took up a good part of the first floor, and a dining room had tables to seat everyone at once.

"We have a garden, flower beds, dogs, and cats, and a local farmer loans us horses if we have students who want to ride. His cow comes to visit whenever she can. She is a genius at getting through the fence."

"What part do the animals play in the school?" Mrs. Wooster asked.

"They add to a home atmosphere we try to provide. As we are a vocational school too, the animals help the students learn responsibilities they may meet once they leave. We have built on the ideas of the Industrial Home for Deaf Mutes in Massachusetts."

When they returned to the sitting room, Mrs. Callahan motioned to Grace. "Why don't we go in another room so we can talk. Please excuse us."

Grace followed her, Mrs. Wooster squeezing her hand as she walked by. It was a shame Jonathan's mother wasn't more like Mrs. Wooster.

Mrs. Callahan motioned for Grace to sit in a chair facing her. "You speak quite well for someone born deaf. You must have worked very hard."

"I—we, my mother, my sister, and I did work hard. And I keep practicing all the time. I know it is sometimes hard for others to understand me."

"I'm sure you've had some interesting experiences."

Grace half smiled and gave a little nod.

"I'm going to ask you some questions that might not make a lot of sense but will give me a good idea of your signing skill."

At the end of the questions, Mrs. Callahan complimented Grace on her dexterity. "You sign so gracefully too. You and your mother are to be commended. We have learned some new things that I know you will pick up easily." She studied Grace for a moment. "I'm wondering if you would consider being a teacher's assistant with second-level returning students. You can study with the advanced level students at the same time to improve your own skills. This would help with your school expenses, although I am not able to waive them all. Would this be satisfactory?"

"Why, I . . . ah, I am so surprised. But yes. Yes, I would like that." *And here I was afraid I would not even be accepted.* "How much would I need to pay?"

Mrs. Callahan named a sum, and Grace nodded again. Using her graduation money, she could pay most of it herself.

"Our first quarter lasts until Christmas. Could you possibly move here within a week?"

"As far as I know." *I wish it could be tomorrow.*

"Very good." She stood. "I am looking forward to working with you."

"But is this all?"

"I have learned that when I meet someone well qualified, I snap them up before someone else gets them. I don't usually get someone of your caliber just walking through my door."

Tears sprang up at her words. Within these walls Mrs. Callahan considered her of high caliber, whereas outside she was defective or inferior. She felt all the tension she had been holding in these many days slip away.

"Thank you. What do I need to bring?"

"Only your personal things. You will probably have a roommate, but I haven't assigned rooms yet. Mostly we wear waists and dark skirts. You will be responsible for your own laundry. If you want to bring anything extra for your room, like pictures or remembrances of home, just remember your roommate will have some too. We provide the books and all the school supplies."

Grace walked with her head high into the sitting room. "Could I move here within the week, or would that be an imposition?"

"Wonderful. Of course you can," Mr. Gould said as he rose.

"I will be a teaching assistant, so I can afford my own expenses."

"I told you I would gladly pay your way."

"You already did so with my graduation gift."

"We'll discuss this later. Good day, Mrs. Callahan. Mrs. Wooster and I will be in contact with you soon."

"Thank you." She showed them to the door. "Miss Knutson, please have someone call me to let me know when you can arrive."

"I will, Mrs. Callahan. Thank you so much."

"Congratulations," Jonathan said rather formally as they went down the walk.

She studied his face. Was he not happy for her? What was wrong? After all, this was why he brought her to New York, wasn't it?

27

Blessing, North Dakota

NO WONDER SHE WAS HAVING TROUBLE leaving the threshing crew in God's hands this year. Haakan had confessed not only to being tired, but he'd used the word *exhausted*. Was it age creeping up on him or was something wrong? And she'd kept missing Elizabeth to ask her opinion before the men left.

She glared down at the letter in her hand. She'd tried reading between the lines by lamplight for the last hour, because she'd awakened and not been able to go back to sleep. Usually when she woke in the night like this, she prayed for those who came to mind and went soundly back to sleep. But not this time. She stared out the window. Not even the tiniest crack of light in the east.

She picked up her Bible from the nightstand and flipped to Jesus' words: *I will never leave thee, nor forsake thee.* Usually they brought all the comfort she needed. *Lord, I know you keep your promises, and right now I ask you to heal whatever it is that is making Haakan feel so exhausted. Help him to sleep the deep sleep of healing and awake full of energy. I can't be there, but you are, and I have to trust you in this. You know my heart. I am having trouble with trust right now.* The same feeling she'd had at the slaughter of the cattle was poking at her, trying to take over.

"I do not live by feelings. I live by faith in Jesus Christ, the Son of the living God." She repeated the words aloud to re-brand them into her mind and heart. "My heavenly Father has plans for good and not for evil."

Will you trust me? floated in on the breeze that stirred the curtains.

"I will trust you. I will trust you. I do trust you. I am trusting you." She repeated the phrases as she refolded Haakan's letter and slid it back into the envelope. "Please bring him home safe."

She overslept for the first time since she couldn't remember when. Astrid had bacon fried and eggs ready to fry next, with bread toasting on the rack over the open back lid.

"I was about to go wake you. Are you all right?"

Ingeborg finished tying on her apron. "Ja. I woke up and couldn't go back to sleep. Then when I did, I guess my body decided to catch up." The cat chirped as he wound himself around her skirt.

Astrid pointed to the envelope on the table. "There's a telegram for you there."

Oh no. Ingeborg's heart fell even with her knees. "Why didn't you wake me?" She stared at the yellow paper as if it were a snake coiled and ready to strike.

"Don't worry, Mor. You'll like it. Were it about Pa, I would have brought it to you. Mr. Valders delivered it."

Ingeborg walked to the table and reached for the envelope. Since when did telegrams have good news?

DEAR MRS. BJORKLUND STOP PLEASE MEET MY EMIS-SARY AT WESTBOUND TRAIN TODAY STOP HAS SOME-THING FOR YOU STOP WITH DEEPEST GRATITUDE STOP DAVID GOULD

Ingeborg read it again and looked up to find Astrid watching her. "What do you think it is?"

"How would I know?" She flipped the toast onto a plate, slid two fried eggs and bacon next to it, and handed the plate to her mother. "Coffee will be ready in a minute or two."

"I was going to pickle beets today."

"I'll dig them right after we eat, and we can at least get them boiling. I have eggs to take to town, so we'll have to take the buggy."

"Meet his emissary? Something he couldn't just put in a box or crate and send?"

"Are we going to say grace?"

"Ja, of course." Together they repeated the prayer, their voices almost lost in the cavernous stillness of the house. Astrid got up to get the coffeepot and fill their cups.

"When do you think the crew will be home?"

"Your pa didn't say but most likely not for at least two weeks. He said the harvest is good, so that means they won't be home early. Thank you, Lord, for a good harvest." That would help compensate for the earlier losses. "I keep thinking I should start looking for cows to buy, but I don't even know where to begin."

"Andrew said he and Pa would go looking after harvest."

"He did? Well, nice to tell me."

"Maybe they were hoping to surprise you and I just let the cat out of the bag."

"Maybe. I'm thinking not to replace the sheep. We can buy a few fleece to card and spin our own yarn."

"We can buy already spun too, remember?"

"I know, but somehow that seems a waste."

Astrid propped her elbows on the table so she could hold her coffee cup to her lips more easily. "Mor, we have to keep up with the times. Would you want to give away your sewing machine, your washing machine?"

"Don't be silly." Ingeborg mopped the last of the egg yolk with her toast and pushed her plate away. "We need to watch those beans that are drying on the vines too. Might be time to pick them before they drop their seeds."

"You do that while I dig the beets. The beans can finish drying on the front porch." Astrid stacked the plates together and carried them over to put in the dishpan on the stove.

"Maybe I should go over and help Kaaren. Now with school start-ing, she and Ilse will be doing it all." She thought a moment. "And I think we'll take some of the beet greens in to Elizabeth. Inga really likes them."

"Inga really likes anything her grandmother likes."

Several hours later, with the cooked beets cooling, washed beet greens in a basket, and a crate of eggs for the store, they drove the horse and buggy down the lane. Usually they had at least one of the men home, but this year with no cows to milk and other livestock to take care of, even Trygve and Samuel had gone along. They'd be com-ing back soon to start school, but it saved hiring another man they could not afford. While school had already started, frequently the older boys began late due to harvest.

"I forgot to check the snare line." Astrid stopped the horse and turned around at the junction of lane and road. She had put it out the night before, since they were so low on meat. She stopped by the barn, climbed down and ran through the open pole gate to head for the riverbank, where Samuel usually ran a snare.

Ingeborg thought of going up to the house and slipping the skins off the boiled beets but instead leaned against the back of the seat, studying the empty barn. What if they didn't buy any cows until next year? But they had far more than enough hay for the horses. Was the return on the cheese business necessary? What if they let it go? The thought choked her like hands around her throat. The December shipments would clean out the cheese house.

"Dear Lord, what are we to do?"

One good thing about keeping excessively busy, one didn't have much time to ponder the future. As if her worrying would make one iota of difference.

Astrid came back shaking her head.

They wouldn't be having rabbit tonight.

When they heard the far-off wail of the train whistle, Astrid hup-ped the horse into a trot. But at Ingeborg's reminder of the eggs, she slowed him to a fast walk. They arrived at the station just as the train squealed to a stop. While Astrid tied the horse at the hitching post, Ingeborg walked to the platform.

When a man came down the stairs looking around, the only one disembarking, she walked over to him.

"Are you Mrs. Bjorklund?" He touched the brim of his felt hat.

"Ja, I am."

"I am Mr. Harry Burke, and it is my pleasure to bring you something Mr. Gould hopes you will receive without complaint."

"Without complaint?" *Whatever does that mean?*

"Come with me."

Astrid joined them, and they moved down the track to where a cattle ramp was being pushed up to the train car. Ingeborg and Astrid exchanged questioning looks until Mr. Burke appeared at the top of the ramp with a black and white Holstein cow on a tether and led her down. He handed the rope to Astrid.

"I'll be right back."

"A milk cow." Ingeborg couldn't get her mouth to shut.

Burke reappeared, this time with a gold and cream Guernsey. He handed Astrid another rope and walked back up the ramp.

Ingeborg took the rope and stroked the Guernsey's soft neck. Between the tears, she murmured, "Aren't you beautiful?"

This time Mr. Burke appeared with a young bull on a lead. "Both the cows are already bred, and this young fellow should be up to the job when he is needed. The Holstein is due in December and the Guernsey in February, so you should have milk clear through. Mr. Gould said to contact him if you decide to buy more replacement stock. He has a ready seller. Do you have any questions?"

Ingeborg sniffed and mopped her eyes with her free hand.

The station agent came out of the office, shaking his head. "Well, I'll be. Fine looking stock you got there. Wait until Haakan hears about this. You going to tie those three behind your buggy, or do you need some help getting 'em home?"

"I milked them this morning and poured the milk into a can. You want to take that too?"

Ingeborg turned to Astrid. "We'll have cream again and butter." She huffed a breath. "Thank you, Mr. Burke. You can tell Mr. Gould that his payment will come in December."

"That means a wheel of cheese," Astrid said to the man, who was about to argue.

"If you don't need me, I'm to go to the boardinghouse for a good dinner and catch the afternoon train heading east. Thank you, Mrs. Bjorklund, and the best to you."

Ingeborg watched him stride off. *Uff da, what a surprise.*

The station agent took the young bull's lead. "I'll tie up this one."

After leaving off the eggs at the grocery store, they drove by Elizabeth's with the basket of greens, and the three bovines put down their heads to graze at the grass in front of the fence.

Thorliff charged out the door. "What in the world?"

"A thank-you present from the Goulds." Astrid headed inside with the basket of greens. "We were going to stay but not now."

Thorliff looked the stock over, shaking his head and stroking his chin between thumb and forefinger, a trait he had picked up from Haakan. "Leave it to Mr. Gould."

Ingeborg pointed to the ten-gallon milk can. "From this morning's milking. Go get a container and I'll leave some with you."

"Gamma!" Inga shrieked from Astrid's arms on the front step.

"Coming." She turned to Thorliff. "You stay with the cows."

"We sure know who comes first around here."

"Never a doubt."

"Gamma, cows."

She kissed the rosy little cheek. "Yes, and milk for Inga and butter and cream and . . ." She took the child from Astrid and danced them around the yard in a circle. Astrid disappeared into the house again. "And pudding and cream pie and . . ."

"Gamma, pet cows."

"Not this time but soon."

Astrid returned from the house with Elizabeth in tow and a pot to pour the milk into.

"If only we had ice, we could make ice cream," Ingeborg said.

"We have ice," Elizabeth said. "I bought a block from the ice wagon yesterday."

"Good. Come for supper and come early enough to bring ice, and we will make ice cream. I'll let Kaaren and Ellie know."

Within a few minutes they were waving good-bye and slowly plodding home. Cows did not move fast.

After they let the animals loose in the corral, they leaned on the pole gate and watched the three drink from the tank and then walk around the corral, immediately pulling grass from between the lower rails.

"Should we let them in the pasture or put them in the barn to feed on hay?"

"What a quandary!" Ingeborg grinned at her daughter. "Maybe we should tether them up by the house and knock down some of that grass."

"Ingeborg!"

They heard Ellie call and saw her striding across the field with Carl on her hip.

"Come celebrate. We have milk and cows for more."

Barney outran them and ducked under the fence rail to go sniff his new charges. The bull backed off and shook his head while the cows ignored him and continued wrapping their long tongues around mouthfuls of grass and yanking it in.

"Now, if that isn't a lesson in life. The bull gets all huffed up, and the cows keep on doing what needs to be done."

"Mor!" Ellie and Astrid said at the same time, shock turning mouths and eyes into big Os.

That night Ingeborg wrote Mr. Gould a thank-you letter and told him how nice Mr. Burke had been, even to saving the milk in the can for that day.

The cows have settled in nicely, but then cows are easy to please—good pasture, a can of grain, and getting milked two times a day. Our cattle dog, Barney, was teaching them the rules here, and they were perfectly amenable to that. The girls named the bull Buster, and he is content in his pasture also. Kaaren said to thank you too, as now she no longer has to worry about milk for the schoolchildren.

The men are not back from threshing yet, but the boys will be home next week to start school.

We all miss Grace, and Jonathan created his own place in our hearts, so we miss him too. What a good worker that young man is. Again, our thanks, and we pray God's blessings on all that you do. You have been such a good friend to us all these years, and we thank you for that too.

With all gratitude,
Your friend,
Ingeborg Bjorklund

She knew Mr. Gould would not accept payment, even when they could afford it, since he had stipulated the stock as a gift. So how to repay him as a gift? Send a supply of cheese on a regular basis? Maybe Grace could let her know if, in fact, cheese was a regular part of the Gould family diet.

She addressed and sealed the envelope and propped it against the glass sugar and creamer Haakan had given her. Symbols of two important men in her life. Her sons were the symbols of their father Roald. She had kept the bit of the mule's bridle that they found and had given Roald's pocketknife to Thorliff. With no grave to wear a headstone, it was as though Roald Bjorklund had just disappeared from the face of the earth in that winter blizzard. Except in her memories.

Thorliff remembered some things about his real father and Kaaren of course remembered her first husband's brother too, but with Roald's brother Carl and his mother, Bridget, gone to heaven, his sister Augusta in South Dakota, and brother Hjelmer in Bismarck, there was no one else here who had known him well.

He had been a good man, stern and without much laughter. Duty came first, along with the drive for land.

She blew out the lamp, musing her way to bed, a bed that seemed empty without Haakan. "Come home soon," she whispered into the night air as she looked at the stars. "Father God, watch over him." A chill shivered up her spine, and she crawled under the sheet. "Please bring him home safe."

28

New York City

THE HOUSE SEEMED EMPTY WITHOUT HER.

"I miss Grace." Mary Anne leaned against Jonathan's knee as he sat in a chair out on the flagstone terrace, reading.

"Me too."

"When you go to Princeton, I'm going to be all alone."

"How can you say that? David and Daniel are still here."

She gave him a look that made him nod.

True, they didn't have a whole lot to do with their little sister. In fact, even when they were home, the rest of the family seldom saw them. They went to a different school than Mary Anne did, and David was hoping to move to a prep school if his father and mother agreed on it. So far, that wasn't happening.

"Do you have to leave on Sunday?"

"Yes. I should have already left."

"But you don't want to go to school there."

"How do you know?"

"I heard you and Father talking."

"Eavesdropping?"

She had the grace to look down, glancing at him out of the corner of her eye. "How else would I know things? Nobody ever tells me anything."

"That's because you are not supposed to be out of the nursery yet."

If looks could scorch, he'd still be smoking. He grinned at her and grabbed her hand. "Let's go play badminton."

"You have to hold the racket in your left hand."

"All right. I suppose you want me to play blindfolded too?"

"Would you?"

"No."

That evening Jonathan's father called him into the study. "I think it is time we picked up our conversation again."

"Yes, sir." Jonathan took the chair his father indicated. Why did he feel like the character in Edgar Allen Poe's story, strapped down on the table with the pendulum swinging back and forth, coming closer with each swing?

"I've been giving our discussion a great deal of thought."

"As have I."

"Good." He paused. "And you've decided you can't wait to get to Princeton?"

His father smiled slightly, so Jonathan knew he was teasing. Perhaps there was hope after all. "No, but I have a proposition to offer." Where had those words come from? He'd never put his ideas into that form before.

His father templed his fingers and tapped his chin. "Go ahead."

"I will go to Princeton and give it my best effort—for one year." His father nodded. "And if at the end of that year, I still have a strong pull to learn about farming, I will transfer to an agricultural college."

His father's slow nod and thoughtful stare sent hope shooting from heart to brain.

"I trust you will keep your word on doing your best?"

"I always keep my word. You taught me there is no other way to succeed."

"Have you looked into other colleges?"

"No, sir. But I will send for information. I thought perhaps you might do the same."

"Your mother is very much against this plan, and I understand her dismay. You are her favored son, and she has high hopes of a good marriage for you and great success in both society and the business world."

"I thought that's what I was looking forward to also, but you sent me to North Dakota, and this is what happened."

"She fears that Miss Knutson is the reason you want to take up farming."

"Father, I love Grace, and I want to marry her. As I have not yet spoken to her about this, she has no idea. But that is not why I want to farm. I want to do something that matters."

"You think what I do does not matter?" His eyebrows rose to arches.

"No, but what Mother sees for me in society does not make any difference to those around unless I commit some misconduct and set the entire gentility into a dithering of gossip."

"You have a poor view of your peers."

"I have lived with my peers, and I know their games well. How you manage not to succumb into all that amazes me."

"That is one of the values of wealth, both earned and inherited. I am free to follow my own interests. I am fascinated by railroads and industry. Money equals power, and power used correctly and wisely can make a big difference in this country and society."

"You have a son who wants to follow in your footsteps. In Europe, the second son goes into the priesthood or the military."

"Touché." His father sat forward. "I will agree to your program. I want monthly reports and high scholastic achievement. You will be asked to join a fraternity and get involved in sports. Whether you want to do either is up to you, but if your grades slide, then our agreement is moot and we will have another discussion. In the meantime, I understand your infatuation with Miss Knutson, but you are both too young to think of marriage, so please do not inform her of your feelings."

The word *infatuation* stung like a hornet, but Jonathan clamped his teeth on that and heaved a sigh of relief. He had mountains to climb, but at least they were his mountains. "May I continue to write to her as a friend?"

His father nodded.

"Thank you, Father. I will do my best."

"And I expect no less. I have a feeling you really don't know what best you are capable of yet. Most young people don't at your age." Mr. Gould stood and shook hands with his son. "I will inform your mother—after you leave."

"Thank you, sir." He felt lighter already. Even one day spent in the house when his mother was in a disapproving state was more than he wanted to endure.

When he refused to have a going-away party, his mother stared at him. "But don't you want to say good-bye and good luck to your friends?"

She doesn't realize how many invitations I've turned down in the last few days. He smiled at her and tried to resume his old happy-go-lucky attitude, but he could see she didn't understand. "That's all right, Mother. I've said good-bye to the ones that matter the most." *Grace and Mary Anne.* The others had slipped away, since he chose not to go out to the shore for the last round of before fall celebrations. Out of sight, out of mind seemed an apt phrase as far as he observed. Had he gone along and resumed all his old activities, they would have welcomed him with open arms, but since he didn't . . . Besides, he'd been busy searching for agricultural colleges to attend after his year at Princeton.

He allowed his mother to oversee the packing of his trunks and making sure he had all she was sure he was going to need, including enough formal wear to warrant an extra trunk. Did she think there were balls every night at Princeton? It was not like Harvard, where Thomas had gone, and even there, that wasn't the case. Just hopeful thinking on his mother's part, he guessed.

Once on the train to Princeton, he took out his leather writing case, a gift from his father, and started another page for his letter to Grace. He'd already told her about the agreement between himself and his father. At least most of it.

I'll have to mail this soon or they will charge extra postage. I am on my way south and relieved to have left all the folderol behind me. I wanted to come see you one more time before I left, but there was no time. I spent one day with my father at his office, and it showed me even more clearly that is not where I am meant to be. How I would have loved to see Mrs. Bjorklund's face when the cows and young bull arrived on the train. Mr. Burke said she was raining tears and Astrid's eyes were bright as well.

What have you heard from Blessing? How is your school going? Do you have a tremendous amount to learn? I am full of questions and cannot wait to read a letter written by you. I feel like I've known you for years instead of months.

He closed his eyes and sighed. How he would love to tell her how important she was to him, but he had given his word.

I know building close friendships takes time, so ours will be a long-distance one until I see you in New York again—at Christmastide.

> Your friend,
> Jonathan D. Gould

❧

Grace picked up her pen and dabbed it in the ink. She wasn't sure when Jonathan was going to leave for college but hoped her letter reached him before he did.

Dear Jonathan,

Since before New York, I had never been five miles out of Blessing. Every day here is a new adventure. The students have not yet arrived, so the teachers and assistants are in classes training to teach. Being with others who communicate only with sign, I am afraid I might forget how to speak, but my signing is improving, and I am learning new things. There are some signs now for whole words, which makes communication easier and flows more quickly.

I hope this finds you before you leave for Princeton, but I am sure Mary Anne will make sure there is the proper address on it if not. I cannot thank you enough for encouraging me to come. I will have so much more to use in our Blessing school from my time here. I promised to write to Mary Anne too. Your little sister is a very special young lady, no matter how hard she tries not to be.

Your friend,
Grace Knutson

Dear Mother,

I know you will be happy that I have pledged with the Chi Phi Fraternity, as you hoped. I almost decided to remain independent, but as both you and Father have said, I will make lifelong friends and contacts here.

I have a full schedule and believe I will go out for the rowing team. That is one of the reasons I pledged with this house. They offer a quality training program. I didn't get a lot of choices in studies. Freshmen rarely do.

I hope all is well at home. Tell Mary Anne I will write to her soon.

Your loving son,
Jonathan D. Gould

Grace read her first letter from Jonathan. When she saw the masculine handwriting, she thought immediately of Toby but then reined herself in. Toby would not be writing to her. Toby had no idea where she was even if he did want to write to her. Besides, she reminded herself, Toby said he was in love with someone else. Why did her mind keep going back to him? He just popped back up at the oddest times.

Jonathan was at college, and though Princeton didn't look that far away on the map, there would be no visits. He'd signed his letter *Your friend*. Somehow she'd had the idea that he would like to be more than just friends, but maybe he had changed his mind. She sure hadn't given him any encouragement, especially when she realized how out of place she was in his world. Yet being with him brought joy, excitement, and laughter.

Put thoughts like that away, she told herself. *His mother does not like you at all*. She had made that very clear. Talk about being icy polite. She had that down to a fine art. She wanted a wealthy and prestigious match for her son, not a farm girl from North Dakota who couldn't hear and talked funny.

She folded her letter and put it in the drawer with the ones from home. After bundling her hair in a snood, she made her way downstairs to the dining room. Supper was ready for serving, and she was head of the table tonight. That meant she had to initiate conversation, which would have to be minimal because it was hard to eat and sign at the same time.

If only she weren't so homesick that she sometimes cried herself to sleep at night, it would be almost perfect. At least she had a room of her own—not that a roommate would hear her crying. She hadn't heard from Sophie, even though Grace had apologized for blowing up at her sister before leaving and again in a letter. She hadn't heard from Astrid either, who should have had more free time. Only one letter from her mother, not that there had been time to get much mail, but still she thought every hour of getting on a train heading west. She had been just getting used to things at the Gould house when she suddenly had to move to the school. The relief at leaving Mrs. Gould's politeness had mixed with an onset of the fear of going into a totally new environment. She'd done it, pasting a smile on her face the entire time. *But.* That was always the word. Did she dare tell Jonathan how she really felt? Did she dare tell anyone how she really felt? Especially after the Goulds had been so good to her, showing her around, giving her a new wardrobe, helping her find the school. And there was Mrs. Wooster. She really needed to write a letter to her too.

29

Blessing, North Dakota

THEY'RE HOME. THE MEN ARE HOME. Ingeborg whipped her apron over her head and ran out the door and down the back steps, waving her apron all the time. Wait until Haakan saw the surprise. She wanted to see his face. Oh, she wanted to see all of the dear him.

The steam engine leading the parade chugged its ponderous way to the bottom of the lane, where Haakan swung down from the cab and, waving to Lars, strode up the half overgrown road. He waved his hat to Ingeborg and then caught a ride in Andrew's wagon as it turned in.

The wagon had high sides, not the usual grain wagon. Ingeborg met them at the barn and threw herself into Haakan's arms, hugging him so tight neither one of them could breathe well.

"This is the last year. I don't want you going away like this anymore. I don't." She wiped her eyes on his shoulder and patted his back. "You've lost weight."

"Leave it to my Inge, worrying about me already."

"Already? You think I haven't stopped praying for you the whole time you were gone?" She placed her palms on either side of his face and peered into his eyes. "Are you all right? I've had this terrible feeling."

"Just tired. Andrew, show your mor what we bought."

Ingeborg looked between the slats of the wagon to see three young hogs. "Aren't they handsome." She clapped her hands to her cheeks. "You must come see *our* surprise." She took both their hands and dragged them around to the corral. "Meet Buster. Belle and Bonnie are waiting outside the back door to be milked."

Haakan and Andrew stared at the bull, who gazed placidly back at them while chewing his cud. "Where? How?"

"Come on!" She threw open the barn door to see the two cows waiting outside the barred back doorway. "They already know when milking time is. I was just about to come out."

"A Holstein and a Guernsey? Where did you get them?" Andrew asked.

"At the train."

Haakan stared at his wife. "At the train? In Blessing?"

"Ja. Mr. Gould sent them. A thank-you gift."

"This isn't just a gift. This is life again. We'll have milk and cream again. Hallelujah!"

"I've sent milk around to those with children. All of Blessing is blessing Mr. Gould. We churned butter today, twice. Both of the cows are bred, but Mr. Gould knew we'd need a bull, so he sent Buster too. When he gets a bit older."

"And to think I was wondering what we were going to feed those hogs."

"Let me go on home and see Ellie and Carl, then I'll come back and milk." Andrew gave his mother an arm-around-the-shoulders hug. "That's some surprise."

"You stay with your family. I can milk."

"Your mother and I can milk."

"Are we having a fight over who gets to milk the cows?" Andrew said with a laugh, heading for the wagon. "I'll put the pigs in my barn. See you tomorrow."

"You let our ladies in and I'll go get the buckets."

Haakan gave her a pat on the back of her skirt and headed to unbar the door, talking to the two cows, introducing himself.

"The Guernsey is Belle. She's the one wearing the bell." Ingeborg paused at the door. "Kind of a giveaway."

"Okay."

Okay? Haakan had picked up a new word. She knew what it meant and had heard it used before, but not by her husband. *They're home! They're home! Thank you, Lord, thank you.* She half danced her way to the well house. They had cows and hogs and, most important, each other. *Thank you, God. They are home!*

They caught up some on the news while they milked, the song of the milk in the bucket so welcome, as was the sound of cows munching their grain—all the normal sounds that had been missing.

Ingeborg listened to Haakan tell her about some of the farmers they had threshed for, many of them reeling from the loss of their livestock too. They'd traveled a long way west before there were cattle in the fields and hogs to be bought.

"The Missouri River seems to be the line of demarcation. I talked to one man about buying one of his milk cows, but he was holding out for more than I was willing to pay."

"Have you thought of going back east to buy stock?"

"You sound like you have an idea."

"Might be a way to regain some of our loss. If you brought back several railroad cars filled with livestock, you could maybe get a better buy. Then you could have an auction here in Blessing. Advertise it all over. What do you think?"

"I think I have a very smart wife."

"We could sell to our neighbors at cost. We don't need to make money on them."

"I'll talk with Lars in the morning. I'm sure Thorliff would take care of the advertising." He stood up, removing the bucket of milk and the stool in the same easy motion he always used, but the next thing Ingeborg knew, he was leaning against the barn wall.

"Haakan, what is it?"

"Just stood up too fast. Be fine in a moment."

"When did that start?"

"Some time ago. Long as I move a bit slow, I'm okay." He proved it by hanging the stool on the peg on the wall. "Just getting old, I guess."

Getting old, my foot. That has to be his heart. I'm digging some fox-glove tonight. Soon as it dries, I can pound it to powder. Her mind was off and running on how much of the powder to give him and wondering if the leaves steeped for tea might not help too. *How do I get him to see Elizabeth?*

When she'd stripped the last drop from Belle, she handed her bucket to Haakan and moved to the cow's neck to pet her. "You are beautiful. You know that? I thank God every day for you." The Holstein next to her turned and looked at Ingeborg, as if to say, "My turn too, you know." So Ingeborg stroked both their necks and inhaled the sweet fragrance of healthy cow. So many of their other cows had been raised from calves right on their own place and had become almost members of the family. But these two were a gift, a constant reminder of friendship and God's grace.

She flipped open the stanchions and watched as they both backed up, turned, and made their way to the back door and down the ramp. So many things to be thankful for.

After pouring the milk through the strainer, they set the cans in the cold water, washed out the buckets and tipped them upside down on the shelf to drain, and then shut the door behind them, making their way to the house arm in arm.

"Where's the cookshack?"

"Mrs. Geddick wanted to take it home and clean it up. That woman is such a worker and good cook. Even without butter, milk, or cream, she fed us right well. Ate more rabbit than usual, bought chickens and eggs when we could. Lars shot some grouse out of a tree one night, and we had a feast the next day. Reminded me of our early days here, before we had all that we have now. Ate a lot of beans and rice too."

Ingeborg rattled the stove's grate and added sticks of pitch wood to the coals. "I'd have had supper ready had I known you were near. How does scrambled eggs and toast sound?"

"Anything sounds good. Where's Astrid?"

"At Elizabeth's. Garth Wiste's nephew Nathan fell out of a tree and broke his leg. Astrid's sitting with him tonight. Poor little guy, pretty painful. When I left, she was reading to him."

"That part of her nurse's training?"

"Most likely." She broke eggs into a bowl, beat them to a froth, and added cream and salt and pepper. "I take it those hogs are for breeding?"

"The little boar is from a different farmer, so we can use him when the time comes. I wanted to buy more to raise for butchering but—"

"You could bring home a train car of feeder hogs too. Or butchering size."

"We'll be able to buy hanging halves of pork and beef most likely."

She set the rack over the open back lid and sliced bread for toast. "I tell you, when that first cream soured, Astrid, Ellie, Kaaren, and I made pigs of ourselves spreading that cream on bread and adding chokecherry syrup. Food fit for a queen."

"If we can't buy much meat and there's no hunting, it might be kinda slim around here this winter."

"Remember how Metiz taught us to dry fish? We can do that again."

"I thought of going up into Canada to see if we can bag a moose or two there. Maybe it was too cold up there for the disease to go that far."

She set his plate in front of him and hers across the table. When she sat down, he reached his hands across the table, and she laid hers in his. "I Jesu navn . . ." When they said the amen she squeezed his hands. "Mighty few times it's been just you and me like this."

He nodded and spread jam on a piece of toast. "Any chance we could heat up some water so I can have a bath?"

"I think that can be arranged—if you can stay awake long enough?"

"It doesn't have to be too hot."

He brought in two buckets of water and poured them into the boiler she had set on the stove.

"You want more coffee?"

"With cream?"

"You never drink it with cream."

"I know, but when you go without something for a long time, it becomes more precious."

She looked up to see him studying her, love shining in his Bjork-lund blue eyes. Her heart did a twirl, and she reached up to pat his cheek, and then leaned into his side. How good to have a man who knew how to love and wasn't afraid to show it. He must let them find out what was wrong. She couldn't bear the thought of his leaving her soon. *Please, Lord, heal him.*

30

New York

Dear Mor and Far,

Thank you for your letter. I was beginning to think you had forgotten me, even though I knew you were busy with the new school year starting. Are you sure you don't need me more at home than here? As always, I like working with the younger children the most, although the adult program here is very interesting also. There is a man in the class, Jeremy Penderwick, who has already professed his undying love for me. I, of course, call him Mr. Penderwick, and had to show him the signs for him to declare his love, which might have reduced some of his ardor. He is forty if a day, so you needn't fear my reciprocating his love. I won't tell him that he seems more an uncle in my mind than a suitor.

Grace smiled to herself as she wrote about Mr. Penderwick. Round was the word she most often used to describe him. He even bounced instead of walking sedately. While he had learned to read lips, signing was giving him a way of communicating other than writing notes. She returned to her letter.

How are the twins? You must tell me about them, for

Sophie has forgotten how to write letters. I know she is busy with her family and the boardinghouse but . . .

Forgive me. I wasn't going to complain.

You'd think by now that I'd know Sophie well enough not to expect things like letters. But in spite of telling herself that, hurt crept in, seeping around her defenses like smoke, nearly invisible until you smelled it. Was Sophie still holding a grudge even though she'd said she understood? For all the times Grace had forgiven her, it seemed that Sophie could at least try. But these thoughts were the kind that caused the outburst in the first place. *I guess I still need more work on keeping my thoughts captive to the Lord.*

Tell the boys hello from me. I think of all of you so often and wonder how you are faring with the lack of meat. We eat a lot of soup here, mostly for the evening meal. The people on the staff are friendly, but so far I've not made any close friends. I feel like I'm still here on approval or something.

What I can't say to you, dear Mor, is that I am so lonely I wake up crying in the night. Her gaze focused on the letter propped in front of her, the one she would answer when she finished writing home. She reread her letter, almost tearing it up since it sounded whiny to her, but instead signed her name and folded it for the envelope.

With a whispered sigh of delight, she removed the sheet of stationery with Jonathan David Gould, Esq., embossed at the top and started reading—for the third time, at least. What a release from the continuing ache when his letter had arrived. It had seemed forever for classes to end that day so she could read it.

Dear Miss Knutson,

See, I can be proper if and when I choose to, but to me you are Grace, pure Grace.

Her heart caught—again—on those two words. *Pure Grace.* In the eyes of her family she was Always Grace or Grace Always. The two words had become almost synonymous but no longer. Was that why Sophie had not written to her? Because she had erupted like a volcano when Sophie had said, "But Grace, you always ..." Such a simple statement was surely not a good excuse for the way she'd acted. *Dear Sophie, will you ever forgive me? I understand now how lonely you must've been when Hamre was out on the boat and you were alone and sick.* She returned to her letter. Rereading Jonathan's letter was far more comforting than reliving the last fiasco in Blessing.

I am settling in to college life, although I look at things differently than before I went to Blessing. The high jinks of my fraternity brothers are more a bother than fun, making it hard sometimes to study with the noise and confusion. If I had my way, I would have a room up on the top floor with no space for a roommate, not that our present quarters are large by any means. At least Thomas had prepared me for much of this. I do enjoy the rowing. I am part of a four-man crew, but I enjoy rowing alone the most. Not that I have a lot of time to think, since I am always pushing for better times. All the work I did on the farm was the best preparation I could have found anywhere. I am far stronger than most of the other freshmen. Perhaps we should make farm work a prerequisite for college or even high school sports. Do you think your father and Mr. Bjorklund would approve?

Grace tried to picture a whole team of society sons working on the farm and started to giggle. It would be like the chaos when the sow let the piglets loose.

I am doing as I promised. My grades so far are at the head of the classes. When I get tired, I remind myself of the high stakes and keep the light on.

Just how high were the stakes, Grace wondered. She knew he had to get good grades for his father to approve his changing schools, but he still hadn't told her where or why.

I hope you are enjoying your school and will find a good friend soon. I so look forward to seeing you again at Christmas. I want to show you New York City, all decked out in her finest.

Your devoted friend,
JDG

She read the last two lines again. *Devoted friend.* Maybe there was more to think on here.

The next morning, Miss Parke, the teacher she assisted, handed her a note from the head of the school. *Please see me in my office as soon as you are finished with this class.*

What could I have done wrong? was her first thought. Ever since her stay with the Goulds, she found herself questioning all her actions. At home she always knew what to do. Now she always felt under scrutiny and was exhausted. Something was wrong at home. This thought flashed like a lightning bolt across her mind. But surely if it were an emergency, the woman would have said so immediately. Comforted, she joined the work with the children. *What can it be?* popped in more than she desired.

While older children were boarded at the school, the younger ones came each morning and went home at night. Patiently she helped them form their fingers into the signs, applauded when they remembered the work from the day before, and rocked one who dissolved into tears of frustration.

At the end of the morning session one little girl came up and signed, "Thank you." Grace signed back, "You are welcome," and the little one skipped out the door. Her mother was coming to the evening class for parents to learn signing, one of the changes Grace already planned to put into effect once she went home. It would be much easier to have one class for the parents instead of the tutoring she and Mor usually did with the adults. And then they could open Blessing School for the Deaf to even younger students.

"I'll let you know what happened." She spoke the words for a change, since Miss Parke was not deaf but had learned sign because of a deaf brother.

"I think it will be something good."

"Why?"

"I just do."

For some reason Grace felt more hopeful as she made her way to the main office.

"Good morning, Miss Knutson," the assistant said. "Mrs. Callahan is waiting for you. Go right on in."

"Thank you." Grace sucked in a deep breath as she knocked on the oaken door before opening it. When she peeked around the door, she saw Mrs. Wooster, whose smile warmed her right down to her toes.

"Come in, come in." The elderly woman held out her ring-laden hands.

Grace felt like she should curtsy but instead she took the woman's hands and pressed gently. "What a pleasure it is to see you again."

"My pleasure, and I have so much to tell you. Mrs. Callahan and I have been in constant contact, and thanks to you, I will be able to fulfill some of the needs of this school."

"But I didn't do anything."

"Oh, yes you did. You are giving an old woman a whole new lease on life. After all, what is money good for if you can't use it to make a difference in this world?" Mrs. Wooster's faded blue eyes lit up. "I hadn't given schooling for the deaf any thought until I met you." She motioned to a chair. "Bring that over, and Mrs. Callahan, would you please order tea? I find that I think better with a cup of tea in my hand. Perhaps, dear Grace, you would like to take notes."

"I'll order the tea, but I think Grace would have a better time if she can concentrate on what we are discussing instead of the notes."

"Oh, of course, how silly of me."

Sometime later, when the conversation slowed, Grace took a deep breath and asked, "Am I understanding this right? You want to duplicate the program here at my mother's school in Blessing?"

"Yes, if she would be willing to do that. All the research I have done has made me aware that we need schools like this all across the country. Too many people cannot afford to come east, nor should they have to."

"And you plan to give training for job skills, like Mor has done, only on a more extensive plan?"

"Your Jonathan has given me ideas."

The fact that he was not "her Jonathan" seemed minor at this point, but the comment still made her want to smile. After all, "her Jonathan" had signed his letter *Your devoted friend*.

"Your mother's school has woodworking training, farm labor, and mechanics for the boys, homemaking skills, sewing, and knitting for the girls, correct?" At Grace's nod, she continued, "What if we added bookkeeping and secretarial skills?"

"But there is no space for that kind of thing. Our school is in our home."

"I understand that, but is there room to build more buildings?"

Grace thought a long moment. Putting up more buildings would take up the farmland. What would her father think of that? And the Bjorklunds, for that matter? Everything they did, they did together.

Grace finally answered the question. "Yes, there is land, but my family farms that land. If we used a wheat field for buildings, there would be less wheat grown. You would need to talk with them and explain what you are thinking."

"Of course. Do you suppose they would like an expense-paid trip to New York City to see their daughter and discuss this with me?"

"I think Mor would want to come, but who would run the school in her absence, since I am here? My father has no desire to travel away from Blessing except to work the wheat harvest."

"I see. So we would need to take the plan to the mountain."

Grace shook her head. "There are no mountains near Blessing."

"I'm sorry. That was a bad application of an old saying. I will start by writing to them first thing tomorrow, and I will tell them of our delightful visit. Now I have another question for you."

Grace waited, her hands clasped loosely in her lap. She watched Mrs. Wooster for the slightest indication of what it might be.

"My question is this: Do you believe my investing in the school in Blessing would be a good thing or a bad thing?"

Dear Lord, please give me wisdom, and I need it right now. She looked around the lovely room with the intricate rugs on the floor, a bowl of rust-colored chrysanthemums on the low table, the rich velvet curtains, pulled back now but ready to cover the windows to help keep out the cold at night. Paintings hung on the walls, lit by gaslamps that gave far more light than the kerosene lamps of home. This place had been the home of a wealthy family, and it showed.

"Would it have to be just like this—this fancy?"

"Why, I don't know. Do you not like the beauty of this place?"

"I-I do, but you see, Blessing is a welcoming, homey kind of place, where people all know one another and take care of one another. The students who come there become part of the community like everyone else, since as soon as they can sign adequately, they attend the Blessing school for regular classes. Mor feels that helps them learn to live with everyone rather than being set apart." Where she found all those words, she'd never know. "And they attend the Blessing Lutheran Church along with the rest of us. They are part of a family."

"But you do not feel part of a family here?" Mrs. Callahan signed and spoke both.

Grace felt as though she were wading through North Dakota mud that stuck to her shoes and weighed her down. "I think it is easier to feel part of a family when the family is smaller."

"That is a very good point, something to think on even further." Mrs. Wooster leaned over and patted Grace's clenched hands. "I am grateful you think and speak so honestly. I know there are ways around all the barriers. We will just have to find them."

She paused, studying something only her eyes could see. "I will start with a letter." She turned to Mrs. Callahan. "And we will begin to put our plans in operation here immediately. I will meet with an architect in the next few days and will bring you the plans when he has finished."

"This is most generous of you. I-I hardly know what to say."

"The more we can train teachers, the more we will change the lives of those without hearing. Thank you for giving me this opportunity."

"Would you like to stay for dinner?"

"No thank you. Not today but perhaps another time. I am meeting with Mr. Gould later this afternoon."

Grace darted a look of question at Mrs. Wooster.

"Yes, Jonathan's father. He is interested in my projects as well. It never hurts to have wealthy men working with one. He has opened many doors for me through the years." She rose and beckoned for Grace to walk beside her. "I would much rather lean on a young arm than on that cane of mine. One must have at least a little pride at my age."

She took Grace's arm, and they followed Mrs. Callahan, who held open the door. "I'll telephone you when I am coming again. In the meantime, if there is anything else you would like to add to that list, now is the time to be thinking on it."

"I cannot thank you enough."

"You will help change lives, just as you've been doing for the last ten years. This will just multiply your efforts. Good day."

Mrs. Wooster paused on the stone steps that led down to the gravel drive where the carriage waited, the horses dozing in the sun and light breeze. Autumn had been busy with a paintbrush in the tops of the maple and oak trees, splashing reds, rusts, oranges, and yellows about like a child playing in water. The older woman inhaled with a look of delight. "Nothing smells like fall but fall, and out here the air is so clean it sparkles. Not like in the city." She turned and took both of Grace's hands. "Thank you for humoring an old woman. I will be in contact soon."

"Thank you." Grace felt lighter than she had in days. Maybe instead of crying over what was missing in her life, she should copy Mrs. Wooster and look at the new opportunities instead.

Mrs. Wooster patted her cheek. "And you greet that handsome young man of yours for me. I have a feeling he is going to work into this plan somewhere."

Grace started to say he wasn't her young man but refrained. After all, the way things were going today, who had any idea what could come of the future?

Princeton University
Princeton, New Jersey
November

Dear Father,

We are two months into this semester and I am pleased to say that my grades are remaining at the top in most of my classes. There is one student ahead of me in Greek. I might complain of nepotism, since there is a family relationship, but I will just have to work harder, even though I see no value in learning Greek for a future farmer. My sciences, which might be helpful in some arcane way, are a joy. I am sure that Mother is going to hear any day now that I have been conspicuously absent from the balls and society entertainments. If she questions you, plead hard work as my defense. I just cannot see any sense in spending an entire evening and into the early morning dancing and imbibing. The aftereffects are evident around me, and while I am not a prude and engaging in holier-than-thou practices, I am getting questioning looks.

I have enclosed a list of agricultural colleges for your perusal. The college in Iowa looks interesting, but I still think Grand Forks would be a better option, because they are working with the same soil and climate conditions as Blessing. It is still my first choice, and the overall relationship of the community is so supportive. Maybe I'm wrong and other communities weathered the hoof and mouth plague with as much compassion for one another, but it seems unlikely to me.

I have spent some time assisting the groundskeeper and gardener here on campus. He is a wealth of information on both gardening and field planting, so my learning extends beyond the classroom.

Jonathan paused, thinking of Henry Osbourne, who could make anything grow but words. Unless one wanted to talk horticulture. Jonathan had spent much of Sunday in Henry's presence, planting seeds and transplanting rooted cuttings in the greenhouse. The man even made his own soil.

Give everyone my love and tell Mary Anne that there is a package coming her way that does not have to wait until Christmas to be opened.

Your son,
JDG

Jonathan stretched his arms over his head, pulling against one wrist and then the other. He glared at the three books waiting to be read. More coffee was indeed the answer.

He ambled down the stairs to the dining room, where Mrs. Maguire, their housemother, was just putting out a fresh pot of coffee.

"I thought you'd be down about now," she said, pouring him a large cupful. "Would cream and sugar help with keeping you awake?"

"No thanks, but one of those cookies might."

"Of course. Why else would I have just taken them out of the oven?"

He took cup and plate on a small tray. "You know you spoil us rotten."

"I hope so." Her smile dimmed a mite. "Only some are already so spoiled I fear they might be dropped."

He knew she was referring to the excessive drinking of a certain group, which precluded class attendance or any thought of studying. One of his friends from BB, before Blessing, as he referred to earlier times, was a member of that group and had tried to get him to join in.

He thanked the housemother and made his way back to his room, where his roommate, Bernie Efflinger, snored away. He'd assured Jonathan that the light on wouldn't keep him awake, and it didn't.

He opened his Greek reader and propped it against the others in order to free his hands to hold the coffee cup and take notes. Had he worked this hard in prep school, he'd have graduated with honors. But that hadn't been important to him at the time.

When he finally turned out the light, he barely had time to pray for Grace before sleep hit him. This still caught him by surprise. Bernie grunted in his sleep, and the idea drifted into his drowse that maybe he should be praying for him too.

⁂

The wind had kicked up a chop when he joined his team for the morning workout.

"Was beginning to wonder if you were going to make it," the coxswain commented as they took their places.

"Sorry. I think the alarm woke half the floor before I heard it." He settled into his number three seat, putting his feet in the stretchers and shivering in the mist rising from the canal. The sun had yet to show its face through the fog.

"Okay, men. Let's get warmed up. The Saturday race will be here before we know it, and we want to win."

They pushed away from the dock, and the coxswain picked up the beat.

An hour later and dripping wet from both sweat and the chop, they eased back to the dock and staggered out.

"That was brutal," one of the team members groaned. He leaned over, hands on his knees, to catch his breath.

Jonathan wrapped one leg in front of the other and leaned down to clasp his hands behind his knees to get the optimum stretch in his hamstrings.

"You men need to spend some time in the weight room to build those shoulders. Running will increase your wind and your leg strength. You can't get by with just practice in the scull. And we need to pick up the run distance."

Even though he knew he was stronger than most of the others, Jonathan listened with a questioning heart. Where would he find the extra time? Right now the only thing to cut back on was sleep, of which he was not getting an excess. So what could he speed up? Read faster, write faster, study faster? Whom could he ask for advice?

There was only one thing he knew for certain he could cut out—his time with the gardener. Deciding he would not walk but run to everything, he took off for his room, hearing the catcalls of his teammates behind him. It was a good thing he had no desire for popularity. This would most likely kill any chance of that.

That night he wrote to his parents to give them the bad news.

Dear Mother and Father,

I am sorry to say that I will not be coming home for the Thanksgiving weekend. I know you are planning a dinner and dancing event, but I just don't have the time to spend traveling. If I want to continue to row and keep my grades up, I need every minute I can beg, borrow, or steal to stay at the top of my class. There are several fellows who have made it their mission to unseat me, since the top spots gain extra privileges. Plus some are business majors, who see this as adversarial practice.

I know you will all have a marvelous time and please have an extra serving of pumpkin pie in my stead.

Your ambitious son,

JDG

This letter would probably bring his mother down on the next train.

Sometimes he wondered if he just wasn't as smart as his brother Thomas, who'd not seemed to have any trouble remaining at the top of his class, turning out for sports, and even having time to attend all the balls and social functions. He tapped the edge of the envelope against the side of his finger. How had Thomas done it all? Maybe it was Harvard that was different and he should've gone there after all.

Jonathan scrubbed his fingers through his hair, realizing that he needed a haircut too. The curls were long enough to tie in a bow. The only way to tame them was to keep his hair short. He stared at the face in the mirror. *These are only petty annoyances*, he informed the dark eyes that stared back at him. The circles underneath them made him look like he was ill.

He picked up his Greek textbook and tried to understand the verb forms. Hours later he woke, shivering, with his cheek flat on his book on the desk. Bleary-eyed, he blinked to be able to see the clock—just after three in the morning. He stared at the page number in his textbook. Not that far beyond where he'd started.

He rubbed his temples to try to get his brain functioning. Go down for another cup of coffee? Surely the coffee would be cold by now. Instead, he turned off the gaslamp and slid between the bed sheets with all his clothes on, grateful for the quilt, since the air felt more like winter than fall. Would they still be practicing in the scull when ice rimed the water? At least he wouldn't have to get up quite so early to dress before he headed for the canal in the morning.

"You look like you slept in your clothes," one of the team members commented the next morning.

"Only because I did." Jonathan pulled his wool stocking cap down over his ears. Even running to practice with the cold air stabbing his lungs hadn't sufficiently awakened him. He'd never be able to thank Bernie enough for pulling him out of bed.

"Hit the oars, men. You'll freeze standing around." The coxswain slapped Jonathan on the shoulder. "Ready for the big meet?"

"As I'll ever be." Saturday was only two days away, and he had an exam on Friday afternoon—the test he was studying for last night when he fell asleep on the book. He should be back at the frat house studying right now. He locked his feet into the stretchers and grabbed his oar. "Let's get this over with."

⁓

He knew when he walked out of the classroom the next afternoon that, in spite of his best efforts, he'd not completed all the questions. No matter how long he'd studied the night before, even missing another class to study for this one. Robbing Peter to pay Paul, as the old saying went. And neither Peter nor Paul was appeased.

A letter from his mother waited for him on his desk when he returned to his room. He stared at the handwriting. Why couldn't it have been from Grace? Right now he really needed something to cheer him up, and he knew his mother wasn't the one to do that.

"Hard day?" Bernie dropped his books on his desk. "It is bitter cold out there. Surely they won't have the race tomorrow in this kind of weather."

"We could pray the canal freezes over, but barring that, I think it will go on."

"You'll catch your death out there."

"I sure hope not."

"Just don't go."

"I can't do that!" Jonathan shook his head, giving Bernie a frown. "When you join the team, you agree to practices and meets. Part of the bargain."

"Frostbite won't help your grades any. And that's precluding pneumonia." He headed for the door. "I'll bring you a cup of coffee too. You want anything stronger in it?"

"No, just cream and sugar. I need those extras now." He stared at the letter he'd propped against the lamp. He would read that tomorrow or maybe next week. He didn't want the lecture about family responsibilities and Thanksgiving, which he was sure was the theme.

🙢

They waited an hour for the other school to show up the next morning. At least the walls of the boathouse broke the wind, but the cold penetrated clear to the bones before their coach announced the race was off and they should all go have a warm bath and drink a hot toddy to quicken the warming process.

He woke up Sunday morning with his nose running and chest tight with a hacking cough.

"I'm calling Mrs. Maguire. Perhaps she has some remedy to keep you from getting sicker." Bernie turned from the open door. "You stay in bed!"

That was an order Jonathan was more than happy to obey. As if he had any choice.

"I knew you shouldn't have gone out to the canal yesterday." Mrs. Maguire laid the back of her hand against his forehead. "Hot. I think we better get you to the infirmary immediately."

"No. I can sleep better here." Just those few words sent him into a hacking frenzy.

"Then a mustard plaster it is for you, and I'll mix up some honey and whiskey to cut the phlegm in your throat. I told you you can't go on like this, no sleep, and drinking coffee to keep awake. Come on, Mr. Efflinger, we have a mission to perform. I'll set a chicken to stewing. Nothing works as good as chicken soup."

Jonathan propped some more pillows behind his head so he was almost sitting up. Breathing was easier that way. He couldn't remember when he had felt so miserable. He was never sick.

Coughing woke him later, just as Mrs. Maguire returned to the room.

With the mustard plaster burning his chest and the honey and whiskey in hot water warming his insides, he fell asleep again. During the night he thought he heard Mrs. Maguire say she would call his father, but perhaps he'd been dreaming it.

His father walked into the room the next day to find him half sitting up, being fed chicken soup by the housemother. "Why are you not in the infirmary?"

"I'm getting better care here." Jonathan motioned to his nurse.

"Have you had a doctor check him?"

"Yes. He came during the night and said I was doing all that he could do. He left laudanum to help control the cough, but Mr. Gould is doing better today without that." She held out another spoonful of soup. "This will help him get stronger."

Mr. Gould pulled up a chair by the bedside. "So what brought this on?"

"We had a crew race on Saturday and waited in the cold."

"And he has been burning the candle at both ends." Mrs. Maguire looked to the elder Gould. "If you want my opinion, that is."

Jonathan fought to keep his eyes open and think of a suitable answer for his father, but the effort was too much, and he drifted back to sleep. He kept seeing Grace standing on the shore, and he tried and tried to row over to her. But the wind pushed him back, and the icy cold doubled him over. He tried to call out to her when she began to disappear and remembered she couldn't hear him. Then how could he tell her? He shook his arm in frustration and woke as he felt a soft hand catch it.

"How long have I been sleeping?"

"Four days." Mrs. Maguire held out a spoonful of chicken soup. "Weren't sure you were going to make it for a while there."

"I dreamed Grace was here, then?"

"If Grace is Miss Knutson, you were talking with her a couple of times."

He swallowed another spoonful. "Is it day or night?"

"Night."

He let himself float for a bit. "Was my father here, or did I dream that too?"

"He's sleeping in the guest room. Eat more of this. You need to rebuild your strength."

Jonathan studied the woman who wielded the soup spoon. Lamplight set a halo around her silvering hair, loosely knotted in a bun on her head. "He stayed here?"

"And the doctor's been here several times. He said we were doing all he could do, and it's a good thing you are such a strong young man or we'd be digging a hole for you rather than making chicken soup."

"Hmm. Thank you."

He must have slept, but he wasn't sure, for there she was again, spoon in hand. "Sorry, I must have drifted off."

"I guess so. Morning came an hour ago." She turned at a sound from the doorway. "Good morning, Mr. Gould. This time you get to see the color of his eyes."

"Good. I'll take over, then."

Jonathan watched his father settle into the chair Mrs. Maguire vacated. With his vest hanging loose and the collar of his shirt unbuttoned with no tie, he only faintly resembled the man Jonathan had wanted to please all his life—and never quite measured up. His father also needed a shave. Opening his mouth obediently when the spoon hovered near, he could feel a burning behind his eyes. He could never remember his mother caring for him like this, let alone his father. Their governess had been in charge of the nursery, with a nurse on call when needed. The twins had required far more doctoring than he.

"Why are you doing this?" The words slipped past his reserve.

His father stared straight into his soul. "Because I love you, and I've not taken a lot of time to show it before. The thought of you dying before I grew wise enough to say this was more than I could bear. Mrs. Maguire told me that if I wanted you to live, I'd better get down on my knees and make sure the good Lord knew that I wanted to make amends."

Jonathan tried blinking, but he had no reserve strength to order the tears back. When he raised his hand to wipe them away, it shook so bad, he let it fall back to the bedclothes. Instead, his father wiped his son's tears with the edge of the sheet and, after setting the bowl and spoon on the tray on the bedside table, took Jonathan's hands in his own. "I have watched your dedication to live up to our agreement, and I want you to know that killing yourself to do so is not necessary."

Jonathan smiled when he realized his father was making a joke. "I didn't plan this."

"I know. But I think we need to rewrite our agreement. When you are well, we will discuss it. I think you should come home to recuperate."

"But then I will have failed this semester. Surely I'll be able to return to class in a couple of days." He tried to sit up but collapsed back against the pillows.

"I talked with your professors. You will have until classes resume in January to make up for your lost time. You can take your finals when you return."

"What did you do? Buy them off with a building?"

The burst of laughter from his father made him smile too. He took the next spoonfuls of soup with good grace.

"You really do love Miss Knutson, don't you?"

The question caught him by surprise. Had his father doubted it? Obviously so. But when he thought to the flitting from flower to flower that had been his practice for his prep-school years, which his mother had thought delightful, perhaps his father had not been of like mind. "I told you I did and do."

"You kept calling for her, as if she were lost and you couldn't find her."

What else had he said? How frustrating that he could remember none of it.

"I called Mrs. Callahan to tell Grace and ask her to pray for you also."

The words dropped like petals on a lazy stream.

"You did?" He had never heard his father talk like this of praying before. Granted, they went to church occasionally but only as a social responsibility. Their family name under a plaque on one of the stained-glass windows was as close to community as they came.

"I sent a telegram to the Bjorklunds, asking them to pray too."

That did it. Jonathan's jaw sprung the lock and hung to his chest.

"Mrs. Maguire reminded me that God promised that when two or three agree on something, He will honor those prayers."

"I see." He didn't really, but that seemed a good thing to say. His mind was having a hard time accepting all this information. "So does Grace know I'm still alive?"

"Oh yes. I called to have a message delivered there yesterday when we knew you were on the mend. Mrs. Bjorklund telegraphed a receipt for one of her homemade medicines, and after we found the ingredients and poured that into you, the crisis passed. I will never be able to thank her enough."

Jonathan knew there was a laugh in there somewhere, but he couldn't find it before he slipped into sleep again.

When he awoke a few hours later, a note sat propped against the lamp. This time as he reached for it, his hand held steady. He slit the envelope with a fingernail grown long and read the letter.

My dear Jonathan,

I've been called back to the city—marvelous machines these telephones—but I want you to have some more to think about. I believe you should come home on the train as soon as you are able to travel. We will send someone to assist you. Mrs. Maguire will supervise your care there. She has been a stalwart friend. I release you from your agreement not to mention your feelings to Miss Knutson. I know a letter from you as soon as you can write one would ease her concerns. I sent a message to her again and telegraphed the Bjorklunds, thanking them for their prayers. I guess Mrs. Bjorklund threatened to come and nurse you herself if you didn't improve. I thank our God for the friends He has given us. We will bring in a tutor to help you make up the time if that would be a good idea. Getting well and strong again is your first priority.

I agree with you. Grand Forks sounds like the best school for what you want to do.

Your loving father,
DJG

If he hadn't been lying down, Jonathan knew he would have collapsed.

32

New York
December

Dear Jonathan,

Please get well. Our whole school is praying for you. I've enclosed a note one of my sweet little girls wrote for you. I was so shocked when your father called in the message and so grateful he informed me of what was happening. As Tante Ingeborg has always said, Mr. Gould is a fine man and faithful friend. I believe you take after your father, even though I'm not sure you see that in yourself.

Grace brushed a wisp of hair out of her eyes. *Lord, please bring healing* had been her waking prayer since the telephone call that nearly scared her out of her wits. Mrs. Callahan had knocked at her door that evening just as she was thinking of getting dressed for bed.

"I have a message for you from Mr. Gould," she'd said. "His son Jonathan is terribly ill, and he wanted you to know so you could pray. I told him we would all be praying. I hope that is all right."

"Did he say what was wrong?"

"Pneumonia."

"Oh! Oh, please dear God, not Jonathan." Her mind immediately flew back to the times that Ingeborg and later Elizabeth had nursed people in Blessing, some to live and some not.

"Has he passed the crisis point yet?"

"No, I don't think so. He didn't say. He sounded very worried."

She'd spent much of the night on her knees and searching through her Bible for the promises God had given on healing. Pastor Solberg had given them all a list once, if only she had kept it in her Bible where it belonged. She returned to her letter.

Hearing that you are on the way to recovery has made us all rejoice. Even the smaller children ask me how my friend is.

Thanksgiving here was so different from home. While your family invited me to come there, I decided that here was where I could be most helpful. Some of our students could not go home for such a short time, just like at our school in Blessing. So we had a good dinner here and played games in the afternoon. At least they understand enough signs now that I can read to them, and they can follow the story.

I am looking forward to a letter written by your own hand. However, Mary Anne says she will take dictation and write for you—just in case your hand is too weak.

Your praying friend,
Grace Knutson

She kept herself from writing *Your loving friend*, as that was not appropriate, even though she was his friend. She knew that for sure, and she most certainly had been thinking about him a lot. She couldn't stop thinking about what would have happened if he hadn't pulled through. She felt as if a part of her would have been lost, and she really didn't understand why. Maybe this was what a good friend felt like. Before, her closest friends had also been family. Except Toby. But even during times she had felt the need to pray for him, she had not felt this sense of separation. Maybe it was just the distance, she reasoned.

She slid both pieces of paper into the envelope, addressed it, and set it aside to be mailed when she went down for dinner.

Since Sunday afternoon had become her letter writing time, she wrote one to her mother, another to Sophie, praying once again for an answer this time, and one to Astrid, knowing full well they would share the news, so she made each one different.

"Miss Knutson, would you come see me after supper?" Mrs. Callahan stopped by her chair to ask.

"Of course."

"Now, don't worry. There is nothing wrong."

Grace's heart settled back down out of her throat. This would be a long meal if her worry streak had anything to say about it. One of her Bible verses tiptoed through her mind. *Fret not.* Fret and worry seemed to be twins. One always traveled with the other. At least here they did. They had never seemed to be her insistent companions in Blessing.

She watched carefully as one of the children signed for permission to leave the table. "Why?" she signed back. He wrinkled his forehead, so she signed again, "Why?" and spoke the word at the same time.

He rubbed his tummy and shook his head, then signed, "Sick."

She beckoned him to her side and felt his forehead. Sure enough, he was too warm, and he looked a little green. Just as she rose to take him to the infirmary, he vomited all over her apron and the corner of the table. The shocked look in his eyes would have made her smile if he hadn't been so miserable.

"Don't worry," she signed and reached for an empty bowl, handing it to him to hold in case he needed it. She signaled one of the kitchen helpers to come clean it up, at the same time removing her apron and folding it across the back of the chair. She took his hand and led him out of the room, grateful she'd been able to breathe through her mouth so that she didn't throw up right after him. While the others had stared round eyed, all of them went back to eating.

"Richard had an accident at the table, and he really isn't feeling well," Grace signed when they reached the nurse's office.

"Poor little fellow." Nurse took his hand and felt his head. She signed, "Come with me," and he sent Grace a pleading look, so she went along too. He vomited again when they were getting him into a nightshirt, and he started to cry. Nurse sat down in a rocker and motioned him to climb up in her lap. With a sad look over his shoulder to Grace, he did so and leaned against the woman's soft shoulder.

"I'll let you know how he is."

"Thank you. I need to get back to my table." Grace stopped in the bathroom and washed her hands, grateful for the big aprons that protected her clothes. *Please, Lord, let it be only an upset stomach, not something serious.* Back in the dining room, the mess was cleared away, and one of the older girls had taken her place at the table. Dessert dishes filled with tapioca pudding, topped with crushed peppermint candies, were being served as she sat down in Richard's place.

"Is he bad sick?" signed the girl who always sat next to him. While children were assigned tables, they could sit anywhere they wanted at the table. Until they got into a squabble, and then the teachers and assistants took over.

When the last of the pudding had disappeared, everyone was dismissed and the evening monitors took over. Grace tucked her napkin back into the ring by her place and stood.

"Will you be joining us in the parlor?" Miss Parke asked. "I brought my knitting, and I was hoping you could find where I went wrong."

"I have something else I have to do first, and then I'll come." Some of the teachers had asked her to teach them to knit, and now they met once a week for lessons. Unless there was a problem or other responsibilities to attend to, like now. "You most likely dropped a stitch."

"Or added an extra." Miss Parke shook her head. "You make it look so easy."

"You are doing well. I'll be in soon." All she could think of was the night Mrs. Callahan had come to tell her about Jonathan. Even though the woman had said this was not a bad thing, her stomach

said otherwise. Grace tapped on the office door and opened it enough
to stick her head in. At Mrs. Callahan's smile and beckoning hand,
she entered and took the chair next to the low table that was indicated. She clasped her hands in her lap, the better to keep them from
trembling.

"Now, Grace, I told you not to worry."

"I know." She forced herself to smile.

"I have a problem, and I'm hoping you can help me solve it."

"If I can."

"Here is the situation. Miss Dunkirk has received a letter saying
that her mother is ill and needs her daughter home to help take care
of her. She needs to leave in the morning, and I was wondering if you
would be willing to step into her place?"

Grace stared at her, wondering for a moment if she heard correctly. "You want me to be a full-time teacher?"

"Yes. Starting immediately. And I have a strong feeling that Susan
will not be coming back for some time."

"What about my studies?"

"I am sure you will pick up whatever you may need as you go
along. The rest of us will assist you any way we can."

Grace stared at her mentor and tried to stop her churning
thoughts.

"The pay will be what we always start beginning teachers at." She
named a figure that made Grace swallow quickly.

"Are-are you sure I am worth that?"

"Oh, I am sure. Your patience and gentle spirit have earned you
many accolades from other teachers already."

"I'll still be able to go home for Christmas?"

"Oh yes. The school is closed down for the holidays, starting on
December twenty-first." She paused. "Somehow I thought you were
going to New York City to be with the Gould family for Christmas."

Grace realized what she had said. Home. A wave of homesickness
rolled over her so mercilessly she could scarcely catch her breath. She
straightened her spine and took a deep breath. "That is what I meant,

of course." Like a little child with a stuck-out lip, something inside her insisted, *I want to go home to Blessing. Home is not New York City.*

"Let's walk up to your classroom. I'll send for Susan to join us, and she can show you around. Have you been in her classroom before?"

"No. I've only assisted with the beginning signing classes."

After receiving Miss Dunkirk's schedule and an overview of the class projects, Grace headed back to her room with her mind swimming. But underneath another thought kept nibbling. Maybe, just maybe, with the pay Mrs. Callahan had stated, she could go home to Blessing for Christmas. Yet she had promised the Goulds, especially Jonathan and Mary Anne.

❧

Teaching four classes of primary a day and spending the remainder of the time preparing for those classes gave Grace an increase in respect for all the teachers she had known. There was a big difference between assisting and teaching. By the time she could finally fall into bed, only her prayers for Jonathan's healing occurred before sleep claimed her. And gratitude that Richard was better and a virus had not spread through the classes. So on the third morning she asked their floor maid to wake her half an hour earlier so she could read all the promise verses again and ask for wisdom for herself as a teacher. She flipped pages until she reached Proverbs to remind herself that God gives wisdom to all who ask for it. It sounded like wisdom and insight liked to travel together, so she stored the verses deep in her heart. At the same time, her heart was at war again over promises made and heartache for Blessing. *Please show me, Lord, what is your will. Is it a waste to spend the money going home?*

Still she packaged the presents she had bought for her family and shipped them off, praying over each person, imagining their faces when they opened their gifts.

The final week of school approached and with it finally a letter from Jonathan in his own hand. What a relief that he was strong enough to write himself. *Thank you, Lord, for your healing hand.* At his comments regarding his mother's level of overcare, Grace smiled and then frowned. Mrs. Gould would not be pleased at having Jonathan's attentions upon her at her visit. But she had promised.

Then she opened Tante Ingeborg's letter. She could smell the coffee on the paper and pictured her writing in the kitchen by lamplight. A wave of homesickness struck her again as her aunt's love flowed through the pages. Her aunt informed her that Astrid might try the school in Grand Forks after all, for the winter session—just to see.

Grace grabbed a piece of scratch paper and scribbled out the costs of being at the school until June and added her pay as a teacher. It would be tight, but it was possible. She had already spent her extra money on Christmas presents. Her heart decided. *I have to go home.*

The last two days were spent in class parties and making cookies and candy for the children to take home to their families. She tucked that idea away to use in her mother's school. After all, the children were too excited to settle down anyway, let alone some of the teachers, like her.

She sent two telegrams. One to Jonathan apologizing for not stopping to visit on her way west, as she would not make it home in time for Christmas if she did. He had accepted her news that she was going home so kindly that it hurt to send this telegram. Maybe she could stop on the way back, she thought, to make it up to him and Mary Anne. The other telegram she sent to her family with a sense of excitement, saying she was coming home after all.

After the staff saw all the children off and cleaned up their classrooms, they gathered in the parlor for tea and Christmas goodies, sharing their Christmas plans and appreciating the lack of children's feet thundering vibrations on the halls and stairways. Grace had always thought it interesting that so many deaf children could still create a sense of internal noise just by their busyness.

Mrs. Callahan moved from teacher to teacher, handing out envelopes. "I'm sorry this couldn't be more but know that it comes with my heartfelt gratitude for the superb jobs you all do. I could not ask for a more dedicated staff, and I am grateful to each one of you for the love and care you give our students."

When they all opened their cards, Grace was surprised to find enough money there to pay for her ticket to Blessing. She shot a surprised look at Mrs. Callahan, who just smiled and nodded. A second smaller envelope held her pay, which, since she'd held the teacher position for such a short time, was not much but seemed so, as she'd never worked at a job that paid regular money before. Most of her time in Blessing had always been spent helping out a family member. While Bridget had sometimes paid the girls when they worked at the boardinghouse, this was different. She was not only earning her room and board but enough to pay for her own schooling, and now this on top of all that. God had provided more than she could imagine. Her continuing guilt at not keeping her promise dissolved when she recognized this gift as from His hand.

Grace tucked the envelopes into her skirt pocket. If she wanted to purchase something, she could do that. If she wanted to buy something for someone else or put money in the offering plate, she was free to do so. Or add to her sugar bowl, as her mother referred to the savings she always kept in a sugar tin in the cupboard.

The thoughts leaped and whirled in her mind like the fall leaves playing in a brisk breeze that she'd watched from her window. There would be more envelopes with money in them that she had earned. She accepted the platter of cookies, took two, and passed it on. Nibbling on one while conversation streamed around her, she shut herself off by paying attention to her tea and cookie. Even though she could read both sign and lips, she still struggled to keep up in a large group of people talking. She could start a savings account at a local bank here or at the Blessing Bank, where all the family accounts were held.

Or. Such a special little word, two letters long but ripe with a wealth of possibilities.

But it also would mean staying in New York for a longer time than she had planned.

The next morning the buggy arrived to take Grace and several of the others to the train station. When the train to New York City arrived, she said her good-byes and climbed aboard, taking her valise and a bag holding a blanket with her and a small trunk that the porter loaded into the baggage car. Once seated, she glanced up to find a young man with dark brown eyes smiling at her. She smiled back and settled her bag under the seat, removing a book to read on the journey. The first change of trains would be in New York City. A rush of surprise caught her as she realized how matter of fact her thoughts were. She was traveling alone and did not have that familiar nausea swirling about.

Instead of reading, she watched the farmlands and small towns flow by the window, all the while sensing that she was being watched. Each time she looked up, the young man nodded and smiled at her again.

If Sophie were here, she'd smile and flirt, and soon they'd be talking like old friends. The thought made her smile to herself. Would Sophie still do that now that she was married and the mother of four children? That thought led to another, not one that brought about smiling. Had Sophie forgiven her for her outburst? Another reason to go home. She needed to see Sophie for herself. It was the only way she could know.

She stared at the window, no longer seeing the scenery. The real question lay simmering somewhere beneath the surface, where she did not like to go. Had she forgiven Sophie for leaving her and for leaving home, and not only that but for being Sophie? The words so often heard now only in memories, *"But Grace always . . ."* no longer had a bite to them. She pondered that. When had the change occurred? When Jonathan called her Pure Grace? She repeated *Grace Always* several times and put the words in the context of the event and realized she was right. They didn't hurt any longer. When she thought of Sophie, she wanted to laugh instead of cry. How had this happened? A desire to see her sister rushed through her just as the train entered a tunnel and all went black. They were nearing the station, where she would change trains. *Father in heaven, you worked a miracle and I didn't even know it. Did I forgive Sophie? Oh yes, I did, like you have forgiven me. Those nights of tears are behind me. You were working, and I wasn't even aware. How do you do that?* She put her hands to her cheeks, feeling the trembling smile the thoughts brought, at the same moment using her fingertips to wipe away a couple of joy tears.

The windows lightened again as the train slowed and eased into one of the long slots with platforms on either side that was Grand Central Station. She knew she had an hour or so before her westbound train would depart, so she let some of the other passengers go ahead of her.

The smiling man stopped. "May I help you take your bag down?"

She started to say no but instead said, "Thank you." She caught his surprised reaction to her voice as he held her valise in one hand.

"I'll carry it out for you." His face became a formal mask.

She nodded and, taking her handbag on her arm, walked ahead of him and down the steps, letting the conductor assist her on the steep metal stairs. Once on the platform, she reached for her valise. "Thank you and good day."

He hesitated only a second before handing her the luggage. Then he touched the brim of his hat. "You are most welcome, and I wish you the best on your journey." He looked almost disappointed. Another person for whom she did not measure up. A hollow feeling began inside, but before it could take hold, a picture of Jonathan floated through her mind. He accepted her just as she was. He even called her Pure Grace. A special friend to be sure. Her only regret at going home was not seeing him and Mary Anne. But the hunger for her family was stronger right now, especially with all the decisions before her.

She smiled at the porter who arrived with her trunk and motioned for him to lead the way. Following the stream of humanity into the main station, she admired the way some were dressed in the latest fashions and felt quite at home in the traveling ensemble Mrs. Gould had had made for her. She ran her hands over the dark blue tweed. The jacket was trimmed in black cord, which apparently was no longer the style in New York, but never had she had an outfit so elegant. A little boy and girl caught her attention, and she stumbled into someone standing still. Her valise fell to the marble floor, and she jerked her head up to say excuse me, but the words caught in her throat. "Jonathan—er, Mr. Gould. How did . . . why . . . what . . . ?"

"I came to surprise you." He stared into her eyes, his hands still clutching her arms to keep her from falling. "I guess I did."

"Oh, you did." That look was in his eyes again. The one she had seen Garth give Sophie. No, it couldn't be possible. She became aware of another man standing with him. "Ah, Mr. Gould, how good to see you." *Is my hat on straight? Do I look all right?*

"Our pleasure, Miss Knutson. Jonathan was afraid we had missed you in this stream of people."

"You both came here to see me?"

Mr. Gould picked up her valise as Jonathan tucked her arm through his and turned slightly. He smiled down at her. Were his eyes misty, as she felt hers were?

"But I'm only here for an hour—less now."

"I know," Jonathan said. "We'll take you to your train. I was so looking forward to showing you New York at Christmas."

"I'm sorry, but I-I have to go home."

"I understand, I think."

"Come, let's get out of the way of all these people who are in such a hurry." He waved to the porter to follow them. Mr. Gould led the way, and Grace felt like skipping behind him. When they reached the area near where her train would leave, he found them seats and set the valise on the bench. "I'll go find us all some coffee. Are you hungry, Miss Knutson?"

"Coffee, yes. Food, no thank you." She paused. "Unless, of course, you are hungry." Where were her manners? *Jonathan looks so pale and tired. Is it safe for him to be here? Why is he here?*

Jonathan shook his head and motioned her to sit. They watched his father move away before he pulled a small package from his pocket. "I wanted to give you this in person."

"But I don't have a present for you. I sent it in the mail."

"That doesn't matter. I just wanted to see you." He handed her the square package wrapped in silver paper. "Open it."

"But it's not Christmas."

"I want to watch you open it."

"If you say so, but my mother would scold me for opening a present early."

"Your mother is not here."

Grace unwrapped the package carefully; she'd never had such pretty paper before. The flat box wore the insignia of a jeweler. She glanced at Jonathan, who nodded encouragingly. She flipped the top open to find an oval cameo pin in the form of a young woman with her hair bundled on top of her head. "Jon—er, Mr. Gould, this is far too expensive to give me."

"You call me Jonathan. Mr. Gould is my father." He touched the cameo. "She reminded me of you, and I want her to remind you of me."

"She is lovely."

"Yes, she is."

She glanced up to see him staring at her as she pinned the cameo to her jacket collar. *Did he mean the cameo, or was he referring to me?* The thought made the heat rise on her neck.

"Thank you." *I don't need a reminder, though. I think of you every day. When did that happen? Since your illness. No, before. Ever since you called me Pure Grace.* Her breath caught.

She looked up to see Jonathan's father arriving alongside a white-jacketed waiter carrying a tray holding coffee and sandwiches. Another waiter had brought a folding stool, which he set up in front of them, and the first man set the tray on the stool, creating a table for the three of them.

Grace glanced up to see Mr. Gould's eyes twinkle.

"There are advantages to having wealth." His smile made her smile back. No wonder his son had the ability to fit in anywhere. He resembled his father.

The waiter poured the coffee and passed the cups around, then a plate of fancy sandwiches.

Grace helped herself and sat back to enjoy the impromptu party. Here they were in Grand Central Station with herds of people milling around or purposefully going about their business, and they might as well have been in a drawing room. They had two waiters standing at attention with their legs slightly spread and hands locked behind their backs. Her hand kept reaching up to touch the cameo in case this was all a dream. Such a generous gift. Too generous, and she should refuse. But she couldn't. She saw Jonathan's eyes sparkle with pleasure when he noticed her gesture.

When the call came for her train, Jonathan placed her cup and saucer back on the tray and, taking her hand, pulled her to her feet. Jonathan and his father walked out the concourse to her train and they both helped her onto the train and to her seat.

"Wouldn't you rather have a private compartment?" Mr. Gould asked.

Knowing that he would go buy her a different ticket, Grace shook her head firmly. "This is fine. I like having other people around."

"If you are sure."

How easy it would be to just let them take over. "No, I am sure."

"Remember me while you are in Blessing." Jonathan squeezed her hand as he said good-bye and followed his father out of the car. Both of them stood waving while the train pulled out of the station.

Grace waved back, then sank into her seat. What a surprise. She fanned down the heat that had continued to warm her neck ever since he'd held her hand. The tingle from his touch still lingered. She opened the card inside the cameo box. *Looking forward to a new year together. Love, Jonathan.* She reread it. And read it again.

Blessing, North Dakota

"NEXT STOP, BLESSING."

Grace smiled at the conductor, who had stopped to tell her personally. "Mange takk." The Norwegian phrase slipped out naturally, as if it too had been waiting until she got home.

"You take care now."

"Oh, I will."

As the train squealed into the station, she saw a sleigh and team tied to the railing. She felt her heart surge when she saw her family waiting on the platform. The snow had been shoveled off the platform into mounds on the eastern side of the station. From the looks of it, Blessing had been having a normal year of snow. No one had written about a bad blizzard yet. Grace gathered her things and, after handing her valise to the conductor, stepped carefully down the three stairs and into her mother's arms. Her father, Trygve, and Samuel stood right behind her, waiting their turns to greet her.

"You look different," Samuel said, studying her.

"That's because she left here a girl and came home a young woman."

Her father's words caught her by surprise. She smiled up at him. "Mange takk. I made it in time for Christmas."

"Barely." Trygve took her valise. "Everyone will be at our house tomorrow."

"Everyone?"

"All the Bjorklunds. Penny and Hjelmer and the children even came home." Kaaren took her daughter's hand.

"And Sophie?"

"Them too. And one of Garth's brothers and his family. That's why we are all at our house. It's bigger." Kaaren smoothed Grace's coat sleeve. "This is beautiful. You are beautiful."

"Mrs. Gould made sure I was properly attired." At her mother's slightly raised eyebrow, Grace realized she must have sounded just the teeniest bit sarcastic. Her mother was so perceptive. "She was very nice to me." While she tried to mean the words, what she left out said far more than she wanted. "They are a very generous family."

"We received a letter from a Mrs. Wooster. She thinks you are one of the most remarkable young women she has ever met."

As her father handed her into the sleigh, Grace smiled up at him to receive back the slow smile of his that showed both his love and pride in his daughter. "I missed you, Far."

He shook his head, slowly and gently. "I cannot tell you how much we missed you. The students even left your chair empty. No one ever sat in it."

Grace's eyes misted over. When she settled under the robe with her mother, she turned to ask, "What did you think of Mrs. Wooster's ideas?"

"She most certainly gave us a lot to think on. She said she will be coming to Blessing to talk with us as soon as the weather softens."

Softens. That sounded like Mrs. Wooster. She really had no idea what North Dakota winters could be like. But then, who did if they'd not lived here? So far the winter in New York had been cold, but the wind there was nothing like the northerner that howled down from the polar ice cap, seeking to devour everything in its path.

Far backed the team and clucked the horses into a trot, the sled runners shooshing and the harness bells jingling as they headed for home. Sunlight threw diamond dust across the white drifts, bursts of fire wherever she looked. She'd not seen such a blue sky since she boarded the eastbound train last fall.

"We got three new cows, so you can help milk in the morning if you want to," Samuel said from beside her. He'd tapped her arm to get her attention first, something they all did as a matter of course.

"Thank you for the invitation, but I'd hate to deprive you of the joy of milking." She grinned at him, and he wiggled one eyebrow, the action making her shake her head. How she had missed her brothers too.

Trygve turned from the seat in front beside Far. "He almost forgot how. Complained for days how his hands and arms hurt."

"How's Maggie?" Grace couldn't resist the teasing question since her mother wrote that Trygve had been paying attention to the eldest Clauson daughter.

Samuel dug his elbow into her side, no easy feat since she was wearing her thick wool coat and traveling suit over all the extra under-garments of winter. "Trygve likes to tease but can't take it much."

"Nothing has changed, then." Grace wished she had on a knitted wool hat rather than the fashionable fur that looked good but didn't cover enough. She reached up and pulled her scarf higher over her ears. When they passed the Bjorklunds', she saw Astrid and Ingeborg waving from the front window. They all waved back and swooped into the lane leading to the house. Plain compared to the places she'd seen, but the house seemed to reach out with welcoming arms and remind her there was no place like home.

Her father reined the horses to a stop by the shoveled walk, and Trygve jumped out to assist his mother and sister, while Samuel took the valise and the trunk from the back.

Grace held on to her mother's arm as they made their way to the back porch and up the swept-off steps. Split wood lined both the walls of the house and the porch, ready to be hauled in to fill the woodbox. She stopped inside the door and inhaled lungfuls of all the scents of home at Christmas. Woodsmoke, cinnamon, pine tree,

vanilla, bacon left from breakfast, and fresh bread. Had her mother
stayed up all night to prepare for today, Christmas Eve? She unwound
her scarf and settled it under her collar before reaching up to unpin
her hat. All the time her fingers did their nimble duty, her gaze traveled around the familiar room, seeing as if for the first time the huge
range that cooked food for so many, shined and blacked to glinting.
The red-and-white checked curtains at the windows looked freshly
washed, starched, and ironed. The red geranium on the windowsill
matched the curtains. A dish towel covered the loaves of bread left
cooling on the table, and crocks and tins of cookies and other Christmas baking lined the counter. All so familiar, and all so new.

She hung her coat on the coatrack. "Did my box come?"

"Yes. The presents are under the tree already. I was so sad when
the box came, and I thought you weren't coming home for Christmas." Kaaren hung up her coat and placed her hat on the shelf above
the coatrack, as had Grace. "Your telegram was the best Christmas
present ever."

"I-I have some decisions to make, and I wanted to talk things over
with you and Far first. Letters just didn't seem enough. I know Jonathan—" She saw her mother's eyebrows raise. "I cannot keep calling
him Mr. Gould. That is his father's name, and . . ." She paused and
smiled a gentle smile. "He is my best friend for now, and he was
looking forward to showing me New York City in her 'Christmas
finery,' as he described it."

"Has he recovered from his illness?" Kaaren took down an apron
and tied it over her blue serge dress.

"Not all the way. He is still pale and I think tires easily. He and
his father met my train in New York City so we could visit before I
had to leave again." Grace donned an apron too, after removing her
jacket. She unpinned the cameo and tucked it into her pocket.

"Are you hungry or can you wait for supper?" Kaaren opened the
oven door to check on the ham baking for the next day. The steam
carried the aroma around the kitchen and made Grace's stomach
rumble.

"Can we have cookies and coffee now?"

"Of course. You set out the cups and saucers while I get a new pot started. The men should be in any minute."

Samuel clattered back down the stairs after taking her baggage upstairs. "I put them in your room. Mor and Ilse made you a surprise up there."

"Samuel!"

"I didn't tell her what it is." He dodged his mother's playful swat. "Far said we'd do chores early this afternoon. He didn't figure the cows would mind." While he talked he edged over to the counter and lifted the cover on one of the crocks to snitch a ginger cookie.

"Everyone is coming tonight?"

"No, tomorrow. Church is at six, and one of the new girls at the school, Laurie Clauson, will read her Christmas story as part of the program. Thorliff ran it in installments in the *Blessing Gazette*."

"Really? How good of him." Grace handed a plate to her brother. "See if you can fill this with a variety without eating them all."

"Eating all what?" Trygve and Lars came through the door after stamping their feet on the porch.

"The cookies."

"Are we having lutefisk and lefse for supper?" Grace asked as she put folded napkins at the five places.

"Of course. Far set the lutefisk to soaking yesterday." Kaaren added another stick of wood to the fire.

Sitting around the table, catching up on the news, Grace glanced from face to beloved face. All of a sudden her life in New York seemed another existence, as though she'd dreamed it and here was the reality. Strange, but she'd felt the same there, with this life seeming a dream. Was it always like that—with the two lives connected by more than a thousand miles of railroad track and a mind that encompassed it all?

With the cows milked and chores finished along with the daylight, the family gathered for supper, everyone already dressed for church. As soon as they said grace, Mor pulled the bag of lutefisk from the steaming water in a large pot on the stove and poured the translucent pieces of fish onto a platter. At the same time Grace set the bowls of potatoes and melted butter on the table, where the lefse, pickles, and coleslaw already waited.

"There, and it is just right." Kaaren set the platter in front of Lars. "Not mushy at all." She turned and looked at the stove. "Oh, the beans." The string beans they'd dried over a line in pairs that looked like men's britches had been simmering with bacon, including the rind, and onions. She used her apron as a potholder to carry that bowl from the warming oven. "Now we're set. Help yourselves."

Grace glanced around the table. Five place settings. It just wasn't right without Sophie, but then, there would always be others with her now. How empty the table must have been with both twins gone. Even when the students filled it up. She swallowed quickly and took the platter of lutefisk from Trygve, spooning a fine chunk onto her plate. A quick thought of the Goulds flashed through her mind. She was sure it was safe to say they were not serving lutefisk and lefse for their Christmas Eve supper.

She poured melted butter over her fish and potatoes and slathered butter on her lefse, then sprinkled sugar on it. While her mother and father liked theirs plain, all the children preferred theirs sweeter. To think she had almost missed this traditional supper. She had missed lots of things by being gone. But had she stayed home, she would have missed lots of other things. She put her hand in her pocket, and Jonathan's smile lit up in her thoughts.

"Here, I warmed up the lutefisk if anyone wants more." Kaaren sat back down. "I think the store ran out of lutefisk. I heard someone say they'd not been able to buy as much as they wanted."

"We could have given a couple of our slabs away. We still have enough for at least two more meals." Lars mopped his melted butter up with the last of his lefse. "Just think, in Norway this is a staple winter food, and here we have it just for special meals."

"We dried plenty of fish here too in the early years."

"There is a difference between drying and treating. Makes you wonder whoever dreamed up that idea. Treating fish with poison to make it into something different." Lars shook his head. "You just never know."

Kaaren glanced at the clock. "We better be hurrying along. We can have dessert with coffee when we come home."

"One sandbakkel?" Samuel pleaded, trying to look forlorn.

Kaaren rolled her eyes. "You think you might fade away before we get home, and there will be nothing at the church?"

Grace stood, and the two women cleared the plates away and into the steaming dishpan on the stove.

"We'll do those later."

She stared at her mother. Leave something to later? What other changes had gone on while she wasn't home?

The lanterns on the fronts of the sleighs looked like candles bringing the light of Christmas across the frozen snow. As soon as they tied up the horses and while the men threw heavy quilts over the teams, Grace was greeted like a long-lost celebrity. All the girls, Astrid, Rebecca, and Deborah—crowded around her and hustled her into the church, where they admired her fur hat and muff and asked questions faster than she could answer.

As their families claimed them, she promised to answer more during the coffee hour after the program.

Sophie and her family swept in just before the doors closed. Kaaren nudged Grace to look back. They took the places saved for them, and Grace reached across Samuel to squeeze her sister's hand. She figured her eyes were just as tear filled as Sophie's. She used the tip of her gloved finger to wipe away the moisture that had made it over the edge and trickled down her cheek.

"Sorry we are almost late," Sophie signed. "Getting babies ready for anything on time is a major success." As she passed Hamre down to Mor, Grace held him for a moment. He was so much bigger and even while asleep looked so alert. She felt a soft hand pulling at her and looked down as Linnie scrunched in next to Grace, giving her a big smile.

The congregation stilled when the ushers blew out the sconces on the walls. Two small children walked down the center aisle and lit two candles, then two more and two more, set on stands on either side. Grace knew the piano was playing. She could feel it through her feet. The congregation rose and joined in singing "Joy to the World." Grace followed along in the hymnbook, remembering the times she had signed the carols and the hymns during church. Back at the Fenway School they'd signed the hymns on Sunday, since none of the students could hear.

Trygve read parts of the Christmas story and the age-old play, with all the schoolchildren taking their parts.

A young woman Grace's mother had told her was Laurie Clauson read the final section of her story, "The Lonely Donkey," which had been run in the newspaper. Since they sat close to the front, Grace could follow the story and smiled at the ending. She glanced over to see Samuel staring with puppy love eyes at the reader. Ah, so that was the way it was. Trygve and Maggie, Samuel and Laurie. Did she like him back? Ah yes, that flashed smile at the end said so. How could her brothers have both gotten interested in the opposite sex just this fall? Or had it been going on and she'd been too immersed in her own pain to notice?

Was Toby here? She'd soon know. She wanted to wish him well and really mean it this time. She was grateful for his friendship all these years, but as she remembered Jonathan smiling at her again and the look in his eyes, she realized with Toby that was all it was, a good friendship. She smiled. She surely was remembering Jonathan as he'd asked.

The children all gathered in the front for the lighting of the Christmas tree. The congregation sang "Silent Night" while the candles were being lit, leaving the tree shimmering. Grace felt the tears burning. Tears of happiness were still tears. She glanced at her mother. Sure enough, Mor was mopping her eyes too.

"Whose baby did they use for Jesus in the program this year?" she signed to her mother.

"A new family, and he didn't even whimper. Slept right through the whole thing. Just like this one." Mor kissed Hamre's forehead, and he scrunched his nose like a bunny.

Pastor Solberg and Thorliff were handing out packages from under the tree to all the children, along with an orange and a candy cane.

More signs. "What did they all get?"

"A book—different titles for different grades."

"How wonderful."

As soon as the children received their presents, they ran to their families to open them. Grace watched Grant take his gift to his father and hand one to his little sister. What a sweet little boy he was, she thought.

When the presents were all given out, Pastor Solberg invited everyone for coffee and desserts down in the basement, and everyone stood, turning to their neighbors and friends to wish them "God Jul" and "Merry Christmas." Grace and Sophie came together like two magnets with open arms for hugs and smiles with damp eyes.

"I have missed you so." Sophie leaned back so she could watch Grace's eyes.

"Me too. Oh, me too." They hugged again.

"You look so lovely, so fashionable and grown up."

"The babies have grown so much." Their words tumbled over and around each other. Joy started to fuss, so Sophie took her back from Garth, who took his turn greeting Grace. Grant pushed his way through the crowded aisle and looked up at her.

"You went away and never came back."

"I am back now." She leaned down to give him a hug.

"You going to stay?"

Grace caught her breath. Did she want to stay? Or did she want to return to New York and her school and Jonathan? "For a little while."

"For Christmas?"

"Yes."

"Good. See, I got an orange and a candy cane." He showed her his treasures. "Sissy did too, but Hamre and Joy are too little." He slid his hand into hers. "Ma brought cookies. Come on."

As she allowed him to lead her toward the stairs to the basement, she saw Toby up ahead, watching her with a smile that curved his cheeks.

"Welcome home, stranger."

There was no one with him. The thought flew by as Grace smiled back. "It's good to see you. Merry Christmas." She waited for the familiar longing, but there was none.

"Merry Christmas to you too. I hear you are doing well in New York."

"I am. I love my school." She glanced down at the tug on her hand. "I'm being called."

"No. You are being dragged." He smiled again and turned when someone spoke to him.

Grace sucked in a deep breath and felt herself go lighter and lighter. The pain, the longing for him to pay attention to her, was gone. She nearly danced down the stairs. It was good to see him, yes. He looked . . . what? Older? She couldn't decide. But she was free. And freedom felt like dancing, like giggling, like twirling in place, like flopping in the snow and making a snow angel.

Grant dropped her hand and made his way to the table spread with plates of cookies and sliced quick breads and a beautiful braided stollen. Julekake and iced cakes were sliced and ready to be served, and a huge crockery bowl of warm applesauce waited for ladling. He picked up two cookies and brought one of them back to her.

"Here. Merry Christmas." They took their first bites together, his eyes dancing above the gingerbread man he had chosen. They both bit off the heads. She could see he was laughing. The wish to hear his little boy laughter caught her by surprise. She was so used to not hearing that she'd given up wishing differently a long time ago. But with children it was different. Was it all children? No, on second thought, those related to her were more important.

"So is this the new man in your life?" Thorliff asked.

"I think so." She swung Grant's hand and glanced up to see Toby talking with one of the men. "I really think so." But a picture of Jonathan flashed through her mind, of his sitting beside her, giving her his present in the train station. Her fingers caressed the cameo now at her throat. Waiting for her in New York. *"Remember me,"* he had said. *Looking forward to a new year together.*

And then she knew. So was she. She'd come home to be a snow angel and then leave again for a new beginning. To a man who loved her just as she was, whether in Blessing or in New York. Just Grace, or as he had said, *"Pure Grace."*

DON'T MISS

Rebecca's Reward

Watch for this compelling novel,
the fourth in the DAUGHTERS OF BLESSING series

Nineteen-year-old Rebecca Baard has experienced more than her share of sorrow. Now she's afraid to open her heart to love. Besides, no man has shown enough interest in her to come courting. So Rebecca's friends set out to remedy the situation, concocting social events to attract all the eligible bachelors in Blessing and advising her in the use of feminine wiles. But even the best of intentions can't keep events from taking a most unexpected turn.

Can Rebecca overcome her fears, or will she settle for something less than love?